BETTER
the feel good place

Lincolnshire
COUNTY COUNCIL

Working for a better future

Lincolnshire Libraries
This book should be returned on or before the due date.

To renew or order library books please telephone 01522 782010
or visit https://capitadiscovery.co.uk/lincolnshire/
You will require a Personal Identification Number
Ask any member of staff for this.
The above does not apply to Reader's Group Collection Stock.

EC. 199 (LIBS): RS/L5/19

Bat
Her
the
Orig

The

LOST

CITY

Amanda Hocking lives in Minnesota, had never sold a book before April 2010 and has now sold her millionth. She is 'the most spectacular example of an author striking gold through books', according to the *Observer*. In her own words, Amanda is an obsessive tweeter, John Hughes mourner, man devotee, Muppets activist and unicorn enthusiast. books include the Trylle trilogy, the Kanin Chronicles, Watersong series, the Valkyrie duology and the Omte ins trilogy.

By Amanda Hocking

Freeks

The Trylle trilogy
Switched
Torn
Ascend
Trylle: The Complete Trilogy

The Watersong series
Wake
Lullaby
Tidal
Elegy

The Kanin Chronicles
Frostfire
Ice Kissed
Crystal Kingdom
Kanin: The Complete Chronicles

The Valkyrie duology
Between the Blade and the Heart
From the Earth to the Shadows

The Omte Origins trilogy
The Lost City
The Morning Flower

The

LOST
CITY

Omte Origins Book One

Amanda Hocking

PAN BOOKS

First published 2020 by Wednesday Books
an imprint of St. Martin's Publishing Group

First published in the UK 2020 by Pan Books
an imprint of Pan Macmillan
The Smithson, 6 Briset Street, London EC1M 5NR
Associated companies throughout the world
www.panmacmillan.com

ISBN 978-1-5290-0130-3

1 3 5 7 9 8 6 4 2

A CIP catalogue record for this book is available from the British Library.

Printed and bound by CPI Group (UK) Ltd, Croydon, CR0 4YY

Visit **www.panmacmillan.com** to read more about all our books
and to buy them. You will also find features, author interviews and
news of any author events, and you can sign up for e-newsletters
so that you're always first to hear about our new releases.

The

LOST
CITY

prologue

Ten Years Ago

"Tell me about it again," I entreated—begged, really, in a small voice, small especially for a girl like me.

Mr. Tulin, on the nights he had a little too much hot tea and brandy, would tell me stories of other, less fortunate babies. One had been left out for the wolves, another drowned in the icy river. Still another was killed by an *angakkuq*, this time to be mashed into a paste for one of her potions.

On the other nights, he'd try to convince me there wasn't any time for a story. But I'd beg and plead, and his eyes would glimmer—already milky with cataracts, lighting up when he spoke about monsters. I would pull the covers up to my chin, and his normally crackled baritone would go even lower, rumbling with the threat of the monsters he impersonated.

I was never sure how much he'd made up or what had been passed down to him, as he'd weave through all sorts of patchwork folklore—the monsters and heroes pieced together from the neighboring Inuit, our Norse ancestry, and especially from the troll tribe that Mr. and Mrs. Tulin belonged to—the Kanin.

But I had a favorite story, one that I asked for over and over again.

This one I loved because it was about me, and because it was true.

"Which one?" Mr. Tulin asked, feigning ignorance as he lingered at my bedroom door.

It was dark in my room, except for the cast-iron woodstove in the corner. My room had been a pantry before I was here, before Mr. Tulin had converted it into a tiny bedroom. Outside, the wind howled, and if I hadn't been buried underneath the blankets and furs, I would've felt the icy drafts that went along with all that howling.

"The day you met me," I replied with unbridled glee.

"*Well, you turned out to be a big one, didn't ya?*" That's what Mr. Tulin liked to say, particularly when I was scooping another helping of potatoes on my plate at the supper table, and then I would sheepishly put half a portion back, under the sharp gaze of Mrs. Tulin.

But he wasn't wrong. I was tall, thick, and pale. By the age of nine I was nearly five feet tall, towering over the kids in the little schoolhouse.

Once, I'd overheard Mrs. Tulin complaining aloud to a neighbor, saying, "I don't know why they chose our doorstep to leave 'er on. By the size of her, her da' must be an ogre, and her ma' must be a *nanuq*. She'll eat us out of house and home before she's eighteen."

After that, I tried to make myself smaller, invisible, and I made sure that I mended all my clothing and cleaned up after myself. Mrs. Tulin didn't complain too much about me after that, but every once in a while I would hear her muttering about how they really ought to set up a proper orphanage in Iskyla, so the townsfolk weren't stuck taking in all the abandoned strays.

I didn't complain either, and not only because there was nobody to listen. There were a few kids at my school who served as a reminder of how much worse it could be for me. They were sketches of children, really—thin lines, stark shadows, sad eyes, just the silhouettes of orphans.

"You sure you wanna hear that one again, *ayuh*?" Mr. Tulin said in response to my pleas.

"Yes, please!"

"If that's the one the lil' miss wants, then that be the one I tell." He walked back over to the bed, limping slightly, the way he did every time the temperatures dipped this low.

Once he'd settled on the edge of the bed, his bones cracked and creaked almost as loudly as the bed itself.

"It was a night much like this—" he began.

"But darker and colder, right?" I interjected.

His bushy silver eyebrows pinched together. "Are you telling it this time?"

"No, no, you tell it."

"*Ayuh*." He nodded once. "So I will, then."

It was a night much like this. The sun hadn't been seen for days, hiding behind dark clouds that left even the daylight murky blue. When the wind came up, blowing fresh snow so heavy and thick, you couldn't hardly see an inch in front of your nose.

All over, the town was battened down and quiet, waiting out the dark storm. Now, the folks in Iskyla had survived many a winter storm, persisting through even the harshest of winters. This wasn't the worst of the storms we'd faced, but there was something different about this one. Along with the cold and the dark, it brought with it a strange feeling in the air.

"And a stranger," I interjected again, unable to help myself.

Mr. Tulin didn't chastise me this time. He just winked and said, "*Ayuh*, and a stranger."

The old missus, Hilde, and I were hunkered down in front of the fireplace, listening to the wind rattling the house, when a knock came at the door.

Hilde—who scoffed whenever Tapeesa the angakkuq spoke of the spirits and monsters—shrieked at me when I got up to answer the door. "Whaddya think you're doing, Oskar?"

"We're still an inn, aren't we?" I paused before I reached the door to look back at my wife, who sat in her old rocker, clutching her knitting to her chest.

Well, of course we were. Her father had opened the inn years ago, back when the mines first opened and we had a brief bout of tourism from humans who got lost on their way to the mines.

But that had long dried up by the time Hilde inherited it. We only had a dozen or so customers every year, mostly Inuit or visiting trolls, but whenever I suggested we close up and move south, Hilde would pitch a fit, reminding me that her family settled Iskyla, and she was settled here until she died.

"Course we're an inn, but we're closed," Hilde said. "The storm's too bad to open."

Again the knocking came at the door, pounding harder this time.

"We got all our rooms empty, Hilde!" I argued. "Anyone out in this storm needs a place to stay, and we won't have to do much for 'em."

"But you don't know who—or what—is at the door," Hilde stammered, lowering her voice as if it would carry over the howling wind and out the door to whoever waited on our stoop. "No human or troll has any sense being out in a storm like this."

"Well, someone has, and I aim to find out who it is."

I headed toward the door, Hilde still spouting her hushed protests, but my mind had been made up. I wasn't about to let anyone freeze to death outside our house, not when we had ample firewood and room to keep them warm.

When I opened the door, there she stood. The tallest woman I ever saw. She was buried under layers of fabric and fur, looking so much like a giant grizzly bear that Hilde let out a scream.

Then the woman pushed back her hood, letting us see her face. Ice and snow had frozen to her eyebrows and eyelashes, and her short wild hair nearly matched the grizzly fur. She wasn't much to look at, with a broad face and a jagged scar across her ruddy cheeks, but she made up for it with her size.

She had to duck to come inside, ever mindful of the large bag she carried on her back.

"Don't bother coming in," Hilde called at the woman from where she sat angrily rocking. "We're closed."

"Please," the giant woman begged, and then she quickly slipped off her gloves and fumbled in her pockets. "Please, I have money. I'll give you all I have. I only need a place to stay for the night."

When she went for her money, she'd pushed back her cloaks enough that I could see the dagger holstered on her hip. The fire glinted off the amber stone in the hilt, the dark bronze handle carved into a trio of vultures.

It was the symbol of the Omte, and that was a weapon for a warrior. Here was this giant troll woman, with supernatural strength and a soldier's training. She could've killed me and Hilde right there, taken everything we had, but instead she pleaded and offered us all she had.

"Since we're closed, I won't be taking any of your money." I waved it away. "You need sanctuary from the storm, and I'm happy to give it to you."

"Thank you." The woman smiled, with tears in her eyes, and they sparkled in the light like the amber gemstone on her dagger.

Hilde huffed, but she didn't say anything more. The woman herself didn't say much either, not as I showed her up to her room and where the extra blankets were.

"Is there anything more you'll be needing?" I asked before I left her alone.

"Quiet rest," she replied with a weak smile.

"Well, you can always holler at me if you need anything. I'm Oskar."

She hesitated a second before saying, "Call me Orra."

"It's nice to meet you, Orra, and I hope you enjoy your stay with us."

She smiled again, then she shut the door. That was the last I ever saw of her.

All through the night, she made not a peep, which upset Hilde even more, since it gave her nothing to complain about. I slept soundly, but Hilde tossed and turned, certain that Orra would hurt us.

By the time morning came, the wind had stopped and the sun had broken through the clouds for the first time in days. I went up to check on Orra and see if she needed anything, and I discovered her gone.

She rode in on the back of the dark storm, and she left before the sun.

Her room had been left empty—except for a little tiny baby, wrapped in a blanket, sleeping in the middle of the bed. The babe couldn't be more than a few weeks old, but already had a thick head of wild blond hair. When I picked her up, the baby mewled, but didn't open her eyes.

Not until I said, "Ullaakuut,"—a good-morning greeting. Then her big amber eyes opened. She smiled up at me, and it was like the sun after the storm.

"That's how we met." I beamed, and he smiled back down at me. Mrs. Tulin wasn't sure if they would keep me, so she wouldn't let him name me yet, but then they called me Ullaakuut until it stuck.

"It was quite the introduction," he agreed with a chuckle.

"Oskar!" Mrs. Tulin shouted from the other room. "The fire's gone cold!"

"I'll be right down!" he yelled over his shoulder before turning back to me. "Well, you've had your story now, and Hilde needs me. You best be getting to sleep now. Good night, Ulla."

"Good night." I settled back into the bed, and it wasn't until he was at the door that I mustered the courage to ask him the question that burned on the tip of my tongue. "How come my mom left me here?"

"I can't say that I understand it," he said with a heavy sigh. "But she'd have to have got a mighty good reason to be traveling in that kinda storm, especially with a newborn. She was an Omte warrior, and I don't know what kind of monsters she had to face down on her way to our doorstep. But she musta known that here you'd be safe."

"Do you think she'll come back?" I asked.

His lips pressed into a thin line. "I can't say, lil' miss. But it's not the kind of thing I would hang my hat on. And it's nothing that you should concern yourself with. You have a home here as long as you need it, and now it's time for bed."

1

HOME

Emma sprinted into my room first, clutching her older brother's slingshot in her pudgy hands, and down the hall Liam was already yelling for me.

"Ulla! Emma keeps taking my stuff!" Liam rushed into my room in a huff, little Niko toddling behind him.

My bedroom was a maze of cardboard boxes—all of my worldly possessions carefully packed and labeled for my move in six weeks—and Emma darted between them to escape Liam's grasp.

"He said he was going to shoot fairies in the garden!" Emma insisted vehemently.

Liam rolled his eyes and brushed his thick tangles of curls off his forehead. "Don't be such a dumb baby. You know there's no such things as fairies."

"Don't call your sister dumb," I admonished him, which only caused him to huff even louder. For only being seven years old, Liam already had quite the flair for the dramatic. "You know, you're going to have to learn how to get along with your sister on your own. I'm not going to be around to get in the middle of your squabbles."

"You don't have to tell *me* that," Liam replied sourly. He stared down at the wood floor, letting his hair fall into his eyes. "She's the one that always starts it."

"I did not!" Emma shouted back. "I only wanted to protect the fairies!"

"Emma, will you give Liam back his slingshot if he promises not to kill anything with it?" I asked her. She seemed to consider this for a moment, wrinkling up her little freckled nose, but finally she nodded yes.

"I was never really going to kill anything anyway," he said.

"Promise!" Emma insisted.

"Fine. I promise I won't kill anything with my slingshot." He held his hand out to her, and she reluctantly handed it back to him. With that, he dashed out of the room, and Emma raced after him.

Niko, meanwhile, had no interest in the argument, and instead made his way over to me. I pulled him into my arms, relishing the way his soft curls felt tickling my chin as I held him, and breathing in his little-boy scent—the summer sun on his skin and sugared milk from his breakfast.

"How are you doing this morning, my sweet boy?" I asked him softly. He didn't answer, but Niko rarely did. Instead, he curled up more into me and began sucking his thumb.

I know I shouldn't pick favorites, but Niko would be the one I missed the most. Sandwiched between Emma and the twins, he was quiet and easily overlooked. Whenever I was having a bad day or feeling lonely, I could always count on him for cuddles and hugs that somehow managed to erase all the bad—at least for a few moments.

But now I could only smile at him and swallow down the lump in my throat.

This—all the scraped knees and runny noses, the giggles and tantrums, all the love and chaos and constant noise of a house full of children—had been my life for the past five years. Which was quite the contrast to the frozen isolation of the first fourteen and a half years of my life.

Five years ago, a Kanin tracker named Bryn Aven had been on an investigation that brought her to Iskyla in central Canada, and when I met her, I knew it was my chance out of that town. Maybe it was because of the way she came in, on the back of a storm, or because she was a half-breed. She was also blond like me, and that wasn't something I saw often in a town populated by trolls and a handful of the native humans of the area, the Inuit.

Most trolls, especially from the three more populous tribes—the Kanin, Trylle, and Vittra—were of a darker complexion. Their skin ran the gamut of medium brown shades, and their hair was dark brown and black, with eyes that matched. The Kanin and the Trylle looked like attractive humans, and the Vittra often did as well.

The Omte had a slightly lighter complexion than that, and they were also more prone to gigantism and physical deformities, most notably in their large population of ogres. With wild blond hair and blue eyes, the Skojare were the fairest, and they had a tendency to be born with gills, attuned to their aquatic lifestyle.

Each of the tribes even had different skill sets and extraordinary abilities. All of the kingdoms had some mild psychokinetic talents, with the Trylle being the most powerful. The Vittra and the Omte were known for their physical strength and ability to heal, while the Kanin had the skin-color-changing ability to blend in with their surroundings, much like intense chameleons.

Iskyla was officially a Kanin town, and the Inuit coloring wasn't much different from that of the Kanin. Most everyone around me had a shock of dark hair and symmetrical features. My noticeable differences had always made me an easy target growing up, and seeing the blond-haired tracker Bryn, I recognized a kindred spirit.

Or maybe it was because I could tell she was running from something, and I had been itching to run since as soon as I could walk. The Tulins had been good to me—or as good as an elderly couple who had never wanted kids could be when a baby is dropped on them. But Mrs. Tulin had always made it clear that I would be on my own as soon as I was ready, and when I was fourteen I was sure I was ready.

Fortunately, Bryn had been smart enough—and kind enough—not to leave me to fend for myself. She brought me to Förening, the Trylle capital in Minnesota, and found me a job and a place to stay with friends of hers.

When I had started as a live-in nanny working for Finn and Mia Holmes, they'd only had two children with another on the way, but already their cottage was rather cramped. Shortly after I moved in, Emma came along—followed by a promotion for Finn to the head of the Trylle royal guard—and Mia insisted a house upgrade was long overdue.

This grand little house, nestled in the bluffs along the Mississippi River—cozy but clean and bright—had enough room for us all—Finn, Mia, Hanna, Liam, Emma, Niko, Lissa, Luna, and me. As of a few months ago, we'd even managed to fit in Finn's mother, Annali, who had decided to move in with them after her husband passed away last fall.

This home had been my home for years, and really, this family had been my family too. They welcomed me with open arms. I grew to love them, and they loved me. Here, I felt like I belonged and mattered in a way that I had never been able to in Iskyla.

I was happy with them. But now I was leaving all of this behind.

2

independence

"But Mom, it's not fair!" Hanna was shouting, her voice reaching the ear-piercing levels of indignation that only twelve-year-olds seemed able to master.

When I walked into the kitchen, her mother was attempting to feed the twins, Lissa and Luna. A bright orange mush—presumably pureed carrots or maybe sweet potatoes—was slathered all over their high chairs and hands, and some had even gotten into Mia's dark hair.

"Hanna, we've already gone over this." Mia's tone was beyond exasperated, but Hanna stood defiantly in front of her, arms folded over her chest as she glared up at her mother. "Your grandparents see you so rarely."

"But it's just turned June, and you're sending me off! Me and my friends already made *so many* plans for the summer—"

"Well, that was silly of you, wasn't it?" Mia cut her daughter's rant short with a gentle rebuke. "You've known about this trip for months."

"But I never *wanted* to do it," she insisted with a whine. "At the very least you should let me stay for the party tonight."

"Ulla's internship starts on Monday, and she's not going to miss it for some party," Mia told her firmly. "Besides, parties at the palace are always so stuffy and boring."

Hanna groaned and rolled her dark eyes dramatically. "You're only saying that because you've been to *so many*."

I glanced over at the invitation tacked up on the corkboard—next to the calendar with reminders for the twins' checkups and Liam's camp schedule. Delicate filigree vines had been drawn along the edges, and at the bottom a rabbit sat front and center, flanked by a fish, a cougar, and a vulture.

Her Royal Highness Wendy Luella Staad
Queen of the Trylle
and Her Husband Loki
request the honor of your presence
at the Quinquennial Jubilee
of
Linus Fredrick Berling
King of the Kanin
with His Wife Ariel
on Saturday, the Eighth of June
Two Thousand Nineteen
at Seven O'Clock
at the Trylle Royal Palace in Förening, Minnesota

"Sorry, kid." I tried to sound apologetic—and I was sorry that Hanna was sad about it, but I was not at all upset about missing the party myself.

I had been to enough of these kinds of affairs to know that Mia was right. They were mostly boring and stuffy. This one was all about strengthening the alliances between the tribes—a shaky bit of peace that had been established during the Invasion of Doldastam that had ended with Linus's ascension to the throne.

Even though I'd grown up as part of the Kanin tribe, Iskyla was so far out and isolated we hardly followed politics, so I hadn't known about all the bits and troubles that led up to the civil war in the capital of the kingdom. An heir apparent felt their place on the throne was unduly set aside, and they plotted a coup a decade in the making. Monarchs were killed, leaders were overthrown, and the Kanin eventually found themselves with a whole new dynasty in place.

That meant the jubilee would be a room full of political frenemies saying nice things to one another and pretending that they actually meant them. It would be even less fun than it sounded.

Especially for someone who stuck out like me. It wasn't just that I was blond. Of all the tribes, the Trylle were the most renowned for their beauty, with so many of the men and women like slender models walking off a runway.

Meanwhile, I had broad shoulders and wide hips with hardly a cinch of a waist in the middle, making my body type "rectangular," as the magazines would helpfully declare, and not so much fat as I was *wide*, although I was a little pudgy, too.

Like many Omte, my face had a slightly squished lopsided appearance. The skewed look on my face was mostly due to my mouth—the left corner of my puffy lips drooped a bit—and my eyes—the left eye was slightly larger than the right, and the left pupil was permanently dilated in a birth defect, making the eye appear darker and even larger than it actually was.

It was only the Omte who were known for their asymmetric features, hulking bodies, and generally going against the grain of Western beauty standards in the twenty-first century. And that was me.

While I still enjoyed putting on a gown and getting all gussied up for big events like the royal party at the palace, the pressure of perfection made my less-than-perfect self uncomfortable.

"But none of the other kids have to go," Hanna said, ignoring me on her unrelenting crusade to get her mom to let her stay home.

"Liam has tracker camp, and everyone else is too young to be away from home for six weeks," Mia reminded her. "Besides, I thought you would enjoy having a break from your siblings."

"Yeah, but I didn't mean that I wanted to get stuck in some boring old house out in the middle of nowhere," Hanna muttered.

When she was pouting like that, slouching and with her bottom lip sticking out slightly, she appeared to be even younger than she actually was. The smattering of freckles across her face only lent itself to her youth, and her bouncy dark brown curls didn't help much either. Her thick eyebrows had started sprouting into a full-on unibrow over the winter—around the same time that I'd had to take her shopping for her first bra—and I'd taught her how to pluck and shape them.

"Have you finished packing yet?" I asked her.

"Have you?" she shot back, and her eyes met mine for a split second, long enough for me to see the hurt flash in them, and I realized that she was upset about more than being away from her friends.

My internship lasted six weeks. On my way there and back, I was dropping Hanna off and picking her up at her grandparents'. When we got back, I was moving out to a little apartment on the other side of town. I already had the first month's rent and security down. Mia and Finn were being kind enough to let me store most of my belongings here while I was on the internship.

So this was my last official day working as a nanny and living with the Holmeses.

"Come on, Hanna." I smiled at her. "We've got a super-fun road trip ahead of us. I already have playlists made for the road."

"Yeah?" She lifted her head slightly.

"Yeah, and how often do you get to be outside of Förening and see the humans in their natural habitat?" I asked, since that was something I'd heard her whinge about on more than one occasion.

She stood up taller. "Yeah? Like we'll be able to eat in a real restaurant with humans everywhere?"

"Yeah, we can eat anywhere you want."

That wasn't a total lie. We could stop at any restaurant, but in my experience, most food prepared outside of troll communities tended to make us sick. Since throughout most of our existence trolls had lived off the grid, hidden away and eating mostly what little fruits and vegetables we could get our hands on, we hadn't adapted well to the rich diets of humans.

"I pick . . . McDonald's," Hanna announced, causing Mia to let out a small laugh.

"Well, if you wanna stop somewhere, you better get finished packing," I told her. "I'd like to make it to your grandparents' before dark, and since we're driving fourteen hours, that means that we need to be on the road"—I glanced at the clock on the wall and groaned—"in fifteen minutes."

Now, bolstered by the promise of forbidden treats, Hanna ran upstairs to her room to finish packing.

3

farewells

We were running an hour behind. I don't know how it had happened, but I was still loading up the Jeep at half-past ten in the morning. Finn had been kind enough to borrow the Jeep from the Queen's small fleet of royal vehicles on the condition that I take Hanna to her grandparents'. It was a more-than-fair trade, so I had happily accepted.

"Okay, I think that's the last of it, then," I said, after carefully stowing Hanna's violin between our bags.

Trolls tended to be hoarders, and I was no exception. One of the more obvious ways this presented itself was how much I overpacked. It didn't help that all my stuff was essentially already packed for the big move, so why not just pile it in the Jeep in case I needed it during the next six weeks? Like literally all my clothing and jewelry. Would I need a winter jacket in June in Oregon? Probably not, but why risk it?

I had finally stuffed the Jeep as much as I could without risking injury or discomfort to Hanna and myself, so I closed the gate and turned back to face everyone. Mia and

Finn had attempted to gather the kids to see us off, but it was hard to keep them all together. Liam and Emma kept running around chasing each other, Niko wandered off after a butterfly, Lissa was asleep in a bouncer, and Luna was fussing, so Mia rocked her gently and sang to her.

Hanna started crying when she realized she hadn't said goodbye to her pony Calvin, so she darted off to do that.

"I bet you'll miss all of this," Finn said as he scooped up Niko before the toddler tumbled into the ditch.

"I don't know if you're kidding or not, but it's definitely going to be bittersweet to be somewhere quiet." I gestured vaguely around at the laughing and crying children who nearly drowned out the sound of the chirping birds and the warm breeze rustling through the trees.

"We were lucky to have you as long as we did," Mia said, and she gave me a pained smile with tears in her eyes. "It may be hard to tell right now, but we really are all going to be lost without you, Ulla. It won't hit the little ones until after you're gone."

"Come on, guys, this isn't goodbye forever," I said as I choked down my own tears. "When I get back, I'll still see you around town."

"I know, and you can always come back and visit," Mia said, and that was more of a command than an invitation. She hugged me then, with Luna letting out an irritated squawk as she found herself smooshed in the center of it.

Niko squirmed in Finn's arms, so I untangled myself from Mia and reached out for him. He let me kiss his chubby cheeks and hold him tightly to me, but only for a second. His attention was entirely focused on chasing butterflies, and he wouldn't stand for being held for another moment, so I set him back on the ground to run circles around his mother.

"We're really going to miss you, Ulla," Finn said, and the honesty of his words made tears spring fresh in my eyes. He wasn't much of an emotional guy, speaking in cool, polite tones that bordered on formal, and he chose his words carefully. That's when I realized: this wasn't the first time I was leaving my home, but it was the first time that I would be missed.

I wiped my eyes roughly with the palm of my hand and chewed the inside of my cheek to keep back the tears. "Yeah, well, thanks again for helping me out so much, giving me a roof and an education and now a Jeep and this internship. I don't know if I ever would've gotten to Merellä without you."

"It's the Queen that deserves all the gratitude for that one." He waved it away like it was nothing, but we both knew the truth. If not for his friendship with the Queen of the Trylle, and her writing a recommendation on my behalf, it would've been near-impossible for a nobody like me to land an internship in Merellä.

"And honestly, Ulla," he went on, "it's not nearly enough thanks for what you've done to help us. I don't know how we could've managed with all the changes we've gone through over the years."

"You only ever get what you give, you know?" I said, awkwardly repeating something that Mr. Tulin used to tell me all the time when I was a kid.

Hanna came running back from saying goodbye to her

pony, wiping at her eyes in a hurry. "Okay, I think I got it all out of my system. We can go now."

After a few more tearful and semi-tearful goodbyes, we finally made our way over to the car. Hanna had hopped in, and I was reaching for the driver's-side door, when I heard someone calling my name behind me.

I turned back to see Bryn Aven. Standing at the top of the hill, looking like a vision in white in the bright sun, and I had to blink to be sure it was her. Her crisp guard uniform made her appear older and slicker than when I had seen her last, but the wry smirk on her lips was unmistakably hers.

"You were gonna sneak off without even saying hello?" she asked.

Without thinking, I raced over to her and threw my arms around her, embracing her in a bear hug that was probably a little too tight based on the grunts she made. It had been years since I had seen her, but my feelings of gratitude, friendship, and (a bit of) infatuation remained wholly unchanged.

Once I released her, Bryn smiled at me and smoothed out her uniform. "Either I've gotten shorter or you've gotten taller."

"Maybe it's a little of both."

"It looks like you're all packed up. Are you going somewhere?"

"Yeah, I have to be in Merellä by Monday morning, and it's over a thirty-hour drive."

She let out a low whistle. "And I thought we had a long trip down from Doldastam. What's waiting for you in Merellä?"

"An internship at the Mimirin."

"*The* Mimirin? As in the Mimirin Talo?" she asked, and the awe in her voice made me blush.

The Mimirin was about the only true neutral space in the troll hierarchy. It was an ancient institution, one that purported to house the entire history of our kind. The Mimirin served as a library, a museum, a university, a research facility, and an opera house.

I nodded. "Yeah, it's the headquarters for the Inhemsk Project, and that's really what I'll be working on."

"The Inhemsk Project is that Vittra group that reassimilates the trolls of mixed blood, right?"

Trolls of mixed blood. That was the new official term, replacing plenty of more derogatory terms, like *halvblud*, half-breed, and mongrel. I didn't know how well it would take off, but it was definitely an improvement. Mr. Tulin had always told me that there was no shame in being the child of mixed tribes, but not everybody felt the same way he did.

"The Vittra started it, but it has no true tribal alliance, like the Mimirin. They're neutral and open to anyone."

When the Inhemsk Project had formed a few years ago, it was initially met with a lot of anger and protests. Historically, trolls of mixed parentage were shunned by proper society as punishment for their parents weakening the bloodlines, and by extension, the psychokinetic abilities in our blood that made us so powerful.

Eventually, though, our society had been forced to accept the harsh reality. With tribes like the Vittra and Skojare experiencing record rates of infertility and infant mortality in recent decades, their populations had begun to dwindle.

The Trylle—while not as plagued with medical issues

as the others—had begun to suffer their own population decrease because of their heavy reliance on the practice of changelings. In recent years, many of the troll children left as changelings declined to come back, choosing instead to live among the humans.

The Vittra were simply the first to realize how dire the situation had become. Queen Sara Elsing worried about the extinction of her tribe—not just the blood and their supernatural abilities but their way of life, their history, everything that made them the Vittra. It would all be gone if they didn't find a way to boost their population.

Now the Inhemsk Project worked at reaching out to all the children of mixed blood, hoping to bring them back into the fold to learn about their history and strengthen our society. Initially, the doors had only been open to mixed trolls—like half-Kanin, half-Trylle—but they'd widened their net to include even the ultimate taboo in our world—a child born of a troll and a human.

The two tribes with the largest self-sustaining population—the Kanin and the Omte—had eventually decided on a stance of indifference. They didn't fund the Inhemsk Project or openly use it, but they wouldn't stop the others from welcoming trolls of mixed blood into their midst.

"You're going to find your family?" Bryn asked.

"Well, I'm gonna try." I shrugged, trying to appear more nonchalant about the whole thing than I actually felt.

"I'd wish you luck, but I know you don't need it. You always were one tenacious kid."

I laughed. "Well, we'll see how far my tenacity gets me."

"I'm happy for you, but I have to admit that I'm a little

disappointed you won't be at the party tonight. I'm King Linus's personal guard, so I'll be working, but I hoped we'd have a little time to catch up."

"Still living the dream, huh?" I commented.

"Something like that." She smiled and lowered her gaze.

"Ulla!" Hanna leaned out the window of the Jeep, looking at me over the top of her cat-eye sunglasses. "Are we going or what? Because if we're staying longer, I'm getting out of the car."

I bit my lip and glanced back at an impatient Hanna. "No, don't get out. I'll be there in a minute." If she got out, it would be at least another twenty minutes before I'd get her back in, and we were already running so far behind.

"Sorry, I didn't mean to hold you up," Bryn said.

"No, don't be silly. We really do need to catch up soon."

"You have my number, and you can call me when you're not swamped with all your work at the Mimirin." Then she hugged me, holding me close for a second. "*Tavvaujutit,*" she whispered, saying goodbye in Inuktitut—*tah-vow-voo-teet*.

"*Tavvaujutit,*" I replied quietly, letting go of my oldest friend. I walked to the Jeep, looking back once to wave at everyone who was still around, and when I got in, I sat for a second and took a deep breath. It was time to leave behind everything I knew to start on my next adventure.

4

fathers

The citadel of Merellä sat right on the ocean in southern Oregon, some two thousand miles away from Förening. Almost right in the middle between the two cities was Eftershom—a tiny Trylle village nestled in the mountains of western Montana. That's where Hanna's grandparents lived, a mere thirteen hours away.

My goal from the start had been to make the trip to Eftershom in one day, and we'd gotten off to a late start, but I still thought it was doable assuming Hanna's pit stops didn't get in the way.

The stop to get fast food had been wonderfully quick, which left me optimistic. Then the three bathroom breaks came after, and that's not counting the time I had to pull over on the side of the road so she could throw up.

"Ugh." Hanna groaned and rested her head against the window.

"I told you that the shake and fries were a bad idea."

I really had tried to talk her out of it, suggesting that she ease herself into new foods with smaller sizes or maybe a salad or fruit. But Hanna insisted that I promised she could eat what she wanted from wherever she wanted, and now she was paying the price.

"Maybe I have the flu." She peered over at me with an eagerness that belied her intentions. "Maybe we should go back so I can rest up, and we can leave tomorrow."

"Nope. We're three hours away. Besides, you wanted to see the outside and the human world." I gestured to the acres of farmland that surrounded us as we traveled down a mostly empty highway. "Distract yourself from your upset stomach by taking in the scenery."

"This is *not* what I had in mind," Hanna muttered. "The gas stations haven't exactly been thrilling either."

"I'm sorry to tell you that humans aren't any more exciting than trolls," I said, and she snorted.

I had never spent much time outside of the troll kingdoms, but Finn's job had once been to go out and collect changelings from the human world, so he'd had to be an expert on their culture and way of life, and he thought it was important that we understood how the other half lived. But no matter how often he tried to teach Hanna that humans were usually just as boring as we were, she remained convinced that they were all jet-setting debutantes.

For a few moments, she sat in silence. I sang along to Sia on my playlist and tried to ignore her scowling and exaggerated sighs.

"You're really gonna make me sit in the car for *hours* feeling like I might throw up?"

"We can pull over if we need to. But if you're really worried, you can look in the back for a bucket or something." I motioned vaguely toward the back of the Jeep.

She groaned but complied. The way she leaned back there—unmindful of her stomach squishing between the seats—confirmed my theory that she was playing up her sickness. But she kept rooting around anyway, sifting through a box behind my seat.

I watched her in the rearview and said, "If you haven't found a bucket or anything yet, you probably aren't going to."

"What's this?" She slid back into her seat, holding up a package that I was very familiar with.

It was wrapped in parchment paper and twine. The paper was torn and tattered from me reopening and reclosing it dozens of times over the past six months, nearly making the Nunavut postal code illegible.

Inside of it was a Moleskine composition notebook I'd gotten brand new after Mrs. Tulin had sent me the package. I bought it the day I decided to make an actual plan for finding my parents, instead of just wondering about them, and I had filled the first few pages with everything I knew or suspected about them.

The notebook just fit inside the envelope Mrs. Tulin had sent, so I stored it in there with all the other memorabilia from my childhood. Along with the notebook, there were my limited medical and school records, a few photographs, and a small painting that Mr. Tulin had done.

"Careful." I watched her from the corner of my eye as she looked it over. "That's everything I know about who I am."

Hanna squinted at the return address. "Who sent it to you?"

"The old woman who took care of me when I was a kid," I explained coolly. "Her husband saved everything from the night I was left with them. He died a few months ago, and she was clearing out the house and thought I ought to have it."

"The old woman?" Hanna asked, crinkling her nose in confusion. "Didn't you call her Mom?"

I shook my head. "It wasn't like that. We weren't a family. We were more like flatmates."

"So they never adopted you?"

"Not really. They gave me their last name, but that was more out of practicality."

And even that was nebulous. I was almost certain that there was never any record of my existence in the human world, since trolls did everything in their power to stay off the grid and outside of human history. Other than changelings— who lived with humans after assuming the human identity of the baby they'd replaced—most trolls would never interact with humans, not in a meaningful way. We very rarely left the privacy of our tribes, except when traveling between our communities, and the governments as a whole—American, Canadian, Swedish, whatever—were never even aware of our existence.

And since I had been abandoned as a newborn in one of the most isolated communities in the five kingdoms, I didn't think there was much of a trail in the troll world, at least before I moved in with Hanna and her family.

"You know I'm adopted. Kinda," she said, then quickly added, "I mean, Mom is my real mom, but my real dad died when I was a baby. I don't remember him at all, and Dad officially adopted me when Liam was born."

She fell silent for a minute, staring thoughtfully at the barren landscape around us. What she'd told me wasn't surprising—it wasn't a secret, Mia and Finn had been up front about it from the start—but this was the first time Hanna herself had said anything to me about Finn not being her birth father, and I wasn't sure how to respond.

But before I could come up with anything, she turned her attention back to me and asked, "What about you? Do you remember your parents?"

I shook my head. "No, I was only a baby."

"And your mom just left you?" Hanna asked, sounding genuinely shocked.

"Maybe."

"Maybe?" she echoed in disbelief.

"An Omte woman left me," I said, elaborating what little I knew. "Mr. Tulin thought she looked like a guard or a warrior. When I was younger, I imagined that she was the guard for a Queen or a Princess, and that she hid me away on the orders of my parents—who I alternated between believing were star-crossed lovers who only wanted to protect me or were selfish snobs who got rid of me to protect their inheritances.

"But the truth is that the woman who left me that night might be my mother or her guard or maybe even a kidnapper," I finished with a sigh. "The only thing I know for sure is that she's the only connection I have to my parents."

"Why do you want to find your parents so badly?" Hanna asked, and I had to look over at her to be sure she was serious.

"Aren't you curious about your birth father?" I asked, incredulous.

"Not really." She shrugged. "Grandpa Johan and Grandma Sarina always try to tell me stories about him, and I don't mind hearing about him, but . . . I don't know him. He's a stranger to me."

Her thick lashes landed heavily on her cheeks as she stared down at her lap. "When they tell me about him, he doesn't sound anything like me. He liked math and chess and some boring game called *hnefatafl*. The only thing we have in common is that we both have freckles."

"Maybe it's different for you because you do *know*," I said. "Even if you don't personally know everything about him, that's your choice. You can call your grandparents or ask your mom if you have any questions."

"That's true. And I already have a mom and a dad, so I don't really feel like I need another one." She paused, then looked up at me as if something just occurred to her. "But you didn't even have one mom or dad."

"Not really," I agreed wearily.

"You know you're a part of our family, right? No matter what you find out about your parents, you'll always have us."

I smiled at her. "Thanks, Hanna. That means a lot to me."

5

Eftershom

By the time we finally reached Hanna's grandparents' house, it was after midnight and Hanna was sound asleep. My GPS stopped working as soon as I got to the edge of Eftershom—I wasn't sure if that was because of the mountains or the cloaking magic causing interference—but Mia had handwritten the directions just in case.

Fortunately, Eftershom was little more than a village with a single road running through it, and Mia's description—"a robin's egg"—aptly described the bright blue little cottage built into the side of a hill.

A light had been left on for me, and I'd barely parked in the driveway before Johan Nordin came out of the house to greet me. He offered to carry Hanna in, but when he saw me lift her up with ease, he stepped aside.

"My wife is asleep," he whispered as he held the front door open for me.

I nodded, and he directed me to a small guest room off the entry. I laid her down and pulled the covers up over her.

"Thank you again for driving all this way," Johan said, speaking in a low hushed voice so as not to disturb Hanna. "My eyes aren't what they used to be, and that's no good for all that driving."

Small oval glasses sat on the end of his nose, and he readjusted them as he grinned at me. It was a thin but cheerful smile, buried in a bushy silver-streaked beard that matched his thick head of hair.

"It's no problem," I reassured him.

"I know that you've had a long drive," he said as he led me away from Hanna's room. "I certainly appreciate if you want to lie down and get some rest. But if you're anything like me and need a moment to unwind first, I ought to let you know that I've just poured myself a glass of wine in the study, and you're more than welcome to join me."

"I always have trouble falling asleep, so that sounds great, actually."

"Wonderful." His smile deepened, and he led me toward the keyhole door at the end of the hall. The door was open a crack, and through it warm amber light danced and weaved, casting inviting shadows.

It was a tower of a room, really—round and rather narrow but stretching up for what seemed like miles. Bookcases curved along the walls, with every inch filled. A kerosene lamp glowed brightly on a drink cart where a decanter of wine sat next to two glasses.

The study smelled of wood (oak, maybe? sandalwood?) and old books and fresh dirt. When he handed me the glass of wine, the rich scent of grapes filled the air, giving the room a heady earthy sense.

He sat down in a distressed leather chair and motioned to the cushioned bench of a built-in nook in the bookcases. "Go on, make yourself comfortable."

"I've been sitting in the car all day, so it's nice to stretch my legs a bit." I took a sip from the wine and languidly walked his room, admiring all the old leather-bound books.

"How are things for Hanna back at home?" Johan asked.

"Good. She seems happy. She has lots of friends, and a pony she adores." I looked over my shoulder at him and laughed. "I'm sure you'll hear all about it while she's here."

He chuckled warmly. "I hope so. And her family treats her well?"

"Yes, of course. I mean, it can be chaotic there with all the kids, but her brothers and sisters are crazy about her."

"Good, good." He stared down thoughtfully at his wine, swirling it around in his glass. "I always knew that Mia would be an excellent mother. My son chose well in that regard."

I pointed to a picture on the mantel above the fireplace. "Is this him here?"

"Yes, that's my son Nikolas with my wife Sarina, two years before he died."

It was a photograph of a woman—sharp, severe, brittle, like shattered glass—and a young man around my age, maybe even younger. Under a mop of wild curls and a constellation of freckles, he had a toothy grin.

"Hanna looks like him," I commented.

He smiled wistfully. "She does. She seems to be far more headstrong than he ever was, but maybe that's for the best."

"Why do you say that?" I asked.

Johan waved his hand vaguely. "He got swept up into the

whole tracker thing, tracking changelings, bringing them home, protecting the realm. That's what got him dragged away from Eftershom and out to . . ." He trailed off and let a heavy silence hang in the air. "Well, out to where he died," he finished finally, and took a long drink of his wine.

"I'm sorry."

He shook his head. "It's not a thing that anyone ever really gets over, losing their only child, but time has a way of making it easier to breathe."

I scanned the shelves around us, looking for anything to change the subject. All I wanted was to unwind after a long day, not make an old man rehash painful memories.

"All these books, are you a writer?" I asked lamely.

"A professor and a historian, actually," he said with some pride. "Eftershom has one of the largest libraries in the entire Trylle kingdom."

I raised my eyebrows. "Really?"

He chuckled at my surprise. "Yes, it seems unbelievable that such a tiny community in the middle of nowhere would hold so much of the Trylle history, but that's precisely the reason why it is. The palace has been burned and ransacked a hundred times, but out here it's quiet and safe."

"Is that why the town was settled in the first place?" I asked.

"No, nothing that logical." He shook his head. "It was just that they'd gone far enough. That's where the name actually comes from. When the leader set up camp, one of the stuffy royal Markis asked, 'Why do we stop here?' And the leader answered, '*Eftersom vi har gått tillräckligt långt*,' which roughly translates to, 'Because we have gone far enough.' "

I laughed. "I suppose that's as good a reason as any."

As I walked around the room, admiring the collection of old books and talking with Johan, my eyes kept being drawn back to one. It was a bit thinner than most of the books, with a faded gray cover, but a gilded symbol on the spine kept catching the firelight. Despite the frayed binding, the symbol itself was crisp and intact, and there didn't appear to be a title or even words of any kind on the cover.

I ran my fingers across it—the soft faded fabric shifted to cool smooth embossing. The symbol itself looked both vaguely familiar and like something I hadn't seen before. It definitely had a Norse flair—maybe a variation of a *valknut* and a horned triskelion—but the inner swirls inside the triangles appeared to be leafy vines, a rather uncommon feature in ancient Scandinavia.

"What is this book?" I picked it up to show Johan, and the lightness of it surprised me. It was as if it were hollow, but when I lifted it, the vellum pages fanned out enough that I could see that it was indeed a real book.

Johan leaned forward and readjusted his glasses. When he saw what book I was holding, he smiled broadly. "Ah, I see you've discovered one of my favorites. *Jem-Kruk and the Adlrivellir.* Have you heard the tale of Jem-Kruk?"

"I don't think so," I said as I carefully put the book on the shelf.

"That's not surprising." He settled back into his armchair.

"It's an old bit of troll lore that has fallen out of favor. I'm sure you're familiar with the troll creation myth?"

"The one with the Orm and all the animals?"

He nodded. "Precisely."

Back in Förening, it was in one of the children's books called *Bedtime Stories for Trolls of All Ages,* and I'd read it dozens of times to Liam and Emma when they were younger.

It was a rather simple morality tale. All of the troll tribes were represented—the Skojare as a shy fish, the Omte as a tough vulture, the Vittra as a clever cougar, the Kanin as a wily rabbit, and the Trylle as a flower-loving squirrel.

At the start of the story, all the animals are pals and love hanging out together until this big snake-like monster— simply referred to as "the Orm"—decided to mess with them. The story left it vague about what his motives were— possibly jealousy or maybe just boredom—but eventually he gossips to all the animals and gets them to turn on one another.

In the book I read to the kids, all the animals become friends again and gang up on the Orm and chase him out of their happy home. But Hanna told me that that's not really how the story goes. In the end, all the animals die except for the cougar, and the Orm laughs at him, so the cougar cuts off his head before dying himself.

"It's a rather nice uncomplicated story," Johan said. "The problem with the story of the Orm is that, because it usually begins with 'Once upon a time,' everyone assumes that that's the beginning of the story. But really the story begins long before that, when the Orm still lived in a land of magic, and he fought a man called Jem-Kruk."

I smirked at him. "You say this like it really happened."

"Who's to say it didn't?" Johan asked, and I would swear there was a twinkle in his eye.

I laughed and shook my head. "Immortal snakes and talking animals? That sounds like the stuff of fairy tales to me."

"What about trolls with super strength?" he countered reasonably. "Villages built in secret inside mountains? Kingdoms hidden amongst the humans? That doesn't sound like a fairy tale to you?"

"That's different." I took a long drink of my wine as I tried to come up with an argument.

"How?"

"Because I've seen it. I *am* it."

He cocked his head, staring at me thoughtfully. "Haven't you ever thought that there was more to this world than only what you see?"

"I don't know." I wanted to come up with a better answer than that, but the exhaustion of the day and the wine hit me all at once, and then I was doing the best I could to suppress a yawn. "That's probably too deep a question to be asking me at two in the morning."

"Oh, yes, of course." He stood up and offered an apologetic smile. "I'm sorry. I get carried away talking about my work. You're probably ready to get some rest. We don't have another guest room, I'm afraid, but we do have a very long couch in the living room that my wife has all made up for you."

"Thank you."

6

speed вump

I had driven six hours, which added nearly four hundred miles to the odometer, when I stopped at a little gas station on a deserted stretch of road. I finished filling up the tank when the Jeep started rocking, and a loud banging sound emanated from within. The back gate swung open, and bags came tumbling out onto the ground, along with one very sweaty, disheveled tween girl.

Hanna stood up, dusted off her jeans, and pushed her damp curls off her forehead. "Oh, *jakla,* I seriously thought you'd never stop."

"Hanna!" I gaped at her in disbelief. "What the hell? What are you doing?"

I let out a frustrated sigh. Everything had seemed fine this morning. I woke up later than I'd wanted to after sleeping soundly on Johan's couch, but I'd still had a quick breakfast with Hanna and her grandparents. Hanna was quiet, but more of the shy-awkward type and less of the sulky-quietly-planning-to-run-away kind.

We'd all said goodbye in the driveway, and Johan chatted with me a bit about Merellä and the weather and the roads. I'd *thought* Hanna had gone out to explore the village to avoid a sappy goodbye, because that's what she told us all she was doing.

But apparently that had been a lie.

"I thought you'd gone far enough that it would be safe for me to get out," Hanna said.

I narrowed my eyes. "What do you mean, 'safe'?"

"Well, like you won't turn back." She motioned vaguely to the highway. "I was planning to wait until Merellä, but it was way too hot and cramped back there."

"Hanna, I have to turn back. All you've done is add another . . ." I groaned as I did the math of going to Eftershom and back. "Twelve hours? Ugh. That can't be right."

"Right, and you have to start your internship tomorrow," Hanna said with a waggle of her eyebrows. "You don't have time to go back and forth if you want to get any sleep before then."

"Hanna! What's so terrible about your grandparents that you're trying to hold me hostage over it?"

"I don't know them." She kicked at a rock and stared down emptily at it. "The last time I saw them was two years ago. Grandpa Johan sends me letters, and they call a few times a year, but . . . you wouldn't want to stay with strangers for six weeks, would you?"

"Maybe I'm not the best one to ask, since I moved in with your family pretty fast," I reminded her.

She shrugged it off. "Well, that's different. We have TV and internet."

"Come on, Hanna. You're being ridiculous."

"You don't get it, Ulla. I don't care if they are my family. I don't want to stay with them."

I chewed my lip as I stared down at her. Her arms were crossed over her chest, her chin up, defiant, but her eyes showed what she was truly feeling—fear.

Forcing a young girl to spend time with adults she felt uncomfortable around sounded way beyond my pay grade, so I decided it was time to hand it over to her parents. I called Mia on my cell, and after briefly explaining the situation to her, I handed the phone off to Hanna. Even though I stepped away to give her some privacy, it was hard to ignore her body language—which slowly shifted from slouching and trudging to standing tall with quick steps.

"Here." Hanna skipped over and thrust the phone at me. "Mom wants to talk to you."

"Hello?" I replied uncertainly.

"So, Ulla, I'm so sorry to have put you in this position," Mia said, her voice tight with worry. "I don't want to ask you to do anything that would jeopardize your time at the Mimirin, but I also can't have Hanna left alone on the side of the road in Washington."

"Mia, I would never—"

"No, no, of course not, I know you never would," Mia assured me quickly, then let out a sigh. "We have to figure out where she is going. Where are you staying in Merellä?"

"Just an apartment. I don't know that much about it, and I haven't seen any pictures."

I closed my eyes, trying to remember the listing I'd found online. It had been a few short things: FLATMATE WANTED.

2 BED, 1 BATH, KITCHENETTE. CARRIAGE HOUSE APT W/IN SHORT WALK OF MIMIRIN. After I'd found it, I went to Finn for help, since I'd never rented anything before in my life, and he'd actually set up most of it, gifting me a month's rent as a going-away present.

"Finn helped me out, so he knows all about it," I said.

"Great, wonderful." Mia let out a relieved breath. "That'll . . . hopefully, that should make things easier. So . . . I guess, right now, I think the best thing is for you to bring Hanna with you to Merellä. You have to keep going forward, and we won't be able to make it to wherever you are tonight."

"Yeah, that makes sense," I said, and out of the corner of my eye I saw Hanna twirling about. "I guess I'll call, um, my new flatmate and see how I can make it work."

"Thank you, and again, sorry about all this, Ulla."

"Yeah, I understand. We'll talk more later."

I ended the call and turned my attention back to Hanna. She was smiling widely until she saw my face, and her attempts to appear remorseful only made her look like she was holding back a sneeze.

"Don't do that. Don't pretend that you feel bad." I shook my head and managed a crooked smile. "You owe me big-time for this. Huge."

"I know, I know." She ran over and threw her arms around me. "Thank you so much!"

"Don't thank me so soon. I haven't figured out how you're gonna pay me back yet."

7

merellä

It appeared like a mirage in the dark of night.

There was little to see until a lighthouse, flashing onto angry waves crashing against the cliffside. Miles of empty coastline stretched out before us . . . until it didn't. The air shimmered and bowed, then shadows began to take shape.

"Oh *jakla*!" Hanna said in surprise, and she leaned forward, practically resting her chin on the dashboard, as she watched the cloaking magic fade and the buildings materialize.

Merellä—the ancient city on the sea—loomed before us like a gothic fairy tale. A ten-foot stone wall protected the inland side of the citadel, and to enter we had to pass through a massive gate made of wood and wrought iron. Two guard towers sat on either side, and I had to show them my official acceptance letter from the Mimirin as well as Finn's identification and voucher for me.

The guard handed me back my papers and asked, "Do you know where you're going, miss?"

"Not really, no," I admitted. "This is my first time here."

He tapped the address on my papers. "The place you're staying is in the Olde District, down by the stables. Stay on this road until the Ogden Tower, then take a left down toward Wapiti Way. It's only about a block or so away west of that."

"Thanks." I rolled the window back up and headed off the way he'd pointed me.

I drove slowly down the narrow dirt roads. The village houses along the road were practically built on top of each other, with hardly a gap between neighboring houses. A hazy fog drifted in off the ocean, and the dim kerosene lamps that hung on lampposts only added to the eerie feel.

"Do they have superheroes here?" Hannah asked.

"What are you talking about?"

She pointed out the window, and I looked up to see the dark silhouette perched on the peak of a thatched roof. A cloud shifted over the moon, illuminating the figure and her long, iridescent hair. In the moonlight it shimmered and shifted color like a silken rainbow.

"What the hell—" I slammed on the brakes a split second before I drove into the corner of a house.

Seconds later—barely long enough for me to catch my breath—the fabric roof of the Jeep caved in.

Hanna yelped and crouched down, and I threw the car in park. One of the bags came flying forward, as the figure in the back flailed.

In a clunky but effective move, I opened the door and grabbed Hanna, pulling her out with me. Looking back over my shoulder as I yanked her to safety, I caught a glimpse of the rainbow, then the figure dove out of the Jeep and took off down the street.

"What was that?" Hanna asked. "Is that a troll? Or a unicorn?"

I shot her a look. "Hanna, did you see a horse with a horn?"

"I'm just keeping my mind open. I've never seen anything like that before." She looked up at me. "Have you?"

"No." I shook my head. "Since we don't know *what* that was, I think we should get in the car and get to our apartment and maybe make sure that we lock the door behind us."

Hanna didn't move immediately—instead preferring to scan the skyline for signs of anything else unusual lurking about.

8

Flatmate

"You're late." That was how my new flatmate answered the door.

Hanna and I were huddled up on the landing at the top of the stairs with all of our bags piled around us, and Dagny Kasten—the aforementioned new flatmate—stood just inside, frowning at us. Her long black hair was pulled up into a messy bun, and the old plaid shorts and the pillow imprint on her tawny skin led me to believe she'd been asleep before we got here.

"I'm really sorry about that. We ran into some trouble on the way here," I said, and Hanna was still scanning the nearby rooftops for any signs of the rainbowed creeper.

Dagny narrowed her eyes at Hanna before looking back up at me. "You are the boarder, right? I thought you were coming alone."

"Yeah, I am Ulla Tulin," I assured her, and she relaxed some. "Hanna wasn't supposed to be here, but she's only staying until her parents can come get her."

Hanna smiled up hopefully at her and waved. "Hi, I'm Hanna. I'm twelve, and I'm quiet, clean, and I know how to make a mean carrot cake."

"Well, I don't know where you're gonna sleep, but you might as well come on in." Dagny finally stepped back, letting us into the apartment.

The place was small and rustic. Exposed beams ran along the vaulted ceilings, and the small galley kitchen had butcher-block countertops. Since this was temporary housing, it came sparsely furnished—a lumpy sofa, a battered bistro-style table with four stools, and ratty curtains over the windows. My bedroom was a small, open loft above the bathroom at the back of the apartment, accessible only by ladder. It was large enough for the twin mattress on the floor, a nightstand on one side, and a small dresser at the foot of the bed.

A door off the living room led to Dagny's bedroom that went unseen in the tour, and she immediately declared it was "completely off-limits" to me and Hanna, for any reason, ever.

After that, she gave us a brief rundown of the house rules— which basically amounted to us not touching her stuff, cleaning up after ourselves, and being quiet.

"Any questions?" she asked when she finished.

Hanna's hand shot up. "Do you have rainbow-haired trolls here?"

"Are you talking about those silly troll dolls?" Dagny asked derisively.

"No, we saw . . . *something* when we came into town," I explained. "I think it was maybe a troll or a person, with long crazy rainbow-colored hair."

"The Mimirin is filled with magic and attracts trolls from

all over the world." Dagny shrugged. "With brightly colored hair being so in right now, the wilder coeds here have to find new ways to stand out, so you're bound to see some crazy hair and inexplicable fashion choices while you're here."

"This wasn't just some teenager going wild at college," Hanna insisted. "They were doing parkour on the roofs, and their hair was totally unreal."

"I doubt it's anything more than someone experimenting with potions," Dagny said, and she tried to suppress a yawn. "The guards at the gate may not show it, but the security here is fairly tight. Since most of the protection comes from our supernatural abilities, there isn't much to see, but trust me when I say that Merellä makes sure to keep any really dangerous riffraff out."

"Well, I would like to get in touch with that security, then, to find out who we saw," I said. "When they were doing their rooftop acrobatics, they slipped and fell into my Jeep, seriously damaging the canvas top, and I'd like to get it fixed before I have to head home."

Dagny nodded, and this time she didn't even try to hide her yawning. "Tomorrow I'll take you to the Mimirin, and they'll help you get everything all sorted out. But right now I'm exhausted, so I'm going back to bed. I'll expect you to be up and ready to go by eight A.M. sharp."

"Can do. Thank you."

Dagny paused at her bedroom door. "How long are you staying?"

"For six weeks," I said.

"Oh, you'll be here for the Midsommar festival, then," Dagny commented.

"A festival?" Hanna asked with wide, sparkling eyes. "That sounds exciting. What is it?" But Dagny's only response was closing her bedroom door behind her, so Hanna looked over at me. "Do you know what it is?"

"It doesn't matter, because you won't be here for it," I reminded her.

9

provincial

Dagny led me through the twisting streets of Merellä, carefully navigating along the shops and carts and through all the rush-hour "traffic" of villagers all heading the same place we were. Hanna had been left behind at the apartment to entertain herself with her laptop and Dagny's suggestion of "cleaning." She hadn't been happy about it, but I couldn't very well take her to work with me, and she was old enough to fend for herself for the day.

As Dagny and I passed the third girl in a row sporting unnatural hair color—this time pastel cotton candy—I realized that she hadn't been exaggerating about the wilder fashion sensibilities. Dagny herself wore a bright yellow shift dress, though that didn't clash with the provincial village feel quite as much as some of the other choices I'd seen.

"I didn't think that troll hair held dye that well," I commented.

"They don't use human dye. They use potions here," Dagny explained, sounding bored, and she immediately changed the subject. "That's where I spend most of my time if I'm not working or at home."

She pointed across the road to a large brown building. The sign above the door featured a brightly colored bull's-eye and the name *Merellä Archery Club* in big, bold letters.

"Are you any good with a bow and arrow?" I asked.

"Very," she said. "But I do it because it relaxes me."

I tried to take in all the sights around me, but honestly, it was hard, because I was exhausted. All the driving the last couple days had been particularly draining, and then sleeping in a new bed never went that well for me. Plus, Hanna had kept talking to me from her makeshift bed on the lumpy couch all night.

To make matters worse, Dagny was practically a speed walker, and I had to scramble to keep up with her.

"I don't know if I'll ever be able to find my way here on my own," I said, attempting to make conversation with her in hopes that she would remember I was following her and slow down some.

"You'll get used to it," Dagny assured me flatly.

"How long did it take you to figure it out?" I asked.

"Oh, I knew my way around before I got here."

"How'd you manage that? Did you use magic?"

She snorted. "Hardly. I studied maps and everything I could get my hands on. It took me nine months before I was finally accepted into my program, so I had plenty of time."

"Why did it take so long?"

"*So long?*" she echoed scornfully. "It usually takes over a year for applicants to get in. I was fast-tracked because I graduated the top of my class at the Doldastam royal university."

"Oh, I . . . I didn't realize that, I guess."

"I'm assuming that it didn't take you that long, which means that you either have an *amazing* intellect, or . . ." She paused, her dark eyes appraising me as she clicked her tongue. "*Or* you have connections. So, which was it, Ulla?"

"It's not like that, exactly. I wanted to join the Inhemsk Project to find my parents, and the only way I could do that was through an internship—"

Dagny held up her hand. "I didn't ask *why* you were here, and honestly, I don't care." She turned on her heel and strode ahead.

"Well, it sounded like you cared," I muttered as I hurried after her. She didn't respond, so I decided to change the subject. "What brought you here?"

"I wanted to study environmental effects on parapsychological abilities, particularly in relation to the genetics and biodiversity among trolls, and Elof Dómari is the leading expert in troglecology," she said. "He's been a docent at the Mimirin since 2017, and this is a once-in-a-lifetime chance to work with him."

We'd finally reached the stone fortress at the center of Merellä. It was a massive four-stone Romanesque building, with several towers stretching even higher. Most of the exterior appeared simple and clean, with very few Gothic flourishes to give it an air of aristocracy. The closer we got to it, the more imposing and formidable it felt.

In front of the main entrance into the Mimirin, everyone had to line up to pass through security. At the gates were several guards, running two different kinds of wands over everyone who passed—one that was electronic and scanned for basic weapons, and the other psionic, made with crystals and ancient twisted roots, to check for supernatural threats. The whole process didn't appear much different than when I'd gone through security at the airport, the one time I'd flown.

Unlike airport security, the guards were armed, and they had their weapons on full display. Most of them appeared to either have a dagger or a sword sheathed on one hip, but they all had PSGs—psionic stun guns. They were stocky, nonlethal weapons, usually made from a carved hardwood with four sharp prongs at one end.

"What is a docent?" I asked Dagny, once we'd fallen in beside each other in one of the lines.

"It's like an adjunct professor, but instead of taking a salary, a docent works for free," she explained. "Elof teaches a few classes here in exchange for room, board, and access to their extensive research facilities."

"Are the facilities really that great here that he'd forgo a paycheck?"

"I guess it depends on what you value more—money or the existence of our kind," she said with a cynical smile. "The goal of Elof's research is to discover the sources of our psychokinetic abilities and if there's a relationship with tribal infertility. If we can do that, we might be able to strengthen our blood and our birthright. His work might be our only chance at stopping our own extinction. Personally, I'd take saving our kind over money any day, but maybe that's just me."

"That sounds a little fatalistic to me," I argued. "Things are rough, but that doesn't mean we're going extinct."

"The fact that you're even here is proof that I'm not the only one who's worried."

"What do you mean?"

"You're here for the Inhemsk Project. Do you really think the Mimirin would let in TOMBs like you?" Dagny asked. I must've looked confused, because she clarified, "TOMB is an acronym for 'trolls of mixed blood.' That's what everyone calls the Inhemsk Project members."

"TOMBs?" I laughed dryly. "Everything around here is so Gothic and gloomy. Maybe I can get together with the rest of the TOMBs, and we can start a Joy Division cover band."

Once we finally got through security, we entered the grand main hall, where the barrel-vaulted ceiling stretched out a hundred feet above us. I wanted to take a moment to appreciate the enormity of it all and the history carved into the architecture, but the crowd was pushing me along.

Just around the corner of the main hall was a large room full of tiny lockers, and Dagny quickly ushered me over to them.

"No shoes allowed beyond here," she explained, not that I minded. Like most trolls, I hated wearing shoes, and I was always looking for a way around them.

The lockers had a slot for change, and it cost only two quarters for the entire day. Once a locker was shut, a key was released, and I slid it onto the long chain I wore around my neck, along with the key to the apartment and a stone talisman carved into a small polar bear.

Dagny led me down a long corridor off the locker room,

and then stopped abruptly when the hallway forked underneath an arch.

"Well, this is where we part ways." Dagny motioned down the hall. "The Inhemsk office is the second door on the right."

"Thanks for getting me this far," I said, but she had already started walking in the opposite direction down the hall.

10

ınhemsk

Like many of the other doors I'd passed in the Mimirin, the office door had a frosted stained-glass image inlaid in the wood. This one featured a yellow flower dipped in red blood, and while I wasn't sure what it was in reference to, it seemed fitting for the Inhemsk Project.

I knocked meekly on the door, and a gravelly female voice immediately barked, "Come in!"

I stepped into an office overflowing with paper. Bookcases and mismatched file cabinets were lined up throughout the office, creating a labyrinth of cubicles where half a dozen men and women were typing furiously on old laptops. Files, binders, books, and loose-leaf paper were stacked up all over the desks and any available surface, so it was hard to get a real sense of the size of the office.

The only obviously visible troll was a tall, slender woman in her forties, standing to the side of the desk buried in the center of the room. She held a copper thermos in her hands, the many rings on her long fingers clanking gently against the metal. Her dark brown curls hung stiffly above her shoulders, and she wore a fitted navy blazer with tapered pants, giving her an air of cool professionalism.

From under heavy hooded lashes, her dark eyes stared skeptically at me. "Can I help you?" she asked, in the same gruff voice that had invited me in.

"I'm Ulla Tulin. I'm here for the internship."

"Right." Her thin lips pressed into a tight smile. "The Trylle favor."

I bristled slightly but kept my smile polite. "I wouldn't say that a recommendation letter is a favor—"

She waved her hand. "It doesn't matter. You're here, and we take all the help we can get. I'm Sylvi Hagen, the director of the Inhemsk Project. Unfortunately, I have a meeting, so I won't be able to show you around, but I'll leave you in capable hands."

Sylvi's gaze turned to a young man, mostly hidden behind the stacks of folders and files on the desk nearest to her. In fact, I could only really see his short black curls and sharp eyebrows.

"You have some time now, don't you?" Sylvi asked, absently tapping her rings against her thermos.

"Yeah, of course," he replied without hesitation.

"Perfect." She turned back to me with a bland, tired smile. "So, Ella—"

"Ulla," I corrected her.

"Right. Ulla Tulin, this is one of our researchers, Panuk Soriano."

I stepped closer to Sylvi so I could finally get a real look at him, but he was already getting to his feet. He couldn't have been much older than me, though I suspected that his full cheeks and wide dark eyes gave him a deceptively youthful appearance. He leaned over the desk, extending his arm out toward me, and I realized—with a nervous flurry warming my belly—that he was very handsome.

"Nice to meet you," he said as we shook hands.

"Likewise," I said, swallowing back my nerves enough to manage a smile.

"Great," Sylvi announced abruptly. "I'll leave you two to it, then." Then she walked away, leaving Panuk to sort everything out with me.

"So, Sylvi gave me your file this morning," he explained as he shuffled through the folders on his desk. "But, of course, now I can't find it." He grimaced and shook his head. "I'm sorry about this. Sylvi likes to say that the office is in a constant state of organized chaos, but it's really just chaos."

He let out a self-deprecating laugh, then straightened up and rubbed the back of his neck. "I can't find your file now, but it doesn't matter because I read it earlier, and you're here now, so . . ."

When he looked back at me, an easy crooked smile spread out across his face. "I guess that makes me your official welcome wagon. Welcome to the glamorous world of dusty books and paper cuts. I'm sure you'll come to adore squinting at illegible ancient handwriting well into the wee hours of the morning."

"Wow, I hadn't realized it was so prestigious. Now I feel underdressed," I joked and motioned to my plaid challis shirt and skinny jeans, an outfit that wasn't all that dissimilar from his own flannel and jeans combo.

He looked me over, then laughed again, but this time heartier and warmer. "I think you'll fit in just fine around here."

I tucked my hair behind my ear. "I hope so."

"I should probably start by showing you around." He walked out from behind the desk, coming over to where I stood awkwardly in the middle of the office, and then he gestured vaguely around. "This is the main office, where all the salaried staff have their desks and do their work. But the volunteers and interns spend hardly any time here, so I'll spare you all the gory details of our nightmare filing system.

"You understand how this whole arrangement works, right?" he asked. "Each day you give us seven hours helping to collate our records and enter data, you get two hours of access to our records to look up your family and ancestry."

I nodded. "I gotta put in my time if I want your help."

"That is basically the motto at the Mimirin." He leaned in closer to me, lowering his voice to a conspiratorial tone. "Don't tell anyone I said that. The motto is actually, '*Ex nihilo nihil fit,*' and if the powers that be heard me saying otherwise, they would not be happy."

"They take their mottoes here that seriously, huh?" I asked.

Panuk glanced around before continuing, still in a hushed voice, "Honestly, they take *everything* too seriously." He straightened up. "But don't let me scare you off. Everyone takes it seriously because what we do matters, and there's nowhere else in the world you can get the education you get here."

"Well, that's why I'm here," I told him.

"Perfect." He took a step backward, heading toward the

door. "You'll be working with Calder Nogrenn in the archives, and if you love history, it's a good gig."

He went out into the hallway, holding the door open for me as I followed him. "The only bad thing about the archives is that they are way, *way* down in the basement."

We walked along, and Panuk listed the various amenities as we passed them—restrooms, nearest cafeteria, the rec room with the "good foosball table." In fact, he talked the entire way, helpfully explaining as much as he possibly could, so that when he finally stopped, it felt eerily silent. It didn't help that by then we had started the long descent down the winding stone staircase into the basement.

"So, Panuk?" I began, attempting to restart the conversation so we wouldn't be trapped in an awkward silence. "That sounds Inuit."

"Everyone calls me Pan, actually," he corrected me gently, then sighed. "Sylvi's not so great with names."

"Yeah, I figured that," I admitted with a laugh.

He waited a beat before finally saying, "My grandfather was Inuit."

He said it softly, but not in the conspiratorial joking way he'd spoken before. This was quiet, restrained, like a reluctant confession. He didn't look directly at me as he spoke, instead only peering at me from the corner of his eye.

"*Ullaakuut,*" I said.

He gazed at me with dark eyes, pausing on the step for a moment, until he finally replied with, "*Ullaakuut.*" A slow, crooked smile spread out on his face, and he fell in step beside me. "How do you know Inuit?"

Inuit refers to the indigenous humans of the Arctic regions in North America and the language they speak. In the past, the Inuit may have been called Eskimos, but now that term was generally considered a pejorative. Their people had lived here even longer than the trolls, before we came over with the Vikings, and at various times in our long history we had united with them against our shared enemy of aggressive colonialism.

As such, trolls held a slightly higher opinion of the Inuit than they did most other humans, but that didn't really mean much, considering how little the troll tribes thought of humanity as a whole. But we had managed to fall into an uneasy alliance with the Inuit, working and living together in the Far North when we needed to, and we respected each other's privacy and independence.

"I grew up in Iskyla, so I spent a lot of time interacting with the native humans."

Pan shook his head as he chuckled to himself. "I have to say that is the most unexpected response I've ever gotten to someone finding out that I'm a quarter Inuit."

"How does everyone else react?" I asked, even though I suspected I already knew the answer.

"Well, most trolls aren't so kind when they find I've got human blood," he answered, rather diplomatically.

"I've been here for about two years now, and it has been downgraded to a grudging skepticism from outright disgust, so I guess that's an improvement." Probably realizing what he'd said, he hurried to reassure me with a strained smile. "Don't worry, though. It'll be easier for you because you're a TOMB. The real trouble is when you're a half-TOMB. I'm a KanHu half-TOMB, to be more specific."

"Kanin and human?"

"Yep. And if I recall correctly, you're a Skomte?"

"Yeah." I paused and shook my head. "I mean, I think so. I never even met my parents, so I honestly can't say for sure." When trolls saw blond hair, they thought Skojare, but my strength and facial asymmetry was almost certainly Omte. So, the Tulins had assumed I was Skomte.

"Tomorrow I'll get you set up with a blood test, and then you'll know for sure," he said as we reached the basement. "But we're finally here." He hooked his thumb at two massive arched wooden doors. "Are you ready to see where you're going to spend the rest of your time here?"

11

archival

It was a room of shelves. Floor-to-ceiling—roughly ten feet, ladders needed to reach half the shelves—with archways cut into the bookcases, creating tunnels that ran through row after row of files, boxes, and papers. Most shelves ran parallel to each other, but a few of them crossed this way and that, creating random dead ends and giving it a rather claustrophobic and labyrinthian feel.

The doors opened to the largest of the tunnels, which led straight to the desk at the center. It was a circular desk, and the front side had been intricately carved with scenes from troll history. Vines and trees weaved together in a delicate lattice and connected the various events, bridging the gaps between the ships escaping Scandinavia, to the first settlements in the Arctic, to the battles between the tribes.

Scrolls were set in small piles around the desk, with a man sitting hunched over one in the middle of it all. His right hand was buried in his salt-and-pepper hair, while he used his left to hurriedly scribble onto a pad of paper. The long sleeves of his burgundy caftan hung over his hands, and smudges of black ink stained the golden embroidered designs that ran along the hem.

"And this is where your adventure begins," Pan said to me with faux bravado as we approached.

The man looked up, his eyes crinkling as he smiled, and he set aside his pen. "Well, hello, Pan. What brings you down to the depths of the dungeon?"

"Ah, Calder, you know I can never get enough of your happy face." Pan leaned against the desk, then nodded at me. "But right now I'm showing around the new recruit. This is Ulla Tulin, the intern who'll be helping you. Ulla, this is Calder Nogrenn, our resident history expert, heritage buff, and regular aficionado on all things that go bump in the archives."

"I look forward to helping out and learning from you," I said.

"Then let this be my first lesson to you—beware of Pan's silver tongue," Calder said with a smirk.

Pan rolled his eyes and warned me, "Flattery gets you nowhere with this one. But he is genuinely one of the smartest guys around, and you'll be in good hands with him."

"Now, that part *is* true," Calder agreed with a wink. "What languages are you fluent in?"

"Fluent?" I sucked in air through my teeth. "I'm only truly fluent in English, but I know quite a bit of Inuit, and I've studied all of the old Germanic languages."

"Old Germanic is exactly what we deal with down here." Calder shifted around the scrolls. "Do you think you know enough that you could help me organize these?"

"I'll do my best," I said, hoping I sounded more confident than I felt.

Calder pushed one of the scrolls across the desk toward me, the old paper unrolling to reveal faded black letters scrawled across the parchment.

Pan knocked gently on the desk and straightened up. "I'll let you guys get to work, then." He started backing away, but his eyes lingered on me. "You know where I am if you need anything."

I smiled at him. "I do. Thanks for showing me around."

"What can you make of this one?" Calder asked, tapping the scroll and pulling my attention back to him.

Viliättan Taga

I awkwardly attempted to sound it out. "Miliassnn Togo?"

Calder chuckled and shook his head. "I forget how hard to read these old black letters can be. I've gotten so used to the handwriting of Hilde Nilsdotter, I can read it better than my own."

"Who is Hilde Nilsdotter?"

"You've never heard of her?" He cocked an eyebrow at me. "She is perhaps the most important historian in troll antiquity." He leaned back in his chair and tapped his pen on his paper. "Where were you educated?"

"Mostly in Iskyla, which means practically no education." I fidgeted with the pendant around my neck. "In

Förening, the family I nannied for helped me out with home-schooling."

That was the short version of the story. The longer one was that I'd tried to go to the school in Förening—Finn and Mia had actually insisted on it, if I wanted to stay with them—and I had been so far behind in most of my subjects that it had been impossible for me to follow along. That led to kids bullying me, and the whole situation was untenable.

At least I knew how to read and write, so Finn pulled me out of school. He hired me a tutor who came a few evenings a week, and the rest of the time I fell under the tutelage of Finn, Mia, the local librarians, and online teaching aids and classes. Together it all added up to a rather hodgepodge but somewhat extensive education, which was how I'd ended up semi-fluent in partially dead languages but didn't know the name of a famous historian.

"Ah, yes," Calder said with a sigh. "Iskyla—the frozen village that somehow specializes in letting every one of its inhabitants down."

It was the weary understanding in his voice that suddenly made it all click. His weathered olive complexion, ruddy cheeks, a scar nearly hidden in the wrinkles around his eyes and bushy eyebrows, and his resigned, stoic expression—in his muddy gray eyes I recognized the pain of a thousand icy mornings, of frozen days when the temperatures dropped and the sun never rose.

"You're from Iskyla?" I asked.

He lowered his gaze. "*From* is much too strong of a word, but it's fair to say that I'm well acquainted with it." Then he shook his head and offered me a thin smile. "It's no matter. I've been here in the archives of the Mimirin for almost twenty-five years. And you're here now, which means you've managed to pull yourself out of Iskyla, and I'm happy to help you the rest of the way."

I swallowed the painful mixture of shame and pride, and I fought to keep my expression neutral and polite. "Thanks, but I'm really here to help you."

"And you will!" He flashed an exuberant smile. "I'll give you the tools, and you'll do the work."

With that, he copied the title from the scroll, duplicating the old Norse calligraphy on top, and then translating below in his clear print. When he'd finished, he turned the paper to face me.

"Viliätten Saga?" I read aloud. "The story of the House of Vili?"

He snapped his fingers. "Exactly! Are you familiar with the House of Vili at all?"

"It was the first troll dynasty, right? From back before all the tribes split?"

"Back when we were all known as *ekkálfar*." Calder wrote as he spoke, creating a key between Hilde Nilsdotter's confusing letters to more modern English. "Before it all became a mess of rivalries and lost histories."

I rested my arms on the desk, the smooth dark walnut feeling cool through the thin fabric of my shirt. "But don't you already know about the House of Vili?"

"Yes, but it can be near-impossible to know what you don't know." He peered up at me. "There's an old proverb that my grandmother used to say. 'A foolish man thinks he knows all. A wise man knows he cannot.' "

"I've heard that a few times," I said with a laugh. Finn had been quite fond of telling me something similar when I didn't study enough or failed a test.

"That's why I never stop learning, never stop reading." He gently tapped the scroll with his finger. "This is Nilsdotter's most famous and most extensive work. It's known as the *Heimskaga*."

"The story of the world?" I asked, digging deep into the recesses of the old Norse poems and essays that Finn had made me read.

"Correct," Calder said, sounding impressed. "It took Nilsdotter decades to compile it all, with her writing multiple drafts of the *Heimskaga* through the years, adding new information and correcting previous errors.

"These particular scrolls are from Isarna in Scandinavia," he continued. "In the tenth century there was a great exodus of trolls fleeing the violence and plagues the humans brought with them as they conquered and re-conquered the land around our homes. Thousands and thousands of our kind went with the Vikings to North America, but some—no more than a few hundred—stayed behind in the city that became Isarna.

"Because it's the oldest troll settlement left, it has some of our only records from that era," Calder explained. "The Mimirin recently reached an agreement with Isarna to review some of their ancient records stored there, and they found a whole trove of documents stored away in an old farm cellar.

"These scrolls may not have been read for centuries, their information unseen and thus unrecorded by anyone here at the Mimirin," he went on. "In these unread editions, there may be words, phrases, or even whole passages added or translated differently to give us new insights. There could be things about our history that would have otherwise been lost to us, about our time in Scandinavia and the early years in Áibmoráigi—the First City."

Áibmoráigi was the legendary first city established by trolls, our first home in our recorded history. It was thought to be something like Mesopotamia would be for the humans, but it had been lost for a thousand years.

"So, you scour every version of the *Heimskaga* in case there is something new to be gleaned?" I asked.

"I scour every version of every scroll or parchment that passes over my desk," Calder corrected me. "There is always more to be learned from our past."

"Okay." I nodded. "How can I help?"

"I want you to start by reading through that scroll and transcribe every name listed and everything that's written about them. Once it's all compiled, you can enter that into a database to compare and contrast what's already been documented."

"Sounds easy enough," I said.

Calder chuckled. "Your enthusiasm is admirable, but let's do a trial run first." He pushed the alphabet key toward me and then carefully tilted the scroll. "Why don't you give that a go? Read me the first sentence."

"Okay, um . . ." I began by copying the phrase, carefully transcribing Nilsdotter's words into something I could read.

Within a few minutes, I ended up with the phrase: *Vili hét einn herkonungr; hans synir kölluð Vilfinga ætt, fór til Vesturlands, ok er til sigra allt sem þeir fundu.*

I focused on trying to dig up all the Norse and Swedish Finn had encouraged me to study. " 'Vili is . . . the King. His sons are called the House of Vili . . . and went to *Vestur-lands*?' " I looked up uncertainly at Calder. "Is that the name of a place or is it saying Western Lands?"

"It's referring to North America, but Western Lands is the name given here," Calder explained.

"So his sons went to the Western Lands to . . . fight . . . what they found." I exhaled and said that didn't sound quite right. "*Sigra*. No, not fight. Conquer. To conquer what they found."

"Very good," Calder said. "The most accurate translation would be 'Vili is the one King; his sons are called the House of Vili and went to the Western Lands, to conquer all they found.' "

"Not too bad for my first official translation." I beamed at him.

"Not *too* bad," he agreed guardedly. "But I think your time in the archives should be equal parts transcribing and equal parts studying the languages. The more fluent you are, the more capable you'll be at your work."

12

adjustments

By the time I'd ended my first day of work at the archives, I hardly had the energy to do what I'd come here for: research for any information about my parents.

Calder worked over an hour past the end of his shift, but he still left before I did. Before that, he showed me where the Omte records were kept. In the corner of the archives, through a set of heavy wooden doors, a narrow staircase led down to a dimly lit, temperature-controlled cellar.

"Unfortunately, there isn't much here in the Omte vault." Calder sounded rather grim as he motioned to the sparse shelving. "They're not exactly known for their recordkeeping or sharing with others. But I hope that what we have is enough to help you out."

"Well, I've got nothing now, so even a little something will leave me better off."

He took me back to the shelves labeled NINETEEN-HUNDRED AND NINETY-NINE. Since I had been left at the Tulins' in the fall of 1999 as an infant, it stood to reason that I had been born that year, and I was looking for any pregnancies, births, or unexplained absences during that year.

Calder left me alone to dig through dusty pages of angry chicken scratch. This was yet another way that trollkind's aversion to technology became an inconvenient hindrance. Typing up or even scanning the records into computers would make it all a lot easier, but here they were, all handwritten and stored in a basement.

I worked as long as I could, but I'd only made it to the end of January 1999 when I had to stop. My eyes burned and my lids were heavy, and I was going to have to get up and do it all again tomorrow.

The walk back to the apartment wasn't as bad as I'd feared. It was late, the sun already dipping below the walls that surrounded the citadel, and the streets were much emptier now than they had been this morning. I only made a wrong turn once, and I quickly figured my way back to the right path.

When I finally rounded a corner and saw the carriage house I'd be calling home for the next six weeks, I let out a relieved sigh. That is, until I spotted the battered Jeep, still parked underneath the wooden staircase, and I realized I'd forgotten all about the wild-haired creeper and reporting them to security.

Well, that would have to be a problem for another day. Today I couldn't wait to get out of my skinny jeans and wash the scent of must and dust off me.

The windows of the apartment were open, and when I walked up the stairs I could hear Hanna singing a Taylor Swift song. As I passed the window, a subtle sweetness filled the air, and I inhaled deeply.

It was a wonderfully familiar scent, which instantly brought me back to the long summer days back in Iskyla, when the sun made Mrs. Tulin smile and hum and she'd spend the afternoons baking pastries and tarts for nearly everyone in town.

"Ulla!" Hanna announced, the moment I opened the door. "You're finally home!" She'd been wiping down the counter when I came in, but she paused to smile at me. "There's beet salad in the fridge, and I just pulled the blackberry tarts out of the oven."

"Is that what I smelled?" I asked.

"Yeah, and they taste even better than they smell," Dagny chimed in through a mouthful of food. She sat on the lumpy couch, her feet propped up on the wooden pallet-cinder-block contraption that served as a makeshift coffee table.

"Sit." Hanna tossed the washrag in the kitchen sink, then wiped her hands on a flour-sack towel. "Are you hungry? I'll fix you a plate."

"Um, yeah, I can eat." I gave an uncertain laugh and took a seat on a stool next to the bistro table.

As I watched Hanna run around the kitchen—first handing me a delicate little pastry topped with a dark purple-blue glaze, then carefully piling a plate of deep burgundy beets, sharp green apples, and bright lemon and yogurt cream sauce—I couldn't help but think back to the petulant child I'd been dealing with back in Förening. Hanna wasn't a bad kid, but her mom would probably faint in shock at the sight of Hanna cooking and cleaning without putting on a major protest first.

I took a bite of blackberry tart, deciding that I was old

enough to eat my dessert first, and it was the absolute perfect blend of light flaky crust with a creamy bittersweet sauce. "Wow." I groaned happily between bites. "Oh, this is amazing. You really outdid yourself this time, Hanna."

She shrugged and tried to demur, but her pride was unmistakable in her wide smile. "Well, I figured since I had nothing to do all day, I ought to make myself useful."

"This is definitely a good start," Dagny admitted. She stood up and grabbed her book bag from where it'd been sitting on the floor near her feet. "But like my mother always said, *Fish and houseguests start to smell after three days.*"

"I'll be sure to put on deodorant after I shower," Hanna said with a flat smile.

"Always a good idea," I chimed in.

"I'll be in my room if you need me, and I seriously encourage you not to need me tonight," Dagny said over her shoulder as she walked into her room. While she didn't exactly slam the door, she shut it loud enough that it caused Hanna to jump a little.

"So." She hopped up on the stool across from me and rested her arms on the table. "How was your first day?"

"It was good." I took a bite of the beet salad—which, again, was exquisitely executed, walking that fine, bittersweet line between acidic salt and creamy bland that the subarctic troll cuisine was known for—and I thought over my answer as I ate. "Exhausting, but good. I think."

"Did you find your parents yet?" Hanna asked.

I shook my head. "No, I hardly even had a chance to look."

"Dagny told me that's how things are done here." Her gaze lingered on Dagny's closed bedroom door, and she lowered her voice. "They want to milk you for every ounce of labor they can get, which doesn't leave you with much left over. She said that if you've got stuff you want to do here, you better be willing to fight for it, because they aren't going to give it to you."

"Well, I'm willing to do whatever it is that I have to do," I said, but my words didn't have quite as much conviction as I'd had before I got here. But I assumed that things would get better once I settled, and once I got a few good nights' worth of sleep.

"What do you wanna do after supper?" Hanna propped her head on her hand and stared at me with big, hopeful eyes. "Wanna go out on the town?"

"Actually, I wanna take a nice long shower and then get some sleep."

Her face fell and her more customary whine tinged her words. "Really? But I've been cooped up in the apartment all day."

"I know that sucks." I met her plaintive gaze, and I tried my best to keep my tone as gentle as I could. "But this isn't summer camp, Hanna. I'm here to work. If you wanted to have fun running around and hanging out, you should've stayed with your grandparents."

She rolled her eyes and leaned back away from me. "Oh, that's not fair. I never agreed to go to my grandparents' in the first place. You basically kidnapped me. You can't get mad at me for not taking it lying down."

"I did *not* kidnap you! Honestly, I don't even know what the big deal was. Your grandparents seemed perfectly nice and ordinary. What was so bad about it that you couldn't stay there?"

Hanna stared down at the table and shrugged. "I don't know them."

"You don't know Dagny either, but you seem to be having a fun time hanging out with her."

"That's different," Hanna said, but really, I was a little surprised that she let my description of Dagny as "fun" slip right on by.

"Why?"

"Because." Hanna sighed dramatically. "Dagny doesn't make me uncomfortable like they do."

"How do they make you uncomfortable?" I paused, taking a moment so I could carefully ask, "Do they . . . hurt you?"

"No, no," she replied right away, and then she groaned. "I mean, not like that. It's just that they're always going on and on about Nikolas, and . . . I don't know him, and I don't *want* to know him."

She stared down at her lap, absently picking at her chipped purple nail polish. "I know that he died, and it wasn't like he *chose* to leave me, and my grandparents and my mom have always told me how much he loved me. But . . . he's just some stranger. *Dad* is my dad."

"Have you talked to your mom about how you feel?" I asked.

"No, not really. She always gets so sad and quiet when the subject of Nikolas comes up," Hanna said. "It's easier to avoid talking about him."

"Sometimes you gotta talk about the sad stuff if you

wanna feel better," I said gently, but that only made her sulk more.

"Yeah, well, I'm sure I'll have to do plenty of talking when I get back home," she grumbled.

"Do you know when that'll be yet?"

"No. I talked to Mom today on the phone." Hanna cast a disparaging glare over at the corded telephone attached to the wall. The magic that shielded Merellä also messed with cell phone reception and Wi-Fi, which only encouraged trollkind's reliance on and persistent obsession with paper texts and other outdated modes of technology.

"And?"

"And they're still trying to figure it all out," she said. "With all the royalty in town for the Skojare King's quintessential jubilee—"

"I think it's *quinquennial*, actually," I corrected her, stifling my laugh.

"Whatever." She waved me off. "The point is that my dad can't get away from work, and the twins are teething, and Grandma Annali sprained her ankle this morning. She'll be fine, but it's not a good time. I know that Mom is doing everything she can to get it figured out, but it's probably going to be at least a few more days."

I stood and brought my plate over to the kitchen sink. "Well, you better figure out a fun way to pass the time here."

13

Fables

Calder liked to work with music on, citing the Mozart Effect and its alleged positive influence on information retention. While I didn't think it hurt anything, I wasn't so certain that brash recordings of Bach rattling out of an ancient transistor radio were doing much to help.

Still, I continued making progress, deciphering and outlining the scrolls that had been lent to us from Isarna. We'd been working most of the morning when I came across a name I'd seen before but I didn't know what it meant.

A message did once come from Adlrivellir, in the time after the Battle for the Bifröst. It promised only that the sun sets in the green sky when the good morning becomes the violent night.

"Where is the Adlrivellir?" I asked Calder. "Is it the same as the Vesturlands?"

He sat beside me at the desk, a pair of copper-framed spectacles sitting at the end of his nose. "It's nowhere," he said, without looking over at me or at the scroll I was working on.

"It's a place of fantasy, no different than Mount Olympus or Wonderland."

"Can I ask you something that I've always wondered about concerning troll historians?"

Pushing his glasses up on the top of his head, he answered with a brusque "Of course."

"How do you know how to decipher what's fiction and what's fact when it comes to our history?" I asked. "The humans think all of our stories are just old folklore and myths. Heck, they don't even think we're real."

"Well, I would argue that we're far more observant and intelligent than the humans," he replied with a derisive chuckle.

I bristled and struggled to keep my voice neutral when I tactfully said, "That sounds a tad racist."

It was more than a tad, honestly, and it was the kind of thing I'd heard used a hundred times to dismiss me. Because I was Omte, and everyone *knows* they're the dumbest of the tribes. Because I'm a half-breed, and everyone *knows* that mixed blood makes them weak and stupid. Because I'm from Iskyla, and everyone *knows* that only the unsophisticated and naïve live there.

Because I'm female.

Because I'm asymmetrical and overweight.

Because I'm blond.

Because I'm an orphan.

Because.

Because.

Because.

There were a million reasons why my every thought and

even my existence should be dismissed. Arguing each point and justifying every single thing was too exhausting, and that's why I didn't unload the tirade that was waiting on the tip of my tongue.

But I won't deny that it hurt, that there was a sting as my respect for Calder dipped.

"I'm certain there is a reason that the humans haven't figured us out yet, but writing it off as 'humans are stupid, that's why' seems awfully lazy and disingenuous," I said evenly. "Besides, it's like you said yesterday. You never know what you don't know."

He leaned back in his chair. "You are right. We can't ever be certain of what is truth or exaggeration, not when it comes to our past and the supernatural. Which is exactly why you're here, documenting everything. We're trying to create a picture of the past that's as complete as it can be, but ultimately it's up to each individual beholder what they choose to believe."

"Why do you—specifically, as an individual—think this Adlrivellir place is only the stuff of fantasy?" I pressed.

"Because nobody ever went there," he said simply. "Take the Vesturlands. Vili's sons Alfarin and Valdin were explorers. They went to the Vesturlands, but they also came back. Over the course of the next three centuries there are dozens of stories of adventurers traveling back and forth from the Vesturlands. Until finally Asa the Cold settled Doldastam in the Arctic provinces, creating indisputable evidence that the Vesturlands and North America are one and the same."

"But the Kanin capital is an incredibly obvious example," I pointed out.

"Maybe so," Calder allowed. "But the fact remains. There are several stories *about* Adlrivellir, but in all the tales of explorers, of our trolls and the human Vikings, there isn't a single account of anyone going there *and* coming back. That puts it in the realm of an afterlife story. It is our ancestors' answer to Valhalla."

I considered what he was saying and tried to remember some of the stories I'd heard about Norse mythology and Valhalla. Those weren't something that I'd studied up on, but the fairy tales in *Bedtime Stories for Trolls of All Ages* definitely had a Norse flair to them, and I had spent hours upon hours reading them to Hanna, Liam, Emma, Niko, and the twins.

The doors to the archive swung open, and I looked up to see Pan grinning broadly at us as he walked over. It was the first time I noticed that he had a bit of a swagger to his step. Not too much, but it was right on the line between subtly cool and noticeably dorky. He managed to pull it off, in part because of the way his button-down shirt fit against his broad shoulders and the way his dark eyes flashed when he smiled.

"Hey, hey, hey," he said cheerily and leaned on the desk. "I hope I'm not interrupting your workflow."

"No, I can't say that you were right now," Calder said. "We were having a break."

"I came down here to take Ulla up for a blood draw. Can you spare her for a few minutes?" Pan was talking to Calder, but he kept his eyes on me, and something about that made my skin flush and I lowered my eyes.

"Take as much time as you need. Our work here shouldn't get in the way of Ulla's pursuit." Calder spoke in such a flat way that I couldn't be sure whether or not he meant it sarcastically.

"Thanks, Calder," Pan said as I rolled up my scrolls.

I grabbed my hobo-style bag from where I kept it by my feet, and I draped it over my shoulder as I walked around the desk. "So where are we going for this blood draw?"

"Up to the Troglecology Department. That's where all the blood analysis is." He turned around as he stepped backward, so he opened the door with his back. "Some might even say that's where all the magic happens."

"Blood and magic? It sounds like you've got a D&D tournament going on up there."

Pan laughed. "They wish. What happens up there is a lot more scientific than a role-playing game."

The hallway ended at a very old elevator. Pan had to manually open the ornate brass grille, and inside, instead of buttons, it had a lever that had to be shifted to the floor number. While the elevator was clearly very old, it appeared to be immaculately maintained, with taupe marble floors and a brass bar that wrapped along the walls.

When it first began to move, it jerked upward, and I grabbed the bar in surprise. Pan reached out, putting his hand gently on my arm.

"It's okay," he assured me, his warm voice low and comforting, and I felt a heat flush over me. "It always starts rough, but we'll be fine."

I let out a nervous laugh and tucked my hair behind my ears. "I'm not that used to elevators, I guess."

He moved his hand off my arm, but he leaned on the bar next to me, so his hand was mere inches from mine.

"This place takes some getting used to," he said. "But it gets better. How are things going for you so far?"

"Pretty good," I said with an uncertain shrug.

"But? You seem like you've got something more to say."

I chewed the inside of my cheek. "Calder seems to have a very low opinion of humans."

"Yeah, everyone does around here," he said, his words tinged with a weary kind of apathy. "You can't take it personally. We've been living in a caste system for centuries, and unfortunately you can't eliminate prejudice overnight."

I looked over at him, studying the unusually stoic expression on his face as he lowered his gaze to the floor. "It doesn't bother you? What they say about you?"

"Does it bother you?" He scratched absently at his temple, then looked back up at me. "What they say about you?"

I swallowed hard, then answered honestly, "Sometimes."

"Yeah. Me too," he admitted with a sad smile. "But it is getting better. Twenty-five years ago, I wouldn't even have been allowed *inside* the Mimirin. And now I work here. It's something."

The elevator had finally reached the third floor and groaned to a stop. As Pan opened the doors, he said, "The good news is that happiness and indignation don't have to be mutually exclusive. You can be angry about where we are and frustrated by how far we have left to go, and you can still appreciate the amount of ground that's already been covered."

"That is a surprisingly sunny attitude to have," I said as we walked down the hall together.

"My mom always told me that I had two choices when it

came to my life: let my anger consume and blind me or learn to laugh and keep on fighting."

"Laughter seemed like the easier choice?" I asked.

"The laughter's not bad, but truth is, I really wanted to keep on fighting." He winked at me, then pointed over at a door beside him. "We're here."

14

※

Blood

While most of the Mimirin had been decorated and maintained like it was straight out of a medieval fantasy, the south wing on the third floor housed all the labs and troglecology, so it looked a lot more twenty-first century.

It was an admittedly strange juxtaposition when Pan led me into the docent Elof Dómari's lab and classroom. The stone walls were the same as they were everywhere, but the floor was updated to a slick quartz tile. The original stained-glass windows and vast barrel-vaulted ceiling surrounded sterile islands with shiny lab equipment and bright light fixtures. Most of the islands were bar-height, replete with stools, but a third of them were shorter, designed for the trolls of shorter stature.

All of the classrooms and facilities were built that way. Trolls in general tended to be on the short side, with the exception of the Omte, who averaged over six feet. In contrast, the Vittra had the shortest average height, with the largest birth rate of hobgoblins and trolls with dwarfism. Since the

Vittra provided much of the funding for the Mimirin's programs, it made sense that their facilities were designed specifically with their population's needs in mind.

Elof himself had dwarfism, and he looked about half a foot shorter than Hanna. Other than that, he appeared to be a typical Vittra in his thirties. His rich olive skin complemented his thick russet hair, and the combo of a strong broad jaw, dark deep-set eyes, and a slightly crooked nose—an apparent remnant from a fight years ago—all came together to make him ruggedly handsome, like a troll version of Indiana Jones.

He was sitting at one of the islands, peering into a microscope with his back to us, and across from him was Dagny, taking notes on a pad of paper. Both of them wore matching loose-fitting caftanesque lab coats. The sleeves were cuffed just below the elbows, and the lab coats were made of white linen embroidered with a pale gold quatrefoil pattern.

"Ah, Ulla," Dagny said, hardly even glancing up from her writing. "I thought it would be about time for you to come here."

"You know our eleven o'clock?" Elof asked her and glanced back over his shoulder at me.

"I do." Dagny set down her pen and pressed her lips into a tight smile. "This is my flatmate, Ulla. Ulla, this is Professor Elof Dómari. He has a master's in bioengineering from Stanford University, a bachelor of science in laboratory biology from Jakob W. Rells University of Parapsychology and Medicine, and a licentiate in troglecology from the Mimirin."

It was rare to hear of a troll attending human universities, and he had not one but two degrees from them under his belt. Although, to be fair, the nature of the Rells University as an institution studying the paranormal meant that their student body wasn't made up entirely of humans.

Elof had turned on his stool to face Pan and me, but he looked at Dagny from the corner of his eye. "Thank you for listing my credentials, Dagny, although I don't know if that was strictly necessary."

"It's always more helpful to overexplain than underexplain," she said, sounding unfazed.

"What a wonderful attitude for a teacher but perhaps less so for a student," he muttered, then turned his attention on me. "Are you the one that makes the otherworldly blackberry tarts?"

"No, that's my temporary houseguest," I said, and I wondered exactly how Dagny talked about me and Hanna to others.

"Oh, that's a shame," Elof replied with an embellished frown. "I was going to suggest a trade of pastries for genetic research."

I laughed uncertainly. "Well, I'm sure Hanna would be happy to help me out if there's an offer on the table."

"He's only teasing," Pan said. "Elof will be happy to help you as much as he can."

"That's only because I've always got Pan and Dagny around to keep me on the straight and narrow."

"I don't think most people refer to me as the 'responsible one,' " Pan said with a laugh.

"That's only because you've never partied with the trog majors after they've made a discovery," Elof said with a waggle of his eyebrows.

Dagny looked over at me with a flat expression. "He's exaggerating, but it can get wild here."

"Unfortunately, right now the wildest it's going to get is this lively questionnaire where I ask you everything you know about your family and your lineage while my associate here steals your blood." Elof snapped his fingers at Dagny, and she slid a thin stack of papers across the island to him.

"I'll get the kit," she said and walked over to a cabinet in the corner to start gathering supplies.

"Have a seat. Make yourself comfortable. This whole process takes a bit of time." Elof motioned to the stool beside him. I slipped my purse off and dropped it on the floor, then sat down. "I suppose I should ask you if you're okay with needles."

"I don't love them, but I'm usually okay if I don't look," I said, just as Dagny returned and set down the kit beside me. She put on a pair of latex gloves, then pulled out a massive thick needle. The thing had to be at least nineteen-gauge and over an inch long. "Oh, my *gaad,* is that the needle? How much blood do you need?"

"The size of the needle is based on the Omte's historically tough, deep veins," Dagny explained. "But we do also take a lot of blood."

"The more we take, the more precise the tests can be," Elof elaborated. "At first glance, our blood appears similar to humans', but it's far more complex, and it leaves plenty of opportunities to extract information. Large sample sizes give us near-exponential value."

"Okay. I will try not to focus on the giant stick of metal being jammed into my arm and answer your questions." I tried to keep my cool, but I flinched when Dagny wiped my inner arm with sterilizing alcohol.

"Look over at Pan," she commanded. "Making eye contact with someone else can be very distracting from pain or discomfort. We're social animals, after all."

Pan sat down on a stool across from me. "How you doing?"

"I feel a bit silly," I admitted.

"Don't. It helps," he promised, and I forced myself to meet his gaze.

It shouldn't have been that hard, since he had these amazingly deep dark eyes. They were rich brown, somehow comfortingly warm and endlessly dark. They were the walnut floors in the Tulins' inn, which creaked and groaned when I tiptoed down for a midnight snack with the wind howling outside. They were the black tea that Mia always drank first thing in the morning, before the kids or the sun were up yet, and Niko would sneak out of his bed and snuggle into mine.

The sharp prick in my arm shattered these comforting thoughts, and I flinched. I started to glance over at Dagny's work, the thick needle and the tube filling with my currant-red blood, but Elof cleared his throat and pulled my attention to him.

"So, we'll start with the easy questions," he said. "When were you born?"

I looked back at Pan and kept my expression neutral as I said, "I don't know my birth date, but I was most likely born sometime in the early autumn of 1999, before the middle of October."

Elof jotted down my response. "Where were you born?"

"I don't know. I was only a baby when I was left in Iskyla, up in Nunavut."

"Yes, we are quite familiar with everyone's favorite frozen dumping grounds," Elof replied without even attempting to mask his disdain. "When were you left there?"

"The thirteenth of October."

"Do you know who left you?"

"A woman." I took a deep breath, hoping that would help with the wave of dizziness that passed over me. "She claimed her name was Orra, and she was tall and carried a sword marked with the Omte insignia."

"Did she leave anything else with you?" Elof asked.

"What do you mean?"

"Sometimes babies are left with a blanket or trinket, even a lock of hair," he clarified.

"No," I said, but it took all my energy to force out the words. "The blanket I was wrapped in belonged to the inn where I was left." I paused, forcing myself to dig through the fog of my brain to answer. "When she left me, she left me with nothing. No clothes, not a name, nothing."

"Fortunately for you, we . . ." Elof was still talking, but his voice started to fade out, like he was shouting underwater.

"Ulla?" Pan said, and I was only dimly aware that he was saying my name loudly, almost shouting. I wanted to tell him that I was okay, that everything was fine, but I couldn't form the words.

"Elof, we've got a fainter," Dagny announced flatly, but Pan was already getting to his feet.

"No, I'm . . ." I tried to argue, but my body felt like it was floating away, and the whole room seemed to pitch to the side as my eyes rolled into the back of my head. My body went limp, and I was dimly aware of sliding off the stool, and then strong arms caught me before I hit the floor.

When my eyes fluttered open a few seconds later, Pan's face was the first thing I saw, his eyebrows pinched with worry, and his arms were warm around me.

"Thanks for catching me," I told him groggily, and a relieved smile spread across my face.

"That's why they pay me the big bucks," he said with a light laugh.

Dagny was crouched beside me, wrapping gauze around my arm where the needle had been. Once she was done, Pan helped me back up so I was sitting on the stool, and he hovered beside me, presumably ready to catch me again should I need it.

"I guess these questions weren't as easy as you thought," I said to Elof with an embarrassed laugh.

"You answered them as best you could, and you answered them quickly and correctly. That sounds relatively easy to me," Elof said, sounding entirely unperturbed about the whole thing.

"What he's trying to say is that you aren't the only one who came here with far more questions than they had answers," Pan said gently.

"Did you eat today?" Dagny was finishing up by labeling the vials and cleaning up, but she paused long enough to give me an accusatory glare. "I didn't see you eat this morning."

"I wasn't very hungry," I admitted, suddenly feeling sheepish.

"Pan, get her something to eat," Dagny commanded.

"Right. Of course." Pan touched my shoulder gently. "Will you be okay for a few minutes?"

"Yeah, yeah, I'm fine." I gave him the most reassuring smile I could muster. "I don't think I even need anything to eat. I'm okay."

"No, don't worry about it," Pan said. "I'll be right back."

"Dagny, could you go with him?" Elof suggested. "Grab something for yourself and for me as well."

"Sure thing, sir." Dagny took off her latex gloves, then tossed them in the garbage as she followed Pan out of the lab.

Elof had set aside his pen and paper, and he propped his head on his hand. "Why don't we just talk and relax for a minute? I know these questions can feel intense and invasive, so it's sometimes prudent to take a moment."

"I'm okay, really," I insisted. "I don't even know what happened back there. I'm not usually a fainter, not even over the sight of blood."

"Like I said, this process can take its toll on everyone." Elof leaned forward, studying me. "Your eyes are so fascinating. Firstly, with the sectoral heterochromia."

"The what?" I asked.

"Oh, you didn't realize? Heterochromia is a difference in coloration in the iris of both eyes, such as when the left eye is blue and the right is green. In sectoral heterochromia, a *single* iris contains two completely different colors," he explained.

"With you, it's your right eye." He pointed toward it. "While your left iris is entirely amber, under your right pupil is a little splotch of dark green.

"What's more fascinating, to me at least, is that both of

your pupils appear to dilate, but the left one is consistently much larger than the other, even when factoring in the difference in the size of your eyes," he went on. "How is your vision?"

"It's fine." I shrugged. "I don't really notice anything, but my eyes have always been this way."

"I believe I understand the feeling." Elof tilted his head, as if pondering something while he stared at me. "You really are quite striking, you know that."

"Um . . . I . . ." I shook my head and leaned back away from him, unsure of how to respond. "That's . . ."

"I'm sorry." He waved his hands, as if he could erase his comments from the ether, and he scowled. "That didn't come out the way that I meant it. As a rule, I make a point of not complimenting the appearance of my students or peers, since it's not relevant to the work that we do here. And that's true for you as well."

"But you decided to make an exception?" I asked with an arched eyebrow.

"I suppose I let my fascination get carried away," he said. "We so rarely see any members of the Omte tribe, even TOMBs like yourself. The doors to the Mimirin have been open to all for decades now, but the Omte have not been quick to accept the invitation."

"I think that they've probably accepted the invitation in the exact spirit in which it was given—with resentment and disinterest," I countered.

"Fair point," he conceded. "But to be clear, there are many of us all over the citadel who are genuinely thrilled to have trolls of all walks of life here. It's impossible for us to truly learn about ourselves and where we came from and who we can be if we entirely ignore huge portions of our populations."

"I couldn't agree more."

"Good." Elof smiled. "I look forward to working with you over the coming weeks."

record keepers

Long after my shift in the archives had ended, I was sitting cross-legged on the cold stone cellar floor, struggling to keep myself awake but refusing to give up. Last night, Hanna had relayed Dagny's warnings about how I had to fight for my work, and that's why I kept pushing myself, despite my blurring vision and cellar-dust-induced sneezing. But it was getting harder and harder to fight it. After a long day of reading and translating—not to mention a fair amount of blood loss—my brain felt like mush. All of the Omte records were so scattered and poorly filled out, there was hardly any information to be gleaned from them. (One particularly insightful form was a faded sheet of yellow carbon copy with the words *Torun Winge Says No* scrawled across the lines in big block letters.)

That was the final straw, and I slammed the binder shut, preparing to put it back on the shelf. The gust of the slam caused a piece of paper to slide free, and it fluttered to the floor. It was no larger than a postcard, and most of the info had been blotted out with black ink.

In fact, there was only one line visible, but when I read it, my breath caught in my throat.

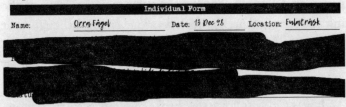

The Offices of Land and Queen
Property Exemption Certificate
Request of Information

Individual Form		
Name: *Orra Fågel*	Date: 13 Dec 98	Location: Fulaträsk

Orra Fågel.

My fingers trembled as I hovered over the name, unable to bring myself to completely touch it, too afraid to confirm it in case this wasn't real, in case this was a strange dream brought on by exhaustion.

I finally let my fingertips graze her name, and my heart skipped a beat when the paper felt solid and didn't give way like a mirage.

"Call me Orra." Mr. Tulin's bedtime story echoed in my head. The Omte woman who had abandoned me had called herself Orra. *Her* name. This could be her. This was the first Orra I had found in the Omte records, alive and old enough to own property around the time of my birth. Old enough to be my mother.

This could be my mother. She might've written this. Nearly a year before I was born, she would've held a pen in her hand, in an office somewhere in Fulaträsk.

It was a long shot, and even if it was her, it told me almost nothing about her. But this was the closest I had been to her in nineteen years, and for a moment I couldn't breathe.

She wasn't a figment from my childhood stories. She was real. She really existed.

I don't know how long I sat like that, staring down at the paper, as if I could somehow memorize every detail of the ink and summon her to life. It was long enough, though, that the cold from the floor had seeped through my jeans, and I was dimly aware of the prickle of goose bumps running up my thighs and my back.

It was Calder's voice that broke my trance, a dry baritone coming from behind me. "You're really burning the midnight oil tonight."

I gasped and looked back to see him standing under the arch at the bottom of the steps, only a few yards from me. "Oh, jeez, you scared me."

"You look like you saw a ghost." His bushy eyebrows pinched together, and his mouth turned down into a scowl.

"Not exactly," I replied, but he wasn't entirely off base.

My mother had always been gone, but that absence had created a form of its own. Like a shadow in the dark I could never quite see, she was a specter hovering over my life, just out of reach.

And this here, the old ink on faded paper—this was the first sign I'd ever really had of her. The first glimpse at the ghost of my mother.

I attempted a half-hearted smile up at Calder. "I didn't realize you were working late tonight."

He leaned his broad shoulder against the weathered arch and crossed one foot over his ankle. "I hadn't really planned on it, but sometimes I get lost in my work."

"Yeah, I know how that goes." I rolled my neck, stretching out the kinks from sitting hunched for so long. "Since you're here, can I ask you a question?"

"I'll help if I can," he replied reticently. "But it's fair to say that we have more information here than one man could possibly memorize, so don't be too shocked if I have to look something up to answer you."

"Yeah, no, of course." I nodded and did my best to keep my voice and attitude super casual. "It's not even about anything specific. I thought you might be able to tell me why something was blacked out."

"Blacked out?" he asked, and he stepped toward me, already peering toward the paper to see what it was.

"Yeah, I hadn't come across it before, but some of this page is blacked out." I gritted my teeth, clamping them together so hard my jaws hurt, and I focused all my energy on keeping my hand steady so that when I held the paper up to Calder he wouldn't see how badly I'd been trembling.

Calder took it from me and stared thoughtfully down at the paper a few seconds before quietly musing, "This shouldn't be here."

"What do you mean?" I stood up—slowly, because my feet had fallen asleep.

"Anything blacked out should be kept with the sealed records in the private vault," he explained.

"A vault? There's a vault of sealed records?" I asked in

surprise. I had thought the whole point of the Mimirin was to discover and share knowledge between all the tribes. A locked vault seemed to contradict that.

"Yes, of course." He smirked, like I was ridiculous for thinking otherwise. "Not everything in our history is accessible for public consumption, nor should it be. Some things are incomplete, inaccurate, or dangerous if they fall into the wrong hands."

"Dangerous? How? Do you have the plans for some kind of psychokinetic nuclear bomb stashed away?" I asked.

"Quite possibly," Calder replied rather seriously, and my smile fell away. "Truth be told, I wouldn't know. Not even I have that level of clearance."

"So you're saying that it's unlikely that I would get access to that vault?"

"No, I'm saying that it's practically impossible for you to ever gain access to that vault, through the proper channels or otherwise. The Information Styrelse takes security and privacy very seriously," he said, referring to the board of intellectuals and influential Merellians who oversaw the operations at the Mimirin.

"Could you tell me why something like this might be blacked out?" I asked.

"I cannot."

"Can't or won't?" I challenged him with a smile, going more for teasing than confrontation.

"I don't know that I would if I could, but I honestly am not capable of it," he said. "There's not enough information here for me to go on, and I'm not privy to the machinations of the Styrelse as to what their reasons may or may not be."

"And how would I go about scheduling a meeting with them?"

He snorted. "You wouldn't." He turned to start walking away, still carrying the paper with Orra Fågel's name on it.

"Where are you taking that? Shouldn't I be putting it back?" I asked.

"Like I told you earlier, this shouldn't be here." He paused, looking over his shoulder at me. "It belongs in the vault, so I'm ensuring that it gets back where it needs to be."

I shoved my hand in my back pocket, attempting my best impersonation of somebody who was totally calm and casual and not at all freaking out about the first clue about her possible-mother being taken away.

"But it was already here," I reminded him with an empty laugh. "What's the harm of leaving it here?"

"What's the help of it?" he countered. "There really isn't any information at all on here, is there?"

"I don't know."

He was right, and I knew he was right, so I squirmed under his disapproving gaze. It was all I could do to keep from running over and snatching it from his hands.

"You know you have a mother, you've told me that you believe her name to be Orra and that she was Omte," Calder elaborated reasonably. "While there is a likelihood that this woman mentioned here may be your mother, it is not a guarantee. Orra may not be a common name, but it's not unheard-of among the Omte. But even if we assume this is your mother—and this paper neither confirms nor denies that it is her—what does it tell you that you don't already know?"

"I don't know . . . ." I sighed and closed my eyes, focusing on slowing the panicked beating of my heart, before I finally said, "That she was real."

"Ulla, of course your mother is real. Trolls haven't yet determined how to self-replicate, so you most certainly had a mother."

"I know." I opened my eyes and exhaled. "Literally, I know that I had to have, but . . . other than the fact that I exist, I've seen far more evidence in favor of Santa Claus being real."

Calder softened. "Your frustration and desperation are understandable, they truly are. And I believe that you will find what you need to know about your parentage within the legal perimeters in which the Inhemsk Project functions. That's where you should be putting your energy and your effort."

"I know that they're using the information—and blood—I gave them to research as much as they can, but this is the only part that I can really do," I said. "The only thing that keeps me from feeling like a bum that expects everyone to do the work for me."

"There's no need for you to feel like that," he said. "This isn't any different than going to see a doctor when you feel ill. Sometimes you have to rely on the expertise of others."

"I guess I don't really like relying on others," I admitted.

"Who does? But that is life."

16

runaway

I had scarcely opened the door and stepped inside the loft apartment when Hanna pounced on me with a bright smile.

"Hey, you're home!" She bounced over from the kitchen and held out a plate of food. "I bet you're hungry, so I made you a plate already. How was your day? Was it busy?"

"Thanks." I set down my bag and tentatively took the plate.

The Karelian pie was a football-shaped crust overstuffed with a savory rice-and-potato mix, similar to a pierogi, and Hanna had stepped up her plating skills by adding a strategically placed evergreen sprig.

Back at home, this was one of my favorite meals that Mia made, but I just didn't have the energy to feel excited about it today.

"Yeah. You look kinda pale." Hanna nodded furiously, making her short curls bob like crazy. "Is that 'cause you had your blood drawn?"

"I don't know. Maybe?" I picked at my plate and walked over to the bistro table. "It was kind of a long day."

"Hanna had a long day too," Dagny chimed in, and I finally looked over to see her sitting on the couch, with her longbow lying across her lap.

"Whoa, what's with the weaponry?" I asked in surprise.

"I practiced at the archery range after work, and now I'm taking care of my bow." Dagny rolled a stick of wax down the taut string of her bow, and then she slowly rubbed it in with a leather cloth. "There's a competition coming up in a week and a half, and I want both me and my bow to be in top shape."

"Okay, that explains that." I set the plate down on the table and looked over at Hanna. "Why did you have a long day?"

"Dagny probably means that I spent the whole day slaving over the pies," Hanna said quickly, and punctuated her statement with a nervous laugh, a combo that caused me to narrow my eyes at her suspiciously.

"No, I mean that you had a long day because you spent the whole day running around town, and you didn't get home until after I did," Dagny replied. "She said she made friends with the girl with the 'trippy hair' that you saw when you first came into town."

"Dagny!" Hanna shouted in horror. "I thought you said you'd keep it to yourself."

Dagny scoffed. "No, you asked me to, and I said that it makes sense that you'd want me to. I never agreed to anything."

Hanna folded her arms over her chest and pouted. "I'm not gonna tell you anything if you just turn around and tell Ulla everything."

"Good," Dagny replied without looking up from her meticulous care of the longbow. "I don't want you to tell me anything. Secrets are for friends. You're not my friend. You're like an invasive species who I tolerate because you make delicious food and your benefactor pays rent."

"That's harsh," Hanna said flatly.

Dagny shrugged. "That's life."

"This is exactly what I'm talking about, Hanna," I said. "You're far too trusting and sheltered if you think Dagny is your friend."

Dagny held up her wax stick, chiming in with a raised hand. "I gotta second that one, Hanna."

"Ugh!" Hanna groaned in frustration. "This is ridiculous! You guys don't need to gang up on me for being nice!"

"We're not ganging up on you, and my complaint isn't that you're nice," I calmly explained. "It's that you tagged along to somewhere you weren't supposed to be, and then you left the safe place where you were supposed to stay to explore a strange city by yourself, and then you attempted to make friends with some daredevil that seriously damaged the car your dad lent me."

She rolled her eyes. "Well, yeah, it sounds bad when you put it like that, but that's not how I meant it."

Dagny interjected, "It doesn't matter what you meant. It only matters what you do. Intentions are the lies we tell ourselves. Actions are the truth."

"So, anyway, what exactly were you doing with the trippy-haired girl?" I asked.

"Her name is Eliana, and she's more than the colors of her hair," Hanna replied coolly. "She's a lost runaway, and she's trying to get by. I think something bad happened to her where she came from, but she doesn't seem to really be able to remember a lot."

"What is she doing here?" I asked.

Hanna shook her head. "I don't know, because she doesn't know. She seems nice but lost."

I'd finally taken my first bite of the pie, and it was every bit as good as I'd hoped, so I let out an involuntary moan. "Sorry. This is really good, Hanna," I said with my mouth full, and I hurried to swallow it down so I could say, "She should talk to security or a doctor or something. They have the resources and knowledge to help runaways and amnesiacs, assuming that's what she really is."

"It's not like that!" Hanna rested her arms on the table and leaned forward, so she could look up at me with big, pleading eyes. "She doesn't know who to trust. She's scared and alone."

"How did you find her?"

"I was wandering around town, and I saw her stealing a mango," Hanna said.

"If she went to a shelter or got help from the proper channels, she wouldn't have to steal."

She exhaled loudly through her nose and narrowed her eyes. "Okay, well, you're obviously never going to believe me, so we should just go find her."

"What?" I said. "Right now?"

Hanna stepped back and put her hands on her hips. "Yes. She needs help, and I'm going to help her. You can go with me tonight, or I'll have to go out by myself tomorrow." She shrugged with exaggerated nonchalance. "Do you wanna meet her so you can see I'm telling the truth? Or you can stay in tonight and worry what I'm up to all day tomorrow."

"Wow, she's really got you over a barrel," Dagny said dryly. I shot her a look, and she got up to store her bow and arrows safely in her bedroom.

I groaned. "This is so unfair, Hanna."

"Yeah, well, life isn't fair, is it?" she shot back. "Do you wanna meet Eliana or not?"

"Sure, let's do it." I wolfed down the rest of my food, then pushed back my stool and stood up, while Hanna let out an excited squeal. "Did you talk to your mom today?"

"Not today," she chirped as she hurried toward the door. "I'll call her tomorrow."

"You can call her now," I suggested.

"No, we've got stuff to do," she replied brusquely. "And if she was on her way to pick me up, she'd have called you."

"That's probably true." I sighed. "All right. Let's go. Let's get this over with."

17

Beasts

"This is where I met her today." Hanna gestured to the wide-open street in downtown Merellä. It was late, so the street was dimly lit with kerosene lamps under the darkening wine-colored sky.

In the mornings and the evenings, when I made my way to and from work, I passed by Wapiti Way. It was one of the main throughways in town, running downhill from the center of Merellä past the Mimirin and down to the coast. Like most of the roads in town, it was made of smooth pebbles, like small river rocks, perfect for barefoot trolls in a hurry.

I had never actually gone down it, though, because it was always so crowded and busy. During business hours, it was lined with vendors selling various wares. Most of them had tents or carts, but some would lay out their merchandise on blankets on the ground, like picnics that were made entirely of plump tomatoes, hemp jewelry, and soy candles.

The buildings that lined Wapiti Way were taller than most of the others in town, made with a kind of mauve stucco. Despite the height, they had very few windows, and absolutely none of those windows were on the bottom two floors. The space that would usually go to windows and doors was instead taken up by awnings for the vendors.

But now the street was deserted. All the carts were gone, and the awnings were folded up. This was the first time I had seen the street empty like this, and I realized that it had to be at least twice the width of the other avenues and alleys that wound out from it.

"Well, she's definitely not here now," I said as we surveyed the vacant road.

Hanna furrowed her brows. "Maybe she's hiding or something."

"Doesn't her hair kinda make her *really* stand out?"

"No, her hair was different." She gestured vaguely around her own bouncy curls and walked ahead down Wapiti Way. "Instead of being all rainbowy, it was like really shimmery purple-silver. I have a nail polish that looks sorta like that, and it's called Gunmetal Lilac. But it's all one color and doesn't change."

"Are you sure it was her, then?"

Hanna walked on ahead of me, peering behind the awnings and checking the walls as if she were looking for a two-inch chameleon instead of a full-sized troll. But she stopped now to glare back at me. "Yeah, of course I am."

"How?" I asked her.

Hanna spoke like it should've been super obvious. "I said, 'Hey, are you that girl that fell through the roof of our car the other day?' And she said, 'Yeah, you're the girl I nearly fell on!' So, that all felt pretty concrete to me."

"Did you ask her about her hair?" I asked.

"Yeah, of course I did! That was the very next thing I asked her. She laughed it off and said she can't stand wearing the same hair twice."

" 'Wearing?' " I arched my eyebrow. "That sounds rather creepy, like she's a monster or an alien wearing a troll costume."

"Maybe she is, but so what? Cosplaying is a super common art form, Ulla." She turned and kept walking down Wapiti Way, so I followed a few steps behind her.

"Be that as it may," I said, "the idea that this Eliana is running around disguising herself and constantly changing her magical hair really does little to pacify my concerns."

"She doesn't seem to be here anyway."

"Did she tell you where she was staying?"

"No, and I didn't ask."

"Why not?" I asked, and Hanna finally turned back to glare at me in frustration.

"It didn't come up."

"It didn't come up?" I echoed, barely containing my own irritation. "What did you talk about?"

"I don't know. Just stuff. Life." She shrugged and stared dejectedly down at the gravel. "We shared a mango."

"But you never managed to ask 'What are you' or 'Where are you from'?"

"How many folks have you met in the past few days?" Hanna countered. "And how many of them have you asked 'What are you' or 'Where are you from'?"

Hanna continued to make an argument for those being incredibly rude questions to ask anybody, but a strange rumbling sound coming from down the road stole my focus. I held my hand up to her and said, "Shhhh."

"You can't shush me just because I'm right!" she protested.

"I'm not," I told her in a hushed, insistent voice. "Listen. What is that?"

She looked toward the sound, a steady rumble mixed with an occasional loud clacking sound, like a faraway avalanche. We both peered up the hill ahead of us, where the sound only seemed to grow louder. Hanna stepped toward it, her eyes locked straight ahead, watching for whatever was about to appear over the horizon.

"Hanna, I think we should get out of here," I said, realizing belatedly that we were right in the pathway of the oncoming rumbling.

"But what is *that*?"

"I don't know, but maybe it's better if we find out from far, far away."

I grabbed her arm, meaning to pull her back, but it was too late.

We saw the horns first—broad, dark bone framed by sharper branches, like moose antlers on steroids. Then it was the massive head, with a narrow snout, calling to mind a giant horse or deer, and the colossal body was covered in thick, chocolate-colored fur. And there were others.

Each one was like a Frankenstein mash-up between a deer and a triceratops with a terrifying dash of woolly mammoth, and now a herd of their mutant offspring were charging right toward us.

I grabbed Hanna, and she squealed as I lifted her up and

threw her over my shoulder. Just as I was preparing to run off down the road, escaping what I assumed was an impending stampede of monster cervids, someone let out a loud whistle.

Out of nowhere, four large dogs came running at top speed. They looked a bit like huskies or wolves, but sleeker and darker. Their coats were dark auburn, bleeding into black for the snouts, feet, and tails.

With a few carefully timed barks and nudges, the dogs skirted around the giant deer, herding them away from us. The deer let out a few deep brays in protest, but otherwise they complied with the dogs rerouting them around me and Hanna, their massive hooves stamping into the gravel a few short feet away from us.

And then I finally spotted the source of the whistle. Pan was grinning as he walked toward us, and two other guys were lingering farther back, giving commands to the dogs and the monster deer. All of the guys wore matching coveralls, and as Pan came closer, I saw that he had a patch on his chest—a dark red heart, more anatomically correct than a cutesy ♥, with large antlers coming from either side.

"Ulla, I think it's safe to put me down," Hanna complained, and I reluctantly set her back on the road.

"Stay out of their way and they won't bother you," Pan said as he reached us. He had a tall walking staff, and he used the end to gently nudge away any of the deer that got too close to the safe little pocket he and the dogs had created around us. "Don't let their size scare you. They're not that different than oversized sheep. A bit more stubborn maybe, but very docile."

"What are they?" I asked.

"We mostly call them 'woollies,' but the official title is giant woolly elk," Pan explained. "Humans called them giant deer, back before they killed them off."

"What do you mean?" I asked.

"They died out in the wild thousands of years ago, but trolls had already started domesticating by then," he said. "We used to breed them for their meat and fur and the purported 'medicinal' benefits from their ground antlers. Now we mostly keep them around out of tradition and to keep them from truly going extinct."

One of the dogs pulled away from the elk, bounding over to check on Pan and sniff around me. This dog was larger than the other four, with a coat of dark fawn with a sable face. Instead of being rigidly pointed like the others', his left ear dropped slightly at the tip.

"Brueger, away," Pan commanded, and the dog darted off after the elk. "Brueger's a good dog, but he might be a little too bonded to me."

"That doesn't sound like a bad thing," Hanna commented.

"It's not, mostly, except for when he needs to focus on the woollies instead of me," Pan explained as an elk drifted closer to us.

Hanna reached out, tentatively running her fingers through their thick fur as they walked by. "Where are you taking them?"

"These giant cows eat grass as much as a regular old Holstein, so we alternate the meadows they eat in to keep them from completely decimating the landscape around here," Pan elaborated. "We can't let them graze too far out from the citadel or the cloaking protections won't hide them from the humans, so that means, to get to the various pastures, we have to herd them through town a few times a week."

"All right, that makes sense," I said. "But how come *you're* the one herding them?"

He smiled sheepishly. "Because my day job does not pay that well, and the late-evening hours as a peurojen don't conflict with the Inhemsk."

"Peurojen?"

He tapped the antlered-heart patch on his coveralls. "A peurojen is an elk shepherd. They give it a fancy title and pretend there's honor in it so they can get away with paying us less," he said with a shrug. "But that's kind of the recurring theme with the Mimirin."

A smaller, antlerless elk broke from the herd to check on Pan. It playfully nuzzled him, licking his curly hair. Pan laughed but leaned away from the attention. "The woollies do grow on you after a while."

Hanna cautiously reached out, and the elk sniffed her hand. With an excited giggle, she started petting the nose, standing on her tiptoes to reach farther. "They seem amazing."

"Yeah, they are pretty special," Pan agreed.

Most of the herd had gone by, so the small elk turned and trotted off after them. One of the dogs was rounding up the last few stragglers, so soon it was only going to be me, Hanna, and Pan, standing alone in the middle of the road, watching the retreating woolly elk.

"I suppose I should let you get back to your job," I said.

"The other guys got it." He waved it off. "I can spare fifteen minutes or so to make sure you guys get home all right."

"I think we can manage," I said.

"I'm sure you can." His expression turned solemn. "But the woollies aren't the most dangerous thing out at night. Not by a long shot."

"Really?" I raised a skeptical eyebrow as I glanced around the quiet street. "Everyone keeps talking about how amazing the security is, and now you're telling me that's not true?"

"Ironically enough, both are true," he said. "The security does an amazing job of keeping new evils and dangerous weaponry from entering the citadel. But in a place as old as Merellä, there's plenty of skeletons and demons that have been buried here for a long time. The gates are locked so danger can't get in, but that means danger can't go out either."

Hanna moved closer to me but tried to keep her expression aloof and tough. "It doesn't seem so bad to me."

"Well, home is that way." I started edging toward it, expecting Hanna to protest, but she stayed close to me. "Is all this buried danger the reason they have a locked vault of secrets?"

Pan shoved his hands in his pockets and fell in step beside me. "I doubt I know much more about the Information Styrelse and their vaults than you do, but I suspect there are many valid reasons why some information needs to be classified."

"Do you come across a lot of classified records?" I asked.

"Me? No, none." He shook his head. "I don't have the kind of clearance for that. Scouring public records and tribal newspapers is, unfortunately, much more in line with my job duties."

"Do you know why some records would be blacked out or redacted?" I pressed.

"I would guess because someone didn't want others to know what it said," he replied with a smirk. "I'm assuming you stumbled across something that's piqued your interest?"

"Just a tax form," I said. "Nothing exciting, and most of it was blacked out, except for a name."

"So what exactly do you do for the woollies?" Hanna asked, returning the conversation to a topic that actually interested her.

As we walked through the quiet, narrow roads back to the carriage house, Hanna interrogated Pan about everything pertaining to the woollies, and he patiently answered her. By the time we reached the wooden staircase that ran up to our apartment door, I had learned that woolly elk live about fifteen years, have one to two babies at a time, that their favorite things to eat are willows and wild roses, and the largest woolly elk ever recorded weighed over a ton.

Hanna took my key and ran up the stairs ahead of us, letting herself into the apartment while Pan and I lingered at the bottom of the steps.

"Thank you for ensuring our safe passage home," I said, and he laughed.

"It was the least I could do."

"I think letting us get trampled by the woollies would've been a little less."

"You only say that because you've never had to clean mushed troll off the bottom of an elk hoof."

I laughed and started up the stairs. "Thanks anyway, even if your motives weren't entirely selfless."

"Hey," Pan called when I'd made it about halfway up the steps. I turned back around to see him leaning on the railing, looking up at me with his dark eyes. "I may not have access to the records you want, but that doesn't mean I'm totally useless. Meet me outside the Inhemsk offices at seven-thirty in the morning, and I'll get you in to see Sylvi."

"Pan, I never thought you were useless."

"Well, I wouldn't completely blame you if you did. After all, you haven't really seen what I can do yet."

"I can't tell if that's supposed to be threatening or if you're bragging."

He shrugged. "Could be both. A threatening brag, like a humble brag's angry cousin."

"It sounds like the best way to impressively scare someone off." I laughed.

"Is it working?"

"Nah, I don't scare easy."

"Good." He smiled up at me. "Neither do I. I'll see you tomorrow."

"Bright-eyed and bushy-tailed."

18

authority

I was definitely not bright-eyed the next morning. Despite my exhaustion, I'd struggled to fall asleep, and I spent the night tossing and turning with nightmares of swirling ink, monster elk, and an encroaching green fog. At least Dagny had been up before me, and after seeing the bags under my eyes, she'd offered me her spare thermos filled with strong lemon nettle tea.

My late start meant that I had next to zero time to spend on my appearance. Ordinarily I wouldn't care that much, but knowing that I was about to see Pan made me feel flustered about how I looked. But I had to make a tough call—either I could put on makeup, or I could show up on time, and I had to pick punctuality.

I threw on a flannel shirtdress, pulled my angry tangles of hair up into a ponytail, and topped off my ensemble with my polar bear talisman necklace and a pair of oversized sunglasses. Then I grabbed my hobo bag, and I was rushing down to the Mimirin, taking long swigs of the nettle tea as often as I could.

Pan was waiting for me outside the entrance to the Mim-irin, just as he said he would be. I tried to apologize for being late, but he assured me I was right on time. We didn't say much as we went through security, and I'd skipped shoes this morning, so we were able to forgo the lockers.

When we were nearly to the Inhemsk offices, Pan slowed his steps slightly and leaned in toward me, speaking just above a whisper. "Okay, so whatever I say in there, go along with it, okay?"

"Why? What?"

"Trust me," he said, then opened the office door before I could argue.

I followed him through the cubicle maze to the door in the back. He rapped on it, then opened it without waiting for an answer.

Sylvi Hagen sat behind a small desk, and she looked up from her paperwork with the same enthusiasm she had the first time I'd met her. Her flat, no-nonsense personality ap-parently translated to her decorating style, which seemed to take a page from "very clean interrogation room on one of those crime scene murder shows."

"Hey, Sylvi, sorry to drop in on you like this, but I thought maybe you could help us out with something." Pan spoke so quickly, the sentence had practically been con-densed into a single word.

"You've only been here for a few days and you already need *more* help?" Sylvi asked.

"I haven't asked for any help, not really," I said.

She snorted. "Your very presence here is asking for help."

Pan closed the door, apparently deciding that the rest of

the office didn't need to hear us. "Sylvi, come on. You don't even know what we're asking yet."

"It doesn't matter *what* it is you're asking," she insisted. "You come here wasting my time first thing in the morning, and you expect me to smile and go along with it?"

"Of course I didn't think that," Pan said. "But you're the only one who can get us in with the Information Styrelse or a Mästare."

Mästares are the prestigious department heads, and along with the Information Syrelse, they were the ones in charge of all the decisions made at the Mimirin.

She laughed darkly. "You think I'm going to help you waste their time on top of mine?"

"I don't understand what's going on or what I've done to make you so angry," I said.

"It's not you," Pan said wearily.

"Don't lie to her, Panuk. It is her," Sylvi said sharply, then turned her bored gaze to me. "Listen, Ulla, you seem like a fine enough girl, and I know you're trying to find your family. It's all noble *Oliver Twist* crap with you, I'm sure."

"I'm sorry?"

Sylvi set her pen down on the desk, then leaned back in her chair. "The Inhemsk Project is the underfunded laughingstock of our society, not only here in Merellä, but throughout the troll world. Most of the trolls don't think we should be here, and they make damn sure we know that whenever they can.

"After a lifetime of ostracization for being half-Kanin in the Vittra kingdom, I finally climbed my way to a position of respectability where I am able to really help others and do work that matters," she continued coolly. "I had to fight every step of the way.

"And then there's you." She looked me over with a derisive grunt, and my stomach rolled. "Who was handed one of the very few internships we are allotted. So instead of getting the most-qualified applicants, we got stuck with you because you're connected to the Trylle Queen, who is apparently allowed to make decisions for us from her lofty palace thousands of miles away."

"I'm not connected to the Queen," I said, hating how small my voice sounded. "I'm the nanny for a tracker, and I had the qualifications to get in."

"Well, then you must have a fairy godmother out there pulling the strings. Either way, you're not here because you earned it." Sylvi looked at me with a smug, self-satisfied grin.

I swallowed hard, taking a brief moment to steel my nerves and gather my wits. I wanted to throw up or cry, but that wouldn't help anything.

Plus, she was wrong. About me. Maybe about everything. And I wasn't about to let her bully me into going away.

"You don't know anything about me or my life," I said, matching her cold confidence with my own. "You know nothing of what I've done, where I've been, or what I'm capable of. And you may be trying to guilt me into leaving out of some twisted sense of entitlement, but I will not be guilted."

Her mask of faux indifference slipped, and her shoulders slacked.

"Sure, I got help on this leg of my journey," I admitted. "But I worked hard to get where I am. I spent my days taking care of babies, and my nights studying dead languages, and now I have the linguistic skills to obtain an internship here. A letter of recommendation doesn't take away from any of that. I came here to find out who I am and who my parents are, and I damn well earned the right to ask that question.

"Now, you can help me, and I'll get out of here as soon as possible," I said. "Or you can walk around with a huge chip on your shoulder, and I'll *draaaaaaagg* out my work all summer, making sure to call home to my friends in high places as often as possible, just to make sure that they know *exactly* how you've chosen to perform your job."

She stared at me, blinking a few times as her lips pressed into a thin line. Finally, she said, "Okay. What is it that you think I can help you with?"

"I want to know why a specific document was blacked out and what the significance of it might be," I said.

"Sure." She smirked. "Would you like the Hope Diamond to go along with that? Maybe the horn of an extinct rhino?"

"We knew that you wouldn't have the answer, but you're the only way that we can get a meeting with somebody who might," Pan clarified.

"You want to see a Mästare?" Sylvi looked at him with her eyebrows arched. "You want to waste what might be your only audience with one on *this* girl?"

Pan crossed his arms over his chest. "Our job here is to unite families and tribes, to find out how we're connected and who we are. So, yeah, I'm going to help do that any way I can, and I would hardly call doing my job a waste of time."

"Okay." She leaned over the desk and picked up her pen

and a scrap of paper. "Tell me what specifically the document is pertaining to, as much as you can."

I repeated the limited information I had about the tax document and Orra Fågel. As I spoke, Sylvi scribbled it down in jagged handwriting.

"All right," she said once I'd finished. "I'll put in a call and see if I can set something up with a Mästare." Then she glanced at Pan. "If you're really insistent on doing all of this, you might as well take her up to the Tower of Avanor. It's tedious and most likely futile, but if there's anything that's public for you to find, it'll be in there."

I smiled thinly at her, but she didn't look at me again. "Thank you."

"Sure. Now get the hell out of my office."

"Wow," Pan said, once we were safely in the hallway, far out of Sylvi's earshot. "You know, I read through your paperwork, but I didn't see that you were adopted by royalty."

"I was never really adopted at all, but I'm blue-collar through and through," I clarified. "The family I nannied for, the dad worked for the Queen. He put in a good word for me and cashed in a few favors because I worked my ass off helping his wife and taking care of their six kids."

Pan's eyes widened. "*Six?*"

"Yeah. Hanna—the girl you met last night—is one of them, so technically I'm still working even when I'm not working."

"You really are dedicated," Pan said.

"Thanks," I said with a laugh. "But the moral of the story is that I don't actually have friends in high places, and I am qualified for my internship—Finn doesn't have enough clout to pull that off. So I deserve to be here as much as anybody else, and I wasn't about to let her push me out."

"Color me scarily impressed."

"I thought it was impressively scared?"

He grinned at me. "I'm more impressed than scared."

"So," I asked as we walked together, "where is the Tower of Avanor, and what is it?"

"Come on. I'll show you."

avanor

The Tower of Avanor was—according to Pan—the tower of our ancestors. It was in the northeast corner of the Mimirin, rising far above everything around it, making it the highest point in all of Merellä.

The tower itself was relatively narrow, with enough room for a thick spiraling staircase around the sides, and that was basically it. The stairs themselves were split up with long landings on a very low incline, and stone bookcases were built in against the wall, curving along with it.

"*Alai*," I said in awe as I gaped at the rows and rows of books that lined the tower. "This is insane." I slowly climbed the steps, running my fingers along the spines.

Most of the books were bound with soft Tralla leather, made from the Tralla workhorses in the north. The leather was rare, since Trallas were revered and illegal to slaughter, so it could only be harvested when the animals died of natural causes. Their leather was prized not only because of its scarcity but also because of its durability and its distinct velvety texture.

"It's all lineage?" I asked.

"Yep. Down in the offices we call this the 'begats.' You know like, Odin begat Thor, Thor begat Magni."

I looked back over my shoulder at him, where he followed a step or two behind me. "Is that all it is? Just long lists of parentage?"

"Sorta, but with a bit more info." Pan grabbed a random book off a shelf, and I stepped to where I could peer over his shoulder. He flipped through the pages—thick papyrus with rough deckle edges.

On the top of each page was the stamp of a Mästare, asserting that they had individually confirmed every line of information on that particular page. Beneath that were columns, filled with meticulous type.

Pan ran his finger down the page and explained, "It's organized by birth date, then it has the name of the troll, followed by their tribe, the city they were born in, and their parents. In a lot of these, especially the older ones, there are a few blanks." He tapped one of the names near the bottom—*Lars Nomen-Valko*. "Nomen-Valko is one of the surnames given if the parents are unknown."

"Yeah, I know what a *Nomen* is." I swallowed hard. "I grew up in Iskyla."

Nomen was the generic name given to abandoned orphans who hadn't been left with a family. Each tribe had their own distinct hyphenate: Nomen-Brun for Omte, Nomen-Valko for Kanin, Nomen-Blár for Skojare, Nomen-Rautt for the Vittra, and Nomen-Grönn for the Trylle.

All my identification and paperwork had been done by Finn and Mia, using the name I had given them, the name I had adopted from the couple who raised me. But they had never actually given me their name, which meant that in these books, if there was a record of me at all, I would just be another anonymous Nomen.

"Yeah, I suppose they're pretty common up there."

"What do they do when the birthday isn't known?" I asked.

I knew what I'd done—or rather, what Mr. and Mrs. Tulin had decided to do, with me. We never really celebrated much, but every year they would acknowledge the day that I'd been left with them—the thirteenth of October in 1999. But I didn't know what the actual protocol was.

"They take a guess on the birth year when necessary, and then for convenience and organization, they put them all under January first," he said.

"Am I in one of these books?"

He nodded right away. "Yeah."

"How can you be so sure?"

"I could say it's because everybody's in here, but the truth is that I looked." He gave me an uncertain smile. "I thought there might be something in there that could help."

"Is there?"

"Not really." He put the book back on the shelf. "Come on. You can see for yourself."

Pan led me up the steps, always scanning the spines embossed with their cryptic Dewey-decimel-esque number system. He grabbed a thin book bound in a charcoal-blue fabric and hurriedly flipped through.

"Here you are," he said once he landed on the right section, and then he handed the book over to me.

Birth Date	Name	Mother	Father	Tribe	Location	Alias
1 Jan 1999	Nomen-Brun, Ulla	Unknown	Unknown	Omte	Iskyla	Ulla Tulin

I read it again, and again after that, and then once more. As if reading it over and over would somehow make the information expand, or as if my mother's name had been printed in disappearing ink and any second it would materialize on the paper. But it never did.

"That's it," I said finally. "That's all there is to know about me."

"Oh, come on, Ulla." Pan bumped his shoulder against mine, futilely attempting to get me to lift my eyes from the line about me. "This was only what was submitted to the officers when they did a census at the turn of the millennium. You're more than a line in a book. Nobody can fit an entire lifetime into twenty words or less."

"You're somebody." I closed the book and looked at him. "So that means you're in one of these."

"Yeah, of course."

"Show me."

He leaned back, appraising me for a moment, then smiled crookedly at my request. "All right. Don't get excited, though," he warned as he headed back down a step. "It's even less informative than yours."

"How is that even possible?" I asked dubiously.

"More of the info is inaccurate or incomplete." He

grabbed his book off the shelf, and within seconds he'd found his entry and handed it over for me to read.

Birth Date	Name	Mother	Father	Tribe	Location	Alias
28 Feb 1998	Soriano, Panuk Elliot	Human	Unknown	Kanin	Unknown	Unknown

"Panuk Elliot Soriano," I read aloud. "That is an interesting name combo. Are you like a Kanin-Inuit-British-Italian Viking?"

He laughed. "Something like that."

"The incomplete parts seem obvious, but which parts are inaccurate?" I asked.

"My mother has been present my whole life, but they didn't bother to put her name there because she's human. My father . . ." He paused and rubbed the back of his neck. "Well, that's more complicated, but they refuse to do a blood test that would confirm it. I've been able to test against extended family members to confirm I'm related, but the kingdom refuses to let me make a real comparison with him."

"Why not?" I pressed.

"Because he's high-ranking and they didn't want to sully his good name by admitting that he had a kid with a lowly human." He kept his eyes downcast as he spoke.

"The good news is that you're more than just a line in a book," I said gently.

He managed a half smile then. "Exactly."

I turned my attention back to all the books, rising high above me and far below. "I wish I had more time to go through these."

"Why don't you spend the rest of the day up here?" Pan suggested.

"What about Calder? Shouldn't I be doing work in the archives?"

"After the way Sylvi talked to you today, I feel like you deserve a day off."

"Wouldn't I get in trouble?" I asked.

He shook his head. "Sylvi won't want to deal with it, at least not today. But this is probably the only chance you'll get for a free day with access to the Tower of Avanor, so I suggest you take it while you can."

I looked again at the books, filled with line after line of information I needed to comb through. "Challenge accepted, then."

"Great. I can go stop by the archives and let Calder know you won't be in when I head back down to the office."

"You aren't staying?" I asked, looking over at him in surprise.

"Can't. I have some pressing paperwork that won't staple itself."

"It sounds scintillating."

He smirked. "You better believe it. But if you give me a few hours, I'll be able to come back and give you a hand."

"No, I don't wanna bother you—"

Pan cut me off with a wave of his hand. "If it was a bother, I wouldn't offer."

"All right. Well, I'll be here, then," I told him with a smile.

"I'll see you later. Good luck," he called over his shoulder as he headed down the stairs, and I turned to plan out my research.

Erring on the side of caution, I decided to cast a very

wide net. Since I was born in 1999, I went on the assumption that the latest my mother could've been born was 1985, with 1949 being the soonest. Odds were that that was too broad, but I didn't want to miss her.

I made myself a little study area next to one of the few windows in the Omte section. There was a wooden bench built in under the large arched window between the bookcases, and I set the small stack of the first few books (1949–1956) beside it. It was significantly warmer up here than it was down in the bowels of the archives, so I rolled up the sleeves on my shirtdress and unbuttoned an extra button, hoping that would cool me somehow.

I took my notepad and pen out of my oversized hobo bag, and then I spent the next several hours scouring the books for every "Orra" I could find, then writing all the information available down on paper.

3 April 1952	Holt, Orra	Omte	Sintvann
28 July 1954	Ecklund, Orra	Kanin	Doldastam
5 March 1958	Lund, Ora	Vittra	Ondarike
18 December 1961	Winge, Orra	Omte	Sintvann
21 September 1966	Lykke, Oralie	Vittra	Mörkaston
16 July 1967	Gribb, Orra	Omte	Fulaträsk
9 January 1969	Fågel, Orra	Omte	Fulaträsk
30 June 1970	Strom, Aura	Skojare	Storvatten

I had even expanded to include variations of spellings and tribes outside of Omte, because the truth was that I couldn't rule anything out. Still, my heart skipped a beat when I finally came across the name "Orra Fågel." That's the name I had seen on the blacked-out Omte form, the one that Calder assured me belonged locked up in the vault.

Her parents had been listed—Osvald and Anne Fågel—but there was nothing more. Without their birth dates, it would be difficult for me to find them, and there was still no real proof that the Fågels were related to me at all.

That had been the culmination of my work that morning. Three hours of reading and searching, and I'd only come up with that short list by the time Pan came back.

"Hey, how's it going?" Pan asked as he approached me.

"Okay. But it would be a whole lot easier if there was a database." I moved a stack of books aside to make room for Pan.

"Yeah, it really would," he agreed as he sat down beside me, his thigh brushing against mine on the narrow bench. "But you try convincing a group of old dudes who sit on an ancient board obsessed with tradition to make a change. They're convinced that if we go online, we won't be able to use magic like we do here, and then the humans would finally stumble upon all our secrets."

"Are they right?"

"We can't really be sure, since they won't even let us try it out," Pan said. "Maybe they are. We have historically had a very difficult time merging our abilities with technology."

"Yeah, I have found that my superior strength has only really been a detriment to technology. And I've got the replacement costs for three phone screens to prove it," I said dryly.

"Did you find any leads yet?"

"I don't know. It's hard to tell at the moment."

"Let me see what you've got." He leaned over, his shoulder pressing against mine so he could inspect my notepad. "That Fågel sounds familiar. Aren't they Omte royalty or something?"

I shook my head. "I grew up mostly with the Kanin and Trylle tribes, so honestly, my Omte history is pretty shaky."

"Royalty tend to have super immaculate records, even for the paperwork-hating, privacy-obsessed Omte." He tapped the page and stood up. "I'll go grab the royal books, and we can see if there's anything more there."

He jogged up the stairs, and a few minutes later he returned with a crisp-looking book with bronzed edges on the pages.

"Oh, it's all gilded and shiny?" I asked.

"Of course it is." He sat back down beside me. "Do you think the information on Kings and Queens can be stored in plain old pages with a boring cover? Please."

I laughed. "How silly of me."

Pan started flipping through the book, running his fingers along the columns as he read the names at lightning speed. "The Elaks have been in power for some time now, but I wasn't completely wrong."

"What do you mean?" I asked.

He tapped the newest entry in the book. "The current Queen Regent of the Omte, her name is Bodil Elak, but her maiden name was Fågel. When was Orra born?"

"In 1969," I said, without even having to check my notepad.

"The good news is that she's in the book," he said. "The bad news is that she—along with her entire immediate family—is dead."

"What?" I leaned over, looking at the multiple entries that ended with a solitary bold word: DECEASED. "Did they all die in a war or something?"

"No, it looks like they were all spread out." His fingers trailed down the years—ranging from 1964 all the way up to the year 2006. "She had four brothers, and all of them died when they were fairly young. Only she and one of her brothers lived past age five."

"Oh, that's awful."

"Unfortunately, this kind of childhood mortality isn't uncommon, especially not for the Omte," he said solemnly. "A lot of the babies and children fail to thrive."

"What about Orra herself? When did she die?" I asked.

"She's listed as having died in 2006 and there's a footnote at the bottom of the page that explains . . ." He squinted and held the book closer to his face to make out the tiny print, and he read aloud, " 'Declared dead in 2006, after missing for years, at the behest of her next of kin, her cousin HRM Bodil Elak, Queen of the Omte.' "

In this case, *HRM* stood for Her Royal Majesty.

"Great. Is there a way that I can contact her?" I asked, then I realized that I hadn't ever tried to reach a Queen before. "Does she take calls?"

"We can put in a requisition through the Inhemsk offices, but I would be surprised if we heard anything back within the next six months, and I am not optimistic that she would reply positively," he said.

"So the first lead I get is actually a dead end?" I leaned back against the window.

Pan closed the book and turned to face me. "Have you eaten anything?"

"That's an abrupt change of subject," I said with a laugh.

"You look like you need a break, and I'm starving. Let me buy you lunch," he insisted. "You gotta fuel your brain if you wanna keep at this for another four hours."

I smiled. "All right. Lunch, it is."

20

Ögonen

Pan led me up to the widow's walk at the very top of the Mimirin. He kept promising, as we climbed the endless narrow stairs, that it would be worth the effort when we finally made it to the top.

We'd gone down from the Tower of Avanor to get our food in the cafeteria, which was on the first floor of the institution, and then we had turned around and gone back up a different set of stairs—this time in the center of the Mimirin—and Pan expected me to climb them all the way to the top, unlike in the Tower of Avanor, where my search had never taken me higher than halfway up.

Finally, though I was struggling to catch my breath, we made it, and Pan opened the hatch that led us up to the roof of the Mimirin. The walk was a narrow pathway, maybe about four or five feet across, that ran along the length of the highest point of the roof of the main building. Either side of the path had wrought-iron railings, preventing someone from sliding over the edge and down the shingles of the roof.

From here, the entire city and the ocean were visible. The first thing I could think of was a Claude Monet painting I remembered from the art magazines that Mr. Tulin kept around the house. The beautiful ocean on the rocky shore and picturesque village around us.

I breathed in deeply, and the air tasted sweeter and saltier up here than it did in the city. "This is *spectacular.*"

"I know. And the best part is that nobody is ever up here."

"Why not?" I leaned against the railing and admired the enormity of the view before me. The ocean, the sky, the city all around me. "I know all those stairs are a deterrent, but this view is totally worth it."

"The stairs don't help any, but the real issue is the Ögonen."

Pan motioned to the octagonal glass atriums that sat at the top of the thirteen towers that ran around the edges of the Mimirin. The towers were all much smaller than the Tower of Avanor—maybe ten feet tall and just as wide.

Each one of the atriums held a tall, sinewy sliver of a trollian being. They stood nearly seven feet tall and couldn't be more than thirty inches around, but it was hard to say for sure, since they had a strange skeletal fluidity to them, like a jellyfish with bones.

The Ögonen were covered in leathery ocher skin, but like it had been stretched out so thin it was slightly transparent. With the afternoon sunlight shining through them, they seemed to be glowing burnt orange. Their heartbeat—a rapid pounding of their curved oblong heart in the center of their shallow chests—was easily visible.

But the eeriest thing about them had to be their eyes.

They came in various shades of brown, and they looked like every other troll's. It was the normalness of it, the ordinary everyday trollian eye, in such an otherworldly being.

Outside of their very distinct appearance, I didn't know much about the Ögonen. They were the androgynous guardians of the Mimirin and the citadel surrounding it, using their very extreme psychokinetic powers to hide everything under a protective cloaking veil.

"What's wrong with the Ögonen?" I asked in a hushed voice. "Do they not like it when we're up here?"

"As far as I can tell, they don't care one way or another. They don't ever talk to me, and other than the occasional look my way . . ." He paused to motion toward a nearby Ögonen, who very slowly turned to stare at us fully, unblinking for several seconds, before slowly turning back around. "That's it. That's the extent of every interaction I've ever had with them."

"What's the problem, then?" I asked, even though I thought I knew. When the Ögonen looked at me, the hair stood up on the back of my neck.

"They kinda weird everyone out, and I know there's a big fear that the Ögonen read everyone's thoughts all the time."

"Can they?" I asked, whispering despite the probable ineffectiveness of that.

"I don't know." He shrugged. "Maybe? Probably? But if they can, I hardly think it matters if we're up here or even down in the cellars. They're cloaking an entire city and all its inhabitants. If they wanna know what you're thinking, they'll know."

"Do they ever speak?"

"Not that I've ever heard." Pan sat down, threading his legs through the railing so they hung over the roof, and I sat beside him, doing the same. "They stand up here, and when they change out shifts, they go to the edge of town, where they have strange homes built into the ground, like rabbit burrows. The powers that be are very secretive about the abilities and activities of the Ögonen. Hell, I don't even know for sure *what* they are."

He reached into the paper sack and pulled out the two veggie wraps on flatbread he'd procured in the cafeteria, along with a couple cartons of water and baked zucchini chips.

"They are trolls, aren't they?" I asked as he divided the food between us.

"They're troll-*like,* that's for sure," he conceded. "And I don't think they're immortal. There's a graveyard in their little neighborhood just for the Ögonen. The headstones have names on them, but they're all basically just one syllable, like Ug or Br or Non."

"That sounds very strange."

He took a big bite of his wrap and waited until he swallowed it before agreeing. "It's a surreal little plot of land, all right."

"How long have you been here?" I asked.

"In the city?" he asked, and I nodded. "Almost two years. Why?"

"You seem to know all sorts of hidden gems, for not being here that long."

He laughed and absently picked at the tomatoes in his wrap. "I guess I'm a naturally curious kinda guy. I like to know as much as I can about as much as I can."

"Me too." I smiled at him. "And I'm curious about you. You seem to be a little secretive and mysterious."

He laughed again, more heartily this time. "No, I'm not. At least not on purpose. It's just easier for me here if I don't talk about myself a lot. But really, I'm an open book. If you wanna know anything, you only have to ask."

"Okay. We'll start easy. Where are you from?"

"Ottawa," he replied, and my eyes widened.

"Wait, you didn't grow up around trolls? Were you a changeling?"

Pan shook his head adamantly. "Nope, not even close. My mom's human, and she grew up in the Inuit village of Iqaluit, which isn't that far from Doldastam. As she grew up, she started trading and working with the Kanin."

Trolls actually had a very interesting relationship with the native peoples of North America. We had lived side by side for nearly a thousand years, and we both had a general distrust of outsiders, which made sense given our respective experiences with conquerors and pillagers.

While trolls generally did our best to remain entirely hidden from all humans, the nature of surviving in the harsh winters of arctic living meant that we had to take all the help we could get. Because of the mutual enemy of overhunting/overmining/overfishing imperialism, we had developed an understanding with the local native humans.

"Eventually my mom actually became an accountant for the royal family, helping them to legally funnel money so they could keep the taxman off their back," Pan elaborated.

"And that's how your mom met your dad?"

"Yep. But things got very complicated very, very quickly."

"Was he a member of the royal family?" I asked, and when he didn't answer right away, I went on, "You said they refused to list him as your father in the Avanor records, so I figured he's gotta be someone with some pull."

He exhaled through his nose and admitted quietly, "He was the King."

"Seriously?"

"Seriously. I didn't fully believe it either, not until I got the blood test with a cousin."

"How did you not know that your dad was King?"

"The King couldn't be involved with a human, not without risking banishment, but he and my mom fell in love anyway, so they had a secret affair. When she found out she was pregnant, she left for a while to protect him, and to protect us, and I was born in Ottawa, but my dad missed us and pleaded with us to come back," he explained.

"I was still a baby when we moved to Doldastam, with him sneaking around to see us when he had the chance," he went on. "But when I was about a year old he fell ill and he died unexpectedly. He didn't have a clear heir, and there was a coup at the palace. I don't remember him at all, and after the uprising, things were really scary and unsafe for me and my mom, so she took me away, and we never went back."

"I'm sorry. That's so sad."

"It wasn't so bad." He sighed and shrugged. "I mean, my childhood was mostly normal, at least for a human. I didn't even know I was a troll until I was a teenager."

"How'd you find out?"

Pan rubbed the back of his neck and grimaced. "It's super embarrassing."

"Okay, well, now I *have* to know."

"Well, I'm Kanin, and even though I'm a half-TOMB, my father apparently had a powerful enough bloodline to pass his abilities on, even to a human," he explained. "I didn't notice anything, not as a kid. But after I hit puberty, I, uh . . . my skin would change color when I saw a pretty girl."

He laughed nervously but went on, "It wasn't like blushing, and it wasn't on my face or anything. My whole chest and sometimes my neck would get all blotchy and start changing to match the color of whatever shirt I was wearing."

"That doesn't sound *so* rough," I said, trying to comfort him.

"Yeah, at least I lived in Canada, so I had a good reason to wear turtlenecks and scarves all the time," he agreed. "I did get a handle on it eventually.

"But right after it started happening, I went to my mom, and she sat down and explained it all to me," Pan said. "I wanted to go back to Doldastam to find out more about what it meant to be a troll, but she was too afraid because of the violence that happened after my father died. Considering that my father's successor was eventually assassinated, she was right to be worried.

"She's still always been nervous that someone would hurt me because of my 'birthright,'" he said with a roll of his eyes. "Being half-human, I have no claim to the throne whatsoever, and I've always known that, and I never even wanted the crown at all.

"After I turned eighteen, I went to Doldastam," he went on. "Things had calmed down in the aftermath of the war, and the new King seemed a lot more progressive. They didn't exactly welcome me with open arms, but they tolerated me, and I was able to learn more about Kanin society and my family. Then I heard about the Inhemsk Project, and I applied and got some killer letters of recommendation, and here I am."

"Can I ask you something without you taking it the wrong way?"

"Sure?"

"Where do you think you fit in?" I asked carefully. "In troll society, I mean."

"Um . . . as of right now, I would say that I don't, not really. But I think there's enough room that I can carve out a little space. It takes more work, but hopefully it'll be easier for the half-TOMBs that come up after me."

"So, you plan on living among the trolls for the rest of your life?" I asked.

"It's hard to say," he replied thoughtfully. "I lived most of my life with humans, but I feel like I make more sense here than I did anywhere else out there." He looked over at me. "Since you asked me, I'll ask you something. Do you think you'll live with trolls forever?"

"I don't know." I leaned against the railing and stared out at the ocean, the waves rolling ceaselessly toward us on the shore. "I guess it really depends on if I find any family and where they live. Right now the only family I really know— the only ones that I could even consider my family—live in Förening, so I'll probably end up near them. Or I might end up somewhere else entirely.

"I don't know," I decided finally. "I'm still figuring out who I am and what I wanna do with my life."

"I'm excited to see where you end up."

I smiled at him. "Me too."

❦

visitors

The afternoon I spent researching had left me in a better mood, even though it had mostly been dead ends. My disposition probably had far more to do with hanging out with Pan than it did with the work I had done, but it still felt good to be doing something.

I was smiling as I climbed the stairs to my second-story apartment, but I paused when I heard something strange. Laughter and voices coming from the open windows. Hanna, and someone I didn't recognize.

My smile fell away, and I hurried into the apartment. When I opened the door, I discovered Hanna sitting on the couch next to a beaming young girl.

But it wasn't just any girl. Her hair was this ombré of pale orange shifting to neon-pastel-pink. It was like she'd had very fine blond hair, then someone had gone over it with a bright pink highlighter. Her face was distinctly heart-shaped, her chin coming to a dainty point. A broad, flat nose sat between her narrow, wide-set eyes. The apples of her tawny brown cheeks were full and prominent, and her top lip was thinner than her bottom, giving her a slightly pouty look.

"Hello!" She practically shouted with glee, and she was already on her feet, rushing over to greet me, before I even had a chance to close the door behind me. "You must be Ulla! It's so great to finally meet you! I mean, I know we bumped into each other before, but that hardly counts, since we did *not* have a proper introduction."

When she spoke, her voice was light and sweet like cotton candy, with a slight accent chaser. It was lyrical but rough, with an exaggeration on the vowels, and I couldn't place it at all.

"Um, hi," I replied uncertainly.

"Oh, my," she said with a small laugh—a giggle, really. "You're so shy, it's wonderful."

I gave her an uneasy smile. "I wouldn't really say I was shy." I slipped my bag off my shoulder, dropping it by the door, and edged my way farther into the apartment.

Dagny stepped out from where she'd been hiding in her room, her face scrunched up in annoyance. "This is what I've been dealing with all afternoon," she said, casting a pointed glare at Hanna and her new friend. "Why haven't you been answering your texts?"

I could only shake my head apologetically. "I don't even get texts here half the time. You know my phone gets almost no reception here, and it drops to literal zero inside the Mimirin."

"We've got to come up with a better system, then," Dagny muttered.

"Sorry," Hanna said with a sheepish smile. "Eliana is so excited for you to be here."

"So, this *is* the infamous Eliana?" I turned my attention back to the girl with her highlighter hair and her megawatt smile.

"That's me!" She laughed again—louder, more boisterous this time. "I want you to know that I'm not bappers. And I'm going to have your carriage fixed up in a real hurry. I don't know how—*yet*—but I'll find a way, I promise."

" 'Carriage'?" I asked.

"Sorry." Eliana looked back at Hanna for help. "What did you call it?"

"It's a Jeep," Hanna supplied.

"Yeah, sorry, I'm not fully adapted to your vernacular." Eliana went over and sat down beside Hanna again. "We don't have Jeeps where I come from."

I cast a glance over at Dagny, whose expression of confused skepticism mirrored my own. When I looked back at Eliana, I tried to keep my voice neutral, casual, and I sat down on the battered old recliner. "Do you have cars?"

Eliana nodded rapidly. "We have a few steam-powered carriages, yeah."

"Where are you from?" I asked.

"I don't know exactly." Eliana shook her head, and over her shoulder I saw Dagny rolling her eyes. "It's far away, and I can't remember how to get back there, so it doesn't really matter."

"Don't you want to get back home?" I pressed. "I'm sure you have family or friends who miss you and are worried about you."

"Of course I do," Eliana agreed with a shrug. "Or I presume that I do. I seem likable enough that at least *someone* would miss me."

"Yeah, I like you," Hanna piped up.

Eliana grinned at her. "So, yes, I do."

"Don't you want to contact them to let them know you're okay? Do you want to check in and see how they're doing?" I asked.

"Not really." Eliana shook her head again. "Since I don't remember them, I don't have anything to miss."

"Um . . . okay?" I didn't know how to reply to that, so I fumbled to come at the topic from another angle. "Don't you have a mom?"

"That is a thornier answer, because I can't say that I know one way or the other," Eliana said, sounding unruffled about the whole thing. "But all living beings that I know of have some kind of parent—every flower started as a seed from another flower."

Then she tilted her head, squinting up at the ceiling as she considered it more. "Although, I suppose if you go back to the beginning of time, eventually there had to be *something* that existed before everything else, but all that is to say, which came first, the morning or the night?"

"Okay, well, I . . . I didn't expect things to get so philosophical," I said.

"Buckle up, because that's all you get from her," Dagny said to me, speaking as if Eliana weren't right there listening to us. "Try and ask her anything. The most basic question you can imagine. And she'll give you that weird riddle and dance."

Now it was Eliana's turn to look confused, her smooth

tawny skin wrinkling. "That wasn't a riddle, and I'm not dancing."

"You don't have family back home," I said, doing my best to figure out who—or what—exactly Eliana was.

"No, I didn't say that," she corrected me politely. "I *said* that I don't know who they are and I don't know how to reach them, so why does it matter?"

"Right, okay, sorry," I said. "What about here, then? Do you have friends? Where are you staying?"

"Of course I have friends." Eliana motioned to Hanna. "Hanna is my friend."

"Anybody else?" I pressed.

"Yes, Zinnia," she replied. "Zinnia sells reasonably priced cloth diapers and cloudberry jam."

"Because those are things that go together, obviously," Dagny muttered under her breath. She stood at my shoulder, as if egging me on to prove that Eliana was . . . different? Lying? Dangerous?

"How long have you known Zinnia?" I asked.

"Hmm." Eliana thought for a second. "Almost as long as I've been here."

"Okay, how long have you been here?"

"Um, maybe . . . two or three times as long as I've known Hanna."

"So, what is that?" I paused, doing quick math in my head. "Six days? Ten days? Somewhere in between?"

Eliana nodded. "Yes, that sounds fair."

Dagny scoffed. "To which one?"

"One of them," Eliana said. "It was almost certainly one of them. Or maybe a little more or a little less."

"I don't mean this to sound harsh, because I'm really trying to understand here," I said as gently as I could. "Are you deliberately being this obtuse?"

"How do you mean?" Eliana asked, innocently enough.

"I told you," Dagny said, her voice lilting in a singsong way.

"Do you understand how to tell time?" I asked Eliana.

"Of course I do. First it's light, then it's dark, and when it gets light again, that's another day."

"You guys, stop grilling her," Hanna interjected plaintively. "She's confused, and you're making it worse."

"No, they're fine. I swear," Eliana insisted with a smile. "You'll know when I'm annoyed, and I'm as happy as a *duzee*."

"When it gets dark, where do you sleep?" I asked.

"Oh, I don't sleep much when it's dark. This place has very intense vibrations, and in the dark they seem so much more mercurial."

"Mercurial?"

"I don't know." Her brow furrowed again. "Uncertain? Unsafe? When you're walking through the forest, and you know that somewhere in the trees, a *kuguar* is watching, stalking you. You can't see it, and you know you can't hide, but you can't be sure which way to run."

" '*Kuguar*'?" I repeated.

"I think she means cougar," Hanna suggested.

"The really big cat with velvety dark brown and honey patches." Eliana held her hands several feet up, indicating a cat at least as large as a golden retriever.

"Could be a cougar," I agreed.

"Could be a leopard," Dagny suggested.

Hanna gave us both an irritated glare. "I don't think it really matters to the story."

"Let's circle back." I folded a leg underneath me and leaned toward Eliana. "If you don't sleep in the dark, do you sleep in the day?"

"I usually climb up to the roofs and I nap when the sun is at its warmest."

"Why roofs?" I asked.

"It's safer in the trees," Eliana said, like the answer should be obvious.

"Where you are from are there lots of dangerous big cats and *kuguars* around?"

"Are you a cat?" Dagny asked, with a level of such seriousness and intensity that I had to struggle not to laugh.

Hanna rolled her eyes. "She's obviously not a cat."

"Maybe it was a body-swapping spell or something," Dagny persisted, undeterred. "I don't know what kind of magical experimentation goes on at the Mimirin."

"I'm not a cat, and as far as I know, I never was one," Eliana assured us.

"As far as you know," Dagny echoed.

Hanna threw her hands up in frustration. "She's not a cat!"

"What do you do for fun?" I asked, trying to lighten the mood some.

"Oh, today we had so much fun!" Eliana clapped her hands. "We checked out all the vendors, and Hanna bought some food. We had the most delicious little cherry tomatoes!"

"Actually, they were just cherries, but they were really tasty," Hanna corrected her.

"Then we watched the most *amazing* thing I've ever seen! It was like this electronic play—"

"Television show," Hanna supplied again.

"Right, show. The colors were so bright, and everyone was so beautiful, and the music was beyond anything I'd ever heard. Everything that happened was all so . . . *visceral*."

"It was *Riverdale*," Hanna explained once Eliana had finished her effusive praise. "I downloaded the series on my laptop before we left, so I'd have something to watch at my grandparents', and that worked out for me, since we have zero Wi-Fi here."

"You should have her watch *Planet Earth* episodes," I said. "That'll blow her mind."

"What's that?" Eliana asked.

"It's a nature documentary that shows real footage and close-ups of the plants and animals on Earth in ways that we don't usually get to see them," Hanna elaborated.

"What's Earth?" Eliana asked.

For a moment we were all speechless, Dagny, Hanna, and I sharing a series of very uneasy, bewildered looks.

"Where . . ." I took a fortifying breath. "Where do you think we are?"

"Isn't this your apartment?" Eliana looked around. "Hanna told me it was."

"No, yeah, this is, but I mean, what do you think is outside of the apartment?" I asked.

"The city of Merellä?"

"And what's beyond that?"

"I don't know." She shrugged. "Some water and some trees. Probably."

"What is it that we live on?" Dagny asked, trying to be more specific. "The dirt ball beneath everything? What do you call the world?"

"Oh, that's easy. Why didn't you ask?" Eliana grinned. "It's Adlrivellir."

22

Helping

An hour later, after many, many circular bouts of conversation, we hadn't really learned much of anything about Eliana. As best we could gather, she had simply appeared here sometime between a week and a week and a half ago. She believed that she came here for a reason, but she couldn't remember what it was.

Despite all that, she was utterly convinced that she'd find what she was looking for and that all of this would work out fine for her.

Then, somewhat abruptly, she'd declared that she'd had enough talking and she wanted to go into the city. We'd tried to talk her into staying, but we weren't about to hold her hostage, so we had to let her leave.

"You guys!" Hanna whirled on me and Dagny the second she closed the door behind Eliana. "You scared her away!"

"We did not!" Dagny sounded genuinely offended. "She left because she was done hanging out here. She didn't seem at all flustered by us."

"Yeah, you said she seemed scared before too, but that's not the vibe I got from her," I chimed in. "She seemed really relaxed. It could be because she was so spacey, but she genuinely didn't seem to mind talking to us."

Hanna's anger was immediately replaced with an excited smile. "So you liked her?"

"I wouldn't say that," I answered as carefully as I could.

"Well, what *did* you think of her?" Hanna asked, her eyes bouncing between me and Dagny.

This was not the first time I'd seen Hanna react this way. Such as three springs ago, when she found an injured fawn in the forest that she had to nurse back to health. Or last fall, when a changeling came home early and Hanna immediately took her under her wing and became her best friend. Heck, even six weeks ago, when a bird's nest fell out of a tree in a storm, Hanna set the little robin nestlings up in her room.

Hanna loved to rescue things. Even if she usually ended up way over her head and needed her parents and me to step in and sort things out. Especially with the baby birds—that ended up being a brutal three weeks, but two of the three babies survived long enough to fly away, so I considered that a win.

Usually Hanna gravitated to adorable, helpless animals, and I guess Eliana did seem to sort of check those boxes. Plus, she had the added bonus of being mysterious, fun, and exotic, and she'd shown up just when Hanna was wasting away from boredom. "I don't know what to think," I replied honestly.

"I don't know about the dream girl, but she's definitely

got the manic pixie part down," Dagny muttered, and I laughed, drawing a glare from Hanna.

"What do you think she is? Really?" Hanna asked.

"Honestly?" Dagny puffed out her cheeks as she exhaled. "My money would be on either some type of dissociative disorder or an extraterrestrial."

I rolled my eyes. "Oh, come on, she can't be an alien."

"Why not?" Hanna asked.

"It seems far more likely that it's something we've already had evidence of—like a psychological disorder or something," I said. "Or it could be a mutation or even a new manifestation of some of the psychokinetic abilities trolls usually have."

Dagny seemed to consider this for a few seconds before saying, "We also can't rule out the third possibility. That she's messing with us for fun."

"That doesn't explain her otherworldly hair," Hanna argued.

I scoffed. "You're pushing your alien bias now."

"No, she could have really high-quality wigs," Dagny said.

"For wigs that nice, the price would be very high," I said, causing both of them to give me odd looks. "What? In middle school, I toyed with shaving my head and going with wigs, but the cost of a really nice one plus the shipping up to Iskyla was murder, so I stayed au naturel."

"Oh, but you have such nice hair," Hanna said with a sympathetic frown.

"Thank you," I said, then cleared my throat. "We can't agree on what *exactly* Eliana is, but I do think we can all agree that she is most likely an alien, a lying criminal, or she's very ill."

Dagny nodded. "Yeah, that seems likely."

"I think we should add 'in danger' or 'on the run,' but I would agree that she seems sick," Hanna said.

"I'll concede to that," I said. "In any one of those three scenarios, our correct course of action would be to go to some kind of authority in town."

"No way!" Hanna yelled instantly. "We can't do that."

"Why not?" I asked.

"What do you mean, 'why not'?" Hanna looked at me like I had suddenly sprouted a new head, and she motioned wildly with her hands as she grew more appalled. "We all saw how uncomfortable she got when you brought up taking her to meet Elof!"

"Yeah, because she's afraid that the *häxdoktor* might want to steal her life force!" I said. "That is one of the worst possible reasons to not go get help, honestly."

That had been one of the stranger tangents she'd gone on during our conversation, when we suggested medical help and Dagny had mentioned meeting with Elof might be a less-threatening avenue to help, since he had some medical training but was not actually a doctor. Eliana insisted she would never trust any *häxdoktors* because they steal life forces. When I tried to get her to define *häxdoktor*, the best I could get was that it was some type of doctor or healer or shaman, and she did *not* like them.

"She'll be so freaked out, though." Hanna's shoulders slumped, and her voice pitched toward a whine. "It'd be so much better if you gave me some time to get to know her better and get her to understand your docent isn't practicing witchcraft."

Dagny stepped over to stand beside Hanna. "I'm going to have to side with Hanna on this one."

"What?" I asked, incredulous. "Why?"

"If she's scared, she'll fight us, and if she fights us, we'll have to go to security instead of Mimirin faculty," Dagny reasoned. "If security gets her, they'll most likely eject her, and then she'll be gone. Maybe forever. With time, even a short amount, I'm certain that we could get her to willingly visit Elof, and he might be able to gather a lot of information from her."

"We could find out who she really is and where her home is?" Hanna asked hopefully.

"Possibly." Dagny shrugged indifferently. "But more importantly, we can find out if she's an alien or a new type of troll."

"And we'll get her someplace safe to stay that's not living on the streets," Hanna said.

"Yes, if that's what motivates you, go ahead and focus on that part," Dagny said. "As for myself, I'll focus on the discoveries we could make with her blood."

"Dagny." I gave her side-eye. "I know we haven't known each other that long, but I gotta say that sometimes you really sound like a comic-book villain."

"Comic-book villains are usually very intelligent, so I'll take that as a compliment."

"Yeah, like the Killer Croc was known for his wits," I said.

"I'm not familiar."

"Never mind."

23

Bazaar

After another long, exhausting morning working in the archives, I was in dire need of a break. Instead of spending the forty-five minutes I was allotted for lunch cooped inside the basement with Calder and eating stale zucchini chips, I decided to head to the bazaar.

The bazaar on Wapiti Way was a loud, bright explosion. It was one part flea market, one part farmers' market, one part carnival, but it somehow added up to a complete spectacle. There were flashes of color everywhere, vibrant fresh vegetables, and bold fabrics and jewelry, everyone haggling over prices and a street artist performing an old troll sailing song and accompanying himself on the mandolin. The scent of sweet fruits, savory herbs, and fermented elk milk all mixed together to create a strange but not entirely unpleasant aroma.

Hanna had asked me for cloudberries to make a crumble, and I was poking through small jute baskets to find the tart honey-colored berries. I'd finally found a basketful that seemed pretty good, so I picked it up and waited my turn to pay the vendor.

"You know how to tell if they're ripe?" A young guy had strolled up beside me, and now he plucked a berry out of the basket in my hand. He was lithe and lean, with enchantingly fluid movements, giving him a swarthy David Bowie vibe.

"Um . . ." I floundered for a moment, suddenly flushed and stammering as he looked at me.

A charming smile played on his lips, smooth and sharp as a blade, and it cut through me as easily as a knife. Dark deep-set bedroom eyes under heavy lashes and thick eyebrows, above pronounced broad cheekbones. His black hair was somehow both lush and unkempt, and it landed at his shoulder.

"When they're more of a yellow-orange than red?" I said finally in a voice that sounded like my own but at the same time far away and a little coy.

"You gotta squeeze them." He held a berry between two fingers. "When they're ready, they're soft and tender in your hand."

I bit the inside of my cheek—deliberately, shocking myself out of my flustered nervous attempts at flirtation—and I slowly regained my cool. "Judging by color seems more hygienic than prodding every berry on the bush."

"To each their own." He tossed the fruit in his mouth, and his grin deepened. "Those are perfect."

"Thanks, I think?" I offered him an uncertain smile. "Are you walking around making sure that everyone only buys ripe fruit?"

"I was passing time, and you looked lost."

"I am not much of an expert on fruit," I admitted.

He licked his lips and shook his head once. "That's a shame. The sweet nectar of a perfectly ripe berry is truly a gift from the gods."

Heat rushed to my cheeks and I looked away, hoping he didn't notice the blush rising. "I don't think I've had any fruit that I'd describe that way."

"It sounds like you haven't ever had an Idunnian pear in prime form," he countered.

I shook my head. "Idunnian pear? What's that?"

"I've searched high and low through this whole bazaar, and I haven't been able to find it," he said with a dramatic sigh. "Apparently it's not common around here. It's one of those things that you don't fully appreciate until it's unavailable."

I took a few bills out of my pocket and paid the vendor before walking away from the booth.

I wasn't sure that he would follow, but he did, and we meandered together through the crowd, occasionally admiring the intriguing wares or more alluring showmen.

"Where I'm from, up in the subarctic, our native cuisine was a lot of salty fish and tubers, and honestly, I don't miss either very much," I said.

He snickered. "I don't think I would either."

"How long have you been in Merellä?"

"Long enough to be homesick but not long enough to have given up hope on finding Idunnian pears. What about you?"

I wasn't looking at him, but I could feel his gaze as he studied me—warm and penetrating—and waited for my answer.

"I've been too busy to be homesick so far, but maybe I just need a little more time."

"It depends on why you left home, I suspect," he said reflectively.

"I don't know." I tucked my hair behind my ears and let thoughts of my childhood wash over me for a moment. "Even when you run away, you sometimes miss where you came from."

"You sound like you say that from experience."

"You look like an experienced guy yourself," I said, evading his question.

"I've always considered myself to have a well-learned but slightly sheltered existence," he said. "Traveling, unfortunately, hasn't been common in my life, but an opportunity came up here that I couldn't miss."

"I know the feeling. What brought you here?" I asked.

"Officially, I'm here for research, but between you and me, I really came here to find myself."

Before I had a chance to ask him a follow-up question, a boisterous trio of lute players circled around us, belting out old Skojare fishing songs.

"Would you want to continue this conversation somewhere a little less . . ." He spoke loudly to be heard over the noise, and he motioned vaguely around us. "We could grab some lunch?"

"Um." I stumbled over my response, and my stomach flipped in anguish as I heard myself turning down his invitation. "I would, but I've actually used almost my entire lunch break wandering through the market, and I have to get back to work."

A thin smile of understanding passed across his lips. "I suppose I should do the same."

"Thanks for keeping me company and giving me some berry tips." I held up my recent cloudberry purchase.

"Anytime. Hopefully I'll bump into you again at the market, and I'll be able to expand my helpful tips to all fruits and eventually vegetables and pastries."

"I'm always happy to learn." I smiled at him. "It was nice meeting you."

"Likewise."

It wasn't until I started walking away that I realized I *hadn't* actually met him. The whole time we'd been talking, we hadn't ever exchanged our names. I turned around to correct that, but he was already gone, having disappeared into the crowd.

24

invitations

At the end of the day, before I even rounded the corner toward my apartment above the carriage house, I could smell the *semla*—a Trylle specialty similar to a cream puff that scented the air all sugary sweet like doughnuts fresh at the bakery—and I heard the loud, abrasive melodic/shrill combo of Hanna and Eliana singing together. Based on the lyrics and inconsistent tune, I guessed the song was a mash-up of an old troll lullaby, the theme to *Fuller House*, and a Taylor Swift song.

When I entered the apartment, Hanna and Eliana were laughing hysterically in the kitchen. Dagny sat on the couch, typing furiously on her laptop while wearing a large pair of noise-canceling headphones.

Dagny glanced up at me, and she moved her headphones so that one ear was open, and she loudly explained, "I want to be pissed at them, I really do, but honestly, they've been plying me with delicious snacks all evening, and I can't bring myself to be angry at anyone who makes food like this. I should've gone down to the archery range by now, but I've been way too content just eating and organizing class data for Elof."

I dropped my bag on the table and walked over to see what trouble Hanna and Eliana were cooking up. "What have you two been up to today?"

"We worked all morning coming up with our friendship song, and then we made *semla*," Hanna announced brightly.

"I also watched another three episodes of that *Riverland* show," Eliana added.

"*Riverdale*," Hanna corrected her.

"Right, that one."

"But we stayed in all day, just like you asked," Hanna said with exaggerated compliance that made me suspicious.

"Technically, I didn't specify that Eliana needed to stay in, since she's a stranger and I have no say over what she does and does not do," I clarified.

Hanna shot me a look. "She's not a stranger, Ulla. She's my friend."

"Right, yeah," I agreed uneasily. "Well, I still don't get to tell her what to do, but it's nice that she helped you honor my wishes, I guess." I took the fruit I'd bought at the bazaar out of my bag and set it on the counter in front of Hanna. "I did get you those cloudberries you wanted."

"Thank you so much!" Hanna said, and Eliana clapped her hands together in delight. "You know, we have been running out of stuff to cook. If you'd allow me out of the apartment, I could pick stuff up myself."

"Leave me a list, and I'll get it for you tomorrow," Dagny said from the couch. "I'm going to the archery range after work, and I can stop by the market on my way home."

"Dagny's got you covered," I said.

"Thanks, Dagny," Hanna replied bitterly.

"It's safer for you both if you stay off the streets," I said.

Hanna's sour mood instantly disappeared, and she started bouncing on the balls of her feet, as if I had suggested the most wonderful thing. "Then Eliana should stay here."

"What? No." I shook my head. "I mean, no. That's not . . . there isn't any room."

"We are already beyond max capacity," Dagny chimed in flatly.

"I like it outside," Eliana said. "The nights are so warm, and the stars are so bright."

Hanna looked gravely at Eliana. "But Ulla's friend Pan said it was dangerous here at night."

"I can handle myself," Eliana said with a shrug.

"You fell through the roof of our Jeep," I reminded her.

"Anyone can slip and fall in any place," she reasoned, unfazed.

"Maybe so, but it's still safer here," Hanna argued.

"Maybe once Hanna is gone, we'll have some room," I suggested.

Eliana's eyes widened, and she shot a look at Hanna. "You'll be gone? What do you mean?"

"I told you, Eliana," Hanna explained carefully. "This isn't my real home. I live in a house in the bluffs on a river, and it's thousands of miles away from here."

Eliana's brow furrowed, but she nodded. "Oh, right. I guess I forgot."

"Have you always had problems with your memory?" I asked.

"And how would I know that?" Eliana looked up at me. "I can't remember. That's the whole point."

A knock at the front door punctuated her statement.

"Are you expecting anyone?" I asked Hanna.

"Nope," she said. "Eliana's the only one I know here, outside of you two."

"I know more than that, but I don't usually have guests," Dagny said with a sharp glare. "I like my privacy."

I started toward the door when Hanna asked, "You're not gonna answer that, are you?"

"I don't see any reason not to," I replied, making sure to keep my voice low so whoever was at the door wouldn't hear.

Hanna cast me a wary gaze, and she leaned toward Eliana, whispering, "Maybe it'll be better if you stay out of sight. Just to be safe."

Eliana shrugged. "Sure, no problem."

She crouched down slightly, barely bending her knees, and then she suddenly sprang up, landing lightly on the balls of her feet on the countertop. Before I could even fully register the awesomeness and near-impossibility of her vertical jump, she was on the move in a flash. She ran at the wall, then kicked off with her foot, and she landed delicately on the narrow railing around my little loft bedroom.

Without even a pause to breathe, she leapt from the railing up to a beam that ran across the ceiling, and she lay down on her back on the beam. Her hands hung slightly over the edge, holding the wood, and I saw her fingers slowly shift color—her normal tawny brown changing to the dark, rugged mahogany of the exposed wood.

"Holy shit," I gasped after Eliana's stunning acrobatic display had come to an end and she was safely hidden.

"Ulla?" Pan called from outside the door, and he knocked again. "Ulla? I needed to talk to you for a second."

I plastered a smile on my face and opened the door. "Sorry for making you wait. Come on in. You remember Hanna, and you already know my flatmate Dagny."

"Hi." He offered a small wave to both of them, then his dark eyes settled on me. "Sorry to bother you at home, especially when it's so late."

"No, it's no problem." I ran a hand through my hair. "You can stop by anytime, day or night." He cocked an eyebrow at me, and my cheeks flushed with warmth. "I mean, not anytime, but if you need something, or, you know, at least call ahead, maybe . . . Anyway, what is it that you, um, needed to talk about?"

"Sylvi made some requests, and she was able to get in touch with a Mästare. After talking, they decided to invite us to morning tea tomorrow at seven forty-five sharp."

"Whoa, wait." Dagny slammed her laptop shut and ditched her headphones completely. "You got a meeting with a Mästare?"

"Yeah, I mean, Sylvi Hagen got it, not me," Pan clarified with a self-deprecating laugh. "I doubt her office would ever take my requests."

Dagny stood up and walked over to us. "Which one is it?"

"Amalie Grímms."

"That makes sense," Dagny said thoughtfully. "She did work in the archives."

"Is Amalie a good one?" I asked.

"*Good* is a very subjective term, Ulla," Dagny replied derisively. "Amalie was orphaned as a toddler, and then chosen from by the Mimirin elite to be raised and tutored for service here. She was the youngest woman ever to become the head of a department, hers being the archives. For the past twenty-three years she's been a Mästare—a position that only one of every twenty heads has even a chance of attaining. She's also rumored to be on the Information Styrelse, but the policy of the Mimirin is never to confirm or deny the identity of the board members.

"*Good* I would say isn't the right word," Dagny said, finishing her rant. "*Formidable* is the one I'd choose."

"Awesome." I smiled thinly. "That all sounds . . . awesome. Will Sylvi be there?"

"I can't say for sure, but I don't think so," Pan said. "It sounds like it will be the two of us and Amalie."

"Great." I swallowed my unease and nodded once. "Great. It's really . . ."

"Great?" Pan supplied with a smile.

"Sorry, I'm a bit nervous, I guess, but that's okay," I said with a tight laugh. "I didn't plan to sleep tonight anyway."

"I get it, but it's going to be fine," Pan assured me, his voice low and soothing. "You just wanna talk to her, get a few answers to some basic questions, and you won't be alone. I'll be there with you the whole time."

I smiled at him, genuinely this time. "I know, and thank you."

"I'll meet you outside of the Mimirin tomorrow. Let's say a quarter after seven to be safe?"

"Perfect," I said. "I'll see you in the morning, then. And thanks for coming out to let me know."

"Cell service can be so sketchy out here, and I wanted to make sure you got the message," he explained.

As soon as he was gone and the door was shut behind him, Eliana dropped down from the ceiling, landing nearly silently in the center of the apartment.

"Okay, seriously, what are you?" I asked.

She glanced around the room. "Aren't we all the same thing?"

"What do you think we all are?" I asked carefully.

"Trollian beings."

"Technically, she's not wrong," Dagny said dryly, but it definitely wasn't the answer we were expecting. Most trolls would say either their tribe or just troll. "How old are you?" I asked Eliana directly. I'd been studying her youthful face. Physically, my best guess would put her in her late teens, but she acted so much younger than that—excitable, naïve, cheerful, and entirely unbothered by very serious things that would bother most everyone else, like pervasive amnesia.

"Um . . . I honestly can't remember exactly anymore. But I think I'm older than Hanna, but younger than Amalie Grímms," she said after some thought.

Dagny stiffened. "You know Amalie?"

"No, I heard you talking, and you said she's had her job for twenty-three years. Twenty-three years ago, I was still a baby. I think." She paused and stared up at the ceiling for a moment. "Or maybe I was Hanna's age."

"Okay, fine," Dagny said, and exhaled roughly. "Eliana

can stay here, but Hanna is the one who has to deal with figuring out the sleeping arrangements."

Hanna squealed in delight. "Yes! No problem!"

"Why the sudden change of heart?" I asked.

"We have a color-changing trollish acrobat who is unsure what planet she is from and refers to herself by a species name we don't really use and can't remember how old she is or anything about herself," Dagny summarized. "At this point it seems irresponsible to let her wander around."

"I will stay here, but on one condition—I don't do any tests or go anywhere if I don't want to." Eliana suppressed her joy and made her stipulations coolly. "No poking or prodding without my agree-ence."

"Agree-ence?"

"I have to say yes to it," Eliana clarified.

"Did you mean agreement or consent?" I asked.

She shook her head. "No, I meant agree-ence."

"This wouldn't, by chance, be your way of saying that you're ready to meet with Elof?" Dagny asked.

Eliana shook her head forcefully. "No, not at all. Not even a little."

"Okay, then. As much as I would enjoy a grammar lesson from you, I need to get to bed, and I suggest that you all do the same. Ulla has a very important meeting in the morning, and I'm certain you would both feel quite terrible if you did anything to jeopardize that."

Dagny turned on her heel and went into her room, just as Hanna and Eliana started jumping up and down excitedly as they planned their first sleepover together.

chambers

The Mästare's chambers were on the highest floor in the northwest corner of the Mimirin. The room was significantly larger than the entire apartment that I now shared with Dagny, Hanna, and Eliana.

Her chambers had been divided into two parts—an office near the front, with a massive rosewood desk and high-backed chairs, and the rear area that was a more relaxed sitting area. Although *relaxed* was definitely stretching the definition of the word.

The design was overtly lush and indulgent. The walls were done in a dark cinnamon Venetian plaster, with the light fixtures and antiques in bronze and copper. In the sitting area especially, there was an explosion of fabric—heavy curtains in vivid shades of indigo and crimson with latkan tassels, dozens of pillows covered in bold satin with metallic trellis patterns, handwoven paisley throw blankets, Oriental rugs in burgundy and deep teal.

Double doors took up most of one wall, leading back into

the Mästare's private apartment. Kitty-corner from that was a velvet love seat. Just above the couch, a detailed woolly elk had been block-printed in burnt orange and ivory on a blue-green fabric and was hung in a bulky frame.

Pan and I sat across from the painting in narrow, firm chairs, and the tea rested on a tray before us on the chunky coffee table. We had been sitting there for ten minutes, since the Mästare's assistant had led us in, and we'd been alone since then, waiting in silence as the air thickened with the scent of the rosewater tea.

Finally the double doors opened and Amalie Grímms came in, offering apologies before she even sat down. "Sorry to keep you waiting. A small, unexpected problem came up this morning, but it's been dealt with."

She was petite, hardly five feet tall, and the layers of violet robes of the Mästare's uniform only succeeded in drawing attention to her diminutive frame. Her hair was dark brown, nearly black, with a few silver streaks running through it, and it was cropped short and left unstyled. Her olive skin was besieged by wrinkles, but her eyes were youthful and bright.

"I hope everything is all right," Pan said. He got to his feet to greet her, so I did the same.

"Sit, sit!" she commanded with a wave of her hands. "Yes, everything is fine. Like I said, it was small, and it's nothing you should concern yourselves with."

"Thank you so much for seeing us, especially on such short notice," Pan said, once she'd settled into the couch across from us.

"I'm not really seeing the both of you, am I?" She turned her sharp gaze to me. "It's only you who had the questions."

I cleared my throat. "I only had one question, really."

"You're with the Inhemsk Project?" Amalie asked.

"I'm interning in the archives, but I've been working with the Inhemsk Project to find my parents," I explained.

Her eyes bounced over to Pan. "You're Panuk, yes? One of the researchers down there?"

He nodded. "That's correct."

"And you're here for spectating, or did you have anything you needed yourself?"

"I only came to help Ulla," he said.

"Mmm." She folded one leg over the other and rested her arm on her knee, then turned to me. "And you're here about the blacked-out records?"

"Yes. I know I might not be able to find out what was blacked out, but I was hoping I could at least understand the *why*."

"The Mimirin—despite all our trappings and assertions that we are an institution of influence—makes much fewer decisions about the law of the land than one might imagine." Her lips twisted into a weary smile. "Even in Merellä, where our pull is arguably the strongest, we are often forced to work within the constraints and limitations of the five tribes.

"What that means is that most of the records that are blacked out or altered in some capacity came to us that way," Amalie went on. "The Omte, in particular, have a tendency to be secretive and withhold information for seemingly arbitrary reasons. They are reluctant to share anything at all with us, and we are honestly grateful for what we do ultimately receive."

"You're saying that you have no idea what it said, and you don't have any way of knowing?" I asked.

"That's partially correct," she allowed. "With the particular record you were interested in—a taxation form with the name of one Orra Fågel—I couldn't be sure, so I did some research myself. I put a call in to the Omte liaison, and I believe they may have been able to answer the question of *why*."

I sucked air in through my teeth, and my stomach dropped.

"Orra Fågel is related to the current monarch of the Omte, the Queen Regent Bodil Elak," Amalie explained. "Cousins, I believe. As private as they are about most things, the Omte protect their royalty even more fervently. In fact, for anything beyond the direct lineage of the throne, they guard all information about the royal family as if it's a trade secret."

"Because Orra Fågel is related to the Omte Queen, I won't be able to find out anything about her?" I asked in disbelief.

"Unfortunately, that seems to be the case," she replied. "Of course, you are free to continue looking here as much as you are able, but I wouldn't want you to get your hopes up that you'll find anything substantial or even interesting."

"She might be my mother," I persisted. "Doesn't that matter at all?"

Amalie shook her head sadly. "I'm very doubtful that the Omte will be forthcoming with you without evidence that you are a direct heir of Orra Fågel's."

"But without access to their records, I won't be able to gather any evidence that I'm related to her," I argued.

"If you're not sure that Fågel is who you're looking for, then perhaps you should move on to other options," she suggested. "Do you have other names on your list of potential mothers?"

"I have some," I admitted grudgingly.

"Perfect." Amalie clapped her hands as if she had solved the whole thing. "If they won't give you evidence, then the only thing you'll have to show the Omte is the absence of evidence."

"How will that work?"

"Look into the other names on your list," she said. "I assume many of the others are Omte, but as long as they aren't related to the Queen, you should have an easier time gathering information. It's likely that one of them will turn out to be your mother, but if not, ruling them all out may help convince the Omte of your relation to Fågel, and they may be willing to allow you to unseal her records."

"That is an awful lot of ifs and mays," I pointed out.

"When you work in the field we do, you learn quickly that it doesn't do well to promise certainties," Amalie said with her weary smile. "Nothing in life is certain, not even the past."

chess

After the meeting with Amalie, Pan took me down to a lounge so I could have a moment to clear my head before I had to go to work. The lounge itself had been the subject of an unfortunate renovation at some point, with my guess being the seventies, if the balding avocado-green carpet was any indication.

There was a kitchenette at one end with badly stained mustard-yellow countertops and a few partially stocked vending machines. Several games were scattered around, between mismatched couches and cracked tables and chairs. The foosball table was in rough shape, but the chess table looked fairly new.

"I know it wasn't what you wanted to hear, but she's not entirely wrong," Pan said as he poured me a glass of water from the tap.

"I know." I took the water from him, drinking it down greedily, and shook my head. "I'm more frustrated that I wasted her time and yours and mine."

"It wasn't a waste of time. You learned some things."

I looked over at him. "Did I? I already knew that Orra was related to the Omte Queen, and I don't know why Sylvi or Calder wouldn't have just told us that the Omte are super secretive."

"Maybe they didn't know."

"But how could they not know?" I argued. "First of all, it's not much of a secret. Like, what would be the point of hiding it? Beyond that, it's something that both Sylvi and Calder should've gleaned from their day-to-day work. Hell, it's already common knowledge that the Omte are cagey and like to keep to themselves, which isn't that much different from how any of the other tribes behave."

Pan leaned against the counter and folded his arms over his chest. "Yeah, that's definitely true."

"So, what was the point of all that? Why did she even agree to see me?"

"I mean, you did sort of demand that Sylvi get you in to see the Mästare," he reasoned.

"But why wouldn't Sylvi have told us what the Mästare said? I wouldn't have kept pressing. And why would the Mästare even entertain us for something as simple and basic as that?"

I set down my water glass so I could gesture with my hands as I grew emphatic. "Picture how that call must've gone down. Sylvi gets her on the phone and says, 'Hey, I got a well-connected intern down here, and she's got some questions about why an Omte record would be blacked out.'

"And instead of Amalie replying, 'Oh, that's because the Omte black everything out related to the Queen, and she's related to the Queen'—instead of answering that way and having Sylvi fill us in, Amalie instead decided to say, 'Ah, I believe I know the reason, but that is much, much too sensitive to pass along to you, the head of one of our departments. No, it is much easier and safer for me to go around you and have a meeting with a TOMB who has only the vaguest and thinnest connections to royalty.'

"Which one of those situations makes more sense to you?" I asked him directly.

"I get what you're saying, that both scenarios you described sound a tad ridiculous, but what is the alternative?" he asked carefully. "What other possible motive could Amalie and Sylvi have?"

"I don't know. I'm not saying that anything nefarious is going on, but the whole situation doesn't quite mesh for me, and I want to know why."

"Fair enough. Where do you wanna start?"

"What do you know about the Mästare? Like, the position in general, not Amalie specifically."

"Do you play chess?" he asked abruptly.

"Um, I have played a few times," I answered uncertainly, but he was already walking over to the chess table. "But it's not something I would say I'm really any good at."

Once he sat down at the table, he gestured to the empty chair across from him, so I joined him.

"You know the basics? The king, the queen, the bishops, the knights, the rooks, and the pawns." Pan lined up the pieces by rank—the tallest ones were the king and queen, a pair of ravens carved into ivory, the king broader and the queen with a dainty tilt of her beak; the bishop was a wolf baring his teeth; the knight was a thick Tralla horse rearing up like it was ready for a fight; the rook was a tall, twisting serpent. "This one right here"—he put his finger on top of a pawn, a delicately carved small deer with slender horns—"that's me. An expendable pawn."

"If you're a pawn, what does that make me?" I asked.

He smirked. "Honestly? You're not even on the board."

"Ouch."

"Hey, nobody ever said that caste systems were kind." He pushed up the sleeves of his flannel shirt and returned his attention back to the pieces. "Above me is the knight, and their equivalent would be all the educators, whether that be teachers, docents, or what have you. There are rankings among them, which vary with position and expertise, but generally speaking the teaching staff are all regarded about the same."

"Only slightly better than you."

"Like I said, nobody ever said it was kind. Anyway, directly above them is the bishop, which are the department managers, like Sylvi or Calder. These are the ones that make sure everything is running smoothly and everyone is getting paid.

"This right here is a Mästare." He touched the top of a rook. "There are two positions above them, but that's not exactly true either. Directly above the Mästare isn't an individual but a group. The queen represents the Information Styrelse."

"Isn't the Styrelse made up of several of the Mästare? Wouldn't that make them their own boss?"

"So the rumors go, but unless you're on the Styrelse yourself, it's impossible to know for sure. The Mimirin charter states that a board of information will be made up of anonymous members of the faculty and elite members of the kingdom. It could be all Mästares. It could be just royalty. It could even be made entirely of janitors. Who can say? But the good news is that there is still one more position above them, to keep them in line."

"The Korva?"

He nodded. "Yep. The Korva is the one that rules them all. The current Korva is Ragnall Jerrick and has been for the past six years."

"How does the Korva get the job? Are they voted in?"

"They are appointed by the Styrelse."

"Uh-huh." My eyes bobbed between the king, queen, and rooks. "The only two positions above the Mästare are chosen by the Mästares? Doesn't that sound a bit like the hens running the henhouse?"

"A little bit, maybe, but aren't the hens the ones most qualified to know how a henhouse should be run?"

"I take it you haven't spent a lot of time in a chicken coop," I said. "Chickens are mostly sweet and docile, but they can be capable of barbaric acts of violence. I once saw the older hens nearly peck a younger red hen to death because she had a solitary white feather on her head. They just kept pecking at it and pecking at it."

"What happened to the chicken?" Pan asked.

"We took her out of the coop and nursed her back to health, and she's essentially a house pet now. The kids named her Dottie, and she sleeps in Emma's room back in Förening."

"At least that story had a happy ending."

"Unlike this one."

"What do you mean?"

"The system you described, there's no way for us to know who's in charge," I said. "As a Mästare, Amalie might actually answer to no one. She could be a member of the Styrelse. She could be best friends with the Korva and got him appointed."

"Or she could be an average employee with no pull or real connection with the board or the Korva," Pan countered. "Sylvi may have oversold your connection to the Trylle Queen, and Amalie was just trying to keep the peace."

I sighed. "That could also be true."

"This isn't a dead end, though, Ulla. You still have a dozen or so names."

"I'm up to eleven now, ten without Orra Fågel."

"So, ten. That's still a lot of Orras to go through, and any one of them could be your mom or know something about her. You could use this time worrying about what Amalie's ulterior motives may be—if she even has any—*or* you could do what you came here to do, and go back to looking for your mother."

"I know you're right, but . . ." I chewed my lip. "I just . . . I felt something when I found that paper, and . . . I always thought I would *know* when I found my mother. That it would be this intrinsic feeling I had inside me, where I knew it was her. And I thought I felt that when I saw the name Orra Fågel. But now I don't know if I did. I don't know if I ever will."

Pan leaned forward, resting his arms on the chessboard. "When I was a kid, my grandpa used to make the most delicious country food. It wasn't one of those big Sunday meal things, but he'd have me and my mom over about once a month, and he'd cook for us. All of it was amazing, but my favorite thing was the *akutaq*—which is sort of like an ice cream made with berries and whipped fat.

"And then after he died, my mom tried replicating his meals, but they weren't the same," he went on. "I looked up recipes and got a country food cookbook written by a local Inuit tribe, and I tried my hand at it. I even went to a food fest in Montreal and tried *akutaq* made by experts and professional chefs.

"Then it hit me: I had tried every conceivable variation of Grandpa's *akutaq*, including one made by his daughter, who had learned to cook it from him. I had to have eaten one that was right. But I didn't recognize it because I had inflated the flavor in my brain, making it this mythical perfect ambrosia.

"I was remembering something that had never existed, something that I had never had, and I would never know when I tasted the flavor my grandfather made," Pan said with a sad wistfulness. "All it is and all it will ever be now is a distorted memory."

"That's dark."

He shook his head adamantly. "No, it's not. I don't want you to get caught in the same trap that I was. Life isn't a fairy tale. Sometimes things happen without intense feelings or magical certainties."

"Thanks. I think I needed the reminder."

"I know. The more you get to know me, the more you'll get used to me being right."

"I think I can manage it." I smiled at him. "But I should

probably get back down to the archives. I've ditched out on Calder enough this week."

"I'll walk you down."

"You don't have to."

"I know. But I want to." He stood up with me. "And it gives me a reason to avoid Sylvi for a little bit longer."

27

ARROW

This was my paper-cuts-and-ink-stains montage. This was nine and a half hours of cold floors and books that smelled like dust and mold. This was translating old Norse so long that the words blurred into one foggy mass of umlauts and overrings. This was the silence that came after the radio broke, when it was only the papery scrape of turning pages and Calder's occasional phlegmy cough.

This was my Friday night. I had been working all day, and I was working well into the evening.

Calder excused himself to go to the storage closet, since we were in need of more pens. It was about ten minutes after he'd left me alone that the doors to the archives groaned open and Dagny walked in. Her black hair had been pulled into a long braid that hung down her back and swayed slightly as she strode over to me.

I sat up straighter and offered a cautious smile. "Hey, what are you doing here?"

"Hanna told me you were working late, and I thought I

ought to bring you some of the ridiculously tasty *dökkt rúg-braud* she and Eliana cooked up today." Dagny set a paper bag down on the desk, and I could already smell the fresh rye bread.

"That's awfully kind of you."

"I did it for myself, really," Dagny admitted and leaned against the desk. "I don't need to eat an entire loaf of that, and if I didn't get that out of the house, I was going to eat an entire loaf of it."

"Well, I appreciate it either way," I said. "How are things going at the apartment? Hanna told me it was going great when I called, but it's hard to know how truthful she's being."

"They haven't broken anything, and they were both home watching some cartoon burgers on Hanna's laptop. It's nice when they watch shows, because Eliana is focused and quiet."

"Do you have any new ideas about what's going on with Eliana?" I asked.

Dagny let out an irritated sigh. "Not really. I ask her as many questions as I can, but she doesn't have the patience for it. It's like she can't hold a single thought in her head for very long, and then she has to flit on to the next thing."

"You think she has some kind of brain trauma or something like that?"

"Since I'm not a medical professional, it would be irresponsible of me to speculate," Dagny answered in her usual cool and collected way. "I also haven't been able to gather enough data to even make a wild guess."

She fell silent for a moment, her jaw tensing subtly and

her eyes narrowing as she thought. "The only thing I will say is that Eliana seems fully capable of caring for herself and performing complex tasks. I can't in good conscience make a case for her being a danger to herself or others, so there really isn't any more I can do except attempt to persuade her to allow Elof to evaluate her."

"What happens when Hanna goes home?" I asked.

"Why?" Dagny asked quickly. "Are her parents on their way?"

"Not as far as I know. I'm supposed to call her mom tomorrow at eleven, and we'll hopefully get it figured out then. But that's not what I meant. After Hanna goes, are you going to kick Eliana out?"

"No, of course not." She shook her head. "I have another four months left here on my term, and I'm fairly confident that in that time we'll be able to figure out who she is and where she belongs. If not, I will try to set her up with housing and a job before I go."

"But you'll let her stay?" I asked in a mixture of surprise and optimism.

"Of course. Beyond my admitted scientific curiosity about Eliana, I worry about her as a sentient being. I wouldn't leave a dog abandoned on the side of the road, and I won't leave her."

"That's nice to know," I admitted, and I did feel a bit of relief. I wasn't sure what would become of Eliana when I left in six weeks, but at least now I knew that she had someone as knowledgeable as Dagny looking out for her.

Calder returned with an armload of supplies from the storage room—pens, paper clips, erasers, pencils . . . really, he must've raided the damn place. He gave a gruff hello to Dagny before taking his seat on his side of the circular desk and beginning to put his haul away.

"So how did your visit with the Mästare go?" Dagny asked, turning her sharp eyes to me.

Calder immediately swiveled his chair toward me. "You visited the Mästare?"

"Yeah, that's why I was late this morning."

"You only said you had a meeting," he said, sounding dismayed.

"You were engrossed in your work," I explained. "I didn't want to bother you with a boring story about a go-nowhere meeting." He also hadn't shown the slightest bit of interest in me or my life, so I hadn't thought to share it with him, but I didn't say that.

"It went that well, huh?" Dagny asked with a wry laugh.

"Which one did you meet with? Was it the archives Mästare, Amalie?" Calder scooted his chair closer to us, apparently not wanting to miss any tidbit about my visit.

"Yeah," I said. "She basically said that the Omte had blacked it out, and she didn't know anything about it, and then that was that."

Dagny frowned. "I'm sorry it wasn't more helpful."

"You've already had a meeting with Amalie?" Calder pressed.

I looked over at him. "What do you mean, 'already'? And she's your boss, I'm sure you must have conversations with her all the time," I pointed out.

He raised his chin slightly and sat a bit taller. "Amalie is a busy woman, and she trusts me to handle the archives with very little intervention. We meet when necessary, yes, but I would never deign to waste her time."

"Anyway," Dagny said and clapped her hand on the desk. "It seems like you have a really fun night here ahead of you. When do you think you'll be home?"

I shook my head gloomily. "I don't know. At least another hour or two."

"They lock us out at eleven, so that's the latest we can be," Calder said.

"There you go."

Dagny nodded and started toward the door. "I'll see you at home."

"Yeah. And thanks again for the food."

Once she'd gone, Calder turned his chair around and went back to organizing his supplies. Since he wasn't actively engrossed in reading or deciphering anything, now seemed as good a time as any to talk to him.

"Can I ask you something, Calder?" I asked.

"Of course."

"Are the Omte private about info on their royals?" I asked, trying to gauge how common the knowledge truly was. I suspected that Amalie had called me for a meeting to tell me something that should've been obvious to Sylvi and Calder, and one way to check that was to see if it really was obvious to them.

He snorted. "They are private about everything."

"Which tribe would you say is the most secretive and reserved?"

"That's hard to say precisely, but the Omte would be the strongest contender for the title," he answered.

"So that's common knowledge, right?"

"I would say it's fairly common, yes," he said, sounding more disinterested as the conversation went on.

"What about the fact that the Omte don't want to share anything about their royalty? Is that common knowledge too?"

"You know, Ulla, I can't really speak to what each individual knows or doesn't know. Especially here in Merellä. Many trolls know many things, far more than what the average troll in the backwoods towns would know."

"No, yeah, of course," I said. "So, what about you in particular? Did you know that the Omte black out info about royalty?"

He finally looked up from his meticulously organized drawer of pens and narrowed his eyes at me. "Is that what Amalie told you? I may have heard that, yes."

"Why didn't you say anything?" I asked.

"I've been answering all of your questions, even as they've begun to get redundant and irritating, quite frankly," he said wearily.

"No, I mean, the other day," I went on, undeterred. "When I found Orra Fågel's taxation paper. You said you didn't know why it was blacked out."

"I didn't. I still don't know why."

"Why didn't you say that the Omte tend to black out info if it's at all connected to the royal family?" I reiterated.

His eyes were downcast again, his attention back to laying his pens in perfect order. "I didn't say that because it didn't seem pertinent. I didn't know that Orra Fågel was related to anyone. I don't know who she is or anything about her. What is it exactly that you're getting at?"

"I don't know, honestly." I sighed and leaned back in my

chair. "I feel like I'm getting a bit of a runaround. I thought the whole point of the Inhemsk Project was to unite families, but it seems like an uphill battle to get even the smallest bits of information."

"That's because your first supposition was incorrect," Calder said matter-of-factly. "The Inhemsk Project does not care at all about you or your family. They only care about two things—your money, and your fertile loins."

"I—I'm not . . ." I stammered and my cheeks flushed. His mention of my *loins* had left me flabbergasted. "I mean, I don't know that I have either. Or that I don't."

"The project was started because we're going extinct, and that means we're also going broke," he explained flatly. "We need money and babies, and we can't afford to turn anyone away. Not anymore. But don't fool yourself for a second in thinking that the Inhemsk cares even slightly about your happiness or your well-being—or even whether or not you ever find another family member."

"That is . . ." I licked my lips. "That is good to know."

"That's one thing I do like about you, Ulla. You're eager to learn."

"Thank you?" I replied uncertainly.

"But you're young and sheltered, and you haven't been here that long." He looked over at me, his glassy eyes resting heavily on me. "Allow me to give you a word of advice. Paranoia is something that comes easy here at the Mimirin. It's a place where competition and rumors run parallel to ground-breaking research and invaluable historical documentation. But you must remember this—just because the walls here can talk doesn't mean that they have anything to say about you."

28

Falling

I was sitting on the floor, leaning back and resting my head on the lumpy couch cushions, while Eliana crouched at my feet. Hanna had suggested that we do something fun, since it was Saturday morning, and I'd had such a long week. That led to Eliana, Hanna, and Dagny taking an excursion to the bazaar to get what they needed to make "organic" nail polish.

I hadn't minded that much, honestly, because it gave me the place to myself for an entire silent hour. I wasted all the quiet time sleeping, but I woke up feeling better and more refreshed when the girls returned from their shopping trip.

Another forty minutes later—and a big mishap involving spilled beet juice that Dagny barely saved from turning into a full-on disaster—I was on the floor, while Eliana painted delicate filigree and Celtic knots in mango yellow over deep burgundy polish.

When the landline rang, Hanna turned and glared at it, as if her mother could suddenly teleport her home. She wouldn't even get up and grab it for me, even when Eliana insisted that I couldn't walk until the polish was fully dry. Dagny brought me the phone, while Hanna sat sulking in the corner.

"Hi, Ulla, I hope things haven't been too stressful for you this week," Mia said cheerily when I answered.

"They have been," I admitted. "But fortunately—or unfortunately, maybe—Hanna hasn't been the cause of most of it."

"I'm glad to hear she hasn't been too much trouble, and I'm still so sorry you have to deal with all of this. Has she been helpful?"

"Yeah, she's been helpful," I said.

"I made her supper every night!" Hanna shouted defiantly, as if I had claimed otherwise.

"What was that?" Mia asked.

"Hanna's just saying that she's been cooking for me a lot, which is true, and it's been very nice of her." I made sure to meet Hanna's gaze as I said the last part and enunciated every word. She just looked away from me.

"Good, good," Mia replied. "But I'm sure what you really want to know is when we're going to get her out of your hair so you can get back to focusing on your work."

"Do you have anything figured out yet?"

"Finn finally has some breathing room in his schedule," Mia explained. "This coming week is still fairly tight, but next weekend is wide open. If you're really desperate to be free of Hanna before then, Finn can pull an all-nighter and get to her, but it wouldn't be until Tuesday or Wednesday at the soonest."

"What day works best for him?" I asked.

"This upcoming Saturday, a week from today. But again, if you need him sooner, he can make it work and he will be there."

"No, Saturday should be fine," I said, while Hanna seethed in the corner.

"Great, Ulla," Mia said, her words awash with relief. "Thank you so much. I know you shouldn't be dealing with all of this, but I'm so grateful for you. I don't know what we'd be doing otherwise."

In the background, I heard familiar babbling—the hallmark of Niko's monosyllabic conversation skills.

"Is that Niko?" I asked hopefully.

"Yeah, he wants to talk to you. Should I put him on the phone?"

I pushed myself up so I was sitting straighter, as if that would somehow help me hear him better. "Yeah, I'd love to say hi."

Within seconds the little boy's voice was chirping in my ear. "Hi, Ulla."

"Hey, little buddy. How are you?" I asked.

"I miss you," he said simply, and immediately a lump formed in my throat.

"Yeah, I miss you, too."

"Yesterday Liam got a big grasshopper, and it was . . ." He kept talking but his words became a jumbled intelligible mess until he finished with, "but I laughed."

"Oh, yeah?" I said.

"Yeah, and Nana tried reading from the *Bedtime Stories* book but she did the wrong voice," he said with exaggerated disapproval.

"Oh, I'm sorry about that. I'll show her what the right voice is when I get back," I promised.

"When will you be back?" he asked, without missing a beat.

"A few more weeks." I exhaled deeply.

In the background I heard Emma shouting, "Is that Hanna? Does Niko get to talk to Hanna? I wanna talk to her!"

Then there was a bit of a scuffle—Niko dropping the phone, Mia telling everyone they needed to wait their turn, Finn telling Liam not to call Emma names, the indistinct babbling of the twins talking to one another—and I felt a pang of homesickness. I missed all the chaos of the kids, even while I was grateful for the calmer pace away from them.

Not that my situation was exactly drama-free, as Hanna was quick to point out by shooting me daggers with her eyes.

"Hanna?" Emma said, finally getting her hands on the phone.

"No, this is Ulla, but I can get Hanna for you."

"Okay, get her, because I need to tell her something," Emma insisted in the same very-serious tone she used whenever she was about to ask for something—like a cookie or to borrow Hanna's markers.

"Sure." I held out the phone to Hanna, careful to keep the long cord from tangling with the vials of organic nail polish. "Emma wants to talk to you."

At first it seemed like Hanna was just going to sit there scowling at me and leave her little sister waiting. But finally she got up to take the phone from me.

"Hey, Em," Hanna answered, followed by a long pause before she replied, "Yeah, of course you can play with my pony. I'm not there, so I'm sure Calvin can use the extra attention."

"What do you think?" Eliana asked me, and she sat back on her knees to appraise her finished work on my toenails.

"Wow!" I said as I admired the detail she'd put into such tiny designs. "It's really amazing, Eliana. You do amazing work. Were you an artist?"

She cocked her head and twisted her mouth as she thought. "Um, I don't know. I feel like I wasn't an artist professionally, but I definitely dabbled in it, I think." Then she shrugged and smiled. "I like doing it, and I'm good at it, so it's the only thing that makes sense."

Eliana began cleaning up the mess, and I helped as much as she would allow. We had just finished when a knock came at the front door. Hanna was busy giving Emma tips on how to play with the pony, and Dagny was in the bathroom.

"Don't get up," Eliana warned me as I carefully pushed myself up to my feet. "Your toes aren't dry yet."

"You can't answer the door, and everyone else is busy."

She tilted her head at me. "What do you mean?"

"The last time someone came to the door, I thought we all decided it was better if you hid," I said. "Since we don't know how to explain you to any kind of Merellä officials."

"Oh, yeah." She nodded. "Yeah, maybe. It's probably for the best, I guess. Okay. You be careful. I'll hide out in the rafters."

I hobbled to the door, stepping carefully on the heels of my feet so I wouldn't muss the polish, while Eliana immediately jumped into her acrobatic routine again—bouncing up on the table and off the walls until she was safely hidden on the beams.

I opened the door to find Pan standing on the landing, his hands shoved into the pockets of his old blue jeans.

"Hey." A warm smile spread across his face when he saw me. "I swung up by the archives, and Calder said he'd given you the weekends off."

"Yeah, he told me something about his last intern having serious burnout, and he wants to keep me fresh for my duration," I said.

One of his thick eyebrows arched skeptically. "But twelve-hour workdays are still fine?"

"They're not 'fine' as much as they are 'mandatory' "—I used my fingers to make air quotes on *fine* and *mandatory*—"but Calder thinks a couple days off a week provides balance. I'm not in a position to complain. I could use the break."

"That's actually why I stopped by." He leaned against the doorframe as we talked. "You seemed so down and tired yesterday. I wanted to take you out and do something fun with you, cheer you up a little bit."

Yesterday, when I had been busy working from dusk until dawn, Pan had stopped down and attempted to invite me to dinner. I'd wanted to join him, but I was also trying to make up for the morning I'd missed when I had met with Mästare Amalie, so I had sadly declined his invitation, and instead, I translated musty documents while eating stale zucchini chips.

I smiled at him. "Thanks, Pan. That's really sweet of you, but you don't have to do that."

"I know. I want to."

"What'd you have in mind?" I asked.

"Well, we could—"

Before Pan could finish his thought, Eliana let out a loud squeal and tumbled off the beam and fell to the floor. She landed on her feet, crouched down in a three-point superhero landing, but her skin and hair were going crazy. It was a kaleidoscope of colors, bright and rapidly shifting, like ripples of water across her flesh and hair.

"Sorry." Eliana stood up slowly, as the explosion of colors slowed and her earlier coloring returned. "A giant spider fell on me, and I got scared."

"Um . . ." Pan gaped at her. "Who is that?"

I stepped back and opened the door wider. "Why don't you come inside, and we'll talk about it?"

29

trust

Eliana sat cross-legged on the couch. Beside her, Hanna apprehensively chewed her lip and kept her gaze on Eliana and Pan, with periodic nervous glances in my direction.

Pan sat on a stool and rested his arm on the table, propping his head up, and he'd taken in the whole story—everything we knew about Eliana and how she'd ended up in our apartment—with a reserved curiosity.

"What do you think?" I asked once we'd wrapped up our exposition.

"I don't know," he said finally, and his eyes were on Eliana. "You really don't remember anything?"

"Not really, but sorta. There's stuff that I *know* or I'll just remember, and then other times . . . I can tell there's something there, inside my head." She moved her hands rapidly around her head, as if to demonstrate. "But it's out of reach. It's hidden behind a murky wall, and I can't get through it, no matter how hard I try."

"What's the first thing you remember?" Pan asked.

"I don't know. I have no idea how to sort my memories chronologically," she explained. "They're random scenes that might connect to others but I don't usually know how."

"What's your first memory in Merellä?" Pan asked, coming at the question from a different angle.

"Um . . . it was dark." Eliana stared up at the ceiling and squinted. "Nighttime. I was sitting on the roof of one of the houses here, watching the stars, and I was thinking . . . I was wondering how I was going to go about finding someone."

Pan sat up straight on the stool. "Who were you trying to find?"

She shook her head. "I don't know. I don't think I even knew then."

"Then how do you know you were looking for someone?" I asked.

"Do you ever walk into a room, and you know that you came in there for something, but you can't remember what it is? It's usually simple or silly, maybe a book or a mango. But you don't know. You can't remember, but deep down you're certain you went in there for something," Eliana explained as best she could. "That there's something that you're missing."

"She might have been coming to see you, Pan," Dagny suggested. She stood off to the side of the room, watching the whole conversation unfold.

"You mean the Inhemsk Project? Does that sound familiar?" Pan asked.

"We already asked her about it," I clarified.

"It sounds familiar now because they've talked about it, but I don't remember hearing of it before. I just knew . . ."

Her brow furrowed as she concentrated. "I think I heard that the Mimirin is where you come to find someone."

"That is true." Pan leaned forward now, resting his arms on his legs. "I can help you find who you're looking for."

"How?" Eliana asked doubtfully. "If I don't even know *who* it is, how can you possibly find them?"

"It's my job," he said matter-of-factly. "Right now I'm helping Ulla try to find her mother, and she has a few leads, but none of them are concrete. All she really knows is that she didn't spring fully formed from the earth, so she has to have a mother out there somewhere."

"How do you know that she didn't?" Eliana asked.

Pan looked confused. "Didn't what?"

"Spring fully formed from the earth?"

He laughed softly. "Because she's a troll, and that's not how trolls are made."

"So, you think I'm a troll?" Eliana reasoned.

"You think you aren't?" he asked.

"No, it's more like Dagny and Ulla don't seem so sure that I am one."

"Her hair is unlike anything we've seen before," I said, simplifying my position on the whole thing. "We didn't want to make any assumptions just because she has some trollian features."

"Her hair is unusual," Pan allowed, staring at her now-vibrant purple locks. "But it might be an advanced psychokinetic color mutation in the Kanin. I'm gonna say the names of some places. Let me know if any of them sound familiar to you. Doldastam. Iskyla. Tramsa. Kalltheim."

She shook her head. "No, I don't think I've been to any of those places."

"That's okay." He gave her a reassuring smile. "I haven't been to most of them either."

"Are you Kanin?" she asked him.

"Partially. But my mother raised me among the humans to keep me safe. Maybe your mother or father did the same. They wanted to keep you safe?" Pan suggested.

"Maybe."

"Do you think you can help her?" Hanna asked, her voice small and anxious.

"I will try, but I have to be honest: It's going to be difficult working with what I have now. Even in my most problematic cases, I have some information to go on—birth dates, city of birth, names of adoptive parents or an orphanage. *Something.*"

Hanna's eyes widened, and she indignantly asked, "So, you won't do anything, even when she needs your help?"

"I didn't say that," he corrected her gently. "I will do my best, but I don't know how much I can do, not without help from other sources."

"Other sources?" I asked, but his gaze had already drifted over to Dagny.

"Like me and my boss Elof," Dagny said.

"You told me that Elof took your blood." Eliana shook her head emphatically. "No, no. I don't wanna do that. I'm not bappers. I don't want anyone stealing my life force."

When we'd first started talking to her about Elof and a possible blood test, I had made the mistake of going through the process, thinking it would ease her fears, but at the mention of blood, she immediately became agitated. And that's how we learned that she hated anything that sounded at all like a *häxdoktor* to her.

"It's just basic science, Eliana," I said as soothingly as I could.

"I don't care what you call it. Stealing my blood and performing all kinds of strange magic on it doesn't set well with me."

"It's not magic. All we do is look at your blood to see what it says about you," Dagny explained, and then motioned toward me. "Ulla is fine."

I nodded. "I had my blood drawn, and nothing bad happened to me. I'm still me, as normal and healthy as I ever was."

"What did your blood say?" Eliana asked.

"Well, she hasn't gotten her results back yet. It takes time, but she should hear back in a few days," Dagny explained.

"Dagny's boss is one of the most well-respected experts of troll biology," Pan said, still speaking in his calm, reassuring tone. "If anyone would be able to help you, it's him. I'm not telling you what to do or where to go. But I am saying that you seem lost, and you have some of the best resources in the world to help you navigate your way back to where you need to be."

She stared at him, chewing her lip, and then she nodded once. "Okay."

"Okay?" Hanna said.

"Okay, what?" Dagny pressed further.

"I'll go with Dagny to meet her boss," Eliana said. "I know I'll find whoever I need to, but I can't ignore the fact that Dagny might be how I do it."

"Great. Excellent. I'm going to call Elof and get a time set up for you to meet him before you change your mind." Dagny was already rushing over to the phone.

"See?" Hanna said with a relieved smile. "I told you there was nothing to worry about. They're my friends too, and none of us would ever do anything to hurt you. We all wanna help you help yourself."

"I should probably get going," Pan said, getting to his feet. "I'm sure I've wasted enough of your time."

I waved that off. "No, don't be ridiculous. If anything, we've wasted yours."

"Why don't you stay for supper?" Hanna suggested. "I've got a goat cheese and fried green tomato casserole all ready to throw into the oven."

"Yeah?" Pan said, looking uncertainly at Hanna and me.

"My mom only taught me recipes big enough to feed a family of ten, so I'm always making too much. There'll be plenty for you," Hanna assured him.

He looked at me, gauging my response. "If you're sure it's no trouble."

"Stay," I told him. "It'll be fun."

30

tabled

It wasn't until the middle of dinner, when Hanna abruptly asked Pan what his intentions were with me—causing him to nearly choke on the sangria he was drinking, and me to blush nearly the same shade of beet-red as said sangria—that I realized that I'd never brought a boy I was dating home.

Back in Iskyla, there hadn't really been any boys worth dating, but once I'd gotten settled in with the Holmeses in Förening, I had dated some. My only semi-serious relationship had been with Callum Janssen when I was sixteen. He was a tracker-in-training, and he'd always been too nervous to come over to my house because of Finn's reputation.

But now, with Hanna attempting to interrogate Pan, I realized that Finn had never been the biggest threat of romantic embarrassment in the household—it was always the kids.

"Hanna!" I gasped, while Dagny chuckled. "Don't say things like that."

"Why not?" Eliana asked, looking around the table. "I don't really understand what she was asking."

"She was just . . ." I cleared my throat and motioned to Hanna. "Well, Hanna, since you asked it, why don't you explain what you meant?"

"It seems like the two of you have been spending a lot of time together lately," she said with exaggerated innocence. "I was wondering if it was normal for you to hang out with interns this much, or if there was something more going on."

"Oh." Eliana's confusion only deepened. "That doesn't sound like a bad question."

"It isn't," Pan said reasonably. "Not really." He shifted in his seat. "I haven't really kept track of how much time I usually spend with interns. When they get here, I do make a point to show them around and help them get settled in. It can be a bit lonely when you first get here, as I'm sure all of us can attest."

"I was too busy with my work to notice any loneliness. But I will admit that it has been more fun since Hanna and Ulla got here," Dagny said, somewhat grudgingly.

"Your intentions are to help her get settled in, then?" Hanna pressed.

"Hanna, will you stop?" I hissed.

"What?" she asked huffily. "Eliana and I have burned through all the shows I had saved on my laptop. I've gotta come up with something to fill the long hours here, and I've decided on gossip and your extracurricular activities."

"I don't have a curriculum, so none of my activities are extracurricular," I pointed out tersely.

"Technically, I think that makes them *all* extracurricular," Hanna countered.

"Dagny, you're the smartest one in the house," I said. "Tell her she's being ridiculous."

"Nah." Dagny stabbed at her food with her fork. "I've decided not to weigh in on any conflicts between the two of you that don't interest me."

"And here I thought I was missing out by not having any roommates," Pan muttered.

"You live alone?" Dagny looked over at him, her interest now piqued. "In Merellä? How'd you swing that?"

"By having a tiny studio apartment that could fit in your living room, and it's above a salmon-tanning shop," Pan explained.

Dagny nodded in understanding. "Oh, yeah, that'll do it."

"Is it expensive here?" Hanna asked.

"Yeah, but most everyone here only stays for a short time," Dagny said. "A thousand a week isn't *that* bad if you're only here for a week."

"And I've been here for about two years, which is why I have two jobs." Pan glanced up at the clock hanging on the wall. "Speaking of which, I hate to dine and dash, but the esteemed work of the peurojen beckons."

"What's a peurojen?" Eliana asked.

"He's like sheepherder but with giant moose elk," Hanna told her.

"Giant woolly elk," he corrected her.

"Oh, like a *geitvaktmann*!" Eliana said brightly.

Hanna looked at her strangely and shrugged. "I have no idea what that is, but sure. Just like that."

"I'll walk you out," I said as Pan got to his feet.

There wasn't even the pretense of privacy in the apartment, so I followed him out to the landing and shut the door behind us.

I tucked my hair behind my ear and smiled at him. "Thanks for being so cool about all of this."

"There's nothing to be cool about." He shrugged it off. "You're just helping a lost girl, and I'm just doing my job."

"Eliana's nervous, but that is understandable, since she can't remember if someone is after her or who she can trust."

"But you trust her?" he asked, quieter now, so no one would overhear.

"Yeah, I think so," I said, keeping my voice low to match his. "She might be wrong about some things, but I don't think she's lying. What about you?"

"I trust you." His dark eyes met mine, and a flush of warmth ran through me. "And that's enough for me right now."

"So, you never did tell me," I said with a coy smile. "What were you gonna do to cheer me up?"

"Nothing too exciting. Grab something to eat at a café in town. Check out the bazaar on Wapiti Way before it closes. Maybe take you to the beach to see the ocean."

"I have been a couple miles from the ocean for nearly a week, and I haven't gone to see it yet," I admitted.

"We'll have to rectify that soon."

"I'd like that."

"Me too." He looked like he wanted to say something more, but he lowered his gaze and started toward the steps. "Have a good rest of your night."

"Yeah, you too."

Pan had only taken one step down before he paused and looked back up at me. "Stay safe."

"You say that like you think I might not be safe."

"Well, I meant it like I would be upset if something had happened to you." He paused. "So. Stay safe."

"I'll do the best I can."

unusual

At the crack of dawn on Sunday morning, Dagny demanded that we all get up and get ready if we wanted to tag along with Eliana to meet Elof. Although, to be fair, Hanna was more of an emotional-support buddy than a superfluous escort. I didn't exactly need to be there either, but with Hanna going, I felt like I had to accompany them to make sure everything went smoothly.

"It's so quiet," Hanna whispered as we walked down the long, open corridors of the Mimirin. None of us had worn shoes, so we breezed right past the lockers.

"On the weekends during the summer, they really try to discourage any unnecessary work around here," Dagny said. "It's the only time they can make repairs and clean things up."

Eliana paused and pointed to the plastic sheeting draped over an archway. Scaffolding and cans of paint poked out from under the corner. "What's back there?"

"That's the main library. There's a lot of original artwork and stained glass that they're restoring."

Apparently unsatisfied with Dagny's explanation, Eliana broke away from us and peered into the work zone. Hanna followed suit—dashing after her—so I went over to take a look myself. Other than the construction equipment—lots of paint cans, drop cloths, and various masonry tools that I didn't recognize—the room was empty. A massive antique bronze chandelier had been lowered from the ceiling and rested in the center of the half-torn-up marble floor tiles.

There were a few built-in bookcases on the far wall, stone shelving with carved endcaps. The rest of the walls were wide open, leaving plenty of space for the beautifully detailed murals of troll history. In the farthest corner our oldest histories and legends were depicted, from building the First City together beside a waterfall to the Viking ships on angry ocean waters, with our ancestors stowed away in the bellies of the ships as they fled persecution in Scandinavia.

As the mural story continued, the dark blue of the water gave way to the stark frozen wasteland of the original North American settlements, and eventually the green grass of summer and prosperity as the tribes began to spread out over the land.

"Isn't a library basically a book atrium?" Eliana questioned.

"Yeah . . . basically," Hanna replied. When I looked at her, she shrugged and muttered, "I assume that it's exactly what it sounds like."

"Where are all the books, then?"

"I don't know for sure, but they store them somewhere safe, maybe in the catacombs," Dagny replied.

"Where are all the workers?" Eliana pressed.

"It's too early. They haven't started for the day yet. Now come on," Dagny commanded. "Elof is waiting for us. We should go."

We made it up to the third floor, where the Department of Troglecology and Elof's lab were located, without any further diversions, which really was saying something. Eliana got distracted by nearly everything she saw, asking a million questions that Dagny answered as quickly and succinctly as she could, but Hanna managed to keep her moving forward, no matter what.

When we finally made it to Elof's lab, he was already there, sitting at an island and looking over paperwork that was spread out before him. He didn't look up right away, so Dagny announced our presence with a bright, "Good morning, Elof. Thank you for fitting us in."

"It is a good morning indeed, Dagny," he said, outmatching her with his own loud cheer. "But it is I who must thank you for bringing this all to my attention. You know how fascinating I find psychokinetic deviations."

"This is Eliana." She motioned to Eliana, who finally stepped out from where she was glued to Hanna's side.

"It's so good to meet you, sir," Eliana said with a dramatically low curtsy.

"It's very kind of you to show me such deference, but I must tell you that I am not royalty and I do not require such displays," he explained to her.

"Oh, sorry." Eliana laughed—her normally airy laugh sounding now tight and fragile. "I assumed based on how Dagny talked about you."

"You mistake respect for mandatory worship," Dagny

said dryly, and she headed back to start gathering the blood-draw equipment.

Elof smirked, then turned his gaze to me. "Ulla, I didn't expect to see you again so soon."

"Have you heard anything yet?" I asked hopefully.

He shook his head. "Not yet, but I promise you that I'll have Dagny alert you the second I hear something."

"So . . ." Eliana walked slowly around the island, her fingers trailing on the smooth gray quartz countertops as she admired the high ceiling far above us. "You're not royalty. Does that mean you're just an ordinary troll?"

"I was once a Markis, but I gave up that title a long time ago," Elof admitted.

Eliana paused and furrowed her brow. "What's a Markis?"

"A Markis or Marksinna is sort of like a Duke or Duchess," he said, and she shook her head. "They are royalty, as you said, and here that means that they usually get more money and respect than the rest of us."

"That doesn't sound fair," she said.

"You really aren't from around here, are you?" Elof said with a bemused laugh, and he looked over at me. "Where was it that you said you found her, Ulla?"

"I didn't," I corrected him. "She found us."

"She fell on the roof of our car," Hanna added.

"Why don't you sit down?" Elof used his foot to gently kick a stool closer to Eliana. She hesitated, chewing her lip as she stared down at it, but she finally took a seat beside him. "Tell me about yourself."

She shrugged. "I don't really know where to start, and I don't know all that much about myself."

"That's not your real hair color, is it?" Elof asked.

She looked up, as if she'd be able to see her long brown hair pulled back into a loose bun. She'd gone for a "natural" color this morning to blend in. "How can you tell?"

"Dagny did tell me that you have unusual hair, but when you get tense, it starts to lose its hold—it ripples a bit at the roots." He leaned forward and used a pen to motion to her hairline, where the dark brown intermittently shifted to a much lighter, brighter hue. "If I can see it correctly, it appears to be a dull . . . chartreuse."

He frowned and sat back. "But that can't possibly be your natural color. I don't think there're any mammals that exist in nature in that spectrum."

"What's chartreuse?" Eliana asked, glancing over at Hanna, who could only shrug in response.

"It's a bright yellow-green," Elof elaborated disinterestedly, and his eyes scanned the lab. "Ulla, can you grab me that textbook off that shelf over there?" He pointed across the room, and I went over to retrieve a book titled *Troglecology: Studying Trolls, Biology, and the Environment in the 21st Century.*

"Thank you," he said as he took the book from me. He tilted the cover toward Eliana—which depicted several trolls of varying complexions, and with plastic smiles, holding a menagerie of animals and plants. Elof tapped the pale lime-green lizard sitting on a blond Skojare student's shoulder. "That little guy there, he's chartreuse."

"Oh, yeah." Eliana's smile brightened, and the rippling of her hair finally stopped as a wave of pale greenish yellow washed all the brown out of her hair. "Yeah! I think that *is* my real color. I'd just forgotten."

"You forgot your own hair color?" I gasped. "How is that . . . that doesn't . . . No."

"Surprisingly, this isn't the first time I've encountered something like this," Elof said as he set the textbook aside. "Once, I was called up to Doldastam to examine an elderly couple suffering from dementia. They had been very powerful color-shifters before, but with time, they'd lost control of it, and it was becoming quite problematic and uncomfortable."

Hanna leaned on the counter next to Eliana, propping her head up on her hand. "How did you treat them?"

"I didn't," he said simply. "I'm not that kind of doctor."

Hanna's dark eyes narrowed. "What kind of doctor are you?"

"The kind that studies troll phenomena and biology," Elof said. "Then, hopefully, the information learned from those studies can be used to find treatments for illness and ways to help our society function better."

"So, you're not going to be able to help me at all?" Eliana asked.

Dagny returned with her phlebotomy tool kit, and then she began to lay out her needles and vials in a precise row.

"I believe I can help you," he answered carefully. "There is solace and knowledge in discovering a diagnosis. But that does not mean I'll be able to cure you."

Eliana frowned and leaned away from him. "Cure me of what?"

"Whatever ails you, I suppose." He held up his hands

with his palms out. "Right now the only thing I know of is that you have fairly severe memory loss. But there might be other things underlying."

"Like what?" Eliana pressed.

He nodded toward Dagny. "That's what we're hoping to find out with the blood draw."

"How are you with needles?" Dagny asked as she wiped an alcohol swab on Eliana's inner arm. "I forgot to ask last time, and Ulla nearly passed out."

I grimaced. "It wasn't that big of a deal."

"I don't think I have a problem with needles, but I can't remember," Eliana said, and she stared down at her arm, watching with mild curiosity as Dagny wrapped a tourniquet around her arm and prepared the needle.

Slowly and carefully, Dagny pressed the needle against Eliana's skin . . . but instead of going in, the tip of the needle snapped off.

"Shit," Dagny muttered under her breath and immediately hurried to switch the needle out.

"What happened?" Elof asked.

"The needle snapped. I'm going to try a needle with a larger gauge."

"That's a good plan," he said, and as Dagny readied the next needle, he pulled Eliana's attention from that and back to him. "Eliana. That's a beautiful name. Do you have a last name?"

"Hanna's tried to explain them to me, but I don't think I fully understand what it is. The only name that I know I have is Eliana."

"You're going to feel a prick," Dagny warned her, and this time the needle slid in easily.

"Oh," Eliana said with a laugh. "That wasn't so bad."

"Oh, wow," Dagny said in a surprised breath, and I looked over to see the liquid slowly filling the vial.

It was as thick as molasses, and that combined with the strange iridescent burgundy color reminded me of an ad I'd seen for slime. But this wasn't slime.

This was coming from inside Eliana's body.

"Is that how your blood always looks?" I asked dumbly as we all gaped at her.

"Yes. I think," Eliana said, but she sounded less and less confident the more she talked. "Blood is the stuff that courses through our veins, right? It's full of food and water and magic for our bodies."

"It definitely seems like it's blood," Elof said, sounding about as convinced as Eliana had.

"What's wrong with mine?" Eliana asked with a panicked tremble. "It looks fine to me. Why are you guys so scared?"

"We're not scared," Hanna insisted without much conviction. "Our blood just looks . . . different."

"I don't like this," Eliana declared, but the thicker viscosity of her blood meant it flowed a lot slower, and Dagny had hardly half a vial filled. "I don't want to do this anymore."

"Eliana, hold on," Dagny said, and she was using both her hands to try to hold her still and keep the needle in. "Let me take it out. You don't want a needle to break—"

"No, I can't. I . . ." Eliana was breathing rapidly, and panicked blotches of dark purple sprang up all over her skin.

"It's too tight in here." I walked over and put a firm hand on her shoulder, hoping to calm her and help keep her from breaking the needle in her arm. "I shouldn't have come here. It's too much and it's all too close."

"Eliana, calm down." Hanna ran around me so she could stand in front of her and tried to force Eliana to look at her, but Eliana kept turning her head away. "Eliana, it's okay."

"No," she said flatly.

"I'm almost done, only a few more seconds," Dagny said.

"What's wrong?" Hanna asked. "What's going on inside your head, Eliana?"

Eliana stared down at the floor, and in a low whisper she said, "I should never have come here."

Then suddenly she sprang up—the needle breaking off in her arm with an audible but tiny *snap*—and before any of us could react, she jumped over the island and raced out of the room. Hanna and I ran right after her, but by the time we'd made it to the door, she had already disappeared.

32

tracking

Hanna ran after Eliana, nearly screaming her name, but Eliana didn't slow, and I took off after them both.

"Hanna! Wait!" I grabbed her arm before she could run off ahead of me again.

"Let me go!" Hanna tried to wriggle away from me, but I was stronger than her, so she could only flail and whine. "Ulla, let me go! She's scared, and she's lost! I can't just leave her!"

"I'm not asking you to!" I argued. "We just need to be smart about this. She's fast, and she can camouflage. She could be anywhere, and it won't do us—or her—any good if we're running around like a chicken with its head cut off."

She took a deep breath and seemed to calm down some, so I let go of her arm. "Eliana's not going to stay in here. She'll want to be outside, where she feels safe."

"Would she go back to our apartment?" I asked.

"Not right now. Not when she's so scared."

"Okay. Let's go outside, then."

Before we headed out, Dagny and Elof joined the search, but we decided to split up so we could cover more ground. Once we were outside the building, they went north, while Hanna and I went south. I kept my eyes up, scanning the rooftops for any sign of Eliana, while Hanna resorted to intermittently shouting her name.

"I never should've listened to you guys," Hanna complained after we'd been searching for about fifteen minutes. "I shouldn't have let you talk her into this."

"Hanna, I know you're worried, but she has been surviving on her own for at least a little bit of time before you found her," I told her gently. "She's got some . . . disadvantages, sure, but she can take care of herself."

"Are you looking for someone?" a woman asked, and I turned to see her standing at the side of the road, carrying a basket of flowers.

"Uh, sort of," Hanna answered uncertainly.

"Are you with the security?" I asked.

"No, I'm merely a concerned bystander," she replied, and to her credit she did look worried—her dark eyes wide and teary above the round apples of her cheeks.

"You don't need to be concerned," I told her with a thin smile. "We've got this under control."

We started to walk away, but she called after us, "I can help you, if you need it."

I looked back over my shoulder, trying to get a read on her.

Her hair—black tight coils—was braided tight to her scalp on one side, while on the other it flowed freely, ruffling slightly in the wind. Her leather pants were tight, squeezing around her legs, and were paired with a loose sleeveless top that showed off her rather muscular forearms.

The youthfulness of her face—the smooth sepia skin and full cheeks—contrasting with the weary concern of her eyes made it impossible to guess her age. Twenties? Thirties?

"Are you a tracker?" I asked.

"That's not my official title, but we have a similar skill set." She smiled and stepped closer to us. "I'm Sumi, and I find things that are lost."

"Even living things, like trolls?" Hanna asked.

Her smile deepened. "Especially trolls. Would you like my help?"

"It can't hurt," Hanna said, looking up at me with pleading eyes.

"So . . . how would it work? What do you do?" I asked.

"Do you have anything that belonged to the missing individual?" Sumi asked.

"She made me this bracelet yesterday." Hanna tugged off the friendship bracelet, made with neon thread and strung with plastic gems and a large bauble with a linnea flower covered in clear resin. "She made this one for me, and it looks just like the one I made for her, but this is the one she handled the most."

"I'm sure that will work fine," Sumi assured her.

She took the bracelet from Hanna carefully, gently, as if handling a priceless heirloom. Delicately, she began winding the thread between her fingers, and her eyes closed. Her expression softened, and her lips relaxed into a sublime smile.

Sumi opened her eyes and announced, "West. She went west."

"Where?" Hanna asked, looking frantically in every direction.

"Follow me." Sumi turned and started following the road down toward the ocean.

"Do you know where she is?" I asked.

"Not exactly, but I'll sense when we get close," she answered, and Hanna was already following her, so I hurried to catch up.

"What is your title, then?"

She glanced over at me but didn't slow her steps. "Pardon?"

"You said that tracker isn't your official title," I reminded her. "What is it?"

"Vizier."

"What?"

"It's like an adviser of sorts," Sumi explained.

"Who do you advise at the Mimirin?" I asked.

"Oh, I don't work for the Mimirin," she corrected me. "I'm not from here."

"I don't think anyone actually is *from* Merellä," I contended. "It seems like everyone is a transplant."

"I would say that I'm more of a tourist," Sumi clarified.

"Are you enjoying your vacation?"

"It's really a working vacation for me," she said with a sigh. "My boss doesn't like to travel alone, but he offers me plenty of time to sightsee and explore the city."

"What have you seen so far?" I asked.

"Oh *jakla*, will you two stop chatting and hurry up?" Hanna shouted in exasperation. "This isn't some casual stroll through the town. Our friend is missing."

"She isn't much farther," Sumi insisted.

Hanna looked up at her sharply. "How do you know?"

Sumi shrugged. "You can trust me or not. I don't really care one way or the other."

Then she stopped short and pointed to the Forsa River—which was more of a wide stream, really, that sliced through the city and flowed out to the sea. "If you follow this river out to the ocean, you should find her."

"Are you sure?" I asked.

"As sure as I ever am," she replied with a small smile. She held out the bracelet to Hanna. "You can have this back."

"You aren't coming with us?" I asked.

"I'm afraid that I have an appointment to keep, but I sense that she is safe and nearby," Sumi said. "You can handle it from here."

"Thank you for your help," I told her, and Hanna was already dragging me away and telling me to hurry, hurry, hurry.

"You are welcome. I wish you luck on the rest of your adventures." Sumi watched us for a moment as we followed the river away.

When we made it to the city wall—and the narrow ledge of a path that ran along the stream and allowed access to the world beyond the city—I looked back to see if she was still there, but she was long gone.

33

brave

It was just beyond the city where we found her, past the small but sheer drop where bright green grass ended and the narrow rocky beach began. Eliana sat on the shore, her back to us, her knees pulled to her chest, and waves lapped at the sand mere inches from her bare feet.

Hanna raced on ahead of me, reaching Eliana much sooner than I did, but I could hear her shouting. "Eliana, I was so worried about you! Why'd you run off like that?"

"It wasn't safe there," Eliana replied, and her words were nearly lost to the sea.

Out here, without the walls shielding us, the Pacific Ocean raged loudly. Right above us the sun was bright and clear, but dark clouds were on the horizon, a storm that was whipping the ocean into angry frenzy.

"What do you mean?" Hanna sat down on the beach beside her, but I stayed a ways back—close enough to hear them but giving Hanna a bit of space to calm Eliana herself.

Eliana looked over at her for the first time since Hanna had come to the beach. "You saw. It wasn't safe."

"I'm sorry I pushed you into that." Hanna's voice cracked with sincerity. "When I did it, it didn't seem so scary, but I didn't count on how different and more frightening it must've seemed for you."

"It's okay." Eliana absolved Hanna with a simple smile and a shrug.

"Why did you come out here?" Hanna asked.

"The water seemed safe, and I had to get away."

"Dagny and Elof don't want to hurt you, and you don't have to—"

"No, I know Dagny wouldn't hurt me." Eliana cut her off. "Not really. It wasn't them."

I stepped closer, inserting myself into the conversation, and asked, "What wasn't them?"

"Who was after me," Eliana replied. "They were different."

"What are you talking about?" I knelt down beside her.

"There were two of them, and they were chasing me," Eliana explained. "That's why I didn't stop. I couldn't stop until I got out to the water, because I knew that I would be safe here."

"Who was chasing you?" Hanna asked.

"Was it security or Mimirin staff?" I added.

"No," Eliana said, then changed her mind and shook her head. "I don't know. I can't really be sure of anything."

"If you don't know who was chasing you, can you at least tell us what they look like?" I asked carefully.

"Yes." Eliana closed her eyes, as if focusing on their images. "One was . . . my shadow, and the other was a dragon."

"A shadow and a dragon?" I repeated.

"And I know what you're thinking," Eliana said and opened her eyes. "The dragon sounds scarier, but no. The shadow is *sooo* much scarier, because I didn't know if I could outrun it. Is it even possible to get away from your shadow?"

"Eliana, you've had a really long, rough morning," I said gently. "Why don't we head back home, you get some rest, and Hanna can make you something to eat?"

"Can I watch my shows on the laptop?"

I smiled. "Yeah, of course you can."

She returned my smile. "Okay. Let's go back."

Before she got up, Hanna took her hand so Eliana would look at her. "You have to promise me that you won't run off like that again, Eliana. I was so scared that I would never see you again."

"Oh, I'm sorry, Hanna," Eliana said. "I didn't mean to make you sad. I'll never, ever, ever leave without saying goodbye. So, if I don't say goodbye, you have to know that I'm not gone for long, and I didn't go very far."

"Promise?"

"Promise. I'll always be close by," she assured her.

Once we got back to the apartment, Hanna busied herself making some kind of sweet-and-tangy popcorn she dubbed "celebratory sparkle corn." I used the landline to call Elof's office and let him and Dagny know that Eliana was safe with us. The conversation was brief, Elof apologizing for the way things turned out today, and he hoped that given some time and space she would be able to return to see him again.

Eliana had settled in on the couch, where she perused through the shows that Hanna had saved on her laptop.

"I'm glad you came back with us." I leaned on the arm of the couch beside her.

"I was always going to come back with you guys. I don't know why everyone thinks I wouldn't."

"Because we don't know much about you," I reminded her.

"I don't know much about me either, but I know that I'm not the type to bolt in the night," Eliana contended.

"I understand that, but you have to be careful about making promises that you can't keep." I lowered my voice now, to above a whisper, so Hanna wouldn't hear over the clatter of the pots and pans.

"What do you mean?" Eliana asked.

"You promised Hanna that you'll always be close by."

"But before that I said, 'unless I say goodbye.' I won't ever leave without telling her. That's a promise I can keep."

"How can you say that?" I asked.

"Because it's true."

"You don't know where you're from, or when you'll go back," I said, doing my best not to sound accusatory. "Today you saw two trolls after you—a shadow and a dragon, whatever that means."

"I've thought about it more, and it wasn't a dragon. Dragons breathe fire and have wings." Eliana said this without looking up from the laptop, her eyes fixed on the images that rolled by as she scrolled through Hanna's shows.

"What made you think it was a dragon?"

"The skin. It was dark and leather, and they were thin but really tall. I think dragons are quite tall."

The first thing that popped into my head was the Ögonen. As soon as she mentioned their skin, I pictured them as I saw them last—standing in their atrium towers along the roof of the Mimirin, the setting sun shining through their thin ochre skin.

"Was it an Ögonen?"

"I've never heard that word before, so I can't say," Eliana replied without giving it much thought.

"Did it look like a dragon mixed with Slenderman, minus the wings and fire?" I asked, floundering for the most accurate description I could come up with.

"I don't know what a Slenderman is, but it was definitely slender."

"What would the Ögonen want with you?" I asked, but I was thinking aloud more than really asking Eliana.

Still, she replied with a curt, "I don't know that it was an Ögonen, and I have no idea what they wanted with me."

"What about the shadow?" I turned my attention back to her. "Why did you call it that?"

"Because she looked like me, only darker."

"Darker? Do you mean like how your skin is darker than mine, or Dagny's is darker than yours?"

"No." She paused her search to give me a look, like I was an idiot. "She didn't have a different complexion. She was *darker*. Like a shadow. And she followed behind me, no matter how fast I ran. Like a shadow."

Eliana's description did little to help me understand what she had seen, but it also seemed like she wouldn't respond well if I asked too many follow-up questions, so I decided my best course was to move on.

"How did you lose her, then? I mean, I'm assuming you lost her, since when we found you, you were alone."

"When I ran past the city walls, she didn't follow me," she said indifferently, like it wasn't much concern of hers why some shadow would pursue her or why it would stop.

"Did she say anything to you?"

"No." She paused, then added, "But the dragon did."

"What did the dragon say?"

" 'Remember the woman in the long white dress.' "

I mouthed this to myself, repeating it, hoping it could dislodge some tidbit of memory that would give it meaning. "Do you have any idea what that means?"

"No, but I've never thought of dragons as making a lot of sense," Eliana said.

"Have you met a dragon before?" I asked skeptically.

"I don't know. Maybe. I've just never thought of them as smart." She looked up from the laptop. "Hey, Hanna, what is *Brave*? Can we watch it?"

"Sure!" Hanna said. "It used to be my favorite movie when I was younger."

"Were either of them wearing a dress?" I asked.

"No." Eliana turned to look at me. "Ulla, can we be done talking about this? I didn't really enjoy my morning, and right now I would like to watch this movie and eat Hanna's sparkle corn."

"Leave her alone, Ulla," Hanna called from the kitchen.

"I didn't say anything more!"

She glared at me as she stirred a bowl of sparkling pink sprinkles. "Good. Don't."

34

symbolic

The remainder of Sunday was restful, but that did little to make the transition to Monday morning easier. I thought that being away from kids would make my time here in Merellä like a vacation, but between the internship in the archives, my investigation with the Inhemsk, and dealing with Eliana and Hanna at home, living with five kids under the age of ten sounded like a piece of cake.

I arrived at the archives in the morning in time to see a batch of fresh crates brought in from Isarna. Calder rubbed his hands together as I pried open the crates, and with a bit of morbid glee he told me, "Another old Marksinna without heirs died, and we're getting all the books in her estate."

Unfortunately, as it would turn out, the Marksinna's collection had been badly damaged by a flood some years back, which meant that we spent the morning wearing rubber gloves and face masks trying to salvage moldy books—most of which were far beyond saving. The only things we managed to save were several morbid scrapbooks of dried, pressed flowers from funerals and headstones, each one labelled *Mourning Flowers*.

I skipped most of the breaks that day at Calder's request, including lunch, but by the afternoon my stomach was grumbling at me so loudly that even he insisted I get something to eat. Since it seemed likely that he would ask me to stay late organizing the new texts, I realized this might be my only free moment to look for info on my parents.

With that in mind, I grabbed a bag of plantain chips from the vending machine and snuck down to the cellar to dig in. I had finally moved out of taxes into a section simply titled INTERCEPTED UNCLASSIFIED COMMUNICATIONS.

I grabbed a stack of binders, set the time on my phone to fifteen minutes (I thought about subtracting the four minutes I spent getting the chips and getting down here, but honestly, I earned the whole fifteen today), and I dug in.

Seven minutes in, I found it. A crisp white half sheet of paper printed with a blotchy pale blue ink.

NorAm Telegram

```
province of fulaträsk 2 dec 1998
c/o p.o. box 117 Catania Springs, La 70750
after much discussion we have decided that an
intervention must be undertaken. a peaceful resolution
is only possible with an intermediary. orra fagel has
been dispatched to the first city as an emissary for
the kingdom.

              h. t. otack, adviser to the king
```

Beneath that, a handwritten message had been scrawled:

Orra has not yet returned. What is the status of her whereabouts?

H.R.M. Bodil Freya Fågel, Consort to the King

8/Nov/1999

Bodil Fågel would one day go on to marry the King and take his name. The Omte tried to block out any communications or documents about the royalty, so this must've gotten through around the turn of the century. Before Bodil was the Queen Regent, and back when she and Orra were low-ranking Marksinnas.

At the very top of the page, halfway covering the name of the communications company, was a red waxy seal, embossed with a familiar symbol.

I had only seen it once before, but it had been just a week ago that I'd first seen the viny triskelion. It was at Hanna's grandparents' house, on the cover of one of Johan's books. *Jem-Kruk and . . .* something.

I read the message over three times before deciding that this was only wasting time. If I wanted to get more info from this, I had to get out of the cellar. I crumpled up my bag of chips and tucked the binder under my arm.

A few minutes later, I was jogging back into the archives.

"Good, you're back," Calder said, without looking up from the book he was translating. "I trust you had a leisurely break."

"Yeah, it was a really leisurely race through a bag of chips and speed-reading in the cellar," I muttered.

He glanced over at me with an arched eyebrow. "What was that?"

"Never mind." I shook my head and gave him a weak smile. "I know you're busy, but can you look at something for a sec?"

He sighed and rested his arms on the desk. "I'll give you twenty seconds, but not a moment more."

"Perfect," I said as I slid the telegram in front of him. "Do you know what the symbol is?"

"The one in wax?" Gingerly, he picked up the paper so he could peer down at it, and then shook his head. "No, I can't say that I do."

"You sure? You've never seen it before?"

"In my work, I see many symbols and shapes that are virtually meaningless—appearing once and then never to be seen again." Calder handed the paper back to me and returned his attention to his work.

"What about Jem-Kruk?" I asked quickly, knowing that my twenty seconds had to be about gone by now, and he shook his head. "And the . . . the Addle-river?"

He chortled. "You mean the Adlrivellir?"

"Yeah, that's it," I said excitedly.

"It's mentioned once or twice in fairy tales," Calder said.

"There's nothing too substantial written on it, and there's no evidence that it ever really existed. And now I think that your twenty seconds is long over."

"Just one more question," I said, and he glared up at me. "Where would I find those fairy tales? If I wanted to read more about Adlrivellir?"

"The catacombs," he replied with tired disinterest. He closed the book he'd been looking through and stood up.

"Catacombs? Like for mummies?"

"No, the Catacombs of Fables—the labyrinthian chambers underground that house all our fairy tales and myths, all the fictions that could be misconstrued with fact to make a confusing and dangerous situation. Accordingly, they're locked away, to protect them and to protect us."

With that, he gathered up his books and turned his back to me as he walked away. "I suggest you get to work now, Miss Tulin. Those books won't translate themselves."

I looked back at the crates, and their stacks and stacks of blurry tax returns and banal correspondence. On the side of each, written in big bold letters, was the place they had come from—Isarna, the troll city in Sweden.

"These are all from Sweden?" I asked Calder's retreating figure.

"You already know the answer," he replied gruffly, and that was enough of a confirmation for me.

In late 1998, Orra Fågel had been sent on a mission to Sweden, by the King of the Omte. A year later, she still hadn't returned, and in 2006, her cousin—Bodil, the Omte Queen Regent—had her declared legally dead.

shadow

"Oh, I couldn't possibly eat another bite." Dagny let out a satisfied groan and pushed her plate away.

"Yeah, you really outdid yourself this time, Hanna," I agreed as I finished scooping up the last few bites of the meal on my fork. The four of us sat around the table eating a delicious veggie pizza.

"The pizza was all Eliana," Hanna demurred. "She has to have the most perfect palate or something."

Eliana grinned. "I don't really understand what that means, but I've taken it as a compliment."

"That's the correct thing to do," Dagny assured her.

A knock at the door interrupted our post-meal recovery haze.

"Ulla, you get it," Dagny commanded as she leaned back in her chair.

"Why do I have to get it?"

"It's probably for you," she said.

"Yeah, it's probably your *boyfriend*." Hanna went all

singsong at the end, the way she did nearly every time she referenced Pan since he'd had supper with us the other night.

"Shush. He's not my boyfriend." I got up and answered the door anyway, but mostly so they wouldn't see the blush forming on my cheeks.

I opened the door, half expecting it to really be Pan, but instead it was Elof Dómari, looking rather uncertain.

"Elof!" I said in surprise, and no sooner had his name left my mouth than Dagny was up and rushing to the door.

"Elof, is everything okay? Did you need me for something?"

"No, everything is fine." He held up his hands in a gesture of peace and reassurance. "I'm sorry to intrude. I just wanted to stop by and check in to see how Eliana was doing."

"Yeah, of course, come in." I moved back and opened the door wider for him.

"Do you want anything?" Dagny asked, hovering beside him. "Tea? Coffee?"

"A raspberry crumble with spicy rose petal foam?" Hanna asked, offering him up the dessert that we'd all had to decline because we were too full.

"I don't think I have ever heard of such a dish, so yes, I absolutely must try that. Assuming, of course, that it isn't too much trouble," he said with a smile.

"If it was trouble, I wouldn't have offered," Hanna told him and headed to the kitchen.

"Thank you." He set his sights on Eliana, the only one still seated at the table. "Hello, Eliana. Do you mind if we sit down and chat?"

"I don't mind as long as you don't jab me with anything," she replied unenthusiastically.

"I promise that I will never lay a hand or an instrument on you without your permission. Not now, not ever," he promised her emphatically.

"I did try to stop the second you asked me to," Dagny added, not for the first time. "I just didn't want to hurt you worse."

"It's okay. I didn't know that I didn't like needles before, but now I do," Eliana said.

Elof climbed up onto the chair beside Eliana—a bit of a difficult maneuver because of his short stature and the bar-height of the stools. I moved toward him, to help him some-how, but Dagny's arm was up in a flash, blocking me, and she shook her head no. Within moments he was comfortably seated next to Eliana, entirely on his own.

"How have you been recovering?" he asked, while Dagny and I hovered in the background.

"Fine," she replied noncommittally. "My arm is healing up fast. I wasn't really that hurt. More freaked out."

"Can I ask what it was that upset you so much?"

"I don't know." She frowned. "It hurt, and I was scared, and . . . I felt like if I stayed there I would die, so I had to run and get away."

"Dagny told me that you ran to the ocean," Elof said.

"I hadn't seen it before. Not up close like that. I've seen it from the top of the buildings before, but it's not the same as being right there and touching it."

"That is very true," Elof agreed as Hanna set a plate with

the raspberry crumble in front of him. "Thank you, Hanna. This looks amazing."

"Eliana did most of the work," Hanna told him.

"Did you?" He took a bite, then let out a pleased moan. "This is delicious. You two are quite the culinary experts."

"We try," Hanna said with a light laugh, and she sat on the chair on the other side of Eliana.

"Were you known for your cooking skills back where you came from?" Elof asked Eliana.

"I don't know. I might've been."

"Did Dagny tell you about the two trolls that Eliana saw after she ran off?" Hanna asked.

"She did mention something, actually." Elof spoke between bites of the crumble, careful never to speak with a mouthful or let a pause go on too long. "Would you want to tell me about that?"

"Sure. I mean, I don't have anything to hide." Eliana repeated the same explanation that she had given the other day—nearly verbatim—about the non-fire-breathing dragon and the "darker" shadow.

"A shadow?" Elof echoed. "Does that mean she copied your every move? Or she was always a step behind you?"

"A little of both, but also neither. She was . . ." She trailed off, searching for the right word, but in the end she finished with a weak, "A shadow."

Elof set down his fork. "All this shadow talk reminds me of a story that my mother read to me as a child."

"What was it?" Eliana asked, her interest piqued at any mention of a new story.

"It was called 'The Markis and the Shadow.' "

Eliana shook her head. "I'm not familiar."

"Would you like to hear it?" Elof offered, and she nodded excitedly.

Once, many years ago, a young Markis in the north traveled south to visit his cousin. He'd only just come of age but he already considered himself a learned explorer, and he wanted to see all the world had to offer.

One night, after he'd reached the southern beach, he sat on the porch of his cousin's house, watching as the sun went down. He watched his shadow grow long, following his every movement, and he imagined that his shadow was another troll, laughing and dancing on the beach around a fire, just as the Markis and his cousin did.

Finally, after the sky was dark and the fire went out, the Markis's shadow disappeared into the darkness, and the Markis went to bed.

When he awoke in the morning, the Markis was surprised to see that his shadow had not returned. He searched everywhere, even in the brightest light, but it could not be found. Try as he might, he could not grow another, so he moved on without it.

Soon after the loss of his shadow, the Markis ran out of money and energy, so he decided to return home to write of the beauty he had seen on his brief travels. He devoted his entire being to the study and creation of beauty and goodness. Over the next seven years, the Markis tirelessly wrote and painted and worked in his garden. His passions paid little, and his inheritance ran out, but the Markis was undeterred, even as he grew poorer and thinner.

One night, a knock in the middle of the night roused the Markis. There on his doorstep stood the Shadow, no longer lost or slight. Through the intervening years, the Shadow had grown robust, his airy darkness taking on a fully trollian appearance, so he looked nearly identical to the Markis—or at least to how the Markis had looked in his prime, some years ago.

The Markis invited the Shadow in, and they stayed up all night discussing what their lives had been. How the Markis's diligent pursuit of purity and beauty had left him penniless and alone, while the Shadow's wanton hunt for excess and debauchery had rewarded him with wealth and adventure.

Despite his comparative misfortune, the Markis insisted that his was the only true way to live fully and appreciate the world. On the contrary, the Shadow argued, it was he who saw the world as it truly was, not the Markis.

The Markis and the Shadow remained friends, and over time the Markis only became sicker while the Shadow only grew fatter. Eventually the Markis became so ill he had no other choice but to accept when the Shadow made him a rather taboo offer.

The Shadow promised to get the Markis healthy and wealthy again if the Markis allowed the Shadow to pose as the Markis and the Markis to pose as a shadow, thereby reversing their original positions. Gravely ill, the Markis soon relented, fading into the darkness as he followed the Shadow's every move.

Now the master in the relationship, the Shadow took the Markis on travels around the world. Slowly, the Markis grew stronger and happier, and it was around that time that the

Shadow met a beautiful Princess. They danced together—all the while, dragging the Markis along with their feet—and the Shadow and the Princess immediately fell in love.

The Markis had had enough of the charade, and before the Shadow and the Princess were to be married, the Markis took the Shadow aside and insisted that they switch back or he would tell the Princess the truth about everything. The Shadow promised that he would, but he wanted to explain it to the Princess himself.

That night, when all the lights were out, and the Markis had disappeared into the darkness that all shadows vanished into, the Shadow was alone with the Princess. Then he confessed his entire story to her—that he was really the Markis, and it was his Shadow that had gone mad, and now he wasn't sure what to do.

The Princess reasoned there was only one thing to do with a deranged shadow like that: to do away with him quietly, putting him out of his misery, before the wedding was under way. After all, they wouldn't want to start their marriage under the dark cloud of accusation.

The Shadow and the Princess were wed the following afternoon, with the Markis executed earlier that morning.

"Your mother used to read you that story?" Hanna asked in surprise.

"That is kind of a dark bedtime story," Dagny agreed.

"It seems to have an awfully ambiguous moral," I said. "Is it an old-timey way of saying, 'Greed is good'?"

"Not exactly. I always took the story to mean that sometimes we can be blind to the darker parts of the world." His gaze rested heavily on Eliana. "To the darker parts of ourselves."

Eliana had been chewing her lip, not saying anything, but she finally nodded. "I think I get it. You can't shy away from the truth just because it's scary or hard."

"That does tend to be the best approach, I've found," Elof said.

"All right." She took a deep breath. "I'll do it. I'll come back to your office tomorrow so we can figure out who I really am. But no more needles."

"Never without your permission, I promise," Elof assured her.

36

Flowers

Dagny left at the crack of dawn for work, like she always did, but Elof had insisted that Eliana needn't rush, so she decided to go a bit later in the morning, when I went to work. Hanna, naturally, wasn't about to let Eliana go off alone—not that Eliana would've gone without her, anyhow.

But I wasn't used to sharing the solitary bathroom, not in the morning with the other three already competing to get ready at the same time, and we ended up finally heading out fifteen minutes later than normal. That meant messy bun with sunglasses and iced lemon tea for the road, and I was still slipping on my jewelry—a few rings and bracelets—as I headed to the door.

"Hey, wait for us!" Hanna complained, shoving her laptop into her backpack as I opened the door. She was bringing it along, so she'd have something to entertain herself with while Eliana was getting examined.

"Yeah, our little legs can't keep up with you," Eliana chimed in.

I looked back at them over the top of my sunglasses. "I'm not that much taller than you two. You can catch up. Come on."

It was a beautiful summer morning, with a warm breeze coming up from the sea and the sun already dancing brightly above us.

At corners and intersections, old wine barrels served as planters, adding cheery color to a crowded pastoral metropolis. All of the quaint homes and centuries-old buildings were built squished together, so there was hardly room for a patch of grass or any plants, really, downtown. On the edges of town, running along just inside the walls, was where the gardens were and where the farmers lived.

So the barrels—each containing a small flowering shrub—were the only real spots of lightness and summer. They were beautiful little plants, with dusky pink bells that smelled sweetly of honeysuckle, and Eliana couldn't resist stopping to sniff every single one.

"What are these called?" Eliana asked, for the third time that morning.

"Still the Linnea twinflower," I replied dryly, then I stopped and turned back to her. "Do you honestly not remember me telling you that two minutes ago?"

"No, I think I do. I just don't remember," Eliana answered vaguely.

"Try repeating it to yourself three times," Hanna suggested. "That's what helps me when I'm trying to remember something."

"Let's talk and walk," I said, and I was already on the move as Eliana repeated *Linnea twinflower* to herself over and over again. I stayed a few steps ahead, weaving a path through the crowd without losing track of Eliana and Hanna, who had gotten into a very focused discussion about the plants.

"Why is it called a twinflower?" Eliana asked.

"Because the flowers—the pink bell parts—there's two of them on each stalk, and they hang in mirrored pairs," Hanna explained. "Like twins."

"Oh."

Eliana fell silent for a moment, long enough that I stopped and looked back to make sure she was still there. She was, but her eyes were downcast and her face was all pinched up in thought.

"Is something wrong?" I asked.

"Yes." She rubbed at her temple. "I guess I don't know what *twin* means."

"It's when two things are identical, like the flowers," Hanna said. "But mostly it refers to two babies that are born at the same time. When three are born together, they're called triplets."

"Like any two babies?" Eliana asked.

"No, siblings. Like sisters."

"Are you sure you're okay, Eliana?" I pressed. "You seem even more spacey than normal."

She tilted her head at me. "How do you mean?"

"You seem to be struggling to understand things and are more forgetful."

"I do have a lot on my mind today," she admitted. "That might explain the forgetfulness. But the understanding . . ." Her frown deepened, and she shook her head. "Maybe it's because twins are such an alien concept to me."

"But . . ." I paused, studying the apparent confusion and frustration on her face. "You understand the idea of *alien,* or at least 'alien concept,' enough to understand that twins are an alien concept to you, but you seem baffled by *twins.* Where you come from is everyone an absolute complete individual, unlike and unconnected to anyone around them?"

"No. No." She shook her head more fiercely now. "I think it's the opposite of that, actually. I feel like . . . I was not the only one. I was part of many. I had many twins."

For some reason, that admission made my blood run cold.

"Do you mean you had twin sisters or had babies that were twins?" Hanna pressed, completely unfazed.

"I don't think I've had any babies, so I must mean sisters," Eliana decided.

"I have three sisters," Hanna said. "Emma is all by herself, like me, but the babies Lissa and Luna are twins."

"All sisters are not twins, but all twins are sisters?"

"Or brothers, or sometimes a brother and sister," Hanna explained. "If you get really technical with intersex and conjoined and all the combos between, there's probably like a hundred different gendered variations for twins."

"You know, if you really wanna know more about twins and sibling biology, Elof is basically an expert on that kinda thing," I said. "So why don't we get over to see him, and you can ask him all sorts of questions, and he can give you real expert answers, not the educated guesses that Hanna and I are giving you."

That got them moving, and it finally seemed like we were really on our way to the Mimirin. We had almost made it to the door—the lines to get through security were mere feet

from us—when a woman handing out flower-chain necklaces shouted at us.

"Are you ready for the Midsommar?" she asked as she
thrust the necklaces at us. "This year's theme is *In Bloom*."

"What is the Midsommar?" Eliana asked, and I groaned
inwardly.

"Only the biggest festival of the summer!" The woman
smiled brightly.

The tiny pink and blue flowers were carefully braided
together to make a chain necklace, each one equipped with a
matchbox-sized square of burlap, and the woman pointed to
it, tapping the message stamped on it in ink. The necklaces
were essentially a rustic take on flyers.

"All the info is right there," she explained. "It's a really
amazing night, and the best-dressed wins an awesome prize!"

"It's this Friday," Hanna announced before I even had
a chance to read it myself. "In a big fancy ballroom at the
Mimirin!"

"Thanks for letting us know, but we gotta get to work." I
grabbed Hanna by the arm—careful not to squeeze too hard
as I pulled her away.

"Did you know about this, Ulla?" Hanna asked.

"Nope."

"Can I—"

"No."

"But I'll still—"

"No."

"What about—" Eliana tried to join in, but I cut her off.

I stopped and faced them both, holding up my hands to
silence them before they even had a chance to start in. "I

am already late for work. I do not have the time or energy to argue about this. Tonight, after I get home, I'll go around and around about this for hours with you, okay? But right now, can we leave it, and let me get in there and get my work done?"

Hanna draped her necklace around her neck and raised her chin haughtily. "Fine. But you know you haven't heard the last of this."

"Yeah," I agreed with a sigh. "I know that."

37

Älvolk

I jogged into the archives, out of breath and sweaty, and Calder was already waiting for me behind the curved desk.

"Ulla, I wanted to speak with you."

"I know, I'm late, I'm sorry." I rushed through my apologies as I slipped off my bag and dropped behind the desk. "I'll cut off fifteen minutes from lunch and tack on another fifteen at the end of the day, so I'm basically throwing in an extra ten minutes as penance."

"Good. But that wasn't what I wanted to talk to you about."

I sat down in my chair and let out a rough breath. "Okay. What is it?

"I wasn't entirely truthful with you yesterday," Calder admitted quietly.

"What are you talking about?"

He paused, finally, almost reluctantly, saying, "When I said I hadn't seen the symbol from that telegram."

"You . . ." I sat up straighter. "Do you know what it was? Er, what it is?"

"It seemed familiar to me. After you had gone for the night, I went down to the catacombs, and it refreshed my memory further. It's the symbol of the Älvolk."

He set a thin book on the desk in front of me. It was little more than a pamphlet, really, held together with flimsy fabric-covered wood. Like the book I'd seen in Johan's office, this one had no title on the cover—just the viny triskelion. Although, this one was only a faded stamp, nothing as glamorous as the gold embossing of Johan's book.

"What are the Älvolk?" I reached for the book, but Calder put his hand on it, stopping me.

"This book"—he paused to tap his fingers on the worn cover—"came from the Catacombs of Fables. You understand what that means, yes?"

"That it's a fairy tale, not a history book."

He raised his eyebrows. "Precisely. With our kind, the lines can get blurred, which makes it imperative that we must always distinguish fact from fiction, truth from lies."

"Critical thinking is great," I agreed hurriedly. "I think I can apply it to old folktales."

"The Älvolk are monklike trolls that serve as the guardians of the Lost Bridge of Dimma," he answered finally.

"I don't know what that is or why it needs guarding."

"Legend has it that the Lost Bridge is the entrance to Alfheim."

"Alfheim?" Unlike the bridge, that actually sounded familiar to me. "Wait. Doesn't that have something to do with Valhalla? I thought that was just human mythology, like Mount Olympus and Wonderland."

"We've lived among them for so long, some of our mythologies cross, which is the only explanation I have for that superhero saga," he said with a dismissive wave of his hand. "Stories of the Älvolk were most popular in the tenth century, when the trolls were traveling with the Vikings. I assume that's how the stories of Alfheim got folded into their Norse mythos."

"Okay, so the Älvolk monks guard the Lost Bridge? That's what this book is about?" I pointed to it.

"This book outlines a series of relatively benign rules and theories on our existence," he said with the same condescension he used whenever he mentioned humans. "You can read it for yourself, but I'm certain, like me, you'll find it to be a benign fable. *This* is not why I remembered the symbol or the Älvolk."

"What do you mean?"

"In your history classes, did you learn of how hard the Industrial Revolution was for trolls?"

"Yeah, our society hasn't really recovered since." It was one of the few world subjects we covered at length in school, just before I left in grade nine, when Finn and Mia started homeschooling me.

"It was especially hard in the beginning, with human technology outpacing our magic and their progress devastating our homes, and our offspring stopped coming back . . ." He let out a rather disgusted sigh. "During times of upheaval, it can be tempting for some to lean on the old ways and myths for comfort.

"That is what some trolls decided to do," Calder went on. "They became followers of the Älvolk, and in depressingly short order they warped into a cult, worshipping a strange dogma that promised eternal life across the Lost Bridge of Dimma. The followers were soon consumed by their deranged pursuit and turned to violent and sadistic means to get their objectives.

"To stop the influence of the cult, the Älvolk and their literature were banned from the Mimirin," he finished grimly.

"Are you worried that me reading one boring old book is going to lead me to join a cult?" I asked.

He managed a thin, humorless smile. "No. But you must always be careful of the information you choose to ingest. That's all."

"I think I can handle it."

"You can't take it with you, but you may read it on your breaks."

"Thank you so much," I said sincerely.

"I'm sure you're excited to get into it, but you made a commitment to the Mimirin, and you have much work to do here," he warned me.

"Yes, of course. Absolutely."

He turned to walk away, saying over his shoulder, "And remember, you promised me that extra fifteen at lunch."

38

disarray

The book was short enough that I hadn't needed an entire lunch break to get through it. It was a few pages of large handwritten commandments, a dozen or so stanzas of clunky poetry, and a few drawings of the Lost Bridge as well as a few sketches of an underground temple in Áibmoráigi, the legendary First City in Scandinavia.

When Calder was in the bathroom, I grabbed my Moleskine notebook from my bag. I always brought it with me in case I learned anything I needed to jot down, and I ripped a few sheets of paper from it. I laid the pages over the drawings and carefully—but quickly—traced them all. When I was done, I discreetly tucked the pages into the notebook and put it back in my bag just as Calder returned.

He got settled into his seat with another of his phlegmy coughs, and I walked over and handed him the book.

He looked at me, his eyes bouncing skeptically between me and the book. "Done already?"

"Yeah, you were right. There really wasn't much to it.

Thank you for digging it up for me. I'm glad I got to see it for myself." I was still holding the book out toward him, and he finally took it, albeit with a dubious expression.

"As am I. I'm always happy to help someone find understanding." That's what he said, but the thin smile on his lips didn't look all that happy.

I took a step backward, toward my side of the desk. "I'm gonna cut my lunch break short and jump back into work so I can get out on time today. If that's okay."

His head was already down, back in his work, and he waved me off vaguely. "If that's what you wish, go right ahead."

On my lunch break, I had called Elof's lab to talk to Hanna and see how things were going. Hanna sounded bored, which was a good sign that nothing traumatic or interesting was happening, and she said that Dagny thought they'd be there until six or seven tonight.

That left me with a marvelous, wondrous plan. If I got out of work on time—at five P.M.—I could have at least forty-five minutes to myself by the time I got home. That would be my first real time to myself since I'd left Förening, and I didn't realize how much I needed it until I saw the opportunity.

I raced out of the Mimirin at 5:01, with my stomach grumbling horribly since I'd almost completely worked through lunch. When I was home I could waste precious minutes of my me-time on cooking or reheating something, *or* I could grab something handy from the food carts that were set up around the entrance to the Mimirin.

The second seemed like the fastest option, so that's what I went with, hurriedly scouring the various food carts and fruit stands that catered to the after-work-in-a-rush folks like myself.

"Looking for cloudberries?" A voice came from over my shoulder, sounding as cool as a garden shower on a hot day.

I looked back to see *him* again. The guy I had met at the bazaar last week. I'd thought of him as a swarthy David Bowie, but seeing him up close again, I realized that description didn't really do him justice. He was uniquely sexy—large Grecian nose, a diamond-shaped face with black hair covering his sharp jawline in a manicured goatee, his long dark hair pulled up into a man-bun.

I attempted to play off my surprise with a crooked smile. "No, I'm all good at the moment. I did have some in a delicious crumble the other day, and I guess I ought to thank you for that."

"No need to thank me." He flashed his smile again—the one that sliced through me like a hot knife, flushing my skin and warming my belly. "I'm always happy to lend my food expertise."

"Oh, yeah?" I glanced around, deliberately looking away from him so I could have a moment to regain my composure. "Do you have any recommendations on what to eat here?"

"Not really. I went with a tofu-radish falafel."

"That sounds a bit weird," I admitted.

"It really is." He scowled. "I don't know what I thought it would taste like, but it is definitely . . . not good."

"All right." I scanned my options, even though I didn't really feel all that hungry anymore—I had an unfortunate nervous stomach that always went nuts around cute boys. "I think I'll play it safe and go with the portabella wrap."

"Do you always play it safe?" He kept his voice light, teasing, but it still felt like an accusation.

I bristled. "I don't know. Maybe when I'm really hungry, and I would much rather have bland food than inedible food. Especially after hearing about your choice."

He held up his hands in a gesture of peace—silver rings adorned his long fingers. "*Ovela.* I didn't mean to come across as so judgmental."

"Not judgmental. Just . . . cliché."

"Cliché?" he echoed.

"Yeah. Like, what's next?" I smirked up at him. "Are you gonna ask me if I wanna dance with danger?"

His eyes narrowed slightly, a hint of a smile still playing on his lips, when he asked, "You think I'm flirting with you?"

"No, I . . ." I floundered for a moment, then shook my head, quelling my insecurity, and I met his gaze evenly and asked, "Aren't you?"

"Maybe I am." He leaned back slightly. "If I was, would you have any pointers on how to proceed?"

"Um." I turned away, under the guise of moving on to check out other food carts, but really it was to get a moment to figure out how to answer his question. "I guess it's better to be real. I'm not that impressed by dramatic displays."

He followed a step behind me, close enough that I could hear him easily but far enough so as not to be imposing. "So, you're saying that you'd rather spend the rest of the evening discussing laundry and the weather than creating an enchanted fantasy world?"

"Just because something's true doesn't mean it's boring,"

I argued. "Sharks, volcanoes, and cloudberry tarts are real, and they're plenty exciting."

"You make a fair point." He paused and let out a resigned sigh. "I have been told that I spend too much time with my head in the clouds."

"I don't know if I have the same problem, but I did just get a similar lecture about how I need to keep myself firmly grounded in reality and how important it is to distinguish fact from fiction."

He frowned—a deep crease across his smooth tawny skin. "That's depressing."

"Isn't it the only way to live?" I asked.

"I don't think that's living at all." He shook his head fervently. "The idea that fact is fact and *everything* else is fiction. That doesn't leave much room for new discovery, does it?"

"How do you figure?"

"The only facts we have are what we've already proven is real." He motioned around us, spreading his long arms wide and stretching them toward the blue sky above us. "Everything beyond that isn't a fact, and by the binary of your logic—fact is fact, and all else is fiction—then everything we haven't seen with our own eyes is imaginary."

He let his arms fall to his sides as he spoke, and closed the distance between the two of us. "But that can't possibly be true, can it?" His words were soft and lilting, as if they meant to float away on the breeze, and his dark eyes locked on mine. "When you look at the stars at night, do you really think to yourself, *Ah, yes, we know all there is to know*?"

"No, of course not." I swallowed, barely holding down

the flutter of the butterflies inside me. "There's millions of stars with the potential for millions of other beings and lives and stories."

"Exactly," he said with a pleased smile. "There's always more beyond the horizon."

"But I'm not going to worry about what might be over there until I get there myself." I lowered my gaze and turned away from him again. "Like how I know I'm going to eat something, even though I haven't decided on what yet."

"If you've got more time, I would recommend the juice cart down the road a ways, right before it turns off onto Wapiti Way."

I looked back at him over my shoulder. "Are you asking me to dinner?"

"As certain as I am that you'd be excellent dinner company, tonight I have somewhere that I need to be." He glanced up at the sky, checking where the yellow-orange sunlight landed on the towers of the Mimirin. "And I'll be overdue if I don't get going."

"Sorry. I didn't mean to keep you."

"No, you didn't." He scratched his temple. "Truthfully, I've been stalling a bit, and it's only partially because I've been talking with you."

"Are you avoiding work?"

"Something like that. I'm a visiting professor of sorts, assisting over the summer, and it wasn't exactly what I signed up for."

"What do you mean?" I asked.

He seemed to hesitate before replying, "It's complicated."

"Sorry, I didn't mean to pry."

"No, it's not that," he was quick to assure me. "I don't have enough time to untangle it all."

"Right, you have to get going."

"I do." He bent low, waving his hand with dramatic flair as he bowed. "Until we run into one another again."

I laughed. "Good luck at your work . . . thing." He winked at me as he walked away.

And then, too late, I realized it had happened again.

I weaved through the crowd after him, but it was still in the midst of the afterwork rush, so I was pushing against the crowd. But he was tall, and the hair knotted up on the top of his head added a couple inches, and I tried to keep my eyes locked on it.

Someone shoved me hard—their shoulder slamming roughly into me. Because of my agitation at fighting the crowd and my natural instincts at being pushed around, I shoved back twice as hard.

Unfortunately, it was once again a case of me not knowing my own strength, and I sent whoever it was flying backward into the crowd, which created a domino effect of innocent commuters falling backward onto the ground.

"Oh, no, I'm sorry," I said as I surveyed the accidental mess I had made, and when I glanced back over my shoulder, the stranger was already gone.

I spent the next ten minutes or so helping everyone up and apologizing for being such a clumsy oaf. By the time I'd finished, he was long gone, and now I was even more tired and hungry, *and* I only had twenty minutes until Dagny, Hanna, and Eliana were due to be done with work.

Hanna had probably stored some leftovers in the fridge

that I could eat cold, over the sink in a hurry, before they got home, which would leave me another fifteen minutes when I could squeeze in a quick soak in a warm bath. I jogged home, pushing thoughts of the handsome stranger and daydreams of flirtation out of my head—at least until I got home and got into the tub. Until then, I would let nothing stop my pursuit of my own private relaxation.

I ran up the steps to the apartment, already pulling my necklace from around my neck for easier access to my keys, and hummed under my breath. It was an old Diana Ross song that Mrs. Tulin would sing on the rare occasions she was happy, usually in the summer when I was helping her hang the laundry out to dry on the line.

And then, just when my key hit the lock, I heard a loud *crash* from inside the apartment. I unlocked the door in a flurry, worried that Eliana or Hanna might've had an accident, but when I opened the door, I was presented with an entirely different situation.

All the cushions had been torn off the lumpy couch, and the dining room table was flipped over. Hanna's (and now also Eliana's) stashed clothes were strewn all over everything. My mattress had been pulled down from my loft and lay askew across the kitchen. The window behind the couch was shattered, the drab curtains blowing in the breeze.

Our apartment had been totally ransacked.

39

ransack

I slammed my open palm on the Inhemsk office door, before slumping against it. The race from my apartment to the office and my growing panic had left me out of breath and a little shaky.

A moment later, the door was pushed open, and I stepped to the side to lean against the wall. Pan poked his head out, and when he saw it was me—all disheveled and sweaty—he immediately rushed over.

"Ulla, what's wrong?" He put his hands on my arms, strong and cool against my clammy bare skin.

"Someone broke into the apartment. I think." I let out a shaky breath and shook my head. "The whole place was trashed, but I didn't see anyone, and I didn't want to stay there, and I don't want Hanna or Eliana walking into that unprepared, but I'm all frazzled so I came here first. I needed to catch my breath and . . . think for a minute. But, crap." I glanced around, searching for a clock. "What time is it? They might be on their way already. I should go up to get them."

"They're with Dagny and Elof?" Pan asked.

"Yeah." I nodded. "They're supposed to be, at least."

"I'll call up there. Come on."

He held the office door open for me, and then I followed him to his desk. He stood behind it as he dialed the landline, while I waited nearby, hugging my arms around me and wondering what the hell had happened at my apartment.

"Hey, Dagny, this is Pan Soriano," he said into the phone. "Are Hanna and Eliana still with you?" He paused. "Good. Can you keep them occcupied for a little bit longer? Ulla's with me, but we'll be up in a while to explain." Another pause. "No, everything's fine. Mostly. I don't know. We'll be up soon. Thanks. 'Bye."

"They're still with her?" I asked the second he hung up the phone. "They're okay?"

"Yeah, they're fine," he assured me as he came around the desk. "Do you want something to drink? Do you wanna sit down?"

I nodded, and Pan put his hand on the small of my back, ushering me to an adjoining break room for some privacy. It was a tiny rectangle of a room that had been another victim of the very unfortunate remodel half a century ago. The good news was that it was empty, aside from a few pleather chairs and a couch—and the permanent scent of stale coffee and cheap tea.

Pan got me a paper cone of water from the water cooler while I sat down on the couch. After handing me the cup, he grabbed a chair and pulled it over. He sat in front of me, leaning forward.

"So, what happened? What's going on?" he asked once I had a drink.

"I don't know. I got done in the archives—a little early, sort of. But then I was outside talking to a professor—"

"A professor?" Pan asked.

"Yeah. I don't know his name, but that's, like . . ." My thoughts lingered on *him*—with the high cheekbones and the smile that always made me blush—but Pan was watching me, his eyebrows drawn together in concern, and I shook my head to clear it. "A whole other thing."

His frown deepened. "Okay?"

"It's not relevant to this," I clarified, and then went on in one long sentence. "I just got home earlier than I usually do, and when I was opening the door, I heard glass breaking, and then I went inside the apartment, it was empty but it was completely trashed. I started going through the mess to see if anything was missing, but then I was worried that something happened to Hanna and Eliana, so I came back here to find you because I didn't know what to do."

"All right." He considered it all for a moment and nodded. "Now we have two options."

"*We?*" I repeated.

"Yeah, I'm assuming you came to me because you wanted my help."

"Yeah, I did," I said. "I do."

His dark eyes held mine as a soft smile formed on his lips. "Good."

I swallowed, then asked, "So, what are the options?"

"In the first option, we go up and get Dagny, Hanna, and

Eliana, and we take the whole troop down to your place to go through it all together," Pan said. "In the second, we go down together, just the two of us, and check it out and make sure it's safe before bringing in the Bobbsey Twins."

"The what twins?" I asked in confusion.

"It was something my mom used to say. She had all these old books about them. It's just human pop culture." He gave me an embarrassed smile and shook his head. "Never mind."

"Well, I choose the second option."

"We should go, then," he suggested. "We can call Dagny from the apartment and let her know they can come home if everything is okay."

The trip back to the apartment seemed to take forever, even though both Pan and I walked quickly. When we got there, I opened the door, but he went in first, announcing his presence with a loud, "Hello," in case anyone was still there.

It was quiet, and everything looked exactly as it had when I ran out. Pan stood with his hands on his hips and let out a low whistle as he surveyed the mess. All the furniture flipped, clothes strewn around everywhere.

"There is an insane amount of clothing here," he said finally.

"Well, there are four of us. Hanna packed a ridiculous amount for the summer."

He looked over at me. "Did Eliana bring in a lot of her own clothes?"

"Not really. She's gotten some things in town, but her wardrobe is mostly pilfered from Hanna and me." I started gathering up the clothing. "She didn't come here with much at all."

Pan righted the couch and picked up a fern that had been knocked over. While he worked on the living room area, I moved on to the kitchen. The biggest thing was my mattress, which I grabbed and essentially threw up into the loft. It landed awkwardly, but I'd deal with getting my room organized later.

On the kitchen floor, the faux-suede box where I stored my necklaces and rings had been tipped over, spilling my modest collection all over. I set aside the clothes and crouched down to start gathering it up.

"Is anything missing?" Pan asked.

"It's hard to say for sure, especially before the others get here and sort through their own belongings. But there isn't anything that stands out to me. My jewelry box was dumped out, and it's all tangled together, but it looks like it's all here."

"What about other valuables? Electronics?"

I stood and looked around the space again, attempting to quickly inventory all of our possessions. "Both Dagny and Hanna took their laptops with them. My phone was in my purse."

"Did you have anything you brought home with you from work?" Pan asked, trying to make sense of *why* someone would've broken into the apartment.

"No, I'm not allowed to. I've taken some notes, but I always carry my notepad with me." I motioned to my bag, where it sat by the door. "Is there a lot of crime in Merellä?"

"I haven't really heard of any break-ins."

"That's not what I asked."

When he looked at me, his eyes were narrowed slightly. "What are you trying to find out?"

"You told me once that the streets weren't safe at night, that Merellä had its own set of danger trapped inside the city walls," I said, reminding him of the conversation we'd had last week.

"Yeah, but I didn't mean burglaries," he said with a sheepish smile. "There's rumors and urban legends about paranormal sightings and unexplained phenomena. The Mimirin's official stance is that the Ögonen's magic interferes with our basic reality sometimes, but I've heard varying explanations about it."

"Ghosts?" I repeated dubiously. "You were talking about ghosts?"

"Sort of." He shifted his weight from one foot to the other and avoided my gaze. "I was mostly just talking out of my ass."

"What?"

"I was making up an excuse to walk you home."

I shook my head, not understanding. "Why?"

"Why?" A nervous laugh escaped his lips, and when he finally looked up at me, his cheeks had reddened slightly. "Are you really gonna make me spell it out for you, Ulla?"

While we'd been talking, the air had changed—feeling heavy and electric around me. I didn't know what Pan was getting at, not exactly, but my heart fluttered, and I knew that whatever he was about to say, I wanted to hear it.

"Maybe," I replied quietly.

"I'm saying—" He spoke slowly, deliberately, and he stopped suddenly when we heard a banging outside.

"What was that? Are they coming back?" I asked, but he had already made for the fire poker by the wood-burning stove.

Within seconds the door burst open and Hanna rushed in, with Eliana and Dagny at her heels.

"Oh, *jakla*, Ulla!" Hanna gasped the very instant she saw the apartment. "What happened? What's going on?"

Dagny looked at Pan and me. "Did you two do this?"

I scoffed. "No, don't be ridiculous."

I explained what had happened—or at least the little that I knew. As I talked, Dagny immediately set to work organizing and cataloging her possessions to see if any were missing. Eliana listened, but she seemed mostly unfazed. She sat back on the couch, suppressing a yawn, and began folding clothes as I got to the end of my story.

"So if you guys notice anything missing, let me know," I finished. "It might help us understand why or who broke in."

"And what good will that do?" Hanna asked.

She'd been standing in the center of the apartment the entire time, rubbing her hands on her bare arms despite the warm summer air coming in through the broken window. Her dark eyes were wide, and they kept darting around the room, lingering on the shadows in the eaves.

"First thing in the morning, we're going to meet with Sylvi Hagen and make a report," Pan said.

"Why not now?" Hanna asked.

"Since nothing's missing, and nobody saw anybody, I don't think there's much anyone can do tonight, but we'll get it on record, and we'll get security checking it out," he explained in a measured tone.

"But what about tonight?" She pointed at the shattered glass. "The window's broken. It's not safe in here."

"We'll fix the window," I promised her. "It'll be safe here."

"I know *dödstämpel*," Dagny interjected. "It's like Vittra *krav maga*. And Ulla here is as strong as a Tralla horse."

"Thanks for that comparison," I muttered.

"Hanna, you don't have to worry." Eliana walked over to her and looped an arm around Hanna's shoulder, gently hugging her close. "I'd never let anything happen to you. As long as I'm with you, I promise you'll be safe."

❦

officials

I toyed with my necklace, sliding the charm along the chain, and my knee bounced up and down, seemingly of its own volition. The chairs outside of Sylvi Hagen's office were made of a rigid plastic that was already causing a dull ache in my lower back, and Pan and I had only been sitting in them for about ten minutes.

"Are you sure we should be meeting with Sylvi?" I asked. "You know, since she hates me?"

"She doesn't hate you," he said gently.

"She doesn't like me."

"Okay, sure, she doesn't like you," he admitted with a sigh. "But this is still protocol. Minor domestic issues like this need to go through your immediate supervisor, and she needs to be the one to requisition security."

I sneered. "If she deems it worthy."

"Right. But she's . . . more impartial than she may seem."

"Really?" I asked skeptically.

"She cares about her job, and she does things by the book.

She just gets annoyed when she feels like someone else doesn't play by the rules." His voice had taken on a resigned irritation.

"You sound like you're talking from personal experience."

He waited a beat before confessing, "She didn't really like me even before you got here."

"I'm sorry to bring down your status," I said, and I meant it. I was only here for a matter of weeks, but this was Pan's job and his home. The last thing I wanted to do was make his time harder once I was gone.

He looked at me with a smile. "You didn't. I made my own choices, and I still think they're the right ones."

Sylvi came out of her office, and she didn't even attempt to smile as she greeted us. Her lips were pressed into a thin line, and she managed to make her brusque invitation to have a seat in her office sound both incredibly bored and deeply offended.

"I would apologize for keeping you waiting, but you've wasted enough of my time in the short time you've been here, so I don't really feel all that sorry about doing the same to you," Sylvi said as Pan and I took our seats across the desk from her.

"It's always good to see you, Sylvi," Pan said drolly.

"Let's cut the pleasantries, shall we?" Sylvi leaned forward, resting her arms flat on her desk, and glared at us. "Something allegedly happened at your apartment?"

"It wasn't alleged. I took pictures." I pulled my cell phone out of my pocket. It didn't have a signal here in Merellä, but it still took pictures. When I held it up for her, slowly flipping through the photos, her expression never changed from bored irritation.

"You were robbed?" she asked.

I put my phone away and sat back in my seat. "No, just ransacked."

"Do you have any enemies?" she asked.

"I've been here for a week and a half," I said with an empty laugh. "That's not a lot of time to make a nemesis."

"You'd be surprised." Sylvi locked her gaze on me when she said that. "So you don't have any idea who would've done this?"

"Not that I can think of."

"What about that strange little vagabond you have living with you?" Sylvi ruffled through some papers on her desk. "The one that's being seen by Elof Dómari."

"Eliana?"

She snapped her fingers and quit her searching. "That's it. What about her?"

"I don't know why she would, but she has an alibi, so it definitely wasn't her," I said.

"But does she have enemies?" Sylvi asked pointedly.

"I don't know," I said, then quickly added, "*She* doesn't know."

"How do you mean?"

I shrugged, not wanting to get into this with Sylvi, especially since she didn't really care anyway. "It's complicated."

"If she's become a bother to you, I'm sure that we'd be able to find housing for her," she said. "I know that Elof finds her quite intriguing, and he'd certainly be able to convince the Mimirin to take her and help her."

"I . . ." I glanced over at Pan, but he looked just as thrown by Sylvi's offer as I felt. "I don't think that's necessary."

"I only suggested it to make your life easier, since you already seem to have so much on your plate, with your work in the archives, your own private investigation into your mother, a trio of flatmates, and now this break-in." Then she waved her finger from one of us to the other. "Not to mention whatever is going on with you and Panuk."

"I'm helping her," he snapped. "The way *you*'re supposed to be helping her."

"On the contrary, I am helping her." She motioned to the papers on her desk, as if they meant something. "You, on the other hand, seem to have taken an unprecedented interest—"

"I'm sorry, Sylvi," Pan cut her off icily. "I didn't realize that you had so little to do here that you could spend all this time making derogatory comments and digging into my personal life."

She twisted her lips into a tight, bitter smile. "Yes, well, I'm sure we all have better things to do. I've made a note of the incident in your file, and I'll send a copy to security for their records, but I doubt anything more will be done with that. So, if that's all you had to tell me, I think this concludes our meeting."

"Great. Thanks," I muttered and stood up.

"Oh, Ulla, I nearly forgot," Sylvi said as I headed for the door. "Elof called down this morning, and he said the results from your blood test are in. You can meet with him at your earliest convenience."

41

❧

RESULTS

We were alone in the lab. Elof sat across the island from me with a manila folder in front of him. Pan had offered to come up here with me, but I didn't want him getting in more trouble with Sylvi, so I told him he could go back to work. Elof had hardly spoken since I'd gotten to the lab, other than telling me to have a seat, and now it seemed he was taking forever to get into it.

Or maybe it only felt that way, because I knew that beneath his fingertips was an answer to the question I'd been asking all my life: Who am I? It wouldn't be the *whole* answer, obviously, but it was part of it. An explanation for things in my life—in myself—I'd been unable to explain.

"I usually start these meetings by explaining the process, so you understand how we came to our results," Elof began finally, and he seemed to be speaking deliberately slowly.

Was this how he always spoke, and I'd just never realized it before? Or was he messing with me for some reason?

"We start with the blood, as you already know," he said, but I cut him off. I couldn't take it any longer.

"So, am I a Skomte?" I asked bluntly.

"You *are* something," he said with a strange smile that did little to ease the growing knot in my stomach.

I licked my lips, and that's when it hit me—he wasn't messing with me. All his words were careful, precise, cautious. He was stalling.

"What does that mean?" I asked.

"You had significant markers for Omte, meaning that one of your parents was almost certainly from the Omte tribe," he said.

I waited for him to say more, but when he didn't, I pressed, "What about my other parent?"

"They're not a troll."

"I'm an OmHu?" I asked in surprise.

"No."

"Okay, can you spit it out and tell me what it is that I actually am?"

"That's the thing." He drummed his fingers on the envelope. "We don't know."

All the air went out of the room, and I could only gape at him and let his words sink in. "Does that mean that I'm like Eliana?" I looked down at my arm, at the blue veins underneath my pale skin, and frowned. "No, that doesn't make sense. I've cut myself plenty of times in my life, and it didn't look anything like her blood." Hers was shimmery, dark burgundy, and viscous.

"There are some . . . similarities," he answered carefully. "But the genetic makeup between trolls, humans, and—and—

well, Eliana is very similar. Our hominid relationship is analogous to the canine one between domestic dogs with wolves, wherein we're the wolves."

"Wolves with psychokinetic powers," I added.

He smiled crookedly. "Yes, that would be a more accurate description."

"But what does that make Eliana in that analogy?"

"I suppose she would be something like . . ." He looked to the ceiling as he thought. "Garm."

"Garm? The Norse hellhound?" I asked, alarmed. "Are suggesting that Eliana is evil?"

"No, no, of course not," he replied quickly. "Garm was the first mythological dog that came to mind. I was merely trying to say that we were unaware that someone like Eliana existed before."

"And you haven't encountered someone like me either, but I'm not the same as Eliana?"

"That's simplifying things a bit, but yes."

"Isn't that a bit strange?" I asked. "That in the same week you discover two trollian beings with blood you haven't encountered before?"

"Not really, when you consider that we've only recently been able to collect and share data," he explained. "For far too long, the Mimirin focused only on cataloging our written history, without doing anything to advance our knowledge. Our scientific studies have been severely underfunded and underutilized.

"It's only been in the last decade or so, as influential tribes began to realize that science might be the only means of combatting their own extinction, that we've made real leaps and bounds in the field of troglecology," he went on. "So we're constantly discovering new information or encountering things we haven't seen before."

"Our entire society is built around who has the purest bloodlines, and you're telling me that nobody has been checking the blood?" I asked skeptically.

"This may come as a shock, but those in power tend not to fund investigations that might prove they're not fit to hold the power they have," Elof said. "The various Markis and Marksinna hold all the wealth and make all the decisions, and their power relies on the presumption that none of their ancestors ever lied or cheated to gain the inheritance given to them by blood. Why would they want to find out that they're not entitled to everything they have?"

"But now they can't have children, and they're willing to risk losing their titles and wealth to find out why," I concluded.

"Exactly. A legacy doesn't mean much if there isn't a future generation to appreciate it."

"So you think that you'll be able to figure out what I am?" I asked.

"Yes, absolutely, I believe we can," he replied confidently. "It's early in the summer yet, and with more time, we will come up with a better explanation."

"Am I . . . am I still a troll?"

"Of course."

"If anyone asks about my tribe, what do I say?" I asked.

"Tell them the truth. You're a troll of mixed blood, raised in a Kanin village, looking for your family. That hasn't changed."

I nodded slowly, not quite sure if I still believed that. But I said, "Yeah, that'll work."

"On the positive side, I am not your only source for information about your past or where you came from," Elof reminded me. "Your parents could shed light on that as well. You're coming at the question from two separate angles, so it should only be a matter of time until you find the answers you're looking for."

42

unknown

I walked down to the archives in a daze. I stared at the floor, only vaguely aware of my bare feet on the cool tile, and I didn't look up until I heard Pan saying my name.

He stood outside the door to the archives, his hands shoved in his pockets and his thick brows pinched in worry.

"What are you doing here?" I asked.

"I wanted to hear what you found out and to see how you were holding up. By the look on your face, I'm guessing it's something not good."

"I don't know." I exhaled deeply. "It's complicated."

"OmHu?"

"No. No." I shook my head adamantly. "Being an OmHu wouldn't be any worse than being a Skomte, so why would I feel bad?"

Many trolls would be disappointed to find out they were half-human, like being human was the worst thing you could be, and I didn't want Pan to think that I felt that way about him. Not for one second since I'd met him had I thought Pan was less than me or not good enough in some way.

"No, you don't have to do that," he admonished me gently. "Not for me. You have every right to feel how you feel about who you are. Does that make sense?"

"I think so."

"What did you find out, then?"

I ran my hands through my hair and groaned inwardly before launching into the vague explanation that Elof had given me.

"So, basically, now I'm even more confused than ever before." I slumped against the wall when I finished. "Before getting my blood drawn, Dagny had explained that they wouldn't be able to use it to directly find my parents." The technology existed, but they didn't have the database or the time to run paternity/maternity tests against every available sample.

I went on, "So I had known going in that this wouldn't be the key to finding my parents, but I did think the blood test would give me some sense of my ancestry. That it could tell me just one little thing about myself." I sighed. "I don't know if I'll ever know who I am."

"Really? You don't know who you are?" He put his hand on the wall beside me and leaned as he spoke.

"You know what I mean."

"I do, but I still think you're wrong. Your parents and your ancestors aren't the definition of you. You're more than the color of your eyes or your super strength or your beautiful smile."

I rolled my eyes. "Okay. Now you're just being ridiculous."

"I'm not." He smiled at me. "I swear I'm not. I don't want you to overlook what you already have and who you are. You have a lot going for you. You're dedicated, you're kind, you're a lot of fun to be around."

"I don't know about dedicated. I'm already late for work." I glanced over at the archives doors.

"I bet you stay late to make up for it."

"Yeah. That's true. But I should get going anyway," I said reluctantly, and he stepped back so I could go to work. "Thanks for coming with me this morning to see Sylvi, and thanks for being here for me now."

"Anytime."

43

advice

I sat on the roof peak above my apartment, under the twinkling stars, anxiously watching my glowing phone screen. Dagny had a cell phone amplifier and she had told me that if I wanted to use it, the roof was the best place to get a signal, so that's why I was up here, waiting for my phone call to go through.

The landline in the house would've been much easier to use, obviously, but it lacked the privacy. Pan had been right— I'd worked late into the evening in the archives to make up for the time I missed. By the time I had gotten home, I'd expected everyone to be all settled in for the night, but it was only Hanna and Eliana at the apartment. Hanna explained that Dagny was still down at the archery range.

With the Midsommar festival coming up, Dagny was trying to get in as much practice beforehand as she could. They had an archery competition that offered presitigous awards, and she really wanted to win one.

Hanna and Eliana had made a fort out of couch cushions

and blankets, and they'd holed up together. When I snuck out to the roof, Eliana was braiding Hanna's hair while Hanna read excerpts from her old battered copy of *Scary Stories to Tell in the Dark*.

With Dagny in her bedroom, and my loft bedroom open to the whole apartment, the roof was the only place I could go to have a private phone call.

"Hey, Ulla," Finn answered, quelling my anxiety with just the sound of his voice—warm and crackling, like a fire on a cold day, so cozy and safe and familiar that it kept even the iciest winds at bay.

When we'd first met, he had seemed rather rigid and aloof, and I didn't know how I would survive under his roof for a week. But I soon learned that his tremendous sense of duty and responsibility came from his deep well of compassion.

"How are you doing?" he asked. "Is everything all right?"

"Yeah, yeah, everything's fine." I wrapped one arm around my knees. "Hanna's good. She's having a great time, I think."

"I'm glad she's doing well, but I'd be lying if I said I wouldn't be happier to hear that she was bored and miserable there. I was hoping it would be more of a punishment for her sneaking out with you," he said, which was just as I expected from him. His approach to parenting was equal parts empathy, mentoring, and strict discipline.

"Believe me, she's had plenty of boredom here," I assured him. "But she has the most uncanny ability to turn anything into a dramatic event."

He laughed softly. "That is definitely one of her talents. How is everything with you?"

"I don't know." The polish on my toenails had begun to chip, and I picked absently at it as I struggled to articulate how I felt. "I don't want to sound ungrateful, because I know you really helped me get into the Mimirin, but . . . I'm starting to wonder if I made a mistake coming here."

"Why would you say that?"

"What if I never find my parents?" I asked, hating how plaintive and small my voice sounded. "What if I'm wasting my time and everyone else's, not to mention resources they're wasting on me? There's this big-time docent looking into my genetics, and he could be spending his time helping Eliana or literally anyone else."

"Who's Eliana?"

"She's the girl that's staying with us," I reminded him. Both Hanna and I had been keeping Finn and Mia apprised of the situation.

"The runaway that Hanna brought in off the streets?"

"Yeah, that's the one."

"Ulla, do you want to find your parents?" he asked pointedly.

"Yes, of course I do," I replied instantly. "More than almost anything."

"Then it's not a waste of time, and if anyone offers to help you or at the very least agrees to it, then you shouldn't worry about it," he said matter-of-factly. "If the docent is looking into your genetics, there's a very good chance that he's learning something from it too, which means that you're helping him."

"I hadn't really thought of it that way, I guess," I admitted.

"Is that why you called?"

"Sorta." I chewed the inside of my cheek. "When is the soonest you can get here?"

"Is Hanna becoming too much of a handful?" he asked immediately.

"No, it's not that at all. She's great, honestly."

"It's currently Wednesday, and I have a meeting in the morning that I can't miss." He paused, and I could practically hear him doing the math in his head. "The soonest I could safely get to Merellä would be late Friday. That's only a day earlier than I had originally planned, and it would be tight, but I could do it if you need me to."

"No, no, it's fine. Everything's fine," I insisted. "I was only wondering."

I'd been about to tell him about the break-in, but I knew that would only make him worry and needlessly rush to get here. I'd already come up with precautions, and I thought I could keep Hanna safe until Saturday.

"Are you sure? You sound anxious," Finn said.

"I am a little," I admitted.

"Ulla, I've known you for over five years. You've lived with me and my family almost the entire time, and I've watched you care for my children and put your whole heart into everything that you do. But I've also seen you be too afraid to ask for help and struggle with feeling that you don't really belong. No matter what happens or what you find in Merellä, you'll always have a home with us."

A wave of homesickness washed over me, and I swallowed back the lump in my throat just enough that I could eke out, "Thanks, Finn."

"Don't give up, Ulla. You want to do this, and you're

more than capable of it, so you should do it. Finish your internship and stay in Merellä. If you're asking for my advice, that's what I'm giving you."

Tears stung my eyes, and I wiped at them with the palm of my hand. "Thanks. I think I really needed to hear that."

"I'm here, anytime you need a pep talk. I'll always be a phone call away."

44

you again

It was already hot outside by the time I made it to work the next morning, but that didn't stop the archives from being freezing cold. I spent most of the day working with a musty flannel blanket around my shoulders, hunched over the desk.

The day dragged by slowly, and it was entirely unremarkable, unless you consider paper cuts and Calder's persistent cough noteworthy. He did seem especially quiet today, saying no more than a dozen words to me, but we weren't exactly the type of coworkers who gossiped over the water cooler.

When the end of my shift finally came, I bolted out of the archives, shouting a quick good night over my shoulder, and Calder only grunted in response. Outside, the evening sunlight felt bright and hot, a rather dramatic change from my long day spent in the archive dungeons. I stopped, squinting into the sun and relishing the feel of it warming my cheeks, but someone immediately bumped into me and snapped at me to get going.

They had a point, so I moved out of the way of the trolls pouring out of the Mimirin and went over to a nearby barrel of Linnea twinflowers on the side of the road. Once there, I pulled off my knit sweater, which left me in a tank top and jeggings.

I had shoved the sweater into my bag and was working on pulling my tangles of hair up into a messy bun when a familiar voice called from behind, "It's you again."

I turned around to see Sumi standing behind me, looking the same as she had when she'd helped Hanna and me find Eliana on the beach: tight leather pants paired with a loose top, and her beautiful black coils of hair plaited tight to the scalp on one side and flowing free on the other.

"Oh, hi." I put my hair up in a flash, suddenly feeling the need to have my hands free, in case . . . In case what, exactly? I didn't know, but the way Sumi looked at me now—an amused smile on her seemingly ageless face but calculating dark eyes—I wanted to be ready for anything. "Sumi, right?"

She nodded once, a fluid, precise movement. "Did you ever find your missing friend?"

"Yeah, we did. And, um, thanks again for that. She was right where you said she'd be."

"Good. I was worried." Then her tone shifted, her voice going low into a whisper, a secret, a warning. "The citadel can be a dangerous place."

"Everyone keeps telling me that."

"Oh?" She blinked at me, that amused smile still locked in place. "You sound skeptical."

I shrugged. "Well, nothing really bad has happened."

"How long have you been here?"

"About a week and a half."

"It's still early, then." Now the smile disappeared, twisting into something more like a grimace or a gash. "You've got plenty of time to discover all that goes bump in the night."

"You sound all menacing all of a sudden," I said, punctuating the sentence with a nervous laugh.

"Do I?" she said with such exaggerated surprise—widening eyes, mouth aghast, apologetic tone lilting toward song—I couldn't help but believe that she'd meant to sound *exactly* as threatening as she had. "I'm merely trying to warn you to keep you safe. The magic here is quite powerful, and it can have a strange effect on things."

"Yeah, I suppose that's true," I agreed, just to move the conversation along, and then casually asked, "How long did you say you were here for, again?"

"I'm not sure. Until my business is concluded. Why?"

"Merellä seems like the kind of place where it's good to have friends." I smiled at her, but it felt forced and tight.

She flashed a matching smile, equally as strained and fake as my own. "I think it's always good to have friends, no matter where you are."

"That is true."

"I should let you get on with your day. I hope you have a pleasant evening."

"Yeah, you too," I said emptily as she turned and walked away.

The wind came up, blowing a chill of salty air from the sea, just before she disappeared into the crowd. It blew her hair wildly, exposing the back of her neck, and the thick black lines of the tattoo on her light brown skin.

It was a tattoo of an ouroboros: a serpentine dragon biting its own tail, so it formed a perfect circle, and this one had a very Norse runic design.

I stared after her, and under the summer sun, my blood ran cold.

When Eliana ran away from the Mimirin, she said she'd been chased by a shadow and a dragon. And Sumi had pointed us right to where Eliana was hiding—just beyond the city walls.

I thought about going after her, grabbing Sumi by the arm and demanding to know what she knew about Eliana, but then I remembered. Eliana and Hanna had stayed home today, and they were at the apartment.

Alone.

45

fear

I ran the rest of the way home, and I even jumped over an overturned cart. My legs burned, and I was drenched in sweat and gasping for breath by the time I raced up the stairs to the apartment, but I refused to slow.

Not until I knew Hanna and Eliana were safe.

I threw open the door, causing Hanna to let out a surprised scream. She'd been sitting on the couch with her legs folded under her, but she jumped to her feet when I came in.

"Are you okay?" I asked between gulps of air. "Where's Eliana?"

"Right here." Eliana stepped out of the bathroom, her long hair a rather somber shade of black today.

"You're both okay?" I put my hands on my hips, surveying the apartment, which looked just as it had when I left for work this morning. "Is Dagny home?"

"No, Dagny's still at work," Eliana said.

"What's going on?" Hanna's voice had taken on a panicked edge. "Did something happen?"

"No," I said, but that didn't feel true to me, not exactly, so I amended, "I don't know." I looked over at Eliana. "You remember the other day when you saw the dragon?"

"Yeah. Why?" Her face lit up, and bright green streaks momentarily flashed through her hair. "Did you see a dragon?"

"I saw . . ." I stopped myself before telling her about Sumi. I wanted to hear what Eliana had to say before I filled her head with my own thoughts and fears. "What did you see? It wasn't a big scaly monster, was it?"

"I don't know." Her face scrunched up. "That day is such a blur to me."

I stepped closer to her, as if that would somehow jog her memory. "Do you remember what you saw? What made you think a dragon was following?"

"I saw . . ." She closed her eyes. "It was before the beach, and I was running through the city, and the world was a kaleidoscope, and . . . and . . ." Eliana scowled as she opened her eyes. "I only know that I ran because I was afraid the dragon was at my heels."

"Ulla, what is going on?" Hanna demanded. "Did you see a dragon or something?"

"Not exactly." I sighed and tucked a loose lock of hair behind my ear. "I don't know. I don't even know if it's related."

"What are you talking about?" Hanna was nearly shouting now, out of fear and frustration.

My earlier panic had subsided, now that I knew Hanna and Eliana were safe. Part of me worried that I'd overreacted to a coincidence, but that didn't erase my very recent memory of how helpless and terrified I had been after talking to Sumi.

"It was this tattoo of a dragon," I explained lamely. "But with the break-in, and knowing you're here alone, and everyone warning me about how dangerous it is here . . . I hate to say it, but I think that we may have to look into alternative housing for Eliana."

"*No!*" Hanna shrieked, like I had suggested murdering a puppy. "No! Why?"

I held out my hands and in the most soothing tone I could manage I said, "I'm not trying to be a jerk, but Hanna, you're under my care. I can't be here with you all the time."

She snorted. "And getting rid of Eliana will make me *more* safe, so I'll be totally alone?"

"First, we're not 'getting rid' of Eliana," I corrected her. "The Mästare already told me that Elof can find her somewhere to stay, and I would never let her go someplace where she wouldn't be safe or comfortable."

"You were already talking about it with the Mästare?" Hanna asked, disgusted.

"No, the Mästare offered the idea, and I turned her down," I said. "But the situation has changed. If someone is after her, she should be somewhere that's safer where they can protect her."

Tears welled in Hanna's eyes, but her expression was that of anger and defiance. "But what about me?"

"Hanna, you're going home on Saturday." I stepped closer to her. "But Eliana will still be here. All alone. Don't you think it would be better that you help her find someplace to stay and get her situated *before* you go?"

She shook her head as a solitary tear slid down her cheek. "Will I still get to hang out with her while I'm here?"

"Yeah, of course you can," I told her.

"Or I can just go back out on my own," Eliana offered.

"No, Eliana, nobody wants that," I assured her. "You're our friend, and we want you to be safe. I have to make Hanna my priority because she's a child, and she's under my care."

It was hard to say for sure how old Eliana was. Her naïveté and diminutive size made her seem younger, but her face was more that of a woman than that of a child, and some of the things she said made me think she might even be older than me.

Hanna wiped roughly at her eyes. "No, she's right, Eliana. This is what's best for you, so this is what we'll do."

"And I won't have to stay if I don't like it?" Eliana asked.

"No, of course not," I said. "You're not being held prisoner. You're still free to come and go as you wish."

She considered this for a moment, then nodded. "I'd like to see where I'm going to be staying before I agree to it. But I'm willing to look."

46

neighbors

Within the hour, the three of us were on the fourth floor, following Elof down a long corridor to the guest accommodations. As we walked, Hanna kept excitedly pointing out the various works of art that hung on the walls.

"It's so beautiful here, Eliana," Hanna gushed. "I'm actually jealous that you get to stay in the Mimirin! It's like living in Cinderella's castle or something."

"Who is Cinderella?" Eliana asked.

"Never mind," Hanna said with a laugh.

"And here we are—room 4113." Elof stopped in front of the door and pulled out a key ring adorned with absurdly large keys.

While we waited for him to unlock the door, I admired the painting hanging nearby. It was simple but beautiful and vibrant—blossoms falling from an apple tree onto a lake, the pale pink flowers floating in a reflection of the blue sky. There was arresting—but strangely familiar—beauty to the quick strokes that had been left in the oil paint.

"Who painted this?" I asked Elof.

The door lock clicked open, and he peered over at the painting. "That one there? I believe it was Claude Monet."

"It's really lovely. I don't think I've ever seen it before." Which actually was saying something.

Back in Iskyla, Mr. Tulin had been something of a failed artist. A few of his paintings hung around the inn, mostly landscapes and animals done in a broad impressionist style. He didn't paint anymore by the time I met him, but he still had his stacks of art books from his youth when he'd been more aspirational. His favorite painter—who would eventually become my favorite as well—had been Monet.

"No, I don't know how you would have," Elof said. "It's been in the Vittra's possession since right after it was painted."

"How did the Vittra get it?" I asked.

"Oh, you know the Vittra," he said with a wan smile. "We have a long history of using whatever means necessary to get our hands on all the shiniest baubles."

"Enough with the painting," Hanna interjected. "Can we see Eliana's room now?"

"By all means." Elof opened the door, and with a showman's flourish he gestured to the room.

It was a spacious room, only a little bit smaller than our entire apartment, and it appeared as if Marie Antoinette had overseen the decorating. A baroque four-poster bed—replete with sheer curtains tied with ribbons to the ornate posts—sat in the center, buried beneath layers of shimmering rose-gold blankets and overstuffed pillows. The walls were covered in a subtle damask pattern with a pale blue sheen, and there was a nice little sitting area with tufted furniture and gilded end tables.

"Wow!" Hanna gasped as she took it all in. "This room is fit for a princess!"

Eliana hopped up on the bed and promptly sank down in the overflowing bedding. "And I finally have my own bed."

"Do you all live like this here?" Hanna asked Elof as she ran her fingers over a velvet chair.

Elof chuckled warmly. "No, no. My room is much more . . . practical. This isn't a residence open to everyone. Even I don't have a room in this wing."

"Why not?" Eliana stood up on the bed and leaned on one of the posts. "How come I get to be here, and you don't?"

"You're an unusual individual with an unusual circumstance, and so that calls for . . . an unusual living situation," Elof explained carefully.

"This is a really nice upgrade, Eliana," Hanna said, as if there were any doubt in our minds. "You should enjoy it while you can. Live it up."

"I do enjoy living it up," Eliana said with a laugh—a melodic burst of happiness. With one hand she hung on to the post of the bed, and extended the other out toward Hanna.

Hanna looked back at me, and I shrugged. This was the room they had given Eliana, and I wasn't going to boss her around in her own space. Hanna took her hand, and Eliana pulled her up on the bed, and the two of them talked and laughed and danced around on the bed.

"I hope you don't mind if I join in." A voice from behind me interrupted their infectious joy, and I turned around to see Mästare Amalie standing in the door, her lips pressed into an indulgent smile.

"Mästare, what a pleasant surprise!" Elof exclaimed, and

he had the breathless stammer of someone genuinely caught off guard by the presence of a luminary. "We're always happy to have a visit from you."

"I had a free hour in my schedule, so I wanted to come say hello to my new neighbor." Amalie looked to where Eliana stood barefoot on the satin sheets, her cotton-candy-pink hair swinging past her shoulders. "Is this her?"

She bounced off the bed and came over to shake the Mästare's hand. "Hi, I'm Eliana."

"I'm Amalie. I've been here for a very long time, and if you need help finding your way around, I live right down the hall."

"Thank you. I do have an unfortunate habit of getting lost, but I promise not to bother you too much."

"Oh, it's no bother at all." Amalie's assurances came with a warm laugh, like a gentle rebuff from a familiar aunt. "I trust that you're satisfied with the accommodations here?"

"Are you kidding?" Eliana glanced around the room. "This place is like the Cindy-bell's palace."

"Cinderella," Hanna corrected her softly.

"Right. Cinderella."

"That's lovely to hear," Amalie replied. "Have you had any improvements with your condition?"

"My memories are still foggy," Eliana admitted, but she tried to adopt a cheery tone when she added, "But we've been working on some memory techniques. I'm hopeful that something will come back soon."

Amalie's smile deepened. "As am I. The Mimirin is the ideal place for you to get well."

47

guardian

We had only been back at the apartment for all of twenty minutes before Hanna started sulking.

She sat on the couch, all splayed out as she stared vacantly up at the ceiling. "It seems so quiet without her."

I hadn't really noticed Eliana's absence yet. Hanna had primarily been sighing and moping, while I straightened up the kitchen and Dagny worked on her laptop, tapping loudly at the keyboard.

"I wouldn't say quiet, but it is more spacious," Dagny countered.

She sat on the floor, her back resting against the couch, so she could use the coffee table as a desk. This was the first time she'd had real access to the table since Eliana had moved in. Usually it was half buried underneath clothing, books, and various electronics.

It was definitely still cramped in the tiny apartment, but it was more "overly crowded" and less "aftermath of a tornado," so that was an improvement.

"Are you sure she's going to be safe there?" This wasn't the first time Hanna had asked this—or even the tenth. But she managed to sound utterly forlorn every time she did, so I stopped wiping down the counters and went over to sit on the arm of the couch beside her.

"She's *inside* the Mimirin," I reminded her. "She'll be safer in there than she is here. Plus, she has the Mästare to watch out for her."

"Do you think she'll be happy?" Hanna asked.

"Of course she will."

Dagny made an irritated clucking sound with her tongue. "You guys are talking about her like she's a puppy that you had to rehome. She's a grown-up. I think." She paused, then shook her head. "Either way, she's a sentient being with free will. She'll be as fine as any of the rest of us."

A loud knock at the front door interrupted Hanna's sullen reply, and she sat up straighter on the couch, asking hopefully, "Do you think that's her?"

"No, we just left her," Dagny reminded her. "It has to be Ulla's boyfriend."

"Ugh." I groaned as I stood up and hoped they didn't notice the subtle reddening of my cheeks. "Shush. We're just friends."

"I think thou doth protest too much," Dagny teased.

Naturally, when I opened the door to find Pan standing on the landing, Hanna burst out laughing, and my face burned.

"Hi!" I smiled at him, and for some reason followed it up with a flustered, "Hello." Then I noticed next to him was the sleek dog with dark fur and one ear droopier than the other. "What's going on?"

"Hey. So, you can say no to this, and it's gonna sound weird, but I came over to lend you my dog." Pan gave me a sheepish smile before bending down to scratch the dog between the ears. "He's technically the property of the Mimirin. Brueger's a Belgian Malinois, and he's been trained to herd and watch over the elk. We got to be buddies, and he usually stays with me at my place. He's a good guard dog, and I know you haven't exactly felt safe since the break-in. So I thought Brueger might help you out."

Before I had a chance to respond, Hanna slid past me and crouched down, squealing in delight as she started petting Brueger. "Oh, that's so cool! He's so cute! We should totally keep him!"

"Hanna, you're leaving the day after tomorrow, and he'd only be staying here temporarily," I reminded her.

"But you're not going to be here the *whole* time." She stared up at me with big brown puppy eyes that had to have made Brueger jealous. "It'd be nice so I don't have to be alone."

I sighed in resignation and turned to Pan. "If it's really not too much trouble."

"I wouldn't have offered if it was," he said with his easy smile.

"What about you?" Hanna looked up at him. "If Brueger's here guarding us, who will keep you safe?"

"My place is actually very safe. The guy who owns it is an ex–Kanin soldier and super paranoid, and added bars over the windows and the whole nine yards. So, yeah, it's basically the coolest bachelor pad ever," he finished with a self-deprecating laugh.

"It's certainly hard to top our bachelorette digs." I motioned to the apartment. "Did you wanna come inside and hang out for a bit?"

He shook his head sadly. "I would, but I have to get up super early in the morning to get the elk ready for the parade."

"There's an elk parade?" I asked, bemused.

"There's a parade in the afternoon for Midsommar, and then later on that evening there's a big party at the Mimirin, and everyone is invited," he explained. "It sounds kinda weird, but it's a lot of fun."

"So you're working through the festival?" I asked.

"Just in the beginning with the elk. Then I'm free."

"I'll see you at the party, then."

His dark eyes sparkled, and he smiled as he said, "It will definitely be a fun time."

48

Night Terrors

A low, rumbling snarl broke through my dream. It was already a half-forgotten memory by the time I opened my eyes—a waterfall on a cliffside, with thunder clapping in the distance, a jagged green bolt of lightning—and then I had the strange disorientation of blinking into the darkness, trying to remember where I was.

It was Brueger's growl that woke me up, and it was his growl now that grounded me back in the quiet little apartment. I sat up in my bed and peered down from the loft. Hanna snored softly from her mass of pillows and blankets she'd buried herself in on the couch, and the door to Dagny's room was shut.

The only one awake down there was Brueger. He stood in the center of the kitchen, the dark fur on his back raised slightly, and both of his ears stood at attention in high alert. His eyes traveled along the ceiling, following something that I could neither see nor hear.

Moving as quietly as I could—no need to alarm Hanna

if I didn't need to—I climbed down the ladder and grabbed the poker from where it sat next to the wood-burning stove. I followed Brueger, watching his gaze and staying a step behind him as he crossed the room.

Then I saw shadows rippling across the floor. I crouched down, trying to peer out the window and into the moonlight, but whoever—or whatever—it was outside making shadows was moving too fast. The shadows leapt around the room, like invisible acrobats were performing a show on the rooftop across from us.

That was more than enough for Brueger, and he let out a loud, angry bark before diving at the window. Thankfully, the old windowpanes held, so there was only the clatter of his claws against glass as he barked and growled.

Hanna screamed, and Dagny rushed out of her room, but the shadows were gone, and Brueger fell silent.

"What's going on?" Dagny asked.

I shook my head. "I don't know."

Brueger began pacing the room, casting confused looks at the ceiling, before finally giving up. He lay down on the floor in front of Hanna, panting and looking around.

"It was probably a raccoon," Dagny muttered between yawns. "But it's good to know the dog kept our trash cans safe."

"Do you think it was Eliana?" Hanna asked. "Or whoever it was that broke into our apartment?"

"Whatever it was, I think it's gone now." I motioned to Brueger, who had finally relaxed, resting his head on his paws and no longer panting or growling. "You should go back to sleep. You don't want to be tired for the festival tomorrow."

"Right. Yeah." Hanna stretched out on the couch, and she let her arm hang over the side so she could absently pet the dog as she fell back to sleep.

Sleep for me wouldn't come so easy. I carried the poker up to the loft with me, and I lay awake for a long time, straining to hear any little noise and wondering what had woken Brueger in the first place.

celebration

After several hours of tossing and turning (while remaining vigilant for possible intruders, of course) I managed to get a few hours' sleep before Eliana came over and the combination of hers, Hanna's, and the dog's excitement made sleep impossible.

"What are you doing here?" I asked her as I peered over the edge of my loft.

Eliana didn't pause scratching Brueger to yell up at me, "Because it's Midsommar! There's *soooo* much fun stuff going on in town, and I don't want to miss a second of it."

"Since when did you become the expert on Midsommar?" I asked her tiredly.

"I'm not, but everyone around town is very excited about it, and there are a lot of streamers."

Midsommar wasn't a holiday we celebrated in the Trylle kingdom. We had adopted Christmas from the humans, since changelings seemed to love it so much, and Yggdrasil Day in the spring, Samhain in the fall, and plenty of days memorializing past monarchs or important battles, and that was plenty.

This was the last day that Eliana and Hanna had to hang out together, and it was a festival I'd never been to before. Because of the Midsommar holiday, nonessential work was closed all over town, and sleeping the day away seemed like squandering a once-in-a-lifetime opportunity.

I dressed in a hurry—throwing on a pair of overall shorts over a crop top and pulling my hair up into a messy bun—and they were already chomping at the bit.

The decorations around town weren't quite as exciting as Eliana had made them sound, although streamers were indeed prevalent. Flower garlands and bouquets adorned every lamppost and street corner, as if summer had arrived overnight with a pastel explosion.

Wapiti Way was the center of morning activities, with the usual market stalls pushed aside for carnival games, specialty food stands, and even a few rides. A wooden Ferris wheel was painted bright pink, and a corner vendor was selling floral wreaths. The whole thing felt like one part county fair, one part Renaissance fair, and one part fairy wedding.

Naturally, Eliana and Hanna were over the moon for it all. It wasn't until late in the afternoon when I managed to convince them to head back to the apartment, so we could take a break before getting ready and heading out to the party.

All of us went to the archery range to watch Dagny compete, and it was actually pretty amazing. I'd never gone to an archery competition before, and Dagny was an impressive shot. For the final feat, small bull's-eyes were placed on strings and moved from side to side, and even with that, Dagny managed to hit three of them dead center. She walked away with the second-highest prize of the day—a silver arrow mounted on a plaque.

"Congratulations!" I told her afterward, and hugged her.

"Thanks." She smiled warmly at me, but she started walking on before I had a chance to say anything more. "Come on. There's not a lot of time."

"What are you talking about?" I asked, and I hurried after with Hanna and Eliana following a few steps behind.

"To get ready for the ball," Dagny called back over her shoulder.

As soon as we got home, Dagny hung up the plaque on the wall, and then immediately darted into her room to get ready. Nearly an hour later, Dagny came out of her room, and my jaw dropped. She wore her long black hair down for the first time since I'd met her, with flowers and ribbons braided in through her waves of hair. She normally wore very little makeup, but now her makeup was a bold avant-garde look, with smoky shimmery white over her eyes and rose-gold foil adorning her cheeks and eyebrows like sparkling flower petals.

Hanna and Eliana stayed around just long enough to marvel at how stunning Dagny looked before immediately dashing to the bathroom to start working on their own hair and makeup.

"You really do look amazing," I told Dagny, once the others had left us alone.

"You like the dress?"

"Your dress is great," I said, and that wasn't a lie, but I honestly hadn't noticed when compared to the dramatic beauty of her makeup and hair. Her dress was gauzy and pink, with bell sleeves and a ribbon tying in the corset waist. "It's simple, but it's perfect."

She gave me a relieved smile. "Thanks. I wasn't sure if it was too much or not enough."

"So what are you all dolled up for? You got a hot date?" I asked, and I was only half teasing.

"No." She shook her head. "I'm an ace, so I don't date. This is for the competition. Whoever is voted the best dressed wins a big cash prize."

"What's an ace?"

"I'm asexual," she replied matter-of-factly as she re-adjusted the flowers in her hair. "That can mean different things for different individuals, but for me it means that I've never been attracted to anyone at all, and I don't feel the urge to be with anyone romantically."

"Oh. That's cool," I said, and then, because that didn't feel like enough, I added, "I didn't know."

"Why would you?"

"I don't know." I squirmed a little. "I just feel like I should say something like how I support your life choices."

"Your support is appreciated but entirely unnecessary," she said, and when I started walking away, she quietly added, "Thanks for being understanding, Ulla."

"Ulla!" Hanna shouted from the bathroom. "Come help us get ready! If we're going to look as fabulous as Dagny, we've gotta get going!"

Eliana and Hanna definitely took Dagny's look as in-spiration, adorning themselves with as many flowers and as much glitter as they could. I, on the other hand, went for a much subtler look, in large part because I hadn't known that I should pack anything so glamorous.

Instead, I went with a simple white crochet romper, which Eliana, Hanna, and Dagny spiced up by sharing all their ribbons, flowers, and glitter with me. In the end, I wasn't as over-the-top as them, but I easily fit in with everyone else making their way down to the Mimirin.

"It's Midsommar, and it's my last day here, so we have to make tonight count," Hanna insisted before making the four of us squeeze in for a selfie.

50

midsommar

Before we left the apartment, Hanna started fidgeting—twisting her rings and tugging at her satin sash—and worried aloud that we'd get lost on the way to the ballroom. Dagny was standing in front of the mirror by the front door, touching up her extensive makeup, and Hanna was growing antsy and anxious.

"There will be a huge crowd of trolls we can follow in," Dagny said, since her assurances that there'd be plenty of signs had done nothing to ease Hanna's concerns.

"Following the crowd doesn't mean I'll get to the right place," Hanna retorted. "They might all be walking off a cliff, for all you know."

"What? Is that a thing that happens here?" Eliana had been busy lacing up the corset-style Victorian gloves that Dagny had lent her, but she stopped and her eyes widened— whether out of excitement or fear, I couldn't be sure.

"No, no, Hanna's being dramatic," I told her soothingly.

"Besides, it's near-impossible to miss," Dagny reiterated as she finished reapplying her eyeliner. "You go in the front door, up the stairs, then go right and through the waiting room, and there you are."

"There's no other turns at all?" Hanna asked.

"Not unless you take a wrong turn at the bathroom and end up in the drawing room. But really, Hanna. You can't get lost, and you'll always be with us." Dagny dropped the makeup into her cosmetic bag, then turned back to face Hanna straight on. "Why are you so worried about getting split off from us?"

"I don't know." Hanna shrugged a shoulder indifferently. "Lots of strange stuff has been happening lately. I like to know all my options."

"Options?" I repeated, confused.

"She means memorizing all the entrances and exits," Eliana supplied when Hanna didn't answer right away. "She's been making me do it at my new place now too."

"I'm just being safe," Hanna said defensively, as if she'd been accused of something untoward. "My dad always taught me to do it, so we'd be safe if there was danger."

"Right, I should've known," I mumbled, which was true enough.

Finn had been through a lot of rough situations, and he'd made it through by obsessing over details and being prepared. On countless occasions, I'd heard him stressing the importance of various safety and danger warnings, not just to the kids, but to me, to Mia, to literally everyone.

"Well, you won't have to worry tonight," Dagny told her with a smile. "There will be guards everywhere, and the Ögonen on the roof."

That calmed Hanna enough. And then we were off,

joining the long procession of elegantly dressed attendees on their way to the Mimirin. The streets were crowded, but most everyone was going the same way, so it didn't take all that long to get down there.

I spotted the guards as soon as we stepped into the Mimirin. Normally they were unobtrusive, standing at the sidelines in bland uniforms. Inconspicuous and vigilant. If I hadn't spent so much time around trackers like Finn, I might not have been so quick to recognize the rigid posture.

But tonight they were on full display for everyone. Crimson satin uniforms—the color of the Vittra, who funded most of the festival—sharply tailored with gaudy embellishments, so they looked like a Victorian cosplay of army men.

The outfits might have been for show, but the swords glinting at their sides certainly weren't. As we passed them, I let myself fall a bit farther behind Hanna and Eliana, letting them enjoy their last night together. We were safe here. I could give them space tonight to have fun without me watching over their shoulder.

The Aurenian Ballroom in the Mimirin was located on the second floor, above the library. It was easy enough to find, even without all the floral and shimmery signs pointing the way—up the main grand staircase, to the right, past the restrooms, and then you were in the elegant waiting room. It was a holding room of sorts, with two sets of floor-to-ceiling doors leading into the opulent ballroom.

The room itself was almost vacantly white, but there were a few subtle touches of pink and red—ruby and rose sapphires adorned the platinum wall sconces, and the marble tiles on the floor had accents of dusky pink stones.

I was a step behind Hanna and Eliana, so I had a front-row seat for witnessing their first look at the festival. Once we'd gotten through the security at the front doors, they'd sidled up together, talking in excited whispers about all the décor and elaborate fashion.

Just outside the ballroom, when their excitement was reaching peak fervor, they clasped their hands together. As soon as they saw inside the ballroom, they gasped in unison, which only caused them to burst out laughing. Then they weaved through the crowd—carefully, since they were still holding hands—until they made their way out to the middle of the dance floor, where other kids and teenagers had already started the circular dancing around the maypole.

By its very nature, the Midsommar festival called for an explosion of flowers. Extravagant bouquets sat on every table, overflowing with lilies, peonies, and roses as large as my fist. Two maypoles stood in the center of the dance floor, decorated with long pastel and floral ribbons.

The Aurenian Ballroom—much like the entirety of Merellä today—smelled of flowers. Sweet and earthy, fresh and bright—like wildflowers and honey and the peach wine that I sipped from a champagne flute. A waiter passed by with the flutes of wine on a silver tray, and I snatched one as Dagny tutted me.

"It's delicious." I held it up, swirling the pale pink liquid in the crystal glass. "You really should try one."

"It's too early. I haven't eaten yet," Dagny said, just as the music swelled.

In the north corner of the room a classical sextet had been set up, with a pair of female vocalists. They were maybe twins, but definitely sisters, with matching diminutive statures and button noses. Not to mention they had equally stunning voices, which they were ably showing off as they sang an old Trylle love song.

"Are you enjoying the music?" Pan's voice behind me, and I turned around to see him looking much sharper than when I'd seen him last, trading in his elk-herding uniform of green velvet slacks and floral suspenders for a slick black suit.

I smiled at him. "I am. I've always liked this song." It was a slow, mournful waltz, but there was something strangely optimistic in the high melody.

"Then it would be a real travesty if you didn't dance to it." He held out his hand to me.

"You don't have to," I demurred.

"I know. I want to."

I placed my hand in his and let him lead me out to the dance floor. As we fell into step together, his other hand slid to the small of my back, and we began to sway and twirl around the room, mindful of the maypole and its zealous dancers.

"This is a very nice song," Pan commented. "I'm not sure if I've heard it before, though."

"They played it all the time at Trylle events I went to in Förening. I don't know how popular it really is outside of that kingdom. It's called '*Den Sista Dansen Utan Dig.*' "

Pan's forehead scrunched in concentration for a moment as he deciphered it. " 'The End of the Dance Without You'?"

" 'The Last Dance Without You,' " I corrected him gently. "But that was pretty close."

"I'm not quite as fluent in other languages as you are," he admitted. "But this sounds like kind of a depressing song."

"It's about a woman whose lover died at sea. She dances on the hills in the morning, the way they did when he was home."

"I stand corrected—it's a *very* depressing song," Pan said.

I laughed. "No, it's not that sad. Like right here." I paused, listening to the operatic lyrics before translating them. " 'And if the sun tomorrow doesn't rise, I still smile that I saw the light. Though the night shall be long, I have our dance to keep me warm. And I know that one day, beyond the dark, I will have my last dance without you.' "

"All right, I guess it has a slightly more optimistic ending," Pan allowed.

"Exactly."

"It probably helps, though, that I'm not dancing alone," he said with a smile that made my heart skip a beat.

"Oh, yeah?"

"Yeah. I'm always in a good mood when I have a beautiful girl on my arm."

I laughed and lowered my gaze, hoping he wouldn't see the blush rising on my cheeks. "Does that happen a lot?"

"Honestly, not often at all. I haven't really been to a lot of dances, outside of a couple of weddings."

"Same. The royalty seem to throw balls and parties every other week, but I've only snagged an invite to a few myself."

The song came to an end, switching to the much jauntier music ideal for maypole dancing, so Pan and I made our way to the edge of the dance floor and separated.

"At least tonight we can get plenty of practice with our dancing," Pan said.

I smiled up at him. "Yeah. I'd like that."

punch-drunk

Another four flutes of peach wine down, and I had to make a break for the bathroom. Dagny was loading up on the crudités while Hanna and Eliana danced, and Pan was chatting with one of his peurojen coworkers, so it was the perfect time to slip out.

I don't know if it was the dancing, the wine, or from Hanna twirling me around the maypole, but I felt dizzy and light-headed in a strangely wonderful way. Deep down, I suspected that that feeling had more to do with Pan than anything else. The way he smiled—so bashful and happy—when I teased him, or the warm palm print I still felt on the small of my back from dancing with him.

In the mirror I could see it on my face—the flush in my cheeks, the delirious sparkle in my eyes, the sleepy smile on my lips.

I was drunk—on the wine, on the night, on Pan.

It didn't really matter what the cause was, anyhow, but I didn't want to act a fool, especially not when things were going so well. To be safe, I needed to sober up. I splashed cold water on my cheeks and decided to take a breather before heading back into the ballroom.

Just outside of the bathroom was a spacious drawing room. It was quiet and sparsely decorated—a few tufted benches, several gilded mirrors, and half a dozen busts of old monarchs. As far as rooms went in the Mimirin, this one was *nearly* unremarkable, aside from one very cool architectural detail: a domed glass window in the center of the floor, giving a view into the library below. Currently, that meant it mostly had a view of the empty shelving and plastic sheeting, since the library was still under renovation.

But directly below the skylight was a pattern inlaid in the library floor, bright copper mixed with red stone to create a map. It was the world, all the major troll communities marked with sparkling gemstones.

The shelves were poised around the mosaic, and there were a few bolt holes drilled into the stone around it, so I wondered if there used to be something there. Maybe a statue or an elaborate light fixture.

I leaned on the railing that surrounded the skylight, trying to deduce what might have been posted down there, when I heard a familiar voice behind me.

"Careful. You wouldn't want to fall through."

And there he was again, Mr. Tall and Handsome himself—the swarthy stranger from the market. Although at this point I had to wonder if *stranger* was still the right word. We were something like acquaintances . . . weren't we?

By then I had been staring at him too long, so I fumbled out a clumsy, "Hey, you," before things got too awkward.

"And hello to you," he replied. His hair hung mostly loose, with a few well-placed braids woven through it, slightly wild and very sexy—not unlike the smile he was giving me now.

"I, um, I didn't expect to see you here tonight," I said, and instantly regretted it.

Why would I say that? It came out as either condescending or threatening, neither of which was what I was hoping for with him.

"And why wouldn't I be?" he asked.

"Oh I . . ." I grimaced, then shook my head. "I don't know what I'm saying. I've had too many glasses of peach wine tonight."

"I was only teasing," he said with a small laugh and stepped closer to me.

Was he taller somehow? Or was it the all-black ensemble stretching out his lean frame?

No, it wasn't that, I realized, when I breathed in deeply. He smelled of fog and leaves and cold springs. And I realized this was just the closest I'd ever been to him.

He was so close, I could touch him. I could reach out and hook my finger through his belt loop, running my—

"No, I know what you meant," he said, interrupting my runaway thoughts, and I jerked my gaze back up to him. "I wasn't sure if you'd be here either." He paused, his dark eyes smoldering. "But I hoped."

"Yeah?" I asked, suddenly feeling breathless. "How come?"

"Because my time in this city has come to an end." His expression turned somber. "But I wanted to say goodbye to you before I left."

"Oh?" I struggled to keep my expression neutral, trying to hide my disappointment. "Why so soon? I mean, I didn't realize it was soon."

"Neither did I. My work is finishing faster than I had thought it would. But you were definitely a bright spot in an otherwise . . . difficult trip."

I was about to protest, argue that I'd hardly spoken with him, but instead I admitted, "I could say the same thing about you."

"It's a shame that we don't have more time."

"You know, there are phones and P.O. boxes. There're ways to communicate no matter how far apart you are," I suggested.

"Communication may be near-limitless, time is unfortunately finite. My life at home is too busy for me to be a worthwhile pen pal."

"Oh." I forced a smile. "I understand."

No numbers, vague details—it painted a clear picture. He was either in a relationship or was royalty, some far-off Markis who couldn't be caught slumming it with a TOMB like me. Either way, I didn't want to be someone's dirty little secret, so maybe it was for the best that my mysterious stranger was leaving.

But somehow that knowledge didn't erase the pang of sadness I felt about his sudden departure.

"I'm glad we got to say goodbye," I said simply, because what more was there that I could really say?

"Me too." He took my hand in his—his skin cool and soft against mine—and for some reason, goose bumps stood out on my arm. "And if we don't meet again, I want you to know that I truly enjoyed knowing you while I did, Ulla." He bent down and pressed his lips—soft, with a warmth that sent heat shooting through my entire body—against the back of my hand in a simple kiss.

"You too," I murmured, in a voice that sounded smaller and lighter than my own.

With that, he turned and walked out of the room, leaving me in a stunned daze. Once he was gone, I leaned back against the railing. It was only then, as my head slowly began to clear, that it hit me.

He'd called me Ulla.

He knew my name. But I'd never told him.

And I still had no idea who *he* was.

I chased after him, running out of the drawing room and back into the ballroom. By now it was crowded, packed even, and I stood on my tiptoes, scanning the crowd for the tall stranger.

When I spotted him, my heart dropped to my stomach. It was worse than I'd thought. He was with Sumi, and they were making a beeline across the room, heading straight toward Hanna and Eliana.

Sumi with her neck tattoo, and him dark and mysterious.

The dragon and the shadow.

52

Dragons

I shouted for them, for both Hanna and Eliana, but my voice didn't carry over the music and the chatter of the crowd.

I started pushing through the crowd, pushing too hard sometimes, based on how far some of the other guests went flying back, but I had to get through.

I don't know if they heard me or if Eliana somehow sensed the danger, but when she finally looked over, she spotted them instantly. She grabbed Hanna by the hand and bolted toward the door.

Sumi and Mr. Tall raced after them, just as a ribbon snapped me across the waist. I'd been so focused on Hanna and Eliana that I hadn't noticed how close I'd gotten to the maypole, and the surprise of the ribbon slamming into my stomach caused me to double over. I fell forward onto the floor, tangling myself further into the ribbon.

The commotion I caused pushing my way through the ballroom and then getting entangled in the ribbon drew the attention of Pan and Dagny, and they rushed over to me.

"What's going on?" Pan took my hand, pulling me to my feet, while Dagny helped unwind the satin from around me.

"They're here, they ran after Hanna and Eliana, we have to stop them," I said in one long, panicked breath.

"Who? Where?" Dagny asked, but I was finally free of the maypole, so instead of answering her, I raced forward.

I didn't make it very far—only to the ballroom doors— when the guards in their shiny red uniforms encircled me.

"You have to help us!" I shrieked at them. "You have to go after them!"

A broad-shouldered guard stepped toward me. His chest was especially festooned with pins and medals, including one that listed his name as Soldatsun. "Miss, you need to calm down so you can tell us what's going on," he said in a slow, condescending tone.

"They're getting away!" I shouted. "Why didn't you stop them?"

"Miss, you need to lower your voice," he insisted firmly.

"Perhaps it's best if I explain." Dagny slid over, putting herself between me and Soldatsun. "Her sister ran off, and she needs to get her."

Dagny was simplifying the story to speed things up, but I couldn't wait any longer. I rushed forward, slamming my shoulder hard into shocked guards and knocking them to the floor.

And then I was running. I jumped over them and bounded down the stairs two or three at a time. Behind me, distantly, I heard Dagny and Pan arguing with the guards.

Between the bottom of the stairs and the main doors was

a line of guards, blocking my exit. They'd checked our bags on the way in, and they would've stopped two panicked girls.

The girls should've stopped and asked for help. Hanna would know that. Finn would've taught her.

Unless Eliana was too scared and didn't know who to trust.

She'd want to keep going. She'd run somewhere she knew, somewhere she liked, somewhere nearby.

The library.

I took off down the hall, and I pushed through the plastic sheeting and promptly tripped over broken hunks of stone flooring.

It was darker in the library than I thought it would be, with the only light coming through the skylight. That should've been enough, but the towering bookshelves, rickety scaffolding, and semi-opaque plastic sheeting made it feel strangely dark and enclosed, like a musty igloo.

Somewhere nearby—muffled through the plastic—a girl screamed, and then there was silence. I sat crouched on the floor, holding my breath and listening, hoping she would make another sound, give me a clue as to which way I should take through this renovation labyrinth.

There was a rustle of plastic—somewhere between close and far away—and that was all I had to go on, so I ran toward it.

Then I saw her, slumped on the floor behind a bookcase. Her legs were all akimbo, with one foot poking out from the shadows and into the light, so her rose-gold nail polish glittered on her toes.

"Hanna!" I gasped and fell to my knees beside her.

A trickle of blood ran down from her temple, and I gingerly put my head to her back, listening for the sound of her heartbeat.

It was there—steady, strong—but I was so focused on listening for it that I didn't notice someone come up behind me until their hand was on my shoulder.

53

pursuit

I screamed and hit back at the figure behind me. My fist collided with an arm—firm under my hand—and Pan let out a pained gasp.

"Oh, Pan! Sorry!" I said in a surprised whisper.

"What happened? Is she okay?" Dagny asked, and she was already pushing me aside as she bent down beside Hanna.

"I don't know. I found her like this."

Dagny put one hand to Hanna's forehead, and with the other gently took her wrist to check her pulse. "Did you move her?"

"No." I glanced back over my shoulder. "Where are the guards?"

"Sealing all the exits," Pan answered. "Dagny convinced them that the duo chasing after them stole expensive jewelry, so they're trying to make sure they don't escape."

"Good. I think," I said.

Hanna groaned and mumbled something about her head hurting.

"You'll be okay—" Dagny's words of comfort were cut off by a loud crash, coming from deeper in the library. A clatter of metal against stone, accompanied by a small scream.

"*Eliana*," Hanna said weakly.

I stood up, but Pan put his hand on my arm, stopping me.

"Wait for the guards. They'll be here any second," he reasoned.

I gently shrugged his hand off. "She could be in danger. I can't wait."

I pushed through the plastic sheeting, with Pan following a step behind, and ventured farther into the darkness of the library. Several feet away, around a bookcase and under some scaffolding, I discovered the cause of the crash—an overturned paint can. White paint pooled all over the floor, followed by a trail of paint puddles and smudged footprints, too smeared to discern how many sets of them there were.

The trail led through another barrier of sheeting, and when I squinted, I could make out the form of someone crumpled on the floor. I crept under the plastic, only to find that it wasn't a body at all—but an abandoned paint-soaked dress.

Suddenly Eliana jumped out from behind a bookcase, swinging a mallet as she did. I managed to grab it—gripping my fist around the rubber hammer—and I stopped it just before it collided with my skull.

Eliana let out a surprised yelp as she let go of the weapon and jumped back from me.

That's when I realized that she'd stripped down to her bralette and panties, with white paint splattered on her exposed arms and legs. Her long black hair had come free from the updo it had been styled in earlier, more paint tangled in the length of it.

"Eliana! It's me!" I set the mallet down behind me, so she would see my empty hands, palm out. "It's me. Are you okay?"

"Yeah. I think. Yeah. Sorry. I thought you were them."

Pan had followed me as I went after Eliana. He slipped off his suit jacket and started undoing the top few buttons of his shirt. He pulled it off over his head, then handed it to Eliana, leaving himself standing in a tank top undershirt.

"Thank you," she mumbled as she slipped it on. "I slipped in the paint, and I was afraid I'd leave a trail of paint for them to find me."

Faintly, the sound of footsteps pounded down the hallway, and the library quickly erupted in noise, as the red guards flowed in, searching the room and shouting their locations.

"Medic!" Dagny yelled, presumably flagging them down. "We need a medic!"

"Where did they go?" I asked Eliana, knowing we had mere moments before the guards rounded us up.

She shook her head. "I don't know. I slipped free after they hurt Hanna."

But it was already too late—the guards had found us, and there was no way we were getting away anytime soon.

54

interrogations

I collapsed back into the hard wooden chair outside the medic office and let out a shaky breath.

"She'll be okay, Ulla," Dagny repeated.

She'd been the one who went back with Hanna, the one who stayed with her after the guards came and took them back here, the one who helped her while I was being questioned.

As soon as the guards had stormed in, they'd detained us and hauled us down for questioning. Not that I could really fault them for that. They were only trying to figure out what the hell was going on and if I was a threat.

I'd answered them honestly—or at least as honestly as I could, given that a lot of what had happened didn't really make sense to me. They scoured the library and all the surrounding areas, and they were still working on a wider sweep of the Mimirin, but there was no sign of Sumi or her swarthy companion.

What we were left with wasn't much. As Soldatsun had

so eloquently put it, "Either they managed to leave here and vanish without a trace from a building surrounded by guards, *or* they were never really here in the first place."

"They were here!" I had shouted at him, sitting on the other side of the cold table in the tiny rectangle of an interrogation room. "I'm not lying!"

"I never said you were," he'd countered.

"I'm not making this up," I'd persisted. "Ask Pan. Ask Dagny. And what about Hanna? Who hurt her?"

"That's what we're trying to find out," he'd replied coolly.

And around and around we'd gone, for over an hour. Eventually they'd cleared me as a nonthreat. As soon as they let me go, I ran straight down to the medical office to find out how Hanna was doing.

Dagny had just come out of the room when I arrived. I sat back in the hard chairs outside the medical office, catching my breath and steadying my nerves, as she stood in front of me, explaining that Hanna was going to be fine. She had a bump on the head, and we'd have to watch for signs of a concussion.

"They're sure?" I asked Dagny again. "She's going to be okay?"

"Yes, they are sure." She spoke slowly, like I was a small child. "A healer came down and checked her over. She'll be fine, minus the major headache. She needs to rest for now."

"What about Pan and Eliana?" I asked.

"You're the first one I've seen."

I looked back down the hall, as if Pan and Eliana would suddenly appear. It was the only way to get into Medical—a narrow corridor at the bottom of the steps and a solitary elevator door, leading into the small but adequate medical wing.

"Are they still with the guards?" I asked Dagny.

She shrugged. "Your guess is as good as mine."

"Were you questioned?"

"Yeah, but I doubt that I was much help. I never really saw whoever it was that was after Eliana and Hanna." She lowered her gaze, pausing briefly before saying, "They told me you knew the guy."

"*Knew* is much too strong a word," I corrected her. "We talked a few times."

"I thought you didn't know anybody else in Merellä," she said pointedly.

"I don't! I don't know him at all. Not really." I sighed. "Nothing he told me about himself was true. But he knew my name."

"I'm guessing you never caught his."

I shook my head. "It doesn't matter. If he'd told me something, it probably would've been a lie anyway."

Dagny stared at me for a moment, and she opened her mouth like she meant to say something more, but the sound of approaching footsteps got our attention. A guard came down the stairs, escorting Eliana. She still wore Pan's dress shirt, baggy over her tiny frame, but they'd supplied her also with a pair of loose gray sweatpants.

"I'll leave you with your friends, then." The guard motioned toward us, then turned on his heel and left Eliana alone with us.

Eliana gave us a sheepish smile. "I didn't know where else to go, so he brought me to you."

"Yeah, of course." I sat up straighter and tapped the chair beside me. "Join us."

"Hanna will be fine, but she needs to rest now," Dagny said, answering the question before Eliana could ask it.

Eliana sat down. "Good. I knew she'd be good."

Dagny was still standing, her arms folded loosely over her chest, and she was looking down at Eliana when she asked, "How'd it go with the guards?"

"What do you mean?" Eliana asked cautiously.

"Do they know who is after you?"

"Um . . ." She shook her head, the white paint dried and clumping in her tangles of hair. "I don't know. They didn't tell me much."

"What about you?" Dagny pressed. "This is the first time you've been up close and personal with them. Did you recognize them?"

"Nope." She shook her head again. "But my memory is so messed up, I didn't expect to remember them."

"Nothing about them seemed familiar?" I asked.

"No, nothing at all." Eliana looked down at her hands in her lap, and she slowly began to peel the white paint off her fingernails and cuticles. "They didn't even say much. Not to me and not to each other."

"So, they were basically silent?" Dagny asked, and she didn't try to hide the skepticism in her voice. "Why did you run from them? If you didn't recognize them and they never spoke?"

"It was just a feeling that I had. Like a gut feeling, that I should run," Eliana replied noncommittally.

The latex paint came off in a long strip, revealing the nail polish underneath. A black lacquer.

With my eyes locked on her slender fingers, I asked, "When did you change your polish?"

"Um . . . what?" she asked in confusion.

"Your polish on your nails." I pointed to them. "They were a different color before."

"Oh, yeah, I made a quick change this afternoon." She self-consciously folded her hands together and gave a wan smile. "Needed a change for the fest."

"The thing is, Eliana, that I saw you and Hanna touching up your polish right before we left tonight. You did matching colors," I said, and she slowly lifted her eyes to meet mine. "And right now I'm willing to bet everything I've got that if we were to go back in there"—I motioned toward the room behind me—"and check Hanna's nails, they wouldn't be black."

A dark realization shifted over Dagny's face, and she moved toward us, blocking a quick escape down the hall if anyone tried to run. "Not even close," she agreed. "They're rose-gold."

Eliana looked from one of us to the other, then she relaxed back into her chair, and a cheery smile spread across her face.

"Okay. You got me. You're quick," she said with a click of her tongue. "I thought I'd pass for longer, but oh, well. I'm not Eliana. I'm her twin sister, Illaria."

55

Helpless

"Don't freak out," she said, and she smiled at me with Eliana's pouty lips and studied me with Eliana's dark caramel eyes.

But it wasn't Eliana. It wasn't her voice now—too syrupy and slightly deeper. Illaria had given up the pretense now that we had seen through her deception.

"I know this is a lot to take in, and it will all sound completely bappers." Illaria held up her hands in an attempt to placate Dagny and me. "But I truly am Eliana's sister, and I only want what's best for her. Right now she's really sick, and I want to get her home."

"That's all well and good," I said. "But why would any of that possibly require you to impersonate your sister? And where exactly is she now? Did your friends take her somewhere?"

"It all seemed easier, really," Illaria said simply, ignoring most of my questions. "If she was missing, you'd be right on our heels. But if I hung around, so that you thought that

Eliana was still here, maybe in a day or two I could miraculously remember everything and leave on my own, and there wouldn't be a need for any more confrontation. We underestimated how quickly you'd become attached to Eliana."

"That doesn't explain where she is now, or why you had to chase and kidnap her," Dagny said. "Once you found her, why couldn't you approach her and talk to her? Why'd you have to resort to sneaking around like this?"

"Because she doesn't know who I am!" Illaria's cheery mask slipped for a moment, letting her frustration escape. "She's really sick, if you hadn't noticed." With a grim smile, she shook her head. "She thinks I'm her 'shadow.'"

Damn. Illaria was the shadow. The dragon and the shadow were Sumi and Illaria.

I'd assumed that the shadow had been Mr. Tall, but Illaria was saying it wasn't him. Who was he, and what did he have to do with all of this?

And Eliana couldn't even remember that she had a twin sister, even when she was face-to-face with her? What was going on with her mind?

"What's wrong with her?" I asked.

"I don't know. That's why we need to get her back home, so we can help her," Illaria said.

"Where is home?" Dagny asked.

Illaria clicked her tongue loudly and exhaled, making a strange sound as the air whistled through her teeth. "It's far, far away, and that's all you need to know right now."

I put my hand on her arm—firm but gentle enough to show her the strength I had coiled inside me. "Maybe reconsider. We'd really like to know more."

Illaria tilted her head, narrowing her calculating eyes at me, and that's when I really noticed the differences between her and Eliana. They were *nearly* identical, but Illaria looked a little bit older somehow, and she had a small scar on her cheek, shaped like a tiny hook. She clicked her tongue again—an odd, loud sound, like a few beats of a metronome.

"I've considered, and the answer is still no," she said coolly.

"Are you ready, Illaria?" Sumi asked, and I looked over to see her standing right at the foot of the stairs that led down into the medical wing, as if she'd materialized out of thin air.

"How'd you . . ." I'd been about to ask her how she did that and where she came from, but I probably already knew as much as she was willing to share with me.

Sumi was a tracker. She'd helped us find Eliana once before—though she didn't take her then, and instead let Hanna and me go after her and bring her to our apartment. Why had she left her then? Why was she here for her now?

She moved closer to us, and that's when I noticed the psionic stun gun in her hand. I'd never been hit with one before. It wasn't supposed to be lethal, but I'd heard that it hurt like hell and then left you incapacitated.

"Where's Eliana?" I asked.

"She's gone," Sumi said, and her tone was almost apologetic. "Jem-Kruk took her home."

"*Jem-Kruk?*" I echoed softly.

The image flashed in my mind—the viny triskelion symbol on the cover of a book, as I talked with Hanna's grandfather Johan in his study. It had been called *Jem-Kruk and the Adlrivellir*, a fable for children. But it was one of those stories that Calder and the Mimirin kept locked up in the catacombs so we didn't mix up our facts with our fiction.

"Sumi, it's time for us to go," Illaria announced.

That was all the instruction Sumi had needed, apparently, because she lunged at Dagny. Dagny readied herself to block an attack, but it was impossible. A purple lightning bolt shot out from the sharp prongs of the psionic stun gun. As soon as they connected with Dagny's arm, her body went slack, and she fell backward.

I was on my feet by the time Dagny hit the floor, and I barely managed to duck out of the way of Sumi's first shot at me. I grabbed Illaria and pulled her in front of me like a shield.

That did not work out as well as I'd hoped, because Sumi instantly dropped down, crouching low, and fired the psionic stun gun between Illaria's legs. It missed Illaria entirely, and I felt it searing straight into my calf.

The pain was brief—albeit intense and white-hot—but every ounce of strength in my body drained out of me, and I collapsed onto the floor. I couldn't move or speak, and I struggled to keep my eyes open.

Sumi crouched beside me, and she gave me a sad smile. "I'm sorry it had to go this way." Her words sounded farther and farther away, like I was slipping underwater. "But if you really care about Eliana, remember to find the woman in the long white dress."

And then everything went black.

56

recovery

"I can't believe you'd let that happen!" Hanna was yelling when I came to. I slowly blinked my eyes until I could make out the stark white ceiling above me.

"Nobody let anything happen," Dagny shot back.

"Guys, calm down." That was Pan, quieter, more composed. From the corner of my eye, I could see him, holding his hands up as he tried to calm them. "You'll wake her up."

"I'm up," I said—croaked, really, since my throat was so scratchy and dry.

I started to sit up, and Pan was there, his hands on my arm and back, helping me. "Easy. Those psionic stun guns can have lingering effects."

"Don't forget that nice metallic lime taste in your mouth," Dagny added dourly, and I already knew exactly what she was talking about. It was a strangely corrosive flavor, like pennies and citrus and battery acid.

"Give her the water," Hanna suggested, and Pan hurried

to fetch me a glass of water from the end table that sat between our beds.

Based on the two hospital beds and the bland, antiseptic décor, I surmised that we were all in the medic office. It was just the four of us—Dagny sitting on the edge of Hanna's bed, Pan beside me handing me the water—but there really wasn't room for much else. It was a small room, with mint-green walls and a narrow counter along the back stocked with gauzes, potions, and other medical supplies.

"So what happened?" I asked, once I'd gulped down an entire glass of water and my voice returned to normal. "Sumi got us with that stun gun?"

"Yeah, the thing knocks you right out," Dagny said.

"That's what happened to me too. But I had the added bonus of hitting my head on the bookcase as I fell." Hanna grimaced and touched the bandage on her temple.

"Are you okay?" I asked.

"I'm fine, except for the fact that you guys let Eliana get kidnapped!" Hanna was nearly shouting by then, and tears were welling in her eyes.

Dagny groaned. "Will you stop?"

"Nobody let them take her," I told Hanna. "Not you. Not us. Maybe . . . maybe Illaria was telling the truth. She looks like her twin sister, and Eliana definitely is sick. Maybe Illaria really did just want to get her home and take care of her."

"But she didn't want to go with them!" Hanna insisted. "She was afraid of them!"

"She doesn't remember them, but that doesn't necessarily mean they're bad," I reasoned.

"Oh, yeah? Then what was with the weapons?" Hanna shot back. "That freaky lightning bolt gun? And this dagger?"

She pulled back the sheet and reached under the hem of her dress to where she had tucked a sheathed dagger into her floral garter. She tossed it on the bed in front of me.

"I got that from Sumi. She had that on her, and I grabbed it before she stunned me. I woke up before the medics came and hid it under my dress. I didn't want them to take it before I got the chance to figure out what it meant."

"I know this symbol," I whispered, tracing my fingertips across the markings embossed in the leather sheath and engraved in the metal handle. It was a viny triskelion, like the one I'd seen before. On the Jem-Kruk book in Johan's office. On the telegram with my mother's name. On the book that Calder had shown me, about the Älvolk cult and the Lost Bridge of Dimma.

"I've seen this before," I said.

Dagny walked over to look at it more closely. "Do you know what it is?"

"Kind of. But I think I know someone who knows a lot more."

myths

Pan and I sat in the tiny kitchen of Calder's suite, while he was back in his bedroom, changing out of an old velour robe into something more presentable. Not that I faulted him for answering the door wearing nothing but a bathrobe. It wasn't even nine-thirty on a Saturday, the morning after the festival, no less, so it was perfectly reasonable for him to be sleeping when we came up pounding on his door.

It had been the middle of the night by the time the medical and security staff cleared us all to go, and we were all exhausted, and Hanna was still recovering. She was leaving the next day, and I didn't want to bring her along on a possibly dangerous goose chase, so we'd decided the best thing to do would be to go to our respective homes and get some rest.

Despite my anxiety about Eliana and the whole situation, the weight of the day hit me at once, and I fell asleep relatively fast. I wanted to believe that Eliana was safe with her sister, that everything Illaria had said was true, but I wasn't about to take her word for it. The only thing I knew for sure was that Eliana was sick and I had to be sure that she was okay.

I'd called Pan this morning at nine—which was the soonest Dagny would allow me to start making calls; anything earlier would be blasphemous. I had only been looking for Calder's address, but he offered to go with me, so I took him up on it.

Hanna begged to go with, but I managed to convince her to stay behind with Dagny and pack up her stuff. Her dad would be here in a few hours, and I reminded her how upset she would be if she left anything important behind, like any of the crafts she'd made with Eliana, and that finally got through to her.

Calder's apartment was located just outside of the Mimirin. Technically it was part of the institution itself, but it was a boxy addition that had been part of the midcentury renovations. These had been built as cheap housing for staff, and that was exactly how they looked—cheap, efficient, stark, unloved.

I didn't know what the other places looked like (although I imagined that they were mostly identical), but Calder's was a tiny two-room apartment. It had a nauseating amount of pea-green fixtures and accents, and there was a great deal of clutter in the form of books, papers, and dusty knick-knacks.

"Much better." Calder came out of his bedroom, having changed into an oddly formal monogrammed pajama set. He ran his hand through his silvery hair and cast a derisive glance at where Pan and I sat at his kitchen table.

"We're sorry again for waking you up so early," I said. "We really appreciate you talking to us like this."

"And I appreciate sleeping in on Saturdays, but here we are." He smiled thinly at me, then went about making himself a cup of tea. He picked up the teakettle from the stove—he'd put it on when he let us in—and poured the hot water over the infuser in his mug.

He turned back around to face us, leaning against the counter and letting his tea steep. "Out with it, then. What is it that you needed so badly this morning?"

"I need you to tell me everything you can about this." I'd been carrying Sumi's stolen dagger in my bag, and I pulled it out and set it on the table. "I need to know about the Älvolk and where they are."

He stared at it for a long moment, not saying anything, and then took a long sip of his tea. "They're not supposed to be anywhere anymore."

"I know, but they are." I tapped the blade. "This was taken from someone last night, someone who helped kidnap my friend."

"True Älvolk are said only to reside in the First City," he said finally. "Although I suppose the followers could reside anywhere. I haven't looked closely at the weapon, but a cursory glance suggests it has markings of an authentic artifact. Someone who had that and not one of the cheap copies that came later, that sounds more like a true believer."

"First City. You mean Áibmoráigi?" I asked.

Calder nodded. "That is the purported home of the Älvolk, so that would be the first place I'd look for them."

"That's somewhere in Scandinavia, right?" Pan asked.

"*Somewhere* being the operative word," Calder said with a wry chuckle. "The location has been lost or hidden—there are stories claiming both. It was done after the Lost Bridge of Dimma fell, and after the Grændöden, the Green Death, wiped out many of the tribe."

"So . . . wait. Is it a real city? Or is it a myth?" I asked.

"Can't it be both?" Calder asked. "I always thought that it was a mixture. It had been a real city, but now it's empty and buried in ice."

"Hasn't anyone tried to find it?" I asked.

"Of course they have. All the tribes have sent expeditions over the years. But as time went on, and the fortunes grew smaller, the search for the First City and the Lost Bridge seemed unimportant. There were rumors that the Omte had a lead on them many years ago, but if anything came of it, they wouldn't be ones to tell."

"So, if I needed to get to Áibmoráigi, how would I do that?" I asked.

He laughed again. "You wouldn't. I don't think it exists anymore. But if you want to find out where it used to be, I would suggest you start with the Omte. They tried to find it longer than anyone else."

"Is there anything else we could go on?" Pan asked. "Any advice at all?"

"I do have some advice, but I doubt you'll take it." Calder shook his head. "Don't go."

Departure

Considering how appalled Hanna had been by the idea of going back to Förening, her reaction to Finn showing up was pretty surprising. All morning long—aside from the brief break I had when I went over to Calder's apartment—I'd been listening to Hanna complain and pout about going home.

But the second Finn got out of his car, Hanna burst into tears and raced down the steps to meet him. He scooped her up, easily lifting her off the ground while they hugged.

I knew how much Hanna loved her family, but it was startling to witness such a transformation happen so quickly. Sometimes I forgot that, despite all her attempts to seem mature and fit in with me and Dagny (and the rather maternal role she'd taken on with Eliana), Hanna was still just a kid. A scared, obviously homesick kid.

Fortunately, even with all the crying (mostly Hanna, but I shed a few, along with Dagny), the goodbyes went fairly fast. Last night, after we'd gotten back from the medic, I'd called Finn and told him about Hanna's recent injury, and he took it in stride. Once he got here and saw it with his own eyes he had a lot of questions, but Dagny swooped in with her biology expertise and medical experience, and she put him at ease. It also helped that Hanna owned up to her mistakes in the whole situation—namely running to the library instead of going to the guards for help.

"I know that things got dicey at the end, but I still want to thank you for helping out so much with Hanna," Finn said, during the few minutes we had alone.

We had finished loading up his vehicle when Hanna realized that she'd forgotten her phone charger back in the apartment. Dagny went with her to help her find it, while I waited outside with Finn.

"I hope you know that I did my best to keep her safe." I stared down at the road, kicking absently at a pebble with my bare foot. "I'm really sorry that she got hurt."

"I know that, Ulla," he said gently. "I try to protect my family as much as I'm able, but the world is a dangerous place. The only way to truly keep my kids out of danger is to keep them hidden away, but that's not what life is for. I want them to be part of the world, and that means sometimes they'll get hurt. I have to prepare them the best I can, and surround them with folks like you."

I smiled at him. "Thanks."

"Do you still think you'll be coming back to Förening when you're done here?" Finn asked.

"I really don't know when I'll be back. I have some things I have to take care of first."

"Just keep us in the loop. We always like to hear how you're doing, and our door is always open for you."

Hanna returned and then it was another ten minutes of hugging, crying, and promises to call. When they finally left, it was bittersweet watching them drive off. I would miss Hanna now, the same way I missed Niko and Emma and all the kids. But it would be a lie if I said that things wouldn't be easier here without Hanna, especially with what I had ahead of me.

As soon as they were gone, I ran back up to the apartment to start packing for myself.

"You're really doing this?" Dagny called up to me. She stood at the bottom of the ladder below my loft, and though I wasn't looking at her, I knew her arms were crossed over her chest.

I knelt on the floor beside my mattress, packing up the last of my stuff. "You know that I am, and you know why I have to."

I'd already gathered up all my clothes and a few other things I needed to take with me. All I had left really were my toiletries in the bathroom and my important papers. In the drawer in my nightstand, I'd saved everything I knew about my parents and the Älvolk.

Most of what I had came from Mrs. Tulin and the package of things she'd sent after Mr. Tulin died. The few pictures they'd taken of me when I was a baby, the medical records from my first few doctor's appointments, Mr. Tulin's handwritten account of the night I had been left at their house, and a three-by-three-inch painting he had done of the woman who had abandoned me there.

The woman who might be my mother. Her hair was shorter and darker than mine, and her cheeks were red and windburned from the cold. She had the look of a soldier after war, battle-weary and haunted.

There were a few other things I'd added to my meager collection since I'd been here. The telegram I'd found mentioning Orra Fågel, the maps and diagrams I'd copied from the Älvolk book, and my Moleskine notebook with my handwritten notes about everything I had learned in the Mimirin.

I grabbed a pen and opened the notebook, preparing to add what Calder had told us about Áibmoráigi. It hadn't been much, but I never knew what would be helpful later on.

But when I flipped to the next blank page—which I'd marked with a ribbon attached to the spine—I found that it wasn't blank anymore. A message had been scrawled across the paper in bold handwriting that I didn't recognize.

> If you ever want to say hello—to me or to
> Eliana—come find us. X Jem-Kruk

I ran my fingers over the long-dry ink, unable to decide which was the most pressing question—*how, when,* or *why* he'd written that note for me. But I quickly decided there was an entirely different question that mattered more: *Where* was he?

There was a knock at the front door, and on her way to answer it, Dagny yelled up to me, "Ulla, Pan is here!"

"I'll be right down."

I closed my journal and carefully placed it in my backpack with the other papers. Dagny let Pan in, and they made small talk about Hanna's departure, while I did one last sweep of my room, making sure that I'd gotten every last earring or electronic charger.

I slung my backpack over my shoulder and climbed down

the ladder to join them. Pan grinned when he saw me, and my stomach flipped when I remembered that I was about to take a very long road trip with him.

"Are you ready?" I asked him.

"Yeah, I think so. I already put my bags in the vehicle, and I called my boss and my landlord this morning, so everything is set."

"You guys are both crazy for doing this," Dagny said with a sigh. "But it's a good kinda crazy. I wish that I could go with you, to find Eliana and to help you find the truth about your parents."

"Elof needs you here," Pan said. "We understand that."

"Yeah, and if you're not here helping him figure out what the deal is with my blood and Eliana's blood, we might never know for sure who we are," I reminded her.

"I know, I know," she said. "Where are you guys headed first?"

"Well, we're starting by visiting the Omte," I said.

"I wish you both the best of luck. And you'll call me if you need anything?" she asked.

"I'll call you even if I don't need anything," I said. She rolled her eyes, and I pulled her into a hug. "Take care of yourself, Dag."

"You too."

When we separated, I looked up at Pan and gave him a nervous smile. "You ready for this?"

He nodded. "Yeah. I'm ready for anything."

TRIBAL FACTS

Kanin—(symbol White Rabbit)

The Kanin are the largest tribe of trolls, with a population approaching fifty thousand. They are also one of the wealthiest tribes, and with their specially trained guard known as the Högdragen, they are arguably one of the most powerful.

The Kanin are also the oldest tribe of trolls. They are descended from the original trolls that traveled from Scandinavia during the Viking Age and founded the city of Doldastam. The tribe officially split in two when the ruling brothers Norund the Younger and Jorund the Elder fought about moving south. In circa 1200 CE Norund stayed in the north, calling his tribe the Kanin and strengthening the city of Doldastam, while his brother went south and established the Vittra tribe and their capital, Ondarike.

Like many of the other tribes, the Kanin still practice changelings, but thanks to their prosperity and large population, they do it more infrequently than they once did. On average, only one out of every ten babies born to a Markis and Marksinna are left with a human host family.

While the Kanin do have some of the minor psychokinetic

abilities trolls are known for, like persuasion and rapid healing, their most powerful ability is that of color-changing. Like a hyper-chameleon's, their skin can change color to blend in with its surroundings, making them nearly impossible to spot.

Doldastam is the capital and largest city of the Kanin, located in the northeastern province of Manitoba in Canada. It was chosen because of its secluded location several miles away from Hudson Bay. When it was originally settled, the subarctic winters meant that the city was entirely isolated from the rest of the world.

The tribe managed to survive thanks to their dependency on changelings sent to the prosperous human cities, as well as their Gotland rabbits and Tralla horses. The Gotland rabbits could handle the harsh cold and reproduced quickly, making the Kanin diet largely carnivorous until they were able to properly set up the community and establish a garden year-round.

Now the Gotland rabbits are revered symbols of the Kanin's perseverance, adaptability, and quick thinking. White rabbits are still bred and owned by many of the Kanin citizens in Doldastam, and now eating them is considered taboo.

The Tralla horses were the only things strong and hearty enough to traverse through the snow in the winters, allowing the trolls to do some trading with the humans. The only road out of Doldastam leads to Churchill, over twenty miles away, and before vehicles were commonplace, the Trallas were the only way the trolls connected to the outside world.

Despite the cold winters, Doldastam enjoys a warm summer and a plethora of wildlife, along with one of the best spots in the world to view the aurora borealis. In fact, the palace in Doldastam was built so the King and Queen's chambers are in the tallest tower to take in the most encompassing view of the beautiful northern lights.

The current royalty in Doldastam is King Linus Fredrick, son of the Markis and Marksinna Dylan and Eva Berling, cousin of his predecessor King Evert Strinne, great-grandson of the beloved King Erland Strinne, and the eighth monarch of the Strinne Dynasty. He married his bride on the twenty-eighth of June in 2017, Queen Ariel Lynn, daughter of Markis Edwyn and Elsa Nylen, and sister to Marksinna Delilah Nylen.

Linus Fredrick, King of the Kanin kingdom, Markis of the Houses Berling and Strinne, Ruler of the Frozen North, the Peaceful, is the thirtieth recognized monarch of the Kanin kingdom. He took the throne on the eighth of June in 2014, after the murder of King Evert and the subsequent execution of his murderers during the Invasion of Doldastam.

Despite his rough start, King Linus has had a rather quiet, peaceful reign, and he plans to continue the prosperity the Kanin are known for.

Trylle—(symbol Green Vines)

The Trylle are the second-largest tribe by population, and they are also regarded as the most peaceful. They practice changelings more than any other tribe, although in recent years under Queen Wendy's reign, the practice has lessened some.

The Trylle tribe was established in 1510 CE when they split off from the Kanin kingdom. The Markis Aldaril became fed up with the inept Kanin King Harald the Coward. Aldaril went south, taking many wealthy and powerful nobles with him, and in establishing the Trylle kingdom he became the first king. He also founded the city of Förening along the Mississippi River, although he originally chose the town of Köldden to be the Trylle capital.

A hundred years ago, Trylle royalty grew tired of the extreme winters of Canada and the relative close proximity to the Skojare capital, Storvatten. Queen Constance Dahl reestablished the more southern Förening as the capital in Minnesota, and she built a palace and all of the governing offices there. As a result, their palace and town are rather modern compared to those of the other tribes.

The Trylle frequently use changelings, requiring them to have many trackers, and therefore the largest army. While the army may not be as skilled as the Kanin's or as strong as the Omte's, they are still considered a force to be reckoned with.

While physically not as powerful as some of the other tribes, most notably the Omte and the Vittra, the Trylle are the most powerful when it comes to psychokinesis. Many of the offspring born to the Markis and Marksinna have abilities that range from controlling fire to moving objects with their minds to precognition.

Their powers have been dwindling over the years, and many believe that it's because of their separation from nature. Historically, the Trylle have been the tribe most connected to the environment, but their pursuit of wealth and treasure has caused a growing schism in their culture.

The current royalty in Förening is Queen Wendy Luella, daughter of the Trylle Queen Elora Dahl and the Vittra King Oren Elsing, and the sixth monarch under the Mógilian Dynasty going back to King Mógil Loren Kroner in the nineteenth century. She is the product of an attempt to align the Trylle and Vittra, making her the only monarch with mixed blood in all the five kingdoms. Queen Wendy was the heir apparent to both tribes after the deaths of her parents, and she chose to serve as the Queen of the Trylle kingdom and allow her stepmother, Sara Elsing, to continue ruling as Queen of the Vittra.

She married her bridegroom on the first of May in 2010, King Loki Nikolas, son of former Trylle Chancellor Alrik and Vittra Marksinna Olivia Staad. With his position as a high-ranking Vittra Markis, their union further secured an alliance between the Trylle and the Vittra.

The son of HRM Wendy and Loki, Crown Prince Oliver Matthew Loren, was born on the sixth of October in 2010, and he will ascend the throne when his mother steps down or upon her death.

Wendy Luella, Queen of the Trylle kingdom, Princess of the Vittra kingdom, Marksinna of the House of Dahl, Ruler of the Riverlands, the Princess of Red and Green, the Mixed-Blood Queen, is the twenty-second recognized monarch of the Trylle. She took the throne on the fourteenth of January in 2010, after the death of her mother and before the execution of her father during the War for the Princess.

Queen Wendy had a tumultuous beginning to her reign, starting with the War for the Princess against the Vittra in 2010, and allying herself with the Vittra and Skojare for the Invasion of Doldastam in 2014. Despite that, she has been working to increase the prosperity of those she reigns over. She has also been developing programs to alleviate the Trylle's dependence on changelings and lessen class distinction.

Omte—(symbol Amber Vulture)

The Omte are a moderately populated tribe, with numbers speculated to be around twenty thousand worldwide, although the Omte's secrecy and antisocial nature make it hard to know for sure.

The Omte split off from the Vittra tribe in circa 1280 CE. Dag, the grandson of the Vittra Queen Bera the Strong, was an ogre, and he thought the Vittra favored the smaller hobgoblins and more conventionally attractive "humanoid" trolls. He took the ogres south, and they crowned him the first King of the Omte when he established the capital city of Fulaträsk.

The only attachment they have to the Old World is their bearded vultures. Trolls had discovered them after a battle in Europe a thousand years ago. The ogres killed many enemies, and the bearded vultures, who survive mainly on bones, helped to clean up their mess. The ogres found that very useful, and they soon domesticated the birds. When they split off from the Vittra, they took only the ogres and the vultures with them.

Since King Dag the First, they have had forty monarchs—much more than any other tribe. The high turnover rate among Omte monarchs is believed to be due to their violent lifestyle, compromised immune systems, and lower intelligence.

Deliberately attempting to separate themselves from the other tribes, the Omte settled farther south than anyone else. While most tribes preferred weather that was like that in their homelands of Scandinavia, the Omte chose the swamps of Louisiana.

Fulaträsk is the capital and largest city in the Omte kingdom, and it has a population of over six thousand, housing most of the kingdom population in a solitary city. It is hidden deep within the wetlands, where most of the inhabitants live in large tree houses or houseboats.

Despite their contrary disposition, the Omte still attempt to leave changelings whenever possible. Their appearance is often disproportionate, with oversized heads, unmatched eye size, and lopsidedness, so changelings are chosen from the most humanoid offspring from high-ranking families.

While the Omte lack the psychokinesis that other tribes possess, they make up for it in brute strength. They are also the only tribe to have ogres, and even the Omte that are more human-looking tend to be very large in stature.

Throughout their history, the Omte have intermittently attempted to align themselves with other tribes, but it usually ends up in a skirmish or even war. Traditionally, they have been very combative with other tribes, but as of late they have preferred to simply isolate and keep entirely to themselves. The other tribes rarely hear from them, and most invitations to visit other kingdoms are turned down by the royal family.

The current royalty in Fulaträsk is Queen Regent Bodil Freya, daughter of Markis Boris and Marksinna Freya Fågel, and widow to King Thor Osvald, son of King Draug and Queen Märta Elak. She became Queen when King Thor the Guardian married his bride on the first of September in 2006, and she became the acting monarch and Queen Regent upon her husband's death on the thirteenth of August in 2011. The Omte kingdom uses male primogeniture succession, so Queen Bodil can only rule until the Crown Prince is of age.

The only son of HRM Thor and Bodil, Crown Prince Furston Thor, will ascend the throne upon his eighteenth birthday, the fourth of March in the year 2028. Since he was only a year old at the time of his father's death, his mother has ruled in his stead as the Queen Regent.

Furston Thor, Crown Prince of the Omte kingdom, Markis of the Houses Elak and Fågel, Ruler of the Untamed Swamps, the Child King, the Fatherless Prince, when he is crowned, will be the eighth King under the Torian Dynasty, which began with King Tor Elak the Vengeful during the Omte civil war at the turn of the twentieth century.

Vittra—(symbol Red Cougar)

The Vittra were once a great tribe, but their numbers along with their powers have been lessening. Many blame it on the cruel reigns of many of the monarchs of the recent Ottarn Dynasty, but they have also been plagued by idiopathic infertility, with increased frequency in the past century.

The Vittra are one of the oldest tribes. They broke off from the Kanin around 1200 CE, when feuding brothers Norund the Younger and Jorund the Elder disagreed about staying in the north. Jorund went south, and he established the Vittra kingdom in Ondarike. He took all of the strongest trolls with him, leading to the ogres and hobgoblins in the Vittra population, until Dag the First split off with the ogres and formed the Omte kingdom.

While the Vittra do possess some psychokinesis, their ability to heal quickly and their superior physical strength are what they are most known for. Despite being the second-oldest tribe, the Vittra have had the fewest monarchs, in large part due to their supernatural longevity. The last king, Oren Elsing, believed himself to be immortal until his execution.

The Vittra are much like the Omte in many ways, both in their excessive strength and their aggression. Like most of the other tribes, the royal families once relied heavily on changelings. Originally it was done to ensure the safety of their offspring, but over the years it primarily became a means to support themselves with human wealth while living as isolated from humanity as they can.

While most Vittra trolls are considered very attractive by human standards, more than fifty percent of their offspring are born as hobgoblins, and nearly a quarter of their attractive populations are born with standard genetic dwarfism. Hobgoblins are short, powerful, dim-witted Vittra with slimy skin and a rank stench, an appearance that matches more typical folklore representations of trolls.

In the last century, the Vittra's inability to consistently produce offspring suitable for changelings has greatly drained their wealth. As a result, the Vittra grew more violent and warmongering, seeking to take the wealth from other tribes. Their main target was the Trylle, chosen because of their larger kingdom and their proximity, with the Trylle capital of Förening being close to the Vittra kingdom, until the recent alliance between the Queen of the Trylle and Princess of the Vittra, Wendy Luella, with her stepmother, Queen of the Vittra, Sara Adrielle.

Ondarike is the capital of the Vittra, located in northern Colorado in a dense forest in the mountains. Most of the population lives inside the sprawling mansion compound that serves as the palace, although the hobgoblins do prefer to live in huts in the ground.

Cougars became the symbol of the Vittra after they settled in

Colorado. Queen Bera the Strong, who helped establish Ondarike, was attracted to the power and grace of the cougar. For centuries after that, cougars roamed the halls of the palace like semi-feral guard dogs. They were never fully domesticated, though, and attacks on hobgoblins weren't uncommon.

It wasn't until King Oren the Cruel's cougar turned on him that that policy changed. He had all the Vittra cougars rounded up and exterminated, and he banned anyone from owning them. Many of the Vittra townsfolk were greatly upset by this, but there was little recourse for civilians under Oren's tyrannical rule.

The current royalty in Ondarike is Queen Sara Adrielle, daughter of Markis Luden and Marksinna Sarina Vinter, and widow of King Oren Bodvar, son of King Bodvar II and Queen Grendel Elsing. She became Queen when King Oren the Cruel married his bride on the second of November in 1996. Upon King Oren's death during the War for the Princess on the fourteenth of January in 2010, his daughter, the heir apparent Wendy Luella, stepped aside and allowed Sara Adrielle to continue ruling as Queen of the Vittra.

Wendy Luella, the only child of King Oren the Cruel and the Queen of the Trylle, Elora, took the throne for the Trylle kingdom on the fourteenth of January in 2010. She maintains the title as Princess of the Vittra, but she has abdicated from the role in everything but name.

Sara Adrielle, Queen of the Vittra kingdom, Marksinna of the House of Vinter, Ruler of the Mountainlands, the Light Queen that Follows the Dark, the First of the Sarafina Dynasty, is the twenty-first monarch of the Vittra. The Ottarn Dynasty, which went back to King Ottar the Awful in the year 1800, died with her husband, and Queen Sara has been ruling as a solo monarch since the fifteenth of January in 2010.

Under Queen Sara's solo reign, the Vittra have seen a great turn in their way of life. Their close alignment with the Trylle has brought in monetary and social aid, with teachers and healers moving to Ondarike to help with the Vittra children and fertility issues.

She's working tirelessly with the Chancellor Ludlow Svartalf, her hobgoblin half brother, on civil rights issues and helping to close the gaps of the caste system and easing prejudices. The In-hemsk Project—an effort to reintegrate trolls of mixed blood and exiled trolls back into society—has largely happened as a result of the Queen and the Chancellor's zealous work. They realize that their way of life will go extinct if they do not open their arms to all other trolls, regardless of race, orientation, or title.

Skojare—(symbol Blue Fish)

The Skojare are by far the smallest tribe, with roughly five thousand trolls left in the kingdom. They are also one of the more isolated tribes, sticking more to the "old ways" than some of the more progressive tribes like the Trylle or the Vittra.

One of the main reasons for their smaller population is their lack of changelings. They are the only tribe to have never used changelings, and as such, they've historically had a much worse infant mortality rate, especially in the earlier years when first settling into North America and medical treatment was scarce.

While most tribes have powers of psychokinesis and superior strength tied to their higher-ranking bloodlines, one-third of the Skojare have gills. It is that attribute that has helped them survive but has also prevented them from leaving changelings, because humans won't overlook a baby with gills.

The Skojare kingdom dates back to circa 1300 CE, when Aun the Blue broke off from the Kanin tribe, heading south from Doldastam for a warmer water source. He took all the gilled trolls with him and established the Skojare tribe and founded Storvatten. He even constructed the beautiful, unique sprawling palace on Lake Superior, where many of the residents reside.

Since they have a more open area on the water, instead of hidden among trees, they do have specialized guards that help cloak their palace with psychokinetic powers.

In the past, their cloaking abilities were unparalleled. Legend has it that long ago a Queen was able to enchant a secret magical lake and hide it among the humans, and some Skojare still search for it to this day. Many have claimed to have been there, but few remember the details.

The most notable feature about the Skojare is their appearance. Other tribes tend to be darker: olive skin; usually brown, green, or gray eyes; brown to black curly hair. The Skojare are pale with blue eyes and blond hair, although their hair is as curly and wild as that of the trolls in other tribes.

They are a primarily aquatic tribe, relying on fishing to sustain them through the long winters. Fishing was also how they managed to support themselves, by trading and bartering with humans for money.

Many years ago, the Skojare used to pillage and pirate to collect resources and treasures, sometimes working with Vikings. In fact, it was the Skojare who originally decided that the trolls should settle in North America after journeying across the sea with the Vikings. All these travels allowed them to build up a stockpile of sapphires and precious gemstones, which is how the Skojare royalty have supported themselves for so long without the influx of riches that comes from changelings in the other kingdoms.

Now the Skojare are considered very quiet and peaceful, due in large part to their small population and nearly nonexistent army. For the most part they keep to themselves, although they do often host parties in the palace, inviting royalty from all over the troll kingdoms.

The current royalty in Storvatten is King Mikko Rune, son of King Rune the Iron Fish and Queen Lucia Biâelse, and the fifth monarch under the Rolfian Dynasty dating back to King Rolf of the House of Leif in the nineteenth century. He married his bride, Queen Linnea Lisbet, orphaned daughter of Markis Devin and Marksinna Ola Ahlstrom and granddaughter of Marksinna Lisbet Ahlstrom, on the twenty-second of June in 2013.

The marriage was arranged by King Rune the Iron Fish before his death, and Queen Linnea was just sixteen when she wed King Mikko, a controversial wedding throughout the kingdoms. While it had once been custom for brides to be chosen as young as fourteen, in the last century most tribes have done away with that practice and insist that bride and groom must be at least eighteen.

The daughter of HRM Mikko and Linnea, Crown Princess Lisbet Mika—affectionately known around the palace as Princess Libby—was born on the third of April in 2017, and she will ascend the throne when her father steps down or upon his death. The Skojare have absolute primogeniture succession, so Princess Libby will rule as the eldest living child regardless of whether or not the King has a son in the future.

Mikko Rune, King of the Skojare kingdom, Markis of the House of Biâelse, Ruler of the Great Lakes, the Absolved King, is the twenty-fourth monarch of the Skojare. He took the throne on the thirteenth of September in 2012, upon the death of his father, King Rune.

King Mikko's rule has had a few controversies, most notably when his brother Prince Kennet got involved in espionage with Kanin traitors. Even with the speed bumps, Mikko's tenure as King is still viewed much more favorably than his father's, who ruled with an iron fist. The King and Queen are trying for a gentler, kinder rule for the Skojare kingdom, and they're working to make strong alliances with the other tribes.

GLOSSARY

Abisko National Park—a national park in the Arctic Circle in northern Sweden. It is located over an hour's drive away from Kiruna Airport.

Adlrivellir—name of a legendary troll kingdom.

Áibmoráigi—the oldest troll establishment on Earth. It is located somewhere in Scandinavia, but its exact location has been lost since before 1000 CE. Frequently referred to as the "First City."

akutaq—a traditional Inuit food often referred to as "Eskimo ice cream." It is not creamy ice cream as we know it, but a concoction made from reindeer fat or tallow, seal oil, freshly fallen snow or water, fresh berries, and sometimes ground fish. It is whipped together by hand so that it slowly cools into foam.

álfar—name given to the trolls from the legendary kingdom of Alfheim.

Alfheim—a mythological realm. To humans, the legend is that it is one of the Nine Worlds and home of the Light Elves in Norse mythology. To trolls, the legend is that it is a utopian kingdom hidden across the Lost Bridge of Dimma.

Älvolk—a legendary group of monk-like trolls, who guard the Lost Bridge of Dimma, along with many troll secrets and artifacts.

angakkuq—an Inuit word that roughly translates to "shaman" or "witch."

ärtsoppa—a Scandinavian soup made of yellow peas, carrots, and onions. Traditional versions have ham, but vegetarian trolls skip that.

attack on Oslinna—a surprise military attack by the Vittra on the small Trylle village of Oslinna, Wyoming, during the War for the Princess. It left the city destroyed since January 2010.

attempted assassination of Chancellor Iver—the attempt on the life of the Kanin Chancellor Iver Aven by the Queen's guard Konstantin Black in January 2010. It was an attack unrelated to the War for the Princess. It was eventually tied to Viktor Dålig and his coup against the Kanin monarchy that lasted over a decade and ended in the Invasion of Doldastam.

Aurenian Ballroom—a grand ballroom in the Mimirin named after the old Vittra King Auren.

Battle for the Bridge—a legendary battle that took place in Áibmoráigi over the Lost Bridge of Dimma that occurred over a thousand years ago. In old myths, it is known as the Vígríðabifröst.

Bedtime Stories for Trolls of All Ages—a children's book of troll fables and stories. It contains an origin story about how all the tribes separated.

beetroot salad—a common Scandinavian dish. It is traditionally made with diced beetroots, apples, vinegar, herbs, olive oil, red onions, yogurt, and lemon zest.

blodseider magick—a type of taboo occult practice in extremist troll sects. The practice of *seiðr* is believed to be a form of magic relating to both the telling and shaping of the future.

Candida viridi—a fungal infection that afflicts trolls, similar to *Candida auris* in humans. The differences being that *C. viridi* is hardy enough to thrive in cold temperatures, and it leaves a greenish tint to the skin of the affected individuals. The fungus causes invasive candidiasis infections in the bloodstream, the central nervous system, and internal organs. With modern medicine it is easily curable, but without proper treatment it is often deadly. Troll historians believe that *C. viridi* is what caused the Green Death (Grændöden) in the thirteenth century, which wiped out most of the trolls that remained in Scandinavia.

Catacombs of Fables—a mazelike vault in the basement of the Mimirin that houses many of the fictional stories of the past, so as not to confuse fact with fiction.

changeling—a child secretly exchanged for another. For trolls, it's an ancient practice, with elite royal families leaving their babies in place of wealthy human babies. The humans unknowingly raise the troll baby, ensuring that the troll will have the best chance of success, with fine education, top health care, and rights to tremendous wealth. When they are of age, they are retrieved by trolls known as trackers, and the changelings are brought back to live with their tribes in their kingdom. The Trylle and the Kanin are the only two tribes that still widely practice changelings.

chromosomes—DNA molecules with part or all of the genetic material of an organism.

Churchill, Manitoba—a small human town in Canada. One must stop in Churchill if venturing to either Doldastam, Manitoba, or Iqaluit, Nunavut, and it may be the easiest way to get to Iskyla, Nunavut, as well.

cloudberries—a plant native to alpine and arctic regions, producing amber-colored edible fruit similar to the raspberry or blackberry. It is commonly used in Scandinavian pies and jams.

Dålig Revolt—the aftermath that took place after the unmarried Kanin King Elliot Strinne died unexpectedly in 1999 without a clear heir. The Chancellor appointed Elliot's cousin Evert Strinne to the throne, overlooking Elliot's sister Sybilla and her three daughters. Sybilla and her husband, Viktor Dålig, contested Evert's appointment, and they staged a revolt that left four men dead, and the Dålig family was exiled.

docent—a member of the teaching staff immediately below professorial rank. In the U.S., it is often a volunteer position, but it can be paid or done in exchange for room and board. At the Mimirin, docents are paid a minimal stipend in addition to room and board.

dödstämpel—a form of martial arts practiced by trolls. The name means "death punch" in Swedish.

dökkt rúgbraud—a Scandinavian dark rye bread.

Doldastam, Manitoba—the capital and largest city of the Kanin kingdom, located in Manitoba, Canada, near Hudson Bay. The Kanin royal family live in the palace there, and the city is surrounded by a stone wall. The population is a little over twelve thousand as of 2019.

Eftershom, Montana—a small Trylle village located in the mountains near Missoula. It is nestled in the convergence of several mountain ranges in western Montana. The terrain is notoriously rough and the winters are brutal. When it was originally settled by the Trylle, a Markis asked, "Why do we stop here?" And the leader answered, *"Eftersom vi har gått tillräckligt långt,"* which roughly translates to, "Because we have gone far enough."

ekkálfar—an old term used for "troll."

Eldvatten—a very strong alcohol made by the Omte. The name literally translates to "firewater." It is also known as Omte moonshine, and it is used in Omte sangria.

ex nihilo nihil fit—a Latin phrase meaning "nothing comes from nothing." It is the motto of the Mimirin.

First City, the—See *Áibmoráigi*.

Förening, Minnesota—the capital and largest city of the Trylle kingdom. It is a compound in the bluffs along the Mississippi River in Minnesota where the palace is located.

Forsa River—the river that runs through Merellä. It is a wide stream that slices the city in half and meets the ocean. The name means "rushing stream."

Frey—a mythological figure. To humans, he is known as the legendary Norse deity of virility and fair weather. To trolls, he is a troll from Alfheim who stayed behind to help rebuild their kingdom after the Battle for the Bridge. He is a prominent figure in the Älvolk cult, the Freyarian Älvolk.

Freyarian Älvolk—the followers of the Älvolk who began following the more extreme teachings of Frey. See *Frey*.

Fulaträsk, Louisiana—the capital city of the Omte, spread out in the trees and swamps of the Atchafalaya Basin in Louisiana.

geitvaktmann—a goat watchman, similar to a shepherd or a peurojen.

giant woolly elk—a name that trolls have given the line of Irish elk they breed. See *Irish elk*.

gräddtårta—a Swedish cream-layer cake. Common during Midsommar.

Grændöden—a plague. See *Green Death*.

Green Death, the—a mass death of thirteenth-century Scandinavian trolls. Troll historians believe that it was an outbreak of *C. viridi*.

häxdoktor—a witch doctor or shaman.

Heimskaga—a collection of ancient troll history, all written by the same troll historian, Hilde Nilsdotter. The name is an anglicization of the Norse words *heim* and *saga*, meaning "the world's saga."

Hilde Nilsdotter—the Scandinavian historian and author of the *Heimskaga*. She was born a Marksinna in 1190 in Sweden. Her husband was a troll ambassador, and they moved to Doldastam in 1211, shortly after their marriage. She used her travels to compile the folklore and histories of her kind, before her death in 1254. She had two children who lived until adulthood: Knut and Norri, the latter of which has lineage that can be traced down to the most recent Kanin dynasty, Strinne, up to and including Linus Berling.

hnefatafl—a family of ancient Nordic and Celtic strategy board games played on a checkered or latticed game board with two armies of uneven numbers.

hobgoblin—an ugly troll that stands no more than three feet tall, known to be born only into the Vittra tribes. They are distinct from Vittra trolls with more humanoid features and attractive appearance who have dwarfism. Hobgoblins are slow-witted, possess a supernatural strength, and have slimy skin with a pimply complexion.

host family—the family that a changeling is left with. They are chosen based on their ranking in human society, with their wealth being the primary consideration. The higher-ranked the member of troll society, the more powerful and affluent the host family their changeling is left with.

Hudson Bay—a large bay in Canada. Doldastam is located on the Manitoba side, with Iqaluit across the bay on the Nunavut side.

Information Styrelse—a board of information (similar to a board of education) in the Mimirin. These boards are subordinate only to their members and the Korva, and they preside over the Mästares and the teaching staff (including docents). The name comes from the Swedish word *styrelse*, meaning "board of directors." The word *information* is the same in both Swedish and English. Each of these boards has thirteen members.

Inhemsk Project—an effort undertaken by the Mimirin in Merellä to help trolls of mixed blood find their place in the troll world. Though it is primarily run by the Vittra, it is open to trolls from any of the five tribes. The main purpose is to combat the dwindling populations of the trolls (due both to issues like infertility among the Vittra and Skojare, as well as changelings choosing to live among the humans or being exiled because of their mixed race). The effort also seeks to reconnect trolls with their heritage and pass along history and culture.

Invasion of Doldastam—the final battle in the Kanin Civil War that ended the war in May 2014. The Dålig supporters were led by Viktor and Karmin Dålig allied with the Kanin guards and the Omte, and the Strinne supporters were led by Bryn Aven and Mikko Biâelse allied with the Skojare, Trylle, Vittra, and many of the Kanin townsfolk. The Strinne supporters were victorious in the Invasion of Doldastam, and the invasion ended with the traitors being executed and Linus Berling coronated as the King of the Kanin.

Iqaluit, Nunavut—the capital city of Canada's northernmost province. It has a large Inuit population, but most residents can speak English. Despite being the largest city in Nunavut, it has a population of over seven thousand. Nunavut has no roads connecting the towns to one another, and it is only accessible by plane, usually flying in from Winnipeg or Churchill in Manitoba.

Irish elk—a species of deer believed to be extinct; also known as the giant deer. It is believed to be one of the largest species of deer, but humans hunted them to extinction in the wild thousands of years ago. The Vittra have secretly been breeding and raising them, where they are known as "giant woolly elk" or "woollies." They stand about 2.1 meters tall at the shoulders, carrying the largest antlers of any known cervid, and they can weigh over fifteen hundred pounds.

irytakki—a language only spoken in Alfheim.

Isarna, Sweden—an island and village in the Kalix archipelago in the Bay of Bothnia in Sweden. It is a Kanin/Skojare co-op, and the largest—and essentially only—troll settlement in Scandinavia, accessible by ferry or boat. The name means "islands of ice." The nearest human settlement is Nikkala, on mainland Sweden.

Iskyla, Nunavut—a small Kanin village, it is one of the northernmost troll communities in the world. Some Inuit humans also live there. It has become a dumping ground for unwanted babies. The name translates to "ice." In 2014, Iskyla had a population of 878.

Jakob W. Rells University of Parapsychology and Medicine—a university in Seattle, Washington. Rells University is renowned for paranormal and scientific studies, sometimes referred to as the Harvard of parapsychology. It was established by renowned telekinetic expert and medical doctor Jakob W. Rells in 1889. Rells presented as human, but he is suspected to have been from the Trylle kingdom.

Kanin—one of the most powerful of the five troll tribes. They are considered quiet and dogmatic. They are known for their ability to blend in, and, like chameleons, their skin can change color to help them blend in to their surroundings. Like the Trylle, they still practice changelings, but not nearly as frequently. Only one in ten of their offspring are left as changelings. The Kanin are also the oldest tribe of trolls, having been the original troll tribe before the brothers Norund the Younger and Jorund the Elder fought about moving south in circa 1200 CE. Norund stayed in the north, strengthening the Kanin in Doldastam, while his brother went south and established the Vittra in Ondarike.

Karelian Piiraka—a Finnish rye pastry. Rye-crusted, handheld pies with rice porridge as the most common filling, but a mix of root vegetables as filling is a frequent variation.

kasteren axe—a small hatchet with curved blades, similar to an ulu knife, with a long, slender handle. Used in the game of *økkspill*. The name means "thrower."

Korva—a title for the Mimirin dean. The name means "crown." The Korva is the highest position in the Mimirin.

Lake Isolera—a secret, magical lake in Ontario, Canada, near Tricorn Lake, and known to the Skojare.

Lost Bridge of Dimma—a legendary bridge in troll mythology— akin to the city of Atlantis or the Hanging Gardens of Babylon— that is watched over by the Älvolk. The bridge was alleged to have connected the ancient troll city of Áibmoráigi to the utopian kingdom of Alfheim, and it was believed to have collapsed before the end of the Viking Age (circa 1000 CE). The bridge was lost and the First City of Áibmoráigi was destroyed during the Battle for the Bridge, also known as Vígríðabifröst.

lysa—a telekinetic ability related to astral projection that allows one troll to psychically enter another troll's thoughts through a vision, usually a dream.

mänsklig—often shortened to *mänks*. The literal translation for the word *mänsklig* is "human," but it has come to describe the human child that is taken when the Trylle offspring is left behind in the changeling tradition.

Markis—a title of male royalty in troll society. Similar to that of a Duke, it's given to trolls with superior bloodlines and their correlating telekinetic abilities. Markis have a higher ranking than the average troll, but are beneath the King and Queen. The hierarchy of troll society is as follows: King/Queen; Prince/Princess; Markis/Marksinna; Högdragen; troll citizens; trackers; *mänsklig*; host families; humans (not raised in troll society).

"The Markis and the Shadow"—a troll reinterpretation of the Danish fairy tale *"Skyggen"* (in English, "The Shadow").

Markis Ansvarig—a position of authority in troll communities, similar to a mayor or chieftain. Literal translation is "Markis-in-charge." It is a position used in cities without any major royals, like King/Queen or Prince/Princess. The female equivalent would be Marksinna Ansvariga.

Marksinna—a title of female royalty in troll society. The female equivalent of the Markis.

Mästare—the title given to prestigious department heads at the Mimirin.

Merellä, Oregon—a large, affluent citadel in Oregon. It is technically under the Vittra rule, but many trolls from tribes all over live there. It is virtually a metropolis compared to most troll towns and villages, and it is essentially a college town built around the Mimirin institution and library. The name means "by the sea." It is one of the oldest cities in North America, having been colonized after the trolls came over with the Vikings. Trolls first arrived in North America in early 1000 CE, and the trolls began moving west to get away from the violence of the Vikings. They settled Merellä around 1400 CE. It remains hidden with powerful cloaking spells by the Ögonen.

Midsommar—a trollized version of the festival "Midsommarafton" or "Midsummer's Eve." It is a summer festival, celebrating the end of the long winter, with flowers, greenery, and maypoles.

Mimirin, the—the great institution and library that holds much of the history of the trolls, located in the city of Merellä. The full official name is "Mimirin Talo," which means "House of Mimir," a reference to Mimir, the Norse god of knowledge and remembering.

Mörkaston, Nevada—a Vittra city located near the Ruby Dome in northeastern Nevada. The name is an anglicized version of *"mörkaste höjden,"* which means "darkest point."

nettle—a stinging herbaceous plant common in Scandinavia. Nettles lose their sting when cooked and can be used in lieu of spinach or any other leafy green. Nettle can also be used dried, as a tea.

Ögonen—the trollian guardians who use their powerful psychokinesis to hide the city of Merellä from humans. They are not considered to be part of any tribe and are almost considered to be something of another species. Their name means "eyes." They are described as sinewy and nearly seven feet tall. They are covered in leathery, ocher skin, but it's so thin it's slightly transparent. They are androgynous, with very humanoid dark brown eyes.

ogre—ogres are similar to hobgoblins, except they are giant, most standing over seven feet tall, with superior strength. They are dimwitted and aggressive, and they are known only to the Omte tribes.

økkspill—a game similar to darts. The name literally means "axe games." It involves a board with three bull's-eyes—in white, black, and gold, respectively—and five kasteren axes.

Omte—one of the smaller troll kingdoms, only slightly more populous than the Skojare. Omte trolls are known to be rude and somewhat ill-tempered. They still practice changelings but pick families of lower class than the Trylle and Kanin. Unlike the other tribes, the Omte tend to be less attractive in appearance. The Omte split off from the Vittra tribe in circa 1280 CE, when Dag felt like the Vittra favored the smaller hobgoblins and more conventionally attractive "humanoid" trolls. He took the ogres and established the tribe in Fulaträsk. Since 1280 CE, they have had forty monarchs—much more than any other tribe. The high turnover rate among Omte monarchs is due to their violent lifestyle, compromised immune systems, and lower intelligence. They are currently in the Torian Dynasty, with the widowed Queen Regent Bodil Elak ruling until her son Crown Prince Furston Elak comes of age in 2028.

Ondarike, Colorado—the capital city of the Vittra. The Queen and the majority of the powerful Vittra live within the palace there. It is located in northern Colorado, near Walden in the mountains.

Oslinna, Wyoming—a Trylle village that was decimated by the Vittra in 2010, but it has been slowly rebuilding. It is near Gillette, Wyoming.

Ottawa, Ontario—a city in eastern Ontario. It is the second-most populous city in Ontario.

Överste—a position in the Kanin military. In times of war, the Överste is the officer in charge of commanding the soldiers. The Överste does not decide any battle plans, but instead receives orders from the King or the Chancellor.

persuasion—a form of psychokinesis that is a mild form of mind control. The ability to cause another person to act a certain way based on thoughts.

peurojen—the one in charge of the giant woolly elk, similar to a shepherd.

precognition—a form of psychokinesis that is knowledge of something before its occurrence, especially by extrasensory perception.

psionic—referring to the practical use of psychic powers or paranormal phenomena.

psionic stun gun (PSG)—a weapon similar to a Taser or stun gun, but instead of electricity, it runs on psionic power.

psychokinesis—a blanket term for the production or control of motion, especially in inanimate and remote objects, purportedly by the exercise of psychic powers. This can include mind control, precognition, telekinesis, biological healing, teleportation, and transmutation.

Rektor—the Kanin in charge of trackers. The Rektor works with new recruits, helps with placement, and generally keeps the trackers organized and functioning.

rose hip soup—a soup common in Sweden, with a deep rosy color and sweet-tart tang. Rose hips, which ripen long after the rose blooms have faded, can be dried to enjoy all year and serve as an important source of vitamin C in northern countries.

Sámi—the indigenous peoples of the Arctic Circle in Scandinavia. Also known as Sami, Saami, or Fenni. They have historically had an appearance similar to Inuit and other First Nation peoples.

semla—a Scandinavian sweet roll made of wheat bread, whipped cream, and almond paste. It is similar to a cream puff.

Sintvann, North Carolina—an Omte city located in the Great Dismal Swamp in North Carolina. The name means "Angry Waters."

Skojare—the aquatic tribe of trolls that is nearly extinct. They require large amounts of fresh water to survive, and one-third of their population possess gills that allow them to breathe underwater. Once plentiful, only about five thousand Skojare are left on the entire planet. In circa 1300 CE, Aun the Blue broke off from the

Kanin tribe, heading south from Doldastam for a warmer water source. He took all the gilled trolls with him and established the Skojare in Storvatten. They have had twenty-four monarchs since 1300 CE, and they are currently in the Rolfian Dynasty, with King Mikko Rune. His daughter, the Crown Princess Lisbet "Libby" Biâelse, is next in line for the throne.

Storvatten, Ontario—the capital and largest city of the Skojare, and it is home to the palace and the Skojare royal family. It is situated on Lake Superior, not too far from Thunder Bay, Ontario, with a population of over fifteen hundred in 2019.

Sverige—the name for Sweden in Swedish.

Tonåren—in the Skojare society, a time when teenagers seek to explore the human world and escape the isolation of Storvatten. Most teens return home within a few weeks. Similar to Rumspringa.

Tower of Avanor—the tower in the Mimirin where the lineage and ancestry records are stored.

tracker—a member of troll society who is specifically trained to track down changelings and bring them home. Trackers have no paranormal abilities, other than the affinity to tune in to their particular changeling. They are able to sense danger to their charge and can determine the distance between them. The lowest form of troll society, other than *mänsklig*.

Tralla horse—a powerful draft horse, larger than a Shire horse or a Clydesdale, originating in Scandinavia and only known to be bred among the Kanin. Once used as a workhorse because they can handle the cold and snow, now they are usually used for show, such as in parades or during celebrations.

triskelion—a symbol consisting of three lines radiating from a center.

troglecology—a branch of biology in the Mimirin devoted to studying the relationships between trolls and the environment around them and with each other. It is derived from the words *troglodyte* (Latin for "troll") and *ecology* (the branch of biology dealing with the relationships of organisms with their environment and with each other).

troll of mixed blood (TOMB)—any troll that has parents that are not of the same tribe. This includes both full-TOMBs (both parents are trolls) and half-TOMBs (one parent is a troll, one parent is a human). By using People First Language, it is more inclusive and socially acceptable compared to *half-breed*, *half-blood*, or *halvblud*. There are fifteen distinct types of TOMBs (ten full-TOMB, five half-TOMB). They are as follows:

- KanHu (Kanin & human)
- KanOm (Kanin & Omte)
- OmHu (Omte & human)
- OmTry (Omte & Trylle)
- Omttra (Omte & Vittra)
- SkoHu (Skojare & human)
- Skomte (Skojare & Omte)
- Skonin (Skojare & Kanin)
- SkoTry (Skojare & Trylle)
- TryHu (Trylle & human)
- Trynin (Trylle & Kanin)
- VittHu (Vittra & human)
- Vittjare (Vittra & Skojare)
- VittKa (Vittra & Kanin)
- Vittrylle (Vittra & Trylle)

Trylle—the beautiful trolls with powers of psychokinesis and for whom the practice of changelings is a cornerstone of their society. Like all trolls, they are ill-tempered and cunning, and often selfish.

They were once plentiful, but their numbers and abilities are fading, though they are still one of the largest tribes of trolls. They are considered peaceful. The Trylle became a tribe in 1510 CE, when Aldaril became fed up with the inept Kanin King Harald. He went south, taking many wealthy nobles with him, and established the Trylle in Förening along the Mississippi River. They have had twenty-one monarchs since 1510 CE, and they are currently in the Mógilian Dynasty, with Queen Wendy Staad. Her son, Crown Prince Oliver Staad, is next in line for the throne.

tupilaq—an Inuit word meaning "witch" or "shaman."

ullaakuut—an Inuit word that means "good morning."

valknut—a symbol sometimes known as the "warrior knot." It consists of three interlocked triangles, and it's frequently seen on Norse artifacts.

Viliätten—House of Vili, the oldest troll dynasty. See *Vilings Dynasty*.

Vilinga Saga—the document that explains the lineage of the troll monarchy that Ulla is archiving. The opening lines of the saga are as follows: "*One war-king called Vili; with his House of Vilings, went to the Western Lands, to conquer all that they would find.*"

Vilings Dynasty—the oldest dynasty in troll history. It is the only dynasty of the united kingdom of trolls. It ran from circa 770 CE with Vili in Áibmoráigi, Scandinavia, and ended with the feuding brothers Jorund the Elder of the Vittra in North America and Norund the Younger of the Kanin in the already established Doldastam, in circa 1200 CE. In circa 1040 CE, Asa the Cold and many of the trolls fled from Scandinavia out of fear of the war on paganism. They sailed with Vikings over to North America and relocated the troll capital from Áibmoráigi to Doldastam.